THE
LAKEBED

Tim Stone

For Lady Gelato of Ferndale Way

CONTENTS

CHAPTER 1. SATURDAY, JUNE 26, 2021.

. . . heals all wounds, Al's father used to tell their country back home. Al, for his part, begged to differ. But he was still young.

So Al had gone west. And now he rode west.

His secondhand Triumph alternately revved and sputtered, passing a small handful of cars heading back to Hynek. The sun had not risen.

The parkway was narrow: only two lanes in each direction and enclosed by Douglas-firs. A mother opossum on the shoulder, with half a dozen fist-sized cubs clinging to her undercoat, stared into the approaching headlight. She dropped to the cement and froze, even as her newborns, oblivious, continued pushing and pulling to secure better positions in her tufts. Al weaved right. A split second slower, roadkill.

Would've been a flattened mother. Another one.

Al winced.

He was on his way to the Hamfield Zoo. A large and well-known institution—a regional draw, in fact—which attracted tourists from throughout the Pacific Northwest, beyond just the residents of Tuckashoa County. The location of job number one.

Parking in the employee lot, Al rested his helmet on the seat and then entered the administration building. No one there yet. Doubling back toward Rocky's enclosure, he saw Bernie's golf cart—overflowing with loose tools and emblazoned with a rainbow-colored Grateful Dead skull—near the Aquarium House. Bernie was an expert in large mammal behavior. But his job was mostly that of repairman extraordinaire. Constructing, improving, and fixing cages, enclosures, and habitats.

And cleaning shit, of course.

Al thought about how, with Bernie, it always came back to shit in some form or fashion. Poop predilection notwithstanding, he liked Bernie a lot.

He entered the Aquarium House, the interior lit by purple fluorescents lining the rear of the tanks. Al looked around. Otto was clinging to a log, his tentacles gently rippling through the water. No Bernie, though.

Al opened a door marked "EMPLOYEE'S ONLY"—Al wished Bernie would just fix that grammar—which led to a cramped room behind the tanks. He recoiled from the smell of mildew and rank shellfish. The beelike hum of electric motors powering the filtration systems grew louder.

A few feet away, two soiled white Reeboks and denim-covered legs protruded from beneath a tank. A deep, paternal voice spoke.

"Ah, Mr. Dragunov. That *is* you, Kemosabe?"

"Indeed it is, sir," Al answered.

"Do me a solid and hand me that wooden plank on the left."

Al found the plank and passed it to an open hand.

The sound of a drill preceded a satisfied, "Bingo."

Bernard Charles Higgins shimmied back and out, extracting his husky frame from the crawlspace. He reached for Al's hand and helped himself up. He had thick salt and pepper hair pulled back in a taut ponytail coupled with a beard that was a sight to behold: a curly grey mass dangling at least a foot from his face. As Bernie himself put it, he was like a bloated cross between Tommy Chong and Ron Kuby.

"And how are we today, Al? Glad to see someone else here early."

"I'm fine, sir. Happy to be here, as always." He meant it.

Bernie had first encountered "Al"—short for Alyosha—while the twenty-two-year-old was working as a cashier in the zoo's cafeteria. Carefully observing him during several lunches, Bernie recognized the urgency, care, and enthusiasm with which Al did his job. He was, in fact, the best damn zoo-cafeteria cashier Bernie had ever seen. And so it was clearly a waste of talent, Bernie had thought, for Al to spend his days selling chicken fingers to grade schoolers. Bernie had introduced himself and the two had chatted about how Al, with his subtle but discernible Slavic accent, had ended up in small town America. Al presented as a quiet, polite, and modest young man, an understated intellect brewing beneath the surface. Bernie knew inherent value when he saw it.

So he'd promoted Al to the newly created role of Assistant Vice Zookeeper, effectively taking him on as a personal assistant at higher pay.

Over the next few months, a friendship blossomed.

The men left the Aquarium House and chatted as they ambled toward Rocky's enclosure. The sun had risen and, at one point, Bernie squinted at the lawn alongside the path. He pointed to a steaming brown mound and shook his head.

"Fucking Mandy," Bernie groaned, referring to the zoo's free range emu. "Downright foul dumps." He smiled and continued walking with a subtle limp. "Good thing I have you, Kemosabe," he said in a pleased tone. "Don't forget about that one."

"Will do, sir," Al said compliantly.

"You know what I didn't know about this job, Al? The amount of doody. I would love a lower doody quotient, know what I mean?"

Al nodded. "You're going to like this one, Bernie. I've been holding onto it. When I was a kid . . ."

"You're still a kid, my man," Bernie interjected.

"Well, a *little* kid, okay? Maybe six or seven. I remember being at the zoo. God, it seemed like a magical place." Al chuckled. "Now I think back on it, the Kiev Zoo is *not* a magical place.

"Anyway, I was with my dad by the elephant cage; we were in a crowd. And one of the elephants picked up something off the ground and flung it toward us and *boom*"—Al clapped—"a big pile of crap hit the woman right next to me. She was stunned. But then, I guess, the absurdity of it dawned on her. And she started laughing hysterically."

"That must have been a scene," Bernie snickered.

"Well, that's not the end of the story. So my dad saw this and ushered me away from the enclosure. He was scared and I didn't get it. Meanwhile, that woman was still laughing. And then suddenly: *boom*!" He clapped again. "The elephant threw a giant rock at her! Hit her right in the head. She went straight down. And my dad looked at me and said—I remember his exact words—'Once you get hit with shit, don't wait to see what's coming next.'"

"He went full Confucius, huh?"

"Yup, and in Ukrainian it kind of rhymes, so it's even better. Really stuck with me."

Bernie nodded thoughtfully. "That's a profound shit story."

"I thought you'd like that one," Al said smiling.

"Sounds like a smart guy."

Al nodded even as his smile vanished. "One of his better traits."

"You said he was kind of like a senator over there, right?"

"Yeah. Before everything changed."

Bernie had walked several feet off the path to the door of a small green shed; he was entering numbers into a combination lock. He opened the door and removed a nine-foot wooden pole; at one end, two metallic jaws enclosed the tip of a spear. The other bore a handle with a trigger. A massive scooper.

"I can hear the pain in your voice when you talk about him," Bernie said.

Al looked at his hands. "Two sides is what he had. No one but our family saw it. My sister never even really saw it; she was so young. He could be this really charming, charismatic guy. And a brilliant extemporaneous speaker. His 'Jekyll,' my mom called it. But when everything went nuts. . ."

They walked in unison to a large circular cage, its circumference two-hundred feet, with thin steel bars spaced five inches apart.

"What was the name of that political party over there you told me about?"

"The Proto Progressives. Prot Progs."

Bernie handed Al the scooper. "Here, take my pole, Kemosabe," he said winking. "That's what she said. Ouch. Way too easy."

"That doesn't make sense, Bernie. More like that's what *he* said."

Bernie ignored him as he circled the cage.

"So your old man was a turd. Hell, my dad used to hit us something good. That was 'parenting' back then," he scoffed. "When I was a kid, the doctor told my mom to smoke Newports to help with her sinuses. They still even have Newports? It's FUBAR, if you know what I mean."

A safety railing lined the front half of the cage. Beyond, a patch of manicured bushes preceded a ten-foot drop into a narrow moat littered with food scraps, wrappers, and personal effects. The moat opened up to the bars of the cage.

Bernie hoisted himself onto the first railing and stepped across the bushes with one leg to the ledge that lined the moat, straddling the gap like a gymnast before shifting his other leg across. Using one hand to grab the tiled roof of the cage and steady himself, Bernie asked Al for the scooper. And warned him to keep an eye out for Rocky.

"So what'd he do?" Bernie asked. "Out with it, boy." He crouched on the ledge and began thrusting the spear, impaling paper cotton candy holders. After a minute, he pointed the tip at Al on the other side of the railing who extracted the rubbish.

Al gritted his teeth even while his eyes never wavered from the cage's interior.

"When I was growing up, Bernie, we had a little patio with a bench on our roof. My mom used to take me up there to see fireworks and stuff like that. Sometimes just to look at the sky. The lights from Kiev drowned out most of the stars, but you could see a few." He registered a sterile laugh. "She used to ask me, 'Who do you think's out there, trying to talk with our people?' She went up there to meditate."

Bernie pointed the spear at Al; Doritos wrappers this time. Cool Ranch.

"The roof made her happy. Especially when the political stuff got out of control. She lost her medical license, like I told you. Anyway." He trailed off.

"They said she . . . jumped."

"Oh, Jesus," Bernie sighed. He craned his neck toward Al. "I'm so sorry, my friend. You should have told me sooner." He turned back to the moat and used the scooper to clamp onto a broken umbrella. "What was her name?"

"Anna."

"Pretty name."

"Pretty person," Al whispered. He continued training his eyes on the cage.

As Bernie swung the pole across the bushes, Al spoke slowly.

"They *said* she jumped."

Bernie's eyes widened as he studied Al's face.

"What, you think someone . . . *pushed* her?"

Al opened his mouth to answer.

But Bernie held up a finger to his own mouth. He gestured for silence.

"You feel that?" Bernie asked.

Al nodded.

The ground was shaking. A subtle rock, but there.

Al turned, trying to pinpoint from where the movement originated. *An earthquake? Some kind of explosion?* He closed his eyes and concentrated, his body gently undulating as the earth pulsed like a beating heart. Bernie, meanwhile, had balanced himself on the ledge with one hand on the enclosure's roof. He had closed his eyes as well. The rocking never intensified and, after twenty seconds, dissipated.

Al opened his eyes and looked at Bernie—and then past him. What he saw terrified him.

$$\triangle \ \triangle \ \triangle$$

Rocky was Hamfield Zoo's thousand-pound polar bear. An international research crew discovered him as a cub in the Bering Strait paddling between distant planks of ice, no mother in sight. With an unusual patch of black fur around one eye, he resembled a massively overgrown albino raccoon.

Rocky did not play nice. As Bernie put it, "That bear carries a wallet. It says 'Bad Motherfucker.'" Rocky annihilated anything unfortunate enough to enter his cage, including a five-hundred-pound female, Paula, which the zoo had procured for mating. After a couple of nose-to-nose whiffs, Rocky reared onto his hind legs, bellowed, and fell forward as Paula scrambled back like a helpless crab. Engulfing her in a hug, Rocky used his tremendous jaws to tear into Paula's neck. He shook his head spastically—the "Rocky Death Shake" as Bernie called it— severing flesh and bone in only two swift motions. Three minutes after Paula's inauspicious introduction, Rocky had torn off her snout and flung it across the enclosure. He chewed on one of her severed hind legs like a rubber bone, his face painted red.

When the gentle tossing ceased and Al opened his eyes, there was Rocky: on his hind legs and stretched fourteen feet off the cage floor. Because the cage was built underground, the top of Rocky—head like an old-fashioned block TV, neck like a pommel horse—was visible just below Bernie's lower half. Rocky was flush against the cage bars: he was reaching for Bernie's legs with both paws. Al could swear the animal wore the grin of an evil clown.

"*Bear!*" Al screamed.

Bernie had seen the handwriting on the wall a split second earlier when Al's eyes lit up like a flicked switch. He'd dropped the scooper and, with both hands, pushed himself away from the cage so that he was balancing upright on the moat ledge. He swiveled one-hundred-eighty degrees and then stepped forward with one leg—a combined set of motions that took one second. He nearly managed to drop from the ledge into the bushes inside the protective railing. But it was too late.

Rocky wrapped his forearms around one of Bernie's knees, who let out a guttural yelp. Like the sucking force of a rocket-powered vacuum, the bear whipped Bernie back-first across the moat and into the bars, holding him in place as if the zookeeper was undergoing crucifixion.

He pulled Bernie's entire left leg through the bars, which caused Rocky to fall backward momentarily by the sudden give. Still using his paws to hold Bernie's leg in place—their girth dwarfing the denim-covered leg like stubby fingers to a toothpick—the bear bit down on the zookeeper's knee and began shaking its head, spraying dribble in all directions. Bernie was splayed across the bars—one leg free and perpendicular to the bars, the other pulled deeper into the cage as the bear yanked and vigorously shook its head.

In the meantime, Al scrambled over the railing and through the bushes.

He's going to eat him alive. I have to get Bernie's hands.

Al hoisted himself onto the ledge, gained his balance, and reached across the gap. Bernie, his face emotionless, grabbed Al's wrist and yelled, "Pull *now*!"

Al hopped backward from the ledge into the bushes and, in a macabre tug-of-war, yanked Bernie toward him. Almost instantly, the polar bear ripped Bernie's leg out of the socket. The abrupt loss of give flung both men through the shrubbery and against the railing.

Jean-covered leg and sneaker in its mouth, Rocky galloped triumphantly around the cage, shaking the booty before hunkering down to eat.

Bernie lay face-first in Al's chest, branches jutting into every nook of their bodies. He pushed himself off Al, reached for the railing, and pulled himself up and over.

Stunned by Bernie's composure, Al rubbed his hands over his clothing, expecting to be drenched in Bernie's blood. Yet he felt dry. He lifted up his head and looked over the railing. "Bernie?"

Dusting himself off with one hand while holding the railing with the other, the zookeeper smiled. His left leg was gone. The torn denim on one side dipped two inches below his groin; the nub was visible where his leg had been surgically removed.

"Helicopter crash," Bernie said, "Kandahar. He can keep the prosthetic, I needed a new one anyway. See, we all got our crosses to bear."

CHAPTER 2. SATURDAY, JUNE 26, 2021.

Job number two.

Hunched over one of the Field Club's slop sinks, Al used a purple sponge to scrub a saucer-shaped metal bowl. He scraped at the grease and breading, which was from artichoke stuffing in the eggplant special. Catching a reflection of himself in the bowl, Al thought of what Dom called him: Drago, referencing a Russian villain from one of the *Rocky* films.

Al had to look up the actor on IMDB. And Dom, for whatever he was, had a point. Exaggeratedly sharp cheekbones, wispy blond crew cut, aquamarine eyes—there was certainly a resemblance. But Al, unlike the movie villain, was no bruiser. He was a string bean: well over six feet and yet one-hundred-sixty pounds soaking wet.

Ugh. Even the momentary thought of Dom battered Al's spirits.

He glanced at the iPatch on the inside of his wrist; an extremely generous birthday present from Bernie.

9:45 p.m. *Fifteen more minutes.*

He was thankful that he didn't have to work even later when the bar got louder and livelier. Fetching empty tumblers as the crowd became progressively drunker, divorced cougars canoodling with preppy twenty-somethings. And the wealthy older men—some divorced, some just unfaithful—picking up women half their age. His parents had once belonged to a country club. He couldn't stomach it sometimes.

As he retrained focus on the plates, Al heard the sound of a strumming harp; it was a message on his iPatch. He twisted his arm and glanced at the wet skin. A banner of elevated holographic text scrolled across.

Yoshi, what are you up to tonight? Grab a late dinner?

Ingo Lee. Only Ingo called him Yoshi.

Al closed his eyes and mind-synced the response.

Sure, but working. Be by at 10:15.

He imagined the index finger of a disembodied hand in a white glove pressing an oversized button marked "SEND." The harp strummed again.

Derik Gange called out from across the kitchen.

"Al, when you're done playing with your wrist, please clean up tables five, seventeen, and eighteen."

Al nodded sheepishly.

△ △ △

The Field Club—officially, the Hynek Golf and Recreation Society—was near Washington's borders with Oregon and Idaho. Renowned for its PGA-caliber course fronting the southern shore of Lake Hynek, the Field Club drew affluent vacationers from around the U.S. It boasted other amenities: an award-winning spa; a private beach (with pink sand imported from Bermuda); two Olympic-size swimming pools; indoor tennis courts. With a fifty-room hotel (all suites) and two dozen standalone bungalows (for those willing to shell out more than $2,500 per night), rich golfers and their families flocked to the Field Club during the late spring and summer.

Not surprisingly, Hynek's tourist-based economy depended on a seasonal influx of spending, from dining and watersports to the ubiquitous "Josie" souvenirs. Josie was a snake-like aquatic creature supposedly spotted on the lake since the pioneers settled there in the early nineteenth century.

The lake's water was an oddity: a sparkling turquoise that shimmered and spangled in the sun. It had a seventy-five-mile circumference, with the lakebed reaching depths that, quite frankly, no one really knew. Some claimed its nadir was deeper than a mile, littered with football field-sized aquatic caves. Josie, after all, had to spend her days somewhere.

The real estate boom more than two decades earlier had yielded beautiful homes along the southern shore, known as the "South Side." In contrast, wealthy families had been building colonial-style mansions on the northern shore since the 1850s—not long after the Tuckashoa tribe inexplicably vanished from Hynek.

△ △ △

Al discarded his speckled white apron and entered the dining hall in black slacks and a teal button-up shirt, the Field Club's color pattern. He made his way to Table 17, a two-seater overlooking the green of the seventeenth hole. Through large bay windows, Al could see the fairway reflected in the moonlight: a straight drive for three-hundred-fifty yards before turning sharply west and disappearing into the cradle of Doursham Forest, which surrounded the water in nearly all directions.

An attractive couple sat at Table 17 with cutlery folded neatly across their plates. The woman had a milky complexion set against flowing strawberry blond hair, and features that were Germanic: tight and efficient. Beautiful symmetry, Al thought.

A well-proportioned nose that curved cleanly at forty-five degrees, albeit the tip pointed just a smidgeon up, and the left nostril bearing a delicate diamond stud. A starlet's full, deep red lips, and oversized, almond-like hazel eyes. Huge eyes. Eyes that, on any other face, would seem almost mask-like. Even alien-like. In a resplendent crimson blouse, her raw beauty nearly paralyzed Al.

The man was like an Abercrombie & Fitch model: late thirties, clean cut brown hair, square jaw, cleft chin. He wore a form-fitting black shirt—slightly too small for someone his size—which accentuated his biceps. Al glanced at the man's shirt and read the unfamiliar cursive print near his heart: "Skadden Arps." His words became audible:

". . . getting too old for this, I really am, Lilly. I've been fighting them for three years, and it's like, 'What do you want already?' Know what I mean?"

"Lilly" raised her eyebrows, shook her head, and expressed token commiseration, but her mind was clearly elsewhere.

Approaching the table, Al smiled meekly and put his head down as he collected and stacked their plates. The man abruptly changed topics.

"So I'm thinking the G-Class. Has a bigger engine than ours. You know the one I'm talking about—the AMG?"

"No, Aiden, I don't." She spoke slowly and lethargically, her voice carrying a lower register crackle. A weak croak, like a dying frog.

The man responded, "For God's sake, Lilly, your vocal fry! Would you please pay attention? You sound like Florida white trash."

Clutching their plates with two half-empty water glasses balanced precariously on top, Al did his best to interject inconspicuously that their waiter would "be right over with the dessert cart." Aiden tipped his head in acknowledgment.

Lilly, in the meantime, shot a disgusted look at her man.

"You *know* it's from the drinking. Asshole."

Aiden grit his teeth and looked straight ahead. "I give you the world and that's my thanks? You've got some attitude on you tonight." Although his tone was measured, he was suppressing an outburst like an unfinished sneeze.

Lilly, for her part, shot a glance at Al. She winked and licked her lips like a gecko.

Did that just happen?

In a slight daze—at once confused and excited—Al turned to head back into the kitchen. But his waist clipped the edge of the table, which shook his entire body. Like a toppling Jenga tower, the plates, cups, and silverware crashed onto the table, with a dirty plate flipping onto Aiden's lap and smearing artichoke paste on his tan khakis. Aiden slammed both palms on the table and pushed back his chair. He swiped at the plate, knocking it to the ground. His jaw flexed.

"What the . . . *are you incompetent?* What's *wrong* with you?"

Al grimaced and stepped backward. He stammered, "Oh jeez, I'm so sorry, sir! I just, I got caught here on the table, and, I—"

Lilly looked amused. She smirked, revealing front teeth stained with cherry lipstick from bottom to top. Al did a double-take at the red teeth before dropping to his knees to collect the scattered items.

Lilly rubbed Aiden's back and spoke to him in a motherly, pacifying tone.

"Just a mistake babe," she croaked, "sim-ple mis-take."

"There's a reason he's bussing tables," Aiden murmured loudly as he used a napkin to dab at his stained shorts. "And your God damn vocal fry! Would you please cut that out?"

By then, another busboy was assisting Al while the waiter apologized profusely and then directed Al back to the kitchen ("you've done enough damage"). Al stood up and walked backward, bowing in deference and repeating that he was "so incredibly sorry."

Aiden never looked up from his lap.

Lilly winked one more time.

Heading through the kitchen and past a door marked "MALE EMPLOYEES' ONLY" (he simply couldn't escape the apostrophe misusage), Al shook his head in frustration. He didn't normally bang into tables and drop plates. Despite his spindly build (his classmates in Kiev used to call him the "mantis"), he was a gifted athlete and hardly a klutz.

Lilly.

The locker room seemed empty. He entered the combination on his locker and peered inside. Everything organized in neat piles: two pairs of clothes; two hardcover books (*The Fabric of the Cosmos* and *Surviving Death*); one slightly yellowed *New York Times* cover folded into a four-inch square (the edition reporting the *Valor's* launch); deodorant; and iron pills. A small photo of Mom and Kaz taped to the back. He stripped off his shirt and took out a clean one.

In the adjacent bathroom, a stall door opened and then slammed shut. The faucet ran.

A few moments later, a hulk of a man entered the locker area.

At least six feet, four inches, dressed in a tight white tee decorated with skulls and graffiti, the man had the upper body of an NFL tight end. An elaborate tattoo of Japanese calligraphy spanned his right forearm from the inside of his wrist to his rippling bicep. He was homely: snub-nose, big lips, hooded eyes, and patches of dense acne on each cheek. The skin on his head, shaved down to the scalp, was cracked and sunburned. As if Shrek had been reared on the Jersey Shore.

The man's face was blank as he left the bathroom, but, upon seeing Al, lit up with a cheerful expression.

"Ivan Drago, there he is! Sup, comrade?"

Al instantly abandoned his plan to change into clean pants. *I have to get out of here.* He shut the locker and tried to straighten his shirt so that he could slide it over his head. Yet he couldn't find the spot where he had ripped off the tag that demarcated the back of the shirt. He frantically traced his finger along the inside of the collar.

Dominick DeRuglia, all the while, stared unashamedly at Al's bare chest, scrunching his cheeks in disgust.

"Bro, what the fuck's wrong with your chest? You mutated or something?"

Al didn't answer. He was referring to Al's *pectus excavatum*—that is, hollowed chest. It was a congenital birth defect that caused the area between Al's pecs to cave in slightly.

"What's up with you, bro? You don't answer me when I talk to you? Bitch ass."

Al pulled the shirt over his head. As he searched for the sleeves, Dom used one hand to push him against the locker. He was as powerful as he looked. Al was like a spider caught in the web of his own clothing, blinded and defenseless. He struggled to pull the shirt down, barking at Dom to stop.

"Or what, bro?"

Once Al got his head through the collar, he found Dom staring at him with narrowed eyes, only a few inches from his face. Five long seconds passed. Dom suddenly lit up with a smile. His oversized teeth were a radiant, unnatural white, like piano keys.

"Just messing with you, Drago! Relax, bro."

Al's mouth was dry and heart was racing. He never had to deal with this kind of stuff growing up. Back home, at Kiev's premier boarding school, he was always popular, admired even. He'd never dealt with a bully until he came to the U.S. *Not true: Dad. But an evil I knew.*

If he'd learned anything from his father at the end, it was that fighting back sometimes only made it worse.

Al did his best to sound calm.

"You must get some strange pleasure from bullying people, huh Dom? Aren't you in your thirties? Don't you think you're too old to act this way?"

A malicious grin was plastered across Dom's meaty lips.

"'Bullying,' is that what this is?" He had Al cornered against the locker. "Maybe I like you. You know, *really* like you."

"You're ga—"

"Fuck no, you fucking faggot."   He slammed Al into the locker for a second time. "You calling me gay?"

I have to do something.

With only inches of space to operate, Al threw a flaccid a jab at the side of Dom's head. In one effortless motion, Dom's left hand swallowed Al's fist and pinned his wrist against the locker.

Al was near his breaking point and ready to scream bloody murder.

"Dom, let me go. *Now.* We're both adults. This isn't secondary school."

Dom blinked twice.

"What's secondary school?"

"High school, I guess. We called it secondary school back home."

"Why'd you come here?"

"A political party got power in the Ukraine. It didn't like Jews. So my family left."

"A heeb, huh? I knew an Israeli guy in New York. He was, like, intense bro."

"More intense than you?"

"I'm like a no-ine, brah," Dom said, strangling his pronunciation of the number nine. "That kike could like, you know, dial it up to an eleven. Maybe twelve. Shit was brolic, know what I'm saying?"

"Honestly, no," Al replied with sardonic dryness.

"Hah," Dom cackled. "You know, Drago, I like you." He sounded sincere. "I think we'd be good together. Like good friends, bro. Wanna get some food?"

Al looked him in the eyes.

"No. I already ate. I just want to go home."

Two Field Club electricians entered the locker room laughing as they discussed a baseball game. Dom, in response, stepped back. He ran his hand over his head and wiped the perspiration onto his jeans.

"Okay, fair enough Drago," he said. He turned and left.

CHAPTER 3. SATURDAY, JUNE 26, 2021.

Please don't let this have anything to do with dogs, Bardo thought.

She rang the doorbell a second time. It was a modest blue cottage in Doursham four miles southeast of the Field Club, nestled among western hemlocks and red cedars. She took a deep breath and scanned the property. A lawn of thick but unkempt grass still benefiting from an unusually rainy May; a recycling bin overflowing with crumpled cans of Miller Lite; two squirrels taking turns chasing one another through the brush, oblivious to a circling red-tailed hawk. And her 2020 black Camaro in the driveway. She admired its curves while checking for dents or nicks. *Flawless.*

Locks on the door began to clink. A stocky, wrinkled man with wispy white hair and pockmarked cheeks cracked it open. He peered out suspiciously. When he recognized his visitor, the old man's look went from grimace to grin.

"Ah, Bardo, it's *you*."   He swung open the door and welcomed her in.

In Hynek, mostly everyone called Michelle by her last name. It seemed to roll off the tongue.

"Come in, come in," his voice trailed off as he turned around.

She followed Cliff Bentwater through a vestibule littered with rubber boots and umbrellas, the floorboard squealing under her chocolate Timberlands.   They entered a small dining room and sat across from one another at an austere wooden table.

In her mid-forties, Michelle Bardo had cropped black hair with mercury streaks, a naturally glossy complexion, and a strong jawline.   Even without a scintilla of makeup or seductive clothing—she wore neither—Bardo was an attractive woman.

"So Cliff, how goes retirement?"   She clapped once and rested her hands on the scarred tabletop.

The man wore a weak, flickering smile.   He couldn't hold Bardo's eyes.

"Same old thing.   Read the different papers, you know. Crosswords and such."   He thought for a second.   "Been fishing quite a bit, actually."

Bardo nodded.   She sniffed twice: stale Marlboro Reds.   And another odd smoky odor, almost like burnt leather with barbeque sauce.

"Best time of year for catching those giant pinks, or so I hear," she offered.

"Can't eat them damn sturgeons, though," Cliff said with a chuckle.   "Sure fun to look at.   *Boy* do they get big."

She nodded and smiled.   "So, pal, what can I do for you today?"

"Well, Bardo, what happened was. Uh. It's that, um.   Why I called you over . . ."

"Say your piece, Cliff."   She stared at his eyes as he looked past her to the window.   Into the lush forest surrounding his plot.

He swallowed.   "You see, the thing is, my hound went missing some time ago."

Bardo's eyes narrowed.

"Retired greyhound, named her Lady." Cliff rubbed his hands together. "Beautiful brindle." He shook his head, staring at the shaggy green beach rug beneath their feet. "Happened only a couple months after I got her." He paused.

"Go on."

"Well, they warned me: don't let her off the leash. Said they're 'sight' hounds. They'll see a hare a quarter-mile off and, if they ain't leashed, just run and run. And then lose track of where they get and so keep on running. And in the winter, especially . . . well, they ain't got almost no body fat."

Cliff twisted his body and reached behind him to a chipped sideboard. He opened a drawer, removed a blue rubber handball, and turned back around.

"Anyway, it was tough to take her out sometimes. Hell, in the winter, I can barely stand in the morning. So the thing is—" He licked his lips and put one index finger in the air. "Let me just say, I only did this once in a blue moon." With his other hand, Cliff squeezed and then released; the elastic ball made a gentle whoosh as it expelled air before snapping back into place.

"*What* did you only do once in a blue moon?"

"Let her off the leash—that's what I'm trying to say. And when I did, I always stood by the door watching like a hawk while she did her business out back. She always came back in, easy peasy."

"I see where this is going."

"I'm sure you do Bardo, I'm sure you do," he murmured, eyes again glued to the rug. "She woke me up one morning before dawn. This was one of the only times I let her out without a leash." He squeezed the ball again. "And then I sat down on the couch and, thing is, I nodded off. Woke up a bit later. She was gone. Plumb gone.

"Those first few days, I looked everywhere. But hell, *you* know how big Doursham is. I figure she chased her own shadow for a few miles and then went to sleep in the cold." His voice cracked as one eye got glassy. "My little Lady slept all nice and peaceful."

"When?" Bardo asked bluntly.

"When what?"

"When did it happen."

"Gosh, must have been, eh, February?"

"February, eh?" She rapped twice on the table. "She left tracks, right?"

"No tracks."

Bardo looked at him incredulously.

"Cliff, there was snow on the ground every day in February. Fresh coat every three days, easy."

He looked up in thought. "Oh, I see whatcha mean. Well, there wasn't no snow Bardo, so I guess it had to be March."

"What time'd you normally walk her in the morning?"

"She'd start nuzzling my face at 6:20, like clockwork."

"So it was dark at some point after 6:20, huh." She rapped two more times. "Must have been January, then. Sun would have been up in March." Bardo paused. "Jeez, Cliff. You should've talked to me sooner. My men could have helped."

He sighed. "I know. Let her off the leash one time, *one time*, and look what happens."

Thou doth protest too much.

Bardo examined Cliff: pushing eighty and barely mobile. Been that way for a couple of years now—at least as long as she'd been in Hynek. A lifetime of cheap steaks, Marlboros, and supermarket-brand ice cream. Not to mention the beer.

This guy couldn't walk a dog every day.

"Let me ask you, Cliff: you keep all of Lady's stuff? You know, food and toys and all that paraphernalia? Or you toss any of it?"

"Kept it all. Thought she might come back."

"Sure you didn't toss anything?"

He nodded confidently. "Got every last thing. Why?"

"Do me a favor, would ya' bub? Show me Lady's leash."

Cliff's head jerked back, eyes widening with nervous realization. He put one hand to his mouth and then retrained his gaze on the rug.

"Uh, the leash. Thing is, I gave the leash to, uh, someone. You know, the person asked for it, so I figured I'd help out with it, cause, you know—"

"Please look me in the eyes when you speak." Her veneer of geniality was gone. "Tell me, Cliff, why would you *just* say you kept everything?" No response. "Don't test my patience. Did you even have a leash? Yes or no."

His pockmarked cheeks flushed bright red. "The thing is that—"

"Yes or no."

"Jesus, Bardo, I wanted your help, not the Inquisition!" He squeezed the ball.

"Stop doing that," she snapped. "And answer me."

His shoulders sank.

"No, okay. I didn't have no damn leash."

"Blue moon, huh?" she sniggered. "The truth will set you free, champ." The less Bardo liked someone, the more she piled on the childish nicknames. Passive aggression, an old flame used to say. She wasn't even cognizant of it.

She reflected anew on the timeline, knocking three quick times on the tabletop. "Just trying to get the facts, bub. You got Lady when?"

"Last October."

"And you were letting her out—with no leash—until she went missing at some point in January. I'll need you to nail down the exact date later, scoop. Hmm. Three times a day, right?"

Cliff nodded.

She whispered to herself, "Approximately three months, three times a day. Roughly, uh, two-hundred-fifty times." *If someone was casing this place, more than enough time to plan and execute an abduction. If.* She noticed one of Cliff's eyes tearing up again. *Shit, didn't mean to ruin the geezer's day.*

"Easy there, compadre. It's terrible to lose a pet, I know." Bardo the Cordial reached across the table and touched his shoulder. "But let me ask you: why call me now?"

Cliff plunged one hand into the pocket of his corduroy slacks and rooted around. He removed a crinkled cigarette and a Zippo adorned with an unusual family crest—four silver discs encircling a crane-like bird. Using the back of his hand to wipe his eye, he asked, "You mind?"

"Your house, skip."

He lit the cigarette, took a drag, and exhaled through his nostrils. After shifting in his seat and clearing his throat, he finally answered.

"I always thought she ran off. That is, up until a few days ago. Lately, I'm thinking, you know what? Maybe she didn't after all."

Bardo furrowed her brow. "And what got you thinking that?"

"Well, Budd told me about the Freeman's black lab."

She grit her teeth. *Fucking Budd.*

"Can you talk about it, Bardo?"

"Not a state secret, amigo. Dog went missing from TJ's lawn. Turned up like it'd been through elevator gears, if you get my drift."

"And so TJ thinks Popper did it, huh?"

"No," she retorted, "I mean, yes—he *thinks*, but he's wrong. My deputy spoke to some folks who saw Popper at the same time the dog turn—"

"But what *I* heard," Cliff drowned her out, "is that TJ saw Popper walking past his place on the same day his lab disappeared. And Popper had this real, you know, shit-eating grin on his face."

Bardo pulled back her index finger. "Number one, when is Popper *not* wearing a shit-eating grin?"

Cliff conceded the point with a nod.

She pulled back her middle finger. "Number two, you're out of your element. Popper's out."

"Well, TJ Freeman don't think so."

Bardo shot him a stink eye. He looked down at his cigarette and tapped ash on the rug.

"TJ and his wife: they're angry, understandably. And there's no question some *mountain lion* did them wrong. The point is that—"

A cracker-thin phone vibrated in the breast pocket of Bardo's shirt. She paused midsentence and checked the screen.

Chief, please call the principal's office ASAP.

Bardo suffered a fleeting pang of anger, as if smacked by a small wave.

She stood up and apologized to Cliff, explaining that she had leave. That she'd have her men keep a lookout for a brindle greyhound.

"And Cliff: get a basset hound next time."

△ △ △

Bardo got in her car, shifted to first, revved the accelerator, and fishtailed out of Cliff's gravel driveway onto the hardtop, just short of peeling out.

Speaking to the infotainment system, Bardo said, "Chevy, call Hynek High School."

"Right away, Michelle," the robotic voice cooed. A ringing phone played through the car speakers.

"This is Principal Lee's office, Patty speaking. How can I help you?"

"Patty doll, it's Michelle. Ken there?"

"Hi Chief Bardo! He's auditing a class at the moment. Did he message you about the church? We're having problems again—they keep going back there. Ken scolded Little Miss You Know Who and some of the other mean girls. But they went right back. He wanted to give you a heads up before he does anything."

Bardo flexed her already pronounced jaw and tightened her grip on the steering wheel.

"That's what I figured, thanks sweetheart. Tell him I'll handle it right now. Bye. Chevy, phone off." The connection beeped and then went silent.

Bardo sunk her nails into the pleather-lined wheel.

"God. Fucking. Damn it." *Just relax.* "Chevy, play *Day after Day.*"

"Right away, Michelle."

The song began:

> *I remember finding out about you,*
> *Every day, my mind is all around you,*
> *Looking out from my lonely room, day after day,*
> *Bring it home, baby, make it soon,*
> *I give my love to you.*

She took a deep breath and struggled to pacify herself in the melody. Her thoughts doubled back to Cliff Bentwater. *Another one missing.* She exhaled. *They brought me here for petty crime, not a serial dog killer.*

Bardo pulled up in front of a small Korean church—United Divine Spirit of Christ's Holy Vessel Fellowship Church of Compassion and Mercy, or known (simply) as UDSCHVFCCM—and got out. She crossed the miniature lawn, straggly and peppered with ragwort, to a narrow cement walkway spanning the church's side. It led to an alley tucked between the back of the building and a stone wall erected at the base of a steep hill. She could already make out a skunky, sour odor.

Around the corner, Bardo found four teenage girls of varying shapes and sizes. One of them—with jet black eyes, olive skin, and a semi-flat pierced nose—held a torch lighter to a partially smoked joint, on the cusp of re-sparking the tip. Upon seeing Bardo, the girl shook her head, annoyed but unflustered. The others were frozen in unadulterated fear.

Shooting daggers at the joint-wielding teen, Bardo barked, "Everyone else, go. *Now!*" The other girls scattered like mice.

Bardo flared her nostrils and ground her teeth. "I recognized Tara Mercer and Edie Vickey, but who's the third one?" Her usually upbeat, faux Midwestern drawl was monotone. And seething.

Fifteen-year-old Sasha Bardo looked up from the joint, which she was rolling impatiently between her thumb and middle finger. She said nothing.

Bardo got to within a few inches of her daughter, like a drill sergeant poised to tear into a subversive recruit.

"*Speak!*"

Sasha exploded into a heaving cough that shot a targeted stream of smoke at her mother's face. Bardo pushed her away, keeled over, and underwent a spastic coughing fit alongside her daughter. They hacked and expectorated like sick old hags.

Bardo eventually looked up.

"For Christ's *sake*, Sash!"

"You scared me!" A smile had already formed at the creases of Sasha's lips.

"Wipe that grin off your face!" She caught her daughter's eyes. "We have these talks, Sash, and you promise me things. And then you go ahead and *piss* all over everything. Do you mean what you promise?"

Sasha appeared unfazed—confident and defiant. Far too much of each for someone her age, Bardo thought.

"Yeah, I mean it," the teen answered in a pestered tone while looking at the joint between her fingers. Then she met her mother's glare. "But then I think to myself, 'What's the point?' We're all gonna die no matter what. We're here for, like, a fraction of a millisecond by evolutionary standards. Life's too short."

"*Your* life's too short. You haven't even been on this earth for two decades. Can you allow for the fact that you don't know everything?"

"And if I get hit by a car tomorrow: you think it'll have been worth it to follow your stupid rules? To not do what I wanted when I had the chance?"

"Sash, when I took you on those ride-alongs in Baltimore, remember all the people in the burnt out row houses? That's *their* philosophy—it's what got them there. If you want anything in this life, you need discipline. Not 'me me me, now now now.' You're too old not to see that."

Sasha shifted her tack.

"Just relax, Mom, Jesus Christ. I was smoking a joint. I didn't set off a dirty bomb."

"You don't even try to hide this stuff. You and your little gang get kicked out of here and go right back. Which is like a giant middle finger to *me*," Bardo pointed at her own chest, "since you know who Ken's calling. Is this to get me out here, is that what it's about? The cursing and the bullying and that fight, and now this?"

She shook her head and scoffed, "It's not about you, Mom. Frankly, I don't give a fu—"

"Shut your filthy mouth," Bardo snapped.

Sasha flinched and quieted for a few seconds.

"I'm gonna talk now, okay Mom? What I was *trying* to say was that I don't do things so you'll come here and yell at me in front of my friends. You ever think it's because *this*"—she pointed at her chest—"is who you adopted? That it's in my DNA?"

Bardo rolled her eyes.

"I don't care what's in your DNA. I raised you a certain way to have certain values."

Sasha snickered. "What, like *your* values? Like last Wednesday when you didn't come home? I've been counting the times, you know. Who you screwing now, Mom? The mechanic? The mailman?"

Bardo slapped her daughter across the face. Sasha cracked an impish grin.

"I could call child services, you know," she muttered. "For that and all the other times. Earth to Police Chief Bardo: parents don't hit kids anymore. And parents don't stay out all night screwing some ran-doh guys."

"You deserved that. And you know what? I can have a life as well."

Sasha gently touched her own cheek. "I miss my Cecil friends," she whined, "you uprooted *everything*. And then you want to know why I act out?"

"Oh, give me a break. You were getting in trouble in Cecil. Remember your little episode with Mrs. Croft during the winter assembly? And now you've got a whole new crew of summer school delinquents. What's your next excuse?"

"Because I'm disturbed? 'I got a social disease!'" Sasha smiled as she sung the line from *West Side Story* in an exaggerated Brooklyn accent.

"Not funny, Sash. You *do* have a social disease," Bardo retorted, although succumbing to her own frustrated grin. She had taken her daughter to see the play when she was only four, but the girl was still quoting it.

"Get to class. And give me the doobie. The lighter too."

Sasha giggled condescendingly. "Here, take the dooooo-beeeee, Mom. God, I can't believe you actually call it that." She slammed the joint and lighter into her mother's hand as she strode past and disappeared around the bend in the church.

These fights wore on Bardo, besieging her psyche. *But not Sasha. The girl's Teflon.*

Every argument went right back to her adoption. Bardo would have never told her about it if Sasha had physically resembled her even slightly. But there was simply no hiding their disparate ethnicities. Sasha was born in Ecuador: a three-week-old left at a Quito orphanage who was filthy, underfed, and riddled with tapeworm. A few months later, by way of a Queens adoption agency, that baby became "Sasha Maria Bardo," the newest resident of Cecil County, Maryland.

By then, Bardo had been a captain in the BPD and nearly a decade into her tenure. She'd earned a reputation in Baltimore as an unforgiving and hands-on leader—she'd continued to lead undercover operations in the field—without a shred of compassion for the endless drug dealers and gang bangers. She had lofty expectations for those she supervised, although she treated everyone fairly if they worked hard. Some of Bardo's lazier cops called her "Captain Cunt" behind her back—and behind the backs of her cadre of fiercely loyal officers.

Bardo examined the half-smoked joint and put the tip to her nose. *I dealt with some punks like Sasha in West Baltimore. Cracked heads back when you still could.* She smiled crookedly. *Yet there's something different about Sasha. Not just her outbursts.* She dropped the joint and used her boot heel to grind it into the dirt. *It's not just the things she does. Well, that's definitely part of it.* She reflected on Sasha's first suspension since their move to Hynek. She'd broken a classmate's nose in two places—and then held the girl down and smeared blood all over her face like some primeval warrior. But she hadn't started that fight, putatively. At least that's what her acolytes had insisted to Ken Lee.

What is it about this girl? It's that she . . . doesn't feel anything. Never scared, sad, truly happy—at least not anymore. And when she gets caught, no shame. No fear of me or any authority, for that matter. No remorse. No empathy.

Bardo believed she had pinpointed it: her daughter felt no empathy. That meant, of course, no conscience.

She felt a powerful high setting in from the gust of secondhand weed smoke. *Fuck.* The sensation contoured to her awareness like a foam mattress. Suddenly, she was no longer Hynek's Chief of Police standing behind an absurdly named Korean church. She was now watching a movie in which Hynek's Chief of Police was standing behind an absurdly named Korean church. She stared slack-jawed at the lighter, turning it over and admiring the design. *Such an interesting shape. So globular. Like a glob of matter. Globular. Glob-u-lar. Gulab-jamon.* Her eyes drifted from the lighter to a vein in her wrist, which she traced along her arm. As she returned to the car, Bardo shook her head and tried to suppress what she was feeling.

It didn't work. All kinds of thoughts, seemingly drawn from the ether, suddenly danced in her mind, catching and then quickly releasing her scatterbrained attention. One was unequivocally the most disturbing: *my daughter is a sociopath.*

CHAPTER 4. SATURDAY, JUNE 26, 2021.

ngo Lee took a drag from a ruby-colored, semi-translucent vaporizer, which was shaped like a cigar. To someone who didn't know Ingo, it was as if he was smoking through his neck. That was because he had no chin: his bottom lip dropped precipitously two inches into a bulbous Adam's apple, a giant knuckle of skin protruding from his neck. Like Al's hollowed chest, the missing chin was Ingo Lee's congenital deformity— albeit one far more conspicuous and off-putting.

Ingo was in a leather computer chair by a wooden desk swiping at a tablet in his lap. A large flat television framed the wall over the desk; it was on mute with commercials playing. Ingo exhaled. The aroma of Hawaiian Punch permeated the room.

Al sat on the corner of a king-sized bed, staring at his wrist and occasionally swiping as well. Several minutes passed with neither man uttering a word.

Al eventually sneezed.

"Bless you," Ingo said without looking up.

He sneezed a second time.

"Bless you again."

Al sneezed a third time.

"Gesundheit."

A fourth.

"You're pushing your luck, Yoshi."

A fifth.

"Christ, sh- sh- sh- shut up!"

Ingo had stuttered all his life. Words beginning with "s" were particularly challenging.

"You got tissues?" Al asked.

Ingo tossed him some napkins. Another five minutes passed without a peep.

"Ss, ss, so you dropped a plate on the guy's lap, huh?"

Al nodded. "I just kind of stood there while he bitched me out."

"Did you tell him to shut his rich ass mouth?"

"You should talk," Al muttered as he looked around the room. "You know, Ingo, if you had a service job—or really *any* job, for that matter—you'd understand the age-old concept of grinning and bearing it. Anyway, it was his wife that had me tripping over myself. *Gorgeous*, man. She was winking at me and licking her lips! What do you think that means?"

"You don't know what *that* means? You must be kidding. That's awesome." Ingo snorted and looked back at his tablet. "But screw women. Well, not literally."

Al chortled while swiping at his wrist.

"Still abstinent, I presume?"

"Not abstinent. Like I ta- ta-, told you: Kakuhido. The Revolutionary Alliance of Men that Women Find Unattractive. Still a standing member. Got my games, food, shelter. Crisp Hynek air."

Al raised his nose and sniffed twice. "What flavor is that again?"

Ingo examined a small glass jar on the desktop. "'Mango Passionfruit Pineapple Piccadilly Surprise.' Want a hit?"

Al shook his head without looking up.

Ingo lived a few miles north of Hynek proper on the bottom floor of his parents' four-story neocolonial. An abyss of unrealized potential, he'd gotten a perfect score on his college admission exam (his claim to fame now half a decade later). After matriculating at Stanford, he dropped out during his sophomore year. He'd taken the principled stand, at least in his mind, that life was simply too short to expend the requisite energy and discipline on undergraduate academics.

A gifted swimmer, he had moved back to Hynek and coached the Field Club's masters swimming program. Six months later, he'd quit. Life was simply too short, in his mind, to wake up so early on weekdays. So, instead, he spent an hour each afternoon tidying up his parents' house under the guise that, during the rest of the day, he was drafting a true crime masterpiece. In reality, he was playing multiplayer first-person shooters and combing the dark web for UFO evidence. And becoming a world-class masturbator.

"When's the Field Club gonna promote you? S-t-t-." He took a deep breath and slowed his cadence. "Sti-ll bussing tables. Such a waste."

"I didn't help my cause today."

"You know what I think about that?" Ingo asked.

"What?"

A strained noise issued from Ingo's chair, alternating between a honk and a whining squeak. Almost like sea lions communicating. Al shook his head.

"Oh, dear God! Your farts today are so . . . eggy!" Al feigned dry heaves.

Wearing a triumphant grin, Ingo swiveled toward the television. "Breathe it in, buddy. It's thera-, thera-, therapeutic."

A commercial for silver bars transitioned to the opening credits of a show called *Ancient Astronauts*. Ingo said, "Mr. Sony, unmute," which triggered sound on the TV. A man in a red bowtie spoke from a stage in a darkened auditorium:

—Cessna 182 piloted by Frederick Valentich, flying from Moorabin, Victoria, to King Island, Tasmania. This was a one-hundred-thirty-mile flight, but Valentich had to pass over the Bass Straight, the channel between Australia and Tasmania. Winds were light on October 21st, with a trace of stratocumulus clouds between five thousand and seven thousand feet. At 7:06 p.m., he saw an unknown object and reported to the Melbourne Flight Service Unit Coordinator, which, serendipitously for our purposes, happened to be testing an archiving program. The audio is a bit gravelly but still audible:

[Valentich:] Melbourne, this is Delta Sierra Juliet. Is there any known traffic below five thousand?

[Melbourne:] No known traffic.

[V:] I am, uh, there seems to be a large aircraft below five thousand.

[M:] What type of aircraft is it?

[V:] I cannot affirm, it is four bright, it seems to me like landing lights. The aircraft has just passed over me at least one-thousand feet above.

[M:] Roger, and it is a large aircraft, confirm.

[V:] Unknown due to the speed it's traveling. Is there any air force aircraft in the vicinity?

[M:] No known aircraft in the vicinity.

[V:] Melbourne, it's approaching now from due east towards me. It seems to me that he's playing some sort of game. He's flying over me two or three times at speeds I could not identify.

[M:] Roger. What is your actual level?

[V:] My level is forty-five hundred, four five zero zero.

[M:] Confirm that you cannot identify the aircraft.

[V:] Affirmative.

[M:] Roger. Standby.

[V:] Melbourne, Delta Sierra Juliet. It's not an aircraft, it is [open microphone for two seconds]...

[M:] Can you describe the, err, aircraft?

[V:] As it's flying past, it's a long shape [open microphone for three seconds] cannot identify more than that [open microphone for three seconds] before me right now, Melbourne.

[M:] Roger, and how large would the, err, object be?

[V:] Melbourne, it seems like it's chasing me. What I'm doing now is orbiting and the thing is just orbiting on top of me, also. It's got a green light and it's sort of metallic-like. It's all shiny on the outside [open microphone for five seconds]. It's just vanished. Melbourne, would you know what kind of aircraft I've got. Is it some type of military craft?

[M:] Confirm the, ah, aircraft just vanished.

[V:] Say again.

[M:] Is the aircraft still with you?

[V:] [open microphone for two seconds]...approaching from the southwest. The engine is rough idling. I've got it set at twenty three, twenty four, and the thing is coughing.

[M:] Roger. What are your intentions?

[V:] My intentions are, ah, to go to King Island. Ah, Melbourne, that strange aircraft is hovering on top of me again [two seconds open microphone]. It is hovering and it's not an aircraft.

The time was 7:12 p.m. After Valentich spoke these last words, Australian traffic control heard a sound, and I quote, "like tin cans rolling around in the bottom of an empty oil drum." He was never seen again. Two search and rescue operations were undertaken immediately, and an investigation followed the next year in 1979. All without success.

Al watched the television, and Ingo watched Al's face.

"High strangeness, huh Yoshi?" Ingo asked. "Makes you wonder what's out there."

"Whatever you say," Al said and winked.

"Don't forget to lick your lips," Ingo countered, muting the television and looking back at his tablet.

"Any job prospects?"

Ingo shook his head. "Still plugging away at the Great American Novel."

"Certainly looks like it," Al said. "Don't you ever want to move out? I mean, the setup is great and everything." He looked around the room. "Way nicer than my place above Budd's. But don't you ever want privacy?"

"In some cultures, children live with their parents their entire professional career. It's the norm."

"Career?" Al scoffed.

"Look, Yoshi, we're in the wake of the Great Recession. I'm still feeling it, at least."

Al shook his head. "You really believe that?"

"Sure," he shot back.

"Dude, you were *nine* in 2008."

"I said '*wake*,'" Ingo retorted. "Look, when I was among the select few who scored perfectly on my college boards, I got a letter explaining—"

"Enough, please. You won, okay? I don't care."

Ingo clicked off his tablet and placed it on the desk. "And what about you, Yoshi? Any closer to finding Nettie?"

"Still working on it," Al replied stoically. He pursed his lips. "I'm hiring a firm to help me track him down. And make sure the meeting actually happens."

"Boba Fett, Inc.?"

"Essentially, yeah. A bunch of investigator types. Ex-police, ex-FBI, those kinds of guys."

"You still haven't told me what you're getting out of this. Sa- sa- say they find your dad and hold him for you in a room, commando st- st- style. You get your meeting. Then what? Some kind of confession—is that what you're after?"

Valid questions, Al thought. And he didn't have answers.

"I don't know, Ingo. I just need to talk with him. For him to answer some questions. To *force* him to answer some questions."

"What's done is done, man," Ingo replied before sucking on the vaporizer, "and your life—your old life—isn't coming back. He did some sh- sh- shitty things and split. But it's the past: no going back. Worry about the future. Just saying."

"Whatever *this* is, I need to do it first before I can move on. Step one is saving the money for Boba Fett Inc. I'm close. The pay bump at the zoo helped."

"They should pay you a lot more. They'd have to pay me a pr-, pre-, pretty penny to get me anywhere near that fucking bear. Did Bernie get his leg back?"

A light rap on the bedroom door preceded a woman's gentle voice.

"Sweetheart, can I come in? I'm coming in."

A petite, attractive middle-aged woman opened the door and stepped inside carrying a laundry basket with folded clothes.

"Hi Al, how are you?"

"Hi Dr. Lee, I'm well. And you?"

"*Please*, Mom," Ingo whined, "wait for me to answer when you knock. Think about it: what you do doesn't make sa- sa- sense. A knock and oral request for permission to enter, but then you just barge in. The key is knocking, then asking for permission, and then *wait-ing* for me to answer. That's the concept behind a request for permission and a grant of permission."

"Get a job, sweetheart."

"I need to write, you know that."

"Slide the manuscript under our door anytime. We'd be thrilled to give you notes." She looked back at Al. "I'm just dandy, Al. Tired of my little snowflake, but otherwise just dandy."

Ingo rolled his eyes.

"Com'on, Yoshi, let's get some food."

Al and Ingo walked south on Luminaire Street, which, after five blocks, turned into a hamlet with a handful of shops and restaurants—a modest commercial area outside Hynek's main drag on Post Road. As they continued south, the houses became humbler than the Lee's.   Post Road, for its part, ran perpendicular to the lake, abutting the western shore. Nearing the water it turned into a pedestrian walkway before narrowing into a boardwalk lining part of the southwestern shore.

They were heading to one of Hynek's three pizza shops, Nardo's. Ingo was dressed as if he had just rolled out of bed: flip flops, mesh shorts, and a hand-me-down rock concert shirt from his father (bearing the faded words "fitter, happier, more productive"). With Korean and French ancestry, Ingo had a slightly oval-shaped face—other than his missing chin—with a sharp and strongly articulated nose. He was just shy of six feet and bulkier than Al's scarecrow-like figure. For someone who spent most of his time sitting in a basement, he was surprisingly toned and muscular. His voice and temperament, conversely, were congruent with a bridge-dwelling troll. The stutter was compounded by his voice's nasally timbre and a cantankerousness that, not infrequently, morphed into outright hostility to the world and everyone in it.

"You working tomorrow?" Ingo asked.

Al shook his head.

"Not Sunday. Monday, yeah; both jobs. We have to install a scratching post for the Bengal tiger."

As they continued south, a sinewy old man with olive skin approached from the opposite direction. In tattered hiking boots and tan khaki shorts, and with a severely lazy eye, it was as if Jack Hanna had hit a terrible wall. As the man got closer the muffled sound of Gerry Rafferty filled the air:

> *When I wanted you to share my life,*
> *I had no doubt in my mind.*
> *And it's been you, woman*
> *Right down the line.*

The man carried a log-like boom box that was four decades old, a relic of a simpler time. He wore a squinty grin as he bobbed his head and ambled along Luminaire. Ingo and Al each acknowledged him with a subtle nod; he reciprocated with the beaming smile of a child on Christmas morning.

It was Popper.

He'd been a fixture in Hynek for decades. Many found him comforting, almost like a security blanket personified. You could travel the world and yet, when you returned, there was Popper, as always, toting around a boom box or pushing a shopping cart. He was mute, perpetually squinting, and known for breaking into glorious smiles.

"Why do people call him Popper?" Al asked as the saxophone from *Baker Street* faded into the distance.

"I dunno. Maybe folks thought he popped some pills and lost his mind or something. My mom said he's been around si- si- since she was growing up."

"You see his teeth, Ingo? Your mom's practice could make a killing if he wasn't a vagrant." Al glanced at his wrist for any recent news about the Valor. "Where do you think he goes at night anyway?"

Ingo shook his head.

They entered the pizza shop. A long line of customers snaked around the counter toward the rear of the store, surprising for that time of night. Ingo shook his head in frustration as they joined the queue. The line advanced quickly, although the woman directly in front of them twice failed to inch forward as soon as the line advanced. Ingo mumbled something inaudibly to himself. When it happened a third time, he sniped to Al about "those people" who "don't know how to wait in lines."

"I mean, how retarded can you be? All you have to do is step forward. Literally."

Al stared at his feet, remembering why he preferred not to hang out with Ingo in public. The woman turned, shot Ingo a dirty look, and muttered "fascist." The very kind of response that was Ingo's catnip.

"Yeah, sah- sah- sah- so what lady?" Ingo countered. "'Fascism will come at the hands of perfectly authentic Americans.' John T. Flynn. Am I authentic enough for you?" The woman's expression changed from one of disgust to mild confusion.

"And yes," he continued, "I voted for Trump. Twice. Pence 2024."

"Enough," Al pled.

They ordered and paid, waited a few more minutes for the slices, and carried their greasy paper bags into the warm night and chorus of crickets. As the men turned right and headed to Luminaire, an electric blue 2013 Infiniti—boasting shiny rims and four darkly tinted windows, with a deep trance bass pulsing from the trunk—sped down the street. The car screeched to a halt in front of Nardo's.

Dom stepped out of the Infiniti and walked around the hood toward the pizza shop. When Al shot a glance behind them, Dom was stopped near the entrance and staring at him like a musclebound owl. Al spun back around.

Shit shit shit. More fodder for our next meeting. Al had considered quitting his job at the Field Club merely to escape Dom and the thought now boomeranged back. But it was easy money and he was close to having what he needed. *Just a little bit longer.*

As they walked north on Luminaire, Popper was now strolling south toward them. A seductive, elfish voice now spilled from his boom box:

> *I'm back at my cliff*
> *Still throwing things off*
> *I listen to the sounds they make*
> *On their way down*
> *I follow with my eyes 'til they crash.*
> *Imagine what my body would sound like*
> *Slamming against those rocks.*

Al noticed as Popper sniffed at the air and, as they passed, glance longingly at their greasy paper bags. A few seconds later Al stopped, sprinted back, and offered Popper a folded paper plate with a slice. The old man accepted the charity with an emphatic smile.

CHAPTER 5. SUNDAY, JUNE 27, 2021.

D om walked slowly down the sixteenth green. He looked at the date on his phone and calculated how long it had been. Three months. He thought about Dad and winced.

A crackling voice issued from the walkie-talkie in his pocket. "Ruglia, you there?"

Dom frowned. He took out the walkie-talkie, clicked the transmitter, and said, "*De*Ruglia, bro. It's *De*Ruglia."

"Whatever. New divots on the fourteenth."

"Roger that."

When Dom had something to gain or someone to impress, he presented as outgoing, sometimes even charming. Otherwise, he reverted to his natural state: nasty and brutish. In this sense, he was something of a gifted actor.

The Assistant U.S. Attorney had gotten the closest to putting her finger on it. At sentencing, she'd argued that he could be "deceivingly pleasant and gregarious, but psychologically and physically abusive to those whom he perceives as weaker." An opportunist with sadistic tendencies, she'd said.

Fuck that bitch. Like being an opportunist is bad?

Dad had taught him to take. His father, uncle, cousins, their associates—they all took.

"In this life, you have to squeeze people, or they'll squeeze you," Dad always told him. Another refrain of Angelo DeRuglia: "When the end comes, the strong will inherit the earth. *We* will inherit the earth." Dom often reflected on those words.

And he just as often reflected on his mother's sayings.

"You're a fucking idiot, Dominick, just like your father. You're an ox." Or, "Is there a brain in that head of yours?" Or even, "You didn't get my smarts, so don't pretend you did." Four-year-old Dom, asking Mom why, unlike the other kids, he had so much trouble spelling. Why words always seemed so jumbled. "Because you're stupider than them. You don't belong with them. You belong at home with me." Lesson learned.

He hopped into the golf cart and drove east along the fairway. Looking to the left past a cluster of maples, a small sailboat and some wind-sailors glided along the twinkling surface of Lake Hynek. Not a cloud in the sky.

Two golfers and a hunched over caddie approached Dom on foot from the opposite direction. Dom waved and smiled, showing his almost blindingly pearly whites.

"Hello gentlemen, beautiful day, huh?" The men nodded and grinned.

The caddie, sweaty and dark skinned, kept up the rear. He motioned to Dom who slowed the cart. Weighed down by two golf bags, the caddie used his head to gesture east. He spoke with a thick Mexican accent.

"Hay un perrito, eh, un dog, on fourteen. Pidiendo comida."

"Huh?"

"Un dog, man. Begg'n for food ahi." He again pointed his chin east.

"Ah, okay. I'll handle it, bro." Dom accelerated east.

△ △ △

Dom neared the men's tee on the fourteenth where two guests inspected their clubs. A three-hundred-twenty-yard hole, the fairway lurched sharply left at half that distance.

A mutt was on its haunches behind the guests, wagging its tail. The animal, a beagle mix, was emaciated, its ribs visibly jagged under a patchy coat of brown fur. Dom approached the tee on foot.

He addressed the men, who were still turned the other way.

"Gentlemen, how are we today? Looks like we got us a little visitor." Dom held out his hand for the dog, which scampered toward him and sniffed excitedly. One of the golfers, a middle-aged black man even taller than Dom, turned around.

"Ah, yes. A cute one, huh? Needs some food. My wife would have a fit if she was here. And I'd have a new pet." He grinned at Dom.

Dom did double take: it was TJ Freeman. In the flesh.

"Yes sir," Dom said respectfully, "this animal needs help, for sure. Mr. Freeman, right?"

He nodded, "Just TJ. Hi there." He extended a hand. "Nice to see some other big guys around here. Sometimes I feel all alone."

Dom chuckled. "Tell me about it, br—sir, I mean. I'm a huge fan. Huge. I'm sure you hear that all the time."

"Never enough, especially these days. What's your name, son?"

"Dominick DeRuglia, sir."

"You play college ball?"

Dom shook his head.

"Just high school football. Fordham Prep in New York."

"Sure, Fordham," TJ responded, nodding. "Where'd you grow up? Let me guess: Westchester?"

"You got it," Dom laughed. "Yonkers. You heard of it?"

"Sure have, Dominick. I have cousins in Mt. Vernon. Small world, isn't it? So how'd you end up out here?"

"My dad, he, um, passed away. Family business went under. And I was, like, uh, looking for a fresh start." *Kind of true. With a liberal definition of "business."* "Can I just say that you were my favorite. You made defense cool. You made people respect good 'D,' sir."

"Another adoring fan, huh?" the second man interjected, who was now looking up from his bag.

"Dominick, this is Jay Taylor, a lawyer friend of mine. We jocks make the money, he steals it." Dom chortled.

"If I had a nickel for every time I heard that one. Dominick, a pleasure." The lawyer shook Dom's hand. "We do have to move along now, TJ. We'll have another couple creeping up on us if we don't keep up our pace."

Dom nodded and bowed reverentially.

"Of course, yes. Sorry to bother you gentlemen. TJ, sir, I'm sure you put up with guys like me all the time; you're very, like, gracious, thank you. And this dog won't be bothering you anymore, I promise you that."

TJ crouched and ran his hand along the dog's spine.

"Wish I had some food," TJ said, "little guy probably doesn't smoke Cubans. What are you going to do with him?"

"Bring him to the clubhouse, feed him, and drive him to, like, a shelter or something."

TJ nodded, satisfied.

"You know Dominick, you're a good dude, I can tell. Everyone hits a patch of bad luck now and then, but you've got the right attitude. Lots of young men these days . . ."

"Lazy criminals," the lawyer volunteered. He was staring at his wrist and swiping.

"A bit harsher than I would have said it," TJ noted, "but yes, that's one way of putting it, Jay. Anyhow, maybe I can throw you some work. Caddying or maybe some light construction work? My wife has these harebrained home improvement projects. We live out on Cedar Drive, which I think everyone and their mother already knows. We're like a stop on everyone's tour of Hynek. Anyway, find me next week; I'm on the links all the time. We'll set something up. Least I can do for a fellow big man, know what I mean?"

Dom nodded, his expression one of earnest gratitude.

"Sir, that would be, like, tremendous, really would. Now please, I insist: get back to your game. I've already taken up too much of your time."

$$\triangle \; \triangle \; \triangle$$

Within minutes, TJ and Jay had teed off, picked up their bags, and walked west along the fairway, waving to Dom as they descended a hill and disappeared. Dom sustained a beaming smile until that exact moment. Not a second longer.

He returned to the cart and removed a half-eaten breakfast sandwich from the passenger seat. From his pocket, he took out a small tool—a five-inch shaft with a switch near one end. Flipping the switch, a razor blade popped out. Dom unhooked the clasp holding the blade inside the shaft. He then wrapped a piece of bacon around the razor and tucked it back into the sandwich.

The mutt was now panting in the shade of a maple. As Dom approached, the dog looked up at him in anticipation. When he revealed the sandwich, it immediately stood, whimpered, and licked its chops. Dom held the food a few feet from its snout, letting the animal accept the scent.

Blood rushed to Dom's groin.

He slowly lowered the sandwich. The dog snatched it out of his hand, chewed twice, and then, like a duck, swallowed it in one fell swoop. For a few seconds, the dog licked its lips and stared eagerly at him.

Then came the noise: a mournful, agonizing moan, almost like a whale. The dog twitched spastically, its body starting to convulse. The animal ran south toward Doursham, its gait devolving into a wobbly stagger as it neared the overgrowth. It vanished past a tree.

Had to put that thing out of its misery. The only humane thing to do.

Dom was erect and throbbing.

CHAPTER 6. MONDAY, JUNE 28, 2021.

Bardo entered Budd's Deli on Post Road. Her brief high was beginning to taper off. A skinny man with a trimmed mustache and throwback Supersonics hat was reading a tablet behind the register. He glanced above the rims of his wire-framed glasses, grunted "Chief," and tipped his head.

"Mr. Hopkins, good day, sir."

Budd swung his stool around to a Mr. Coffee carafe, filled up a paper cup, and handed it to Bardo.

"Chocolate glazed, too," she said.

Budd turned back around and, using a pair of tongs, reached into a display case on the wall; he inserted the donut into a wax sleeve and handed it to Bardo.

"Living the stereotype, huh," Budd muttered.

"Get bent," she retorted. "Oh wait, I think your osteoporosis is already doing that, actually."

"Touché, Chief. Hey, you hear about the quake in Hamfield yesterday?" He spoke slowly. "A small one, but still."

"Yep. Still what?"

"Still, it's strange. When's the last time you heard of a quake this far from the coast? Well, I suppose you're not really the one to ask. Newbie."

Bardo was practically in ecstasy from the donut. She chewed like a cow until the dough had liquefied and then swallowed gradually, allowing the food to linger in her gullet.

"Strange," she said, "would that be strange like, let's see, you telling Cliff Bentwater about how TJ thinks Popper killed his dog? *That* kind of strange?"

Budd peered up from his tablet.

"That a *faux pas*? Didn't realize it was a state secret." He looked back down and swiped twice. "Want to hear about some other strange stuff? Suburbs of Spokane: 'Father arrested, accused of cannibalizing preteen daughter.' That's just swell. Let's see, ah, here's another, this one's out of Portland. 'Unexplained loud booms continue to baffle Portlanders.' Cliff said he was in Portland recently. Maybe he farted."

Bardo chortled, took another bite, and washed it down with a sip of hot coffee. Blowing on the rim, she asked Budd for more.

"Want more, do we? Hmm. How about this: 'Witnesses say deer drowned themselves in Lake Lowell.' Animals acting strangely; that's certainly nothing new. Ah, here's a good one. 'Cordero couple encounter egg-shaped craft while driving near Walla Walla on Tuesday night.' According to the little lovebirds, when they shined their brights on it the thing lifted off the ground and then, quote unquote, 'blinked out of existence.' Sounds credible, huh?"

Bardo licked the frosting off her index finger.

"Krispy Kreme?"

"No, a new one: 'Dough Not Laugh.' Laugh at what, I don't know. Dumb Seattle hipsters. But they're good."

She nodded. "What do you think about all that strange stuff, Budd? We coming to a head or something?"

Budd pursed his lips and considered how to answer.

"Bardo, you'll think I'm a rube if I told you. A handsome rube."

"Please, do shock my conscience."

"Okay, well, what *I* think is that—how does one put it?" He squinted. "You see, the resurrection was the first one of these crazy stories. And I think *he's* finally coming. I think he's drawing power, soaking up energy. All this weird stuff, these are, uh, how best to describe it, let's see. Ripples in the fabric of our space-time. How does that sound?"

Bardo squinted. "You asking or telling?"

"Telling. The way I see it, he's in this other place—right next to us, but worlds away—flexing his muscles. Getting himself pumped up, so to speak."

Bardo knitted her brow.

"You talking about Jesus?"

Budd shook his head. "Satan."

Bardo sipped her coffee. "So these things are disturbances. From Satan. In an adjacent dimension. That's what you're saying?"

Budd nodded.

"And from where, exactly, do these ideas come? You concoct them on your own?"

Budd tilted his head. "Drudge, Alex Jones, Earth Mystery News, Above Top Secret. Don't forget my Catholic upbringing. Kind of a synthesis, I guess you could say."

"And how seriously do you believe this stuff?"

"How seriously do you *think* I believe it?" he said with a crooked grin.

"Budd, you're one of a kind. You're a true bud, Budd. But can I ask you one more thing?"

"Shoot."

"You selling vapes to high schoolers? I'm hearing things."

His head jerked up. "Absolutely not!" he shouted. "Who told you that? Eighteen or no go; I card anyone who looks less than thirty. I'd card you."

"I'm flattered. Just asking. Stay honest, pal, that's all I'm saying. 'Honesty is the best policy.' I think Ben Franklin said that."

Nodding as he tinkered with the credit card reader on the counter, Budd registered a distracted "yup." Then he looked up at Bardo. "You know what OJ Simpson said? 'I'm absolutely, one-hundred percent, not guilty.' What was *his* policy?"

The remark's randomness sent Bardo into a fit of cackling laughter, with Budd impressed by his own comic prowess. Once Bardo had regained her composure she put on a straight face.

"Listen, when I tell you stuff about my cases, I'm doing it in *confidence*. They're not state secrets, but I just won't tell you that kind of stuff anymore. Simple as that."

"Duly noted," he replied as a mother and her eight-year-old son entered the shop. The boy held a flat rectangular object in both hands.

"Stay right here, Noah," the woman instructed as she went to the refrigerator in the back.

Bardo stared at the object. She squinted and suddenly processed what she was seeing.

"Look at that, Budd!" she said in astonishment. "An ant farm! Gosh, I haven't seen one of those since I was little girl. Didn't even realize they still sold 'em."

Noah held the ant farm horizontally in front of him and gazed down on the winding dirt tunnels. The omnipotent boy-king to his colony of insects.

Bardo could just barely make out the black specks scurrying here and there. Or maybe those specks were in her mind.

"Hey there young man," Budd called out, "wha'cha got there? Some little friends, huh?"

Noah looked up and smiled. There was something demented about the boy.

Without warning, he shook the ant farm in a circular and jerky motion—almost violently. And, as if they'd never been, the tunnels vanished.

△ △ △

Bardo entered the police station on Post Road. It consisted of four rooms on the first floor of a building only fifty feet from Budd's. But for a single jail cell with bars facing a bullpen, it could have been mistaken for any run-of-the-mill office.

Winnie Valentino, who double-hatted as a 911 dispatcher and administrative assistant, sat behind a counter near the entrance. She was a small Dominican woman with indigenous features: peanut-shaped black eyes with heavy eyelids, large earlobes, and straight black hair. Unlike Bardo, she could have been Sasha's kin.

"Hola jefe," she said warmly.

"Hi Winnie. Any calls?"

"Nada. It's been a quiet day."

Bardo nodded. "The best kind. The boys?"

"Three on patrol. Justin's on his way back." She was referring to Bardo's deputy, Justin Treanor.

Bardo felt her phone vibrate.

What time u home 2nite Mom?

Bardo typed one word—Why—and tapped "send." It occurred to her that Sasha should have been in class. She was about to type an admonishment when the precinct phone rang.

It was the 911 line. Justin had installed the emergency line so that, unlike the regular one, it pinged crisply like a submarine's sonar.

Ping,g,g,g,g. Ping,g,g,g,g.

Winnie answered.

"Nine-one-one, what is your emergency." She concentrated intently with a knitted brow. "Yes, okay. I see. Mmm hmm. The address?" She began typing and speaking simultaneously. "Fifteen Zamora. That is one, five, Zamora—'z' for zebra— 'Way.' Ma'am, yes. But, okay. Yes. But could you understand what was being said?" A brief pause. "Just a scream, okay. Right. Yes, right away. Thank you ma'am. No, we already have your number in case we need it. That's right, yes. Okay, bye

bye." Winnie turned to Bardo, who watched with inquisitive eyes.

"Diane Hooks over on Zamora Way. Heard screaming. Said it sounded 'frightening.' Lasted about thirty seconds."

Bardo racked her brain and asked, "Who's on Zamora?" Winnie shrugged.

She thought for several more seconds. "Oh, yeah: Scott Maccabee. The pilot. Not sure which one's his. Some of those houses on Zamora get rented out during the season. Could it be a rental?"

Winnie shrugged again. "Should I send one of the boys?"

Bardo glanced at her phone.

Whatever, I don't care Mom.

"No, Winnie, I'll take it. I'll head over now."

△ △ △

Bardo stood in front of 15 Zamora Way. It was small but handsome: a baby blue colonial with a spire rising from the roof like water spouting from a fountain. No sign of life outside the house or on the street; quiet as a mouse. Bardo pondered what she was going to find inside.

Husband choking wife? Wife choking husband? Wife choking wife? Cat choking dog? Husband choking chicken? The weed was still in her system. *Pull yourself together, Michelle.*

She knocked on the front door. Ten seconds and no response. A dog barked a few houses over. Next, she rang the bell, holding her index finger on the button. *One Mississippi, two Mississippi, three Mississippi, four Mississippi.*

"Hello? Anyone home?" A thin pane of stained glass lined the vestibule window. She cupped her hands around her eyes and tried to peer inside. Impossible to see.

I should check with Scott.

She recognized Scott's home one house over. She had first met him at Shaker's, a dive bar in Hamfield that was a magnet for the non-seasonal crowd. A divorced pilot with two adult children, he was a low key guy: soft spoken and to the point. Bardo liked the cut of his jib. She liked it enough, in fact, that she'd gone home with him at the end of a long night of drinking. She remembered them necking with him near the bathroom, and then sharing an Uber back to his place on Zamora. Everything after that was hazy. *He either couldn't get it up or we had amazing sex. One of the two.*

Crossing the lawn to Scott's front door, she heard shuffling inside his single story ranch house. *He must be home.*

Bardo repeated her procedure: *knock knock knock.* Wait. *Ringggggggg.* No answer. She called out. Still nothing. She called louder.

"Scott, it's Michelle. Please, I heard you moving around in there. I just need to ask you something. It'll be quick, I promise." Silence.

Bardo walked along the grass that wrapped around the side of the house. Noticing a window with drawn blinds, she pressed her face against the glass and peered in.

She did a double-take. And then she reached for her gun.

△ △ △

Fighting off the glare from the glass, Bardo made out two silhouettes: the profile of a slightly hunched over man with both arms outstretched, clutching something slumped on the floor as he walked backward a few small steps at a time. That something was a body.

The man was grasping the body by the elbows and dragging it across the floor like a sack of flour—heavy but limp and floppy. Unconscious or dead. If dead, it was recent as *rigor mortis* hadn't set in. Bardo watched for a minute until the man and body disappeared into another room.

The man was clearly Scott. A pit tightened in her stomach.

By now, Bardo was brandishing her .22. She unlocked the safety while using her other hand to retrieve the police radio from her pocket. She clicked "TALK" and whispered urgently.

"Boys, it's Michelle. Respond to 13 Zamora ASAP. Repeat: one three Zamora, 'z' as in zebra." As she spoke, Bardo trotted along the side of the house and through a patch of buzzing gnats.   The passage opened into an unkempt yard where towering western hemlocks lined the perimeter, enclosing the space from the neighboring properties.   The yard abutted Doursham Forest.

"I was just looking through Scott Maccabee's window at him dragging a body through his living room. We have to assume the situation's hostile. Get EMS, too."

Her body was taut as she moved, cat-like, toward a brick patio by a closed screen door. The glass door behind the screen was open.   She tested the handle on the screen door, which clicked and engaged. Bardo stood still for a moment and took a deep breath. *Showtime.*

She cracked the screen door just enough so that she could slip through. Once inside, she carefully set the frame back in place.

Bardo was in a kitchen. Several wrinkled *New York Times* littered a wooden table to her left.   Stools lined a Formica countertop to her right where a half-empty bottle of bourbon rested.   A sink and appliances just beyond the countertop. Straight ahead, a hallway that curved sharply into the room where Maccabee was dragging the body. She now heard it: shuffling and friction against a carpet, and then grunts. Pause. More shuffling and friction. Scott would be coming into sight any moment now. She raised her gun.

Three seconds later, he appeared.

He was hunched over and facing away from Bardo, in a red and white checkered shirt with a collar and short sleeves. The muscles on his back flexed and pressed against the fabric, and he had brawny, hairy forearms. Even his triceps sprouted coarse black hair. The curly brownish hair on his head, meanwhile, was thinning at the crown. He rested for a moment and then continued to pull.

"Scott, do *not* move!" She annunciated each syllable with laser precision.

In mid-drag, he froze.

"Put him down, put your hands up, and turn around. *Now!*"

He complied, gently lowering the person's arms to the floor—a heavyset middle-aged man. Scott then turned: he was broad-shouldered with a wide, freckled face. His hair was in disarray, overgrown and oily. And his cheeks wore at least two weeks of whiskers, which were dark brown with splashes of red.

What stood out to Bardo, though, were his eyes.

Not the sagging black patches underneath (by all appearances, he hadn't slept in days). No, it was the expressive look. A look incongruent with everything else about Scott at that moment. Indeed, notwithstanding all those telltale signs of age and exhaustion, his eyes bespoke a certain youth, even vibrancy. And their color: blue, almost aquamarine. *His eyes look different. Aren't Scott's hazel?*

Scott squinted at Bardo and shook his head.

"How is this poss . . ." His voice faded. "Chief, how are you here? Are you okay? You shoul—"

"Get down on your knees, *now!*"

Scott seemed dumbfounded by everything, as if he had just woken from a long dream. "What? No, Chief, it's me! What day is it? Tell me *now!*"

Scott dropped his arms to his sides. He began to move toward Bardo: one deliberate step after another. But his movements were disjointed and jerky, like an animatronic robot. As if he was suddenly unfamiliar with his own body.

"Put the gun down, Chief, we need to talk!"

Bardo backed up into the screen door. He was only an arm's length away.

"Scott, get the *fuck ba*—"

With his next step, the loafer on Maccabee's left foot twisted to one side on the linoleum floor. As if in slow motion, he wobbled for a second before tipping forward like a downed tree. He was heading straight for Bardo.

As he toppled toward her, Bardo used her left hand to push his body to the right while pressing her back flush against the screen door for balance. With her gun hand, she aimed the top of the barrel for his chin and swung upward.

She connected.

The contact caused her index finger to squeeze the trigger and fire a bullet into the ceiling. But that was only after the barrel collided squarely with Scott's jaw, yielding a distinct popping noise.

Scott dropped face-first to the floor. Bardo's ears rang like a bell.

△ △ △

Bardo checked the lock on the handcuffs one last time. Scott was face down on the linoleum with blood pooled under his head. The pistol whip had not only broken his jaw and knocked him out cold, but also split open his chin. *A concussion for sure, but he'll live.* In applying the cuffs, she had to pinch his husky shoulder blades together behind his back. Once he woke his muscles would nonetheless remain in a deep slumber. He'd be in serious discomfort.

Assured that Scott was at no risk of escaping, Bardo turned her attention to what she now knew was a cadaver. The man had bled profusely from a wound in his upper left chest. *If I had to guess, I'd say stab wound to the heart.* The man's clothing was of very high quality; Bardo touched part of the yellow shirt and guessed it was satin. His pants were silver with a distinctive three-inch strip of glittering gold fabric on each leg, like racing stripes. *Some kind of European style.*

The pants were smeared red, and a crimson trail led out of the kitchen back into the living room. The chest wound was still producing blood, which was soaking through the shirt and onto the floor. Must have been inflicted only minutes earlier, Bardo thought.

She examined the man's face: round, full features. His mouth and deeply set grey eyes—which were wide open—wore a scowl. As if someone had gotten the best of him at the very end. His skin an ashy white, surely attributable, in part, to death, but probably not too dissimilar from the hue when alive. His face and hair were wet.

The man's most prominent feature, by far, was a dime-sized mole on his upper left cheek from which an inch-long strand of black hair unfurled. Bardo could have easily plucked it with her fingers. *Again, some kind of absurd fashion.* She wanted to flip over the body and check for identification to satiate her curiosity, but she knew better. A cavalcade of fire trucks, ambulances, and police cars was en route. *Leave the scene as is.*

Bardo stepped over the man's legs and followed the blood into a narrow hallway, which snaked around a small bend to the living room. The blood continued along the white carpet to the living room's center. And then it abruptly stopped.

She noted the furnishings: dark brown leather couch, two matching armchairs, thin hanging television. Nothing remarkable. A large map of the world on a corkscrew board hung from a wall near the front of the house. The map had pushpins of various colors tacked into it, ostensibly marking places to which Scott had traveled. *Or maybe not.* A few pushpins were in the middle of the Pacific and Indian Oceans.

She returned her attention to the trail of blood. The red smear stopped in the absolute symmetrical center of the square room. *Had to have happened right here.* Bardo looked around for spatter. *Nada.* She contemplated how that would have been physically possible. With a stabbing or gunshot, spatter would have gone, at the very least, a few feet. Yet nothing but a red patch constricted to the dead center. The killing must have happened somewhere else.

But *how?*

CHAPTER 7. MONDAY, JUNE 28, 2021.

Aiden released the oars, which were secured to the small rowboat by rotatable bolts, and let them splash into the placid, shimmering water. The sun had just hit its apex. He wiped the sweat from his brow and removed his Ray Bans, cleaning the lenses with his tank-top. He was pleased with the workout so far, which had toned his arms and upper back nicely. He peeked over the side to catch a reflection of himself in the water, but saw only twinkling aquamarine.

His wife, draped in white fabric just shy of a hijab, sat on a narrow bench at the fore and was leaning back. A straw sunhat hid her red curls while garish sunglasses with dark clamshell lenses masked her face. A hardcover book—*Annihilation*—was open in her lap. She was either deeply immersed or fast asleep.

The sun, situated behind Lilly, beat down on her back. But even in the cocooned shade of her lap, her engagement ring twinkled like a ruby star. It wasn't ruby, though. It was exponentially rarer: painite.

A prized heirloom from Aiden's grandmother Becca, who was a fourth generation Campbell and a member, in good standing, of the Daughters of the American Revolution. Only a handful of painite rocks had ever been cut into faceted gemstones, and this was one of them. Worth more than a Park Avenue townhouse. Aiden had bought Lilly an "alternative" diamond engagement ring—four carats, certainly nothing to sniff at ("at which to sniff," as Aiden would correct his associates)—with the tacit understanding that she'd wear the diamond during their everyday lives, reserving "Big Boy," as he called it, for special occasions. It was just too damn valuable even for someone with Aiden's wealth, which was itself nothing at which to sniff. But he never explicitly instructed Lilly as much, loath to articulate the words and, in doing so, admit that even for him, Aiden James Campbell of East 71st and Park, something was just too damn expensive. As if uttering the thought would reduce his worth by half. So he'd said nothing.

Lilly understood the contours of her husband's ego. She could see them with her eyes closed, like the striations on the wooden steps that led into her childhood bedroom—a room she'd shared with three brothers and one sister. Aiden was far from the richest man in the world, or even in their apartment building. Yet she knew that it was beyond his power to give her the ring with the caveat that she not wear it because it cost too much. She understood this . . . and so wore it everywhere. To the gym, to the beach, on airplanes. On a rowboat.

He made the decisions for them both. What they were doing, when, with whom; their vacations, their restaurants, their circle of friends. Lilly, meanwhile, was his stunning accessory. And wearing that ring was her small rebellion and reminder, to both of them, of her continuing resolve. A small shiv she had plunged into his gut.

Aiden stared at Big Boy. Yet in his peripheral vision, ten feet past his wife, something began to move just beneath the surface. A long and darkened mass pushing the water and sending small ripples in all directions, upsetting the placid sheen. A four-foot row of appendages—bone white and speckled with pink—broke the surface. They were triangular, like fossilized dinosaur teeth, arching upward a few inches in the air before gliding back underwater.

"Lilly!" Aiden tapped the side of the boat. "Lilly, wake up!"

The staccato taps caused her chin to rise an inch, eyes hidden behind the dark shades. Aiden motioned with his head toward her left side. The band of dinosaur teeth made up the spine of a gentle, meandering sturgeon, which had broken the surface only a few feet from Lilly's face. She giggled in delight and reached toward the fish.

The painite's translucence instantly caught the sun, shimmered like lava, and began searing the skin on her finger. She recoiled jerkily and waved her hand in the air.

"Oww!"

Confused and alarmed, Aiden grabbed the sides of the boat and pulled himself toward Lilly.

"What is it? What's happening?" The boat rocked with his movement.

"It's burning! The ring is *burning* me!"

Aiden shifted back to his bench.

"Take it off and give it to me. But be *careful*."

As he spoke, Lilly dipped and then withdrew her hand from the water, and started frantically manipulating the gold band. After two seconds, it came loose and dropped into her palm. Aiden's eyes were glued to her clenched fist.

"Give it to me, Lilly."

She extended her hand toward him.

And then something struck the boat.

Pop!

It was some kind of projectile, as if they'd been hit by tiny cannon fire. The small craft lurched slightly away from the point of impact. Lilly shrieked. Aiden covered his head and dove forward, rocking the boat and tipping Lilly to her right. She tried using one hand to steady herself by grabbing onto the lip of the frame, but the jolt from Aiden's frantic movement sent her toppling into the water.

As the boat steadied itself, Aiden, still shielding his face, scanned his surroundings. His wife bobbed alongside the boat and searched for a way to hoist herself back onboard.

Onshore, hundreds of feet away, two men waved and shouted indecipherably. One held a driver in the air and shook his head, his body language apologetic.

"Aid, what *was* that?" Lilly's glasses were gone and her sunhat floated several feet away. "Are we safe?"

Aiden shook his head angrily.

"Golf ball, Lilly. A God damn golf ball."

Lilly exhaled. "I thought someone was shooting. Help me back in."

He took his wife's hands by the wrists and pulled her chest over the edge of the frame, quickly shifting his weight to the opposite side to steady the boat. He then sat back on the bench. Lilly squirmed forward. She scraped her breasts over the edge and, groaning from exertion, flopped onto the floorboard. She lay panting.

Aiden watched her for a few more seconds before something overpowering occurred to him.

"Lilly, *Lilly.*" His cadence slowed to a trickle. "The ring. You have it, right? *Right?*"

The boat creaked as water lapped against the side. She was silent.

He stood up. His body began to shake; the rage was mounting.

Lilly curled into the fetal position. She knew what came next.

△ △ △

Al scrambled to undress and change into his white smock. He shot an anxious glance at each person who entered the locker room, praying for respite from Dom.

His mind's eye drifted back to the zoo a couple of days earlier—how he almost got Bernie killed. That mindless, thrashing beast.   Bernie had been inches from clearing the enclosure when those paws swallowed his leg. And those black eyes. He swore there was a look of glee. Glee at the chance to tear a man to shreds. But not just any man: the man who had raised him from a cub and fed him every day. *Rocky should be euthanized.* His thoughts circled back to Dom. And his father.

A cascading eruption of sirens fractured his thoughts. One siren, two, three, six. Piercing. *Something big's going down.*

As Al tightened his belt, the sirens triggered a flood of new thoughts. Memories of his mother.

Nothing bad, though.

A stinging sadness was always entwined with these memories, yet these were different—joyful.   When he accompanied her to Paris for a medical conference and, like movie stars, they toured the city in a limousine. When she entered his bedroom and, with sorrowful eyes, whispered that Grandpa Leo had passed to the "spirit plane," as she called it— the place where everyone would eventually reunite.   In the hospital room, when she introduced him to his sister Kaz.

The tragedy always eclipsed these happier memories, but what really *was* the tragedy, he suddenly asked himself. To be sure, he remembered the terrible emotions, but, inexplicably, didn't actually *feel* them. What the police had told him about the incident felt fuzzy, distant, and fleeting, like sand through fingers. Displaced by the tender, better times.

He reached for the curled lobe of his right ear. His mother had always worn a miniature black pearl teardrop on a delicate gold necklace, and he now wore that pearl as a remembrance. A hidden piercing that was his own secret memento, invisible to the world.   The sudden realization was unnerving: it was not there. The pearl was gone. He racked his brain for how this could have happened.

Rocky's cage. When I hit the bushes.

A short brown man entered the locker room and issued a soft "*buenas tardes*," breaking his concentration. Al checked his iPatch: 4:30 p.m. This would be the first of many employees from the golf course soon spilling into the locker room. In other words, Dom was coming. *Rocky and Dom. Dad.*

Al got moving. He clicked the combination lock into place, tucked in his shirt, and headed toward the kitchen.

△ △ △

Al was assigned to bus tables for the first half of the shift and scrub dishes for the second. Dinner commenced shortly before 5:00 p.m. with a room of red knit cardigans and wrinkled scalps. As he collected dishes and cleaned tables, his thoughts wandered to a familiar topic: what the earliest diners were ordering. Tonight, the geriatric patrons at three different tables had ordered the pistachio-crusted salmon. Shortly into his stint at the Field Club, he'd noticed that, on some nights, numerous customers at different tables chose the same dish from the menu. As the chef put it, this or that dish had "won the popularity contest" on a particular night.

He always wondered how that was possible. He hypothesized that, as new customers entered, they overheard the orders from diners who were already seated, saw the dishes being served, or smelled the food—one or all of which influenced their decision-making. Or, more interestingly, perhaps the guests could somehow communicate without speaking. Something physical that other brains could detect and interpret, even if only subconsciously. Some kind of field. This led Al to one of Ingo's paranormal musings: that thoughts could be transmitted over vast distances, and that gifted clairvoyants could perceive events no matter where or even when they transpired. Something about a "shared consciousness framework."

And so Al ruminated as he scurried about the dining room, oblivious to the fact that Lilly was eating alone in a corner. Nor had he noticed that virtually every guest was preoccupied—intensely focused, in fact—on their phones, tablets, and iPatches. Some were standing up and facing away from the dining room, eyes trained on the large monitor above the bar. It was playing Fox News 1, the screen littered with scrolling graphics and newsfeeds. The most prominent said "BREAKING NEWS" in red, white, and blue font. A slideshow of still photographs showed American astronauts standing with helmets at their sides.

Carrying a pitcher of cucumber-infused water, Al wrested control of his focus and squinted at the screen.

"*Valor Crew Disappears. President's Address To Begin Momentarily.*" The words jolted him back to reality. In fact, they whipped his brain into shock.

The Valor was part of Project Infinity, the President's signature space program. It was a manned mission to Mars—the first. The ship carried supplies for the crew to erect and sustain a small outpost, which was a foundational step toward colonizing and then terraforming the red planet. The Valor was three months into its roughly eight-month journey. Al had been paying close attention to its progress because it was the very kind of mission he had once aspired to join. If everything had turned out differently.

Yet the headline was bizarre: the crew "disappeared"? Al considered the verbiage. Not "destroyed," not "lost contact." He knew that cameras inside and outside the ship transmitted video to a semi-live Facebook broadcast, which he sometimes checked . . .

He nearly stumbled into Lilly's table.

Seeing her again was a surprise, but overshadowed by the Valor news. Alone with a tablet, she glanced up with a concerned expression, oversized sunglasses concealing her eyes. Her hair was styled differently: more lustrous and almost ruffled, tumbling onto her shoulders. She recognized Al and grinned bashfully.

"Oh my, hi again," she whispered. Her voice was soft and feminine, in stark contrast to the other night. She swallowed. "Look, I'm sorry for what happened."

Al had nearly forgotten about it.

"Oh, that? It's fine. I'm the one who spilled everything. Your winks didn't help. Bit of a distraction."

Lilly chuckled; her face turned beet red.

"I was in rare form, wasn't I?" she said. "Three Southern Comforts and four Vicodin will do that to you." She paused for a second. "You know what, that wasn't really me. It was my identical twin, Flirtasia."

"Funny you say that," Al parried, "because that wasn't me who spilled everything on your husband. It was my own twin, Intimidated McGee."

Lilly squealed in delight and used her napkin to muffle the sound. When she removed the napkin, she was snorting like a piglet.

"Oh dear Prudence, I'm snorting now, Mr. McGee!" She reached to shake Al's hand. "I'm Lilly Campbell." She glanced at his nametag. "Al. Let's see: short for Alex, Allen, Albert, Alvin, Alejandro, Ali. Waiting for you to stop me, any time now."

"Alyosha." He flashed a mischievous grin. "Alyosha Dragunov." He watched Lilly's eyes as she processed the name. "Did you know," he continued, "that you had lipstick smeared across your front teeth the other night?"

She nodded. "Well, not at first. But I eventually discovered that fact. The gentleman I was with kindly chose not to point that out until the end of our evening. Very sweet."

"Why the sunglasses, Lilly?"

Her grin flattened. She didn't answer.

"Where do you hail from, Al-yo-sha?"

Unsure whether to repeat his question, Al paused awkwardly.

"Uh, I've been in Washington since the beginning of the year. Before that, Ukraine."

"Wow, Ukraine. You speak so well, so natural."

"My mom speaks fluent English and raised me bilingually." He winced at his use of the present tense. *Speaks. Spoke.* "And you?"

"I've always spoken English," she said with a renewed smile. "I'm from the south. Florida. A little town called Quincy. I doubt you've ever been."

"I have not. Is it nice?"

"That's a subjective word. Some folks think so. I never did, but I don't live there anymore. I live in Manhattan with Aiden, who you met the other night under, let's say, inauspicious circumstances."

"Captain of industry?"

Lilly tilted her head expressively. "Lawyer for captains of industry."

"And where is he tonight?"

The inflection in Lilly's voice lowered. "The thing is, I did something stupid today. Lost something very valuable. He's a bit pissed, frankly." She paused. "And anyway, he wakes up so early to golf; he's probably asleep already by now. I'm happy for some me-time." She glanced at her tablet and then looked back up. "You hear about the Valor?"

Al gestured with his chin toward the television over the bar. She craned her neck and saw the crowd gathered and waiting for the President to speak.

"Oh wow, I didn't realize they were playing it here. I've been looking everywhere for more details, but nothing. Just NASA's press release. How does a crew 'disappear'—what does that even mean?"

Al nodded. "I was thinking the same thing. There are video feeds all over the shuttle."

"I know. They apparently went offline at some point. Very freaky."

Al pointed to the TV again. "He's about to speak."

The bartender unmuted the giant monitor. The entire restaurant, staff and guests, stared as the President took to the podium.

> *President: My fellow Americans. I come to you today with dispiriting news. As you know, the Valor and its brave crew embody humanity's first manned mission to Mars—the first time*

that human feet, American feet, will touch that alien planet. The men and women on Valor possess, in the truest sense, the qualities that the ship's name connotes: courage and unmitigated dedication to the exploration and expansion of our frontiers. Our frontiers as both Americans and humans.

It is, therefore, with the deepest regret that I must now report: we have lost contact with the Valor's crew.

At 6:38 this morning, our communications systems in Houston sustained a brief, but complete, interruption. This lasted approximately four seconds. Upon resuming, Mission Control could no longer re-establish audio, video, or biometric contact with the crew.

To be clear, the Valor is intact and, by all indications, undisturbed. The communications and data-gathering instruments on the ship appear, presently, to be operating effectively. But the six crew members are not inside the ship. Simply put, we do not know their fate at this time. For lack of a better word, they disappeared.

Now, needless to say, we have an army of talented scientists and engineers working tirelessly to determine what happened—to locate these brave Americans and to understand the physical explanation. I have confidence that, with a little more time, we will, at the very least, gain some valuable insight into this event. I'll now turn it over to Bill Mitchell, NASA Director.

Bill Mitchell: Thank you, Mr. President. Hello everyone. I lament having to address you and the American people under these circumstances, but I hope to at least answer some of your questions. Bear in mind that everything is a work in progress, an investigation in progress. Yes, you first.

Reporter 1: Director Mitchell, NASA has bio-tracking technology to remotely monitor the vital signs of each crew member. What do those instruments show?

BM: They register nothing. Now, this could stem from either the crew no longer wearing the devices, which are either embedded in their clothing or worn against their skin in various places. It could also indicate, uh, that the crew members have, uh, expired. We do not have a way to distinguish between the two, at least at this moment.

R2: Do the cameras inside Valor record every square inch of space in the ship? What I mean is, could they be somewhere in the ship, but just beyond the cameras' range?

BM: The answer is no, the internal cameras do not provide absolutely full interior coverage. For example, we don't have cameras inside the toilet stalls. Certain storage areas are unmonitored as well. So, I guess, by extension, is it possible that all six of them are somehow clustered in one of those spaces? Theoretically, yes. Do I think that's the case? Not at all. Remember, too, there's no gravity, so unless they were alive and hiding in these unmonitored spots, we'd see evidence of the crew moving past a camera. Eighty percent of the interior is under observation. And the ship has thermal imagers. We'd be registering body heat, which we are not.

R3: Do we know what caused the communications interruption? Was there anything visible or audible that preceded it? Anything out of the ordinary, I mean?

BM: Well, that's two discrete questions, so let me start with your second one: was there anything we saw or heard or that registered on our instruments. Frankly, we don't know yet. The Valor collects and analyzes tens of thousands of different kinds of data points at any given second. We're using automated and manual processes to check that data for anomalies; staff in Houston and Cape Canaveral are working around the clock. So I'll have to get back to you on that one as we make progress.

I will say that roughly ten seconds before the black out, forward-facing cameras outside the ship recorded a brief—quarter of a second—flash of light. We don't know what that means, and we're working to figure it out.

As to your first question, the cause. Given the kind of disturbance and its length, which was very brief, we're considering a disruption in the electromagnetic field, which could

*result from a solar flare, among other potential causes. So
these two issues do overlap, to some degree. Again, we need
more time.*

R3: How could a solar flash cause the crew to vanish in thin air?

BM: I have no idea.

*R4: Where is the crew, Mr. Mitchell? What do you think
happened? Are they still alive? Is that even possible?*

*BM: Folks, this is uncharted territory. We've never dealt with
anything like this before. This is a singular, anomalous event.
I don't have any theories at this point.*

*Our crew is in deep space—deeper than humans have ever gone.
Are we dealing with some kind of, I don't know, unknown force
out there, a pocket of dark matter? Something that uniquely
affects living tissue? I mean, I just don't know. I'm not a
biologist, although we have a team of biologists considering the
implications. What we do need, I can say, is more time. I don't
know if the crew is alive. Either way, my prayers are. . .*

The bartender muted the television as the press conference
cut back to the news studio.

Reflexively, Lilly took off her sunglasses and put two fingers
to the edge of her eye in thought. She looked at Al with
incredulity and shook her head. They locked eyes and shared
the moment's enigmatic implications.

And then Al noticed the skin under her left eye. A waxy layer
of makeup covering swollen, purplish flesh. She caught his
wandering glance and quickly replaced the sunglasses.

"Where were *you*," she asked, "when you found out that the
Valor's crew disappeared?"

Al nodded. "I know. I have goosebumps. What do you think
it means?"

She flexed her jaw, pondering the question.

"I think it means we don't know nearly as much as we're
convinced we do. Kind of a reminder that there's still some
mystery out there."

"Watching the NASA Director speak," he said, "that look on his face. It was like a caveman trying to explain the physics of lightning and thunder. Something just happened, but what the hell just happened. You know?"

She nodded.

"I have a friend who probably has some theories already," Al noted.

"Truther?"

He tilted his head. "Something along those lines, yeah." Al glanced at the time on Lilly's tablet. "Believe it or not, I have to finish my shift." He flashed a grin. "People need food spilled on them."

Lilly smiled even as her eyes betrayed disappointment.

"It'd be nice to keep talking with you, Al. You're easy to talk to."

He nodded. "Good thing is, Mrs. Campbell, you'll have the pleasure of watching me work. Maybe you can give me notes, if we talk again."

"I'd like that."

Al filled up Lilly's water glass and then returned to the kitchen. She watched him every step of the way.

△ △ △

Al wished he'd worn his iPatch. He had left it in his locker cognizant that, of late, he'd been losing himself in the device. He could only imagine what Ingo had written by now.

He contemplated the Valor. This anomalous event, as the NASA Director styled it, was a step toward something radically different. Al could feel it: a transition to something new. He couldn't tell whether the change was in his own life—a personal juncture of some sort—or a change for everyone. At the same time, he had a nagging sense of *déjà vu*.

And Lilly. Still in such a daze from the Valor, he reflected on their conversation—on the naturalness and fluidity with which they communicated. He felt a spark, for sure. More like a tingling interconnectivity. A Pop Rocks attraction, their fields crackling and entangling, exploring one another.

A gruff but friendly voice interrupted his reverie.

"Señor Dragunov, earth to Señor Dragunov."

It was Derik Gange. In a physical sense, Derik was the antithesis of Al: short and portly with a torso like a beer keg and a full head of thick black hair. He had an upturned snub nose that was almost piggish.

"Earth to Señor Dragunov," he repeated.

Al snapped back to the here and now.

"Derik, sorry sir. Taken aback by the Valor news, that's all. Just need to fill up the pitchers and then I'll be back on the floor."

"Al, do me a favor: we got a late afternoon delivery of some greens. I'll put Chris on the floor and you go grab the stuff. UPS left three crates by the range," he pointed to the back door. "Leave the crates, just bring in the greens."

△ △ △

Crowbar in hand, Al stared at the crates. A lone lettuce leaf poked through a wooden slit. He wedged the crowbar under the lip of the crate and began to shimmy.

It was the tail end of dusk, with scattered pockets of glowing magenta to the west in an otherwise black sky. The driving range behind the crates extended to the southern shore of the lake. Netting on each side kept the balls confined, but the tees themselves faced the water with no net. The ablest golfers—those who could drive the ball two-hundred-seventy yards—got the satisfaction of hearing the faint plunk of their ball enter the water, like a penny in a fountain. The Field Club scraped the lakebed each year and recovered several thousand practice balls.

The range was closed and empty, save for one cart combing the landscape to retrieve balls. The last shift.

Al pried open the first crate and discovered a large plastic bag brimming with lettuce heads. Sifting through the heads, he noticed a brown thumb-sized object. A dead water bug of considerable girth.

He sprung back in surprise and shuddered, his upper body twitching as if doing the electric slide.

Didn't have those in Kiev, that's for sure. He took a breath, regained his composure, and peered at the front of the crate. "*Producto de Guatemala.*" Using the crowbar like a reaching wand, he balanced the insect on the sharpened prong and gently dropped it onto the gravel driveway.

Poor little guy. He inspected the creature and noticed a checkered pattern of yellow and red along its tail. *Kind of pretty in its own wa—*

As if the foot of an angry god, a large black Nike high-top crashed down on the insect and pulverized its exoskeleton, the sound like a tearing parasol.

The sneaker was attached to a muscular white leg with a calve like a ham. The leg fed up to white khaki shorts, a teal polo shirt, bulging forearms and biceps, and, finally, the bald head of Dominick DeRuglia. His mouth wore a hyena-like grin. The light from an overhead electric lamp illuminated a weeping cold sore on his upper lip.

Dom was sweaty. The range cart—the one that had been off in the distance collecting golf balls—was parked a few feet away.

"You're welcome, *brah*," he snickered, dragging his shoe across the gravel and turning the mangled insect into paste. Al took a step back, tightening his grip on the crowbar.

"Dom. I didn't see you there."

"Shagging balls. Saw you and wanted to say hello to my *brahhh*." He perverted the word "brother" beyond any conceivable recognition. "What's in the crates?" On a dime, Dom's tone changed from menacing to cordial.

A bully's mind games. He would have licked my boots in Kiev.

Al's heart was racing, his palms instantly wet.

"Just some vegetables." He tested Dom's mood. "You hear about the Valor?"

"What the fuck is that?"

"The spaceship that's going to Mars."

"What about it?"

"The crew disappeared. The President just spoke."

Dom bared his teeth like a dog. The crinkling of his lip caused the sore to drizzle puss. Like a human-dragon chimera, Dom's tongue, surprisingly slender and adroit, shot out of his mouth, traced the top lip, and lapped up the syrupy liquid. Al had to suppress a gag.

"You staring at my cold sore, Drago? You're gonna make me self-conscious, *brahhhhhhh*." The viciousness returned. Al retreated a step.

"I need to get these veggies inside."

"You want to kiss me—big smooch on my cold sore? Is that what'cha want, Putin?"

Al shook his head and took another step back. Dom took two steps forward.

"It hurts me when you blow me off like you did the other night. You think I'm so stupid. Well I'm not. People think I am. But they're wrong."

Four seconds of silence.

Out of nowhere, Dom bent over guffawing, holding onto his knees as if in the throes of some epic punchline.

This man will eventually kill me.

Dom recovered his composure and stood up. With a beaming smile, he said, "Ah, bro, we're too funny together. I'll help you with the veggies." He reached out. "Give me the crowbar. I'll pop the other crates mad quick."

Al shook his head. "No thanks. I can do it myself."

"Let me help you. Give me the crowbar."

Al continued shaking his head. His muscles tensed.

"You ungrateful prick," Dom barked, "I'm your friend, trying to *help* you. I'm trying to be magonious, magnonious, magonia, whatever the fuck that word is. Give me that crowbar." He crept forward in half-steps. Al took a deep breath.

"Don't make me do this, Dom." Crowbar in hand, Al cocked his arm and readied himself. *Draw from my pool of fortitude, as Mom always says. Said. Says.*

Dom was again smiling effusively.

"Oh, you're gonna hit me? Oh yeah, Drago, let's party bro!"

What happened next, at least in some parallel multiverse, was at once gruesome and well-deserved. But in this here and now, a frustrated Derik Gange defused the encounter. Like a ravioli with arms and legs, he waddled over to the crates, his body language bespeaking impatience. He tapped Al on the shoulder.

"Seriously, Al, what's going on with you? It's like you got sucked into a time warp. Carlos just ran out of iceberg."

Like a cat in a dog's presence, Al's body and mind were taut and ready to strike, his shoulders pinched together. Derik's tapping and voice barely made a dent. The tension was palpable.

"What's going on here?" Derik's tone shifted from irritation to concern.

Dom's expression, and the timbre of his voice, changed instantly; he was suddenly soft-spoken and even mildly articulate. He reached out to shake Derik's hand.

"Hi, I don't think we've met, sir. I'm Dominick DeRuglia. I do landscaping."

Derik shook his hand. "Pleasure, Dominick."

"I apologize for keeping my buddy Al, I'm totally to blame. I saw him unpacking the crates and drove over here to ask him about the Valor. Then we started chatting about the Mariners. Again, it was, like, totally my fault."

Reassured, Derik nodded. "It's okay. Al, please just pick up the speed."

"Al, talk to you later, brother. Mr. Gange, good meeting you." Dom got into the golf cart and accelerated into the night. Derik hustled back toward the kitchen.

In what was left of the dusk, Al could just make out Dom's silhouette: left arm protruding from the cart, middle finger straight up in the air.

CHAPTER 8. TUESDAY, JUNE 29, 2021.

Another cloudless morning.

Aiden walked along the fairway parallel to the lake, its inimitable aquamarine twinkled as if sprinkled with fairy dust. The temperature was relatively low (only in the high sixties), but would climb to the eighties by noon. He paused to scan the lake: a boardwalk a few miles to the west, lined with seafood restaurants and tiki bars; the north shore dotted with white colonials that, from more than twenty miles away, resembled grains of salt peppering the green landscape; and even further north Shendo Ridge, a striking mix of bare rock and verdant shrubbery that evoked China's Yellow Mountains. The incline continued as Shendo stretched east for several miles before tapering off into forest.

It was only 6:30 a.m., but the lake traffic was already bustling. Sailboats, jet skis, canoes, kayaks, a smattering of powerboats. Half-a-dozen kayakers, like a flock of oversized geese, paddled near the shore and waved to Aiden. He ignored the friendly gestures and continued walking, caddy-less.

He'd spent yesterday afternoon and evening making urgent phone calls and visiting Hynek's town hall. The upshot: a three-man salvage team from Tacoma would be arriving in a few hours, and he'd negotiated an "emergency scuba permit" with the town. Big Boy was on the lakebed somewhere. At best. In his mind's eye, that fossil of a fish with the polka-dot spine had swallowed his sinking treasure. He shuddered.

When Lilly realized what had happened, she'd opened her mouth several times but produced no words. He couldn't stop himself from hitting that pretty face. Not the first time he'd done so. Probably not the last.

And then he'd spent the next five minutes in a tantrum: wielding an oar like an axe and swinging at the water until his arms were noodles. Neither of them spoke a word. Aiden had sat in silence, contemplating next steps. Moments later, he was having his secretary track down reputable scuba crews in the Pacific Northwest. If all went smoothly, Aiden thought, he should have the ring back in a few hours.

He exhaled as he approached his ball on the fairway, unshouldered his bag, and lay it across the grass. He tried to focus on enjoying the round.

Lilly was always mystified why he didn't use a caddie or a cart. But for Aiden, the exertion of hauling the bag was part of the appeal. A day of traversing the course with a thirty-pound pack was hardly a cakewalk. Eighteen holes left him drained and was not unlike a full day on the slopes: muscles blissfully sore and appetite voracious. Coupled with weightlifting every other day, he'd be returning to work in peak form.

He couldn't help but grin. He was looking forward to that first day back. Perhaps he'd check in at the office in his favorite tight black shirt. That new young associate, the Russian one. She'd probably need to assist him with an "emergency" motion. He was truly skilled at formulating legal emergencies. She'd have to drop whatever she was doing to assist him. They'd need to work together closely. Aiden tried to recall her name. *Isabelle. Belle, she goes by.*

A few feet shy of a sand trap, Aiden approached his ball. He chose an iron and then unhatched the bag's kickstand. Crouching behind the ball and facing the green, he considered the angle. He then stood up and assumed his stance, wiggling his butt like Derek Jeter. He took a deep breath and prepared to swing—it called for a half-powered chip shot.

Yet he froze. A curious sound: chattering and squeaking.

From a patch of thick overgrowth near the shore, two large raccoons emerged and scampered frantically across the fairway between Aiden and the green. Three cubs in tow and scrambling to keep up. The animal family paid Aiden no mind as it continued south toward an adjoining fairway that spilled into Doursham. Aiden's jaw dropped.

A new sound brought Aiden's attention to Lake Hynek: frenzied splashing. As far as he could see, small fish were dancing in and out of the water, just barely breaching the surface before disappearing again. It gave the water a carbonated appearance. Or as if the lake was an enormous boiling cauldron.

Aiden's mouth suddenly dried, his palms became clammy, and his heart began racing. Whatever these animals felt, he now felt it too. Something was about to happen.

△ △ △

Michelle Bardo, Justin Treanor, and three Hamfield officers returned from Budd's to the Hynek stationhouse, coffee cups in hand. The Hamfield men had helped Bardo and Justin begin processing the scene at Scott Maccabee's house. All five had then spent the night in the fishbowl.

Bardo knew how to run a homicide investigation—she'd cut her teeth in Baltimore—but she was nonetheless appreciative for the help. Her old chief used to say, "Every investigation's a story that's already been told." But this story was like nothing she'd ever handled before, and the more brains on hand, the better.

In Baltimore, the scenario inexorably spoke for itself: a shootout between rival gang members; an insult at a basketball game igniting a brawl, with shots fired during the melee; some poor schmoe immigrant (a Jamaican with three jobs) shot to death during a robbery. They were typologies for a reason. In Hynek, however, Bardo had a bona fide mystery on her hands, at least until Scott spilled his guts. A well-respected and reputable local citizen—a pilot, no less—dragging a corpse through his living room. Discovered by pure chance.

No murder weapon, no obvious motive—hell, no clue about the victim's identity—and blood spatter that, in Bardo's eyes, didn't make a lick of sense. Almost impossibly and illogically contained. As if the stabbing happened somewhere else and the men then materialized in Scott's living room through a tear in space. Bardo was flummoxed and needed help. The Hamfield officers represented step one. Step two was a seasoned three-person forensics unit from Olympia that would be arriving in a few hours to collect blood and DNA samples and to help analyze the scene.

Scott, for his part, was sleeping soundly in the bullpen drunk tank; he'd been passed out since Bardo's gun met his jaw. By not bringing Scott to a hospital, Bardo was bucking procedure, but she had an ER physician visit and examine Scott while he was handcuffed to the creaky cot. The doctor's opinion: probably a concussion, but compounded by sleep deprivation. Scott had sagging bags under his eyes; his brain badly needed this rest.

The doctor had advised Bardo to let him sleep. Once he woke, keep him that way for at least twenty-four hours. He'd need to have his jaw examined.

And so the five cops waited patiently for Scott to open his eyes, while they napped intermittently and traded goofy insults. At around 3:00 a.m., Scott had mumbled some words in his sleep. Bardo had rushed to the cell and listened; he'd sounded agitated. She had managed to discern a few cryptic statements:

"How'rehold-enme?" "Icunseethaworld, so pretty." *Did he say something about a 'pretty world'?*

Justin sat at the desk on the far side of the room catty-corner to the drunk tank, his legs folded across the desktop and husky frame pressing down on the wobbly office chair. It was a precarious balancing act. He blew into his cup and then sipped, making a crude slurping noise.

"Pardon me," Justin announced.

They had eaten pizza only two hours earlier, and Justin—having put down four slices with mushroom and sausage—belched loudly, causing his body to spasm and hot coffee to spill on his hand. He lowered his feet, quickly stood up, and blew forcefully on his hand. "Cocksucker!"

One of the Hamfield officers, Josh Urban, chuckled.

"Don't hurt ya' self, Justin," Josh said, "we need your sixty IQ if we're gonna solve this thing." The other cops laughed. Bardo, who was in her office with her eyes closed and door open, cracked a tiny smile.

"Hey Josh," Justin retorted, "sixty's not my IQ, it's my dick size. Just ask Mrs. Urban."

"That doesn't even make sense," Josh replied.

Justin chortled, amused at his own absurdity. He added, "They don't call me the 'Comeback King of Washington' for nothing," which compounded the goofiness. The other officers were giggling as well, the lack of sleep taking its toll on their faculties.

A hoarse, gravelly voice spoke

"How did I get here?"

Scott Maccabee was awake.

△ △ △

As if bounding off a trampoline, Bardo leapt out of her office.

"Scott, hey, good morning. How do you feel?"

"Disoriented. A lot of pain." He squinted and massaged his temples, scrunching his face. With his palms shielding his eyes from the light, he asked, "Shelly, where are we, the station? What am I doing here?"

Justin, by now standing behind Bardo with coffee still in hand, whispered, "*Miranda*, Chief."   Bardo nodded without turning around.

"Scott," she said, "we arrested you last night in your home, and I need to read you your rights before we talk any more. Just procedure; have to do it, pal. Scott, you have—"

"*Christ, Shelly!*" Scott snapped, shooting daggers at Bardo. "Did you hear what I said? I don't know *how* I got here, I don't understand what's happening. Tell me what's happening. I was just somewhere so far away you wouldn't bel—"

"We can't talk, Scott, unless you agree on paper to talk. And the Constitution requires you to agree knowingly and intelligently, which means I have to read you these rights, and you have to say 'yes,' and then you have to sign a little form"— Justin waved a paper in the background—"and then we can talk. Fair enough?"

Scott gritted his teeth and snorted. "Fair enough, yeah. Do it."

Bardo read the *Miranda* warnings, Scott said "yes" several times, and then he signed and dated a form. Scott handed the form through the bars.

"Can you please just tell me what I'm doing here and why I'm handcuffed to this cot?"

"Why don't you start by telling me the last thing you remember."

The trace of a grin formed on Scott's upper lip.

"Shelly, you won't believe a God damn word. I'll tell you, though. But first, I need to know how I ended up here. *Please.*" His elbows were on his knees and he stroked the growth on his face. He stamped a foot while repeating "please."

Bardo nodded.   "I responded to your neighbor's house yesterday afternoon. We had gotten a call about some shouting. No one was at your neighbor's, so I walked next door to check with you. I rang the bell and no answer, but I heard movement inside. I went around the side to see if you were in the back. I looked in a window and saw you dragging someone—a *body*, Scott—through your living room."

Scott's eyes telegraphed shock.

"I went inside the back door and told you to stop, but you didn't. You fell right into me. So I pistol whipped you. You've been asleep since." She paused. "Not ringing a bell?"

"Who's the dead guy?" Scott asked.

God, he seems sincere.

"Well, Scott, that's something we're hoping you could help us answer."

△ △ △

Scott pursed his lips in thought. "It started, let's see, about two weeks ago. You know what I do for a living, Shelly, and I'm sure you all know as well." He glanced at the other officers. "In any case, I'm a commercial pilot. The first 'event,' I guess you'd call it, happened when I was about to start a route back from Baton Rouge.

"I was at a lunch counter at Ryan Field, which is the main airport down there. It all began when this Delta counter-girl ran up to me. Looked like she'd seen a ghost, but doing her best to act composed, bless her soul. She kind of stutters to me, 'Captain, we have a situation at one of the gates. We're just trying to get some pilots' opinions, maybe those with a military background.' She looked terrified. I was in the California Reserves so I thought, hell, maybe I can help out with whatever this is.

"We go onto the tarmac and there are, maybe, I dunno, a couple dozen folks out there. At least four other pilots, a bunch of mechanics, various other Delta staff. Baton Rouge is a Delta hub.

"Everyone's got their backs to the runway. And they're all staring up into the sky above the terminal." He rubbed his hands together. "Shelly, you know when a cat sees a bird? How its eyes widen and neck constricts. You know what I mean?

That's what it looked like: a bunch of transfixed cats out there on the tarmac. No one saying a word. Just staring. Up.

"So let me say this: there's heavy cloud cover that day. No sun. The clouds were low, maybe fifteen-hundred feet. And just below the clouds, there's this, this—let's call it a *thing*." He cleared his throat uncomfortably. "It was metallic looking."

One of the Hamfield officers sighed. "Give me a fucking break," the officer muttered.

Bardo spun around. "Keep your mouth shut or get the hell out." The officer bowed his head in acquiescence. "Go on, Scott," she said.

"So, anyway, the thing was revolving, spinning." He put his index finger in the air and used his other hand to trace a circle around it as if spinning an invisible record. "It was about the size of an apple at arm's length, to give you some perspective. It was close and big. It was *not* a drone, it was *not* a blimp, it was *not* a balloon, so don't go there. It was seamless. Like a large silver egg or Tic Tac. The air was a little hazy beneath it, like those wavy lines that emanate from a hot road. This was a solid craft."

"Where's this going?" Justin interjected. "How do we get from Baton Rouge to your living room?"

He looked at the deputy. "You asked what happened. It started in Louisiana."

The officers' chairs formed a semicircle around the door to the cell, as if Scott was a preacher in the throes of a morning sermon—albeit imprisoned by his own flock. Justin, at the right edge of the semicircle, stared back. His stomach churned loudly.

Bardo examined her deputy: broad-shouldered and burly, ebony skin, and a fleshy face with babyish features. A strange combination, at least she always thought. In his early forties with a wife and three young kids, Justin had been interim chief when the mayor recruited Bardo to combat growing petty crime—a trend linked to the opioid epidemic hammering Hynek and every other nearby town. When Bardo arrived from Baltimore, she wasn't expecting much from Justin Treanor. But he'd won her over. An intuitive investigator with a sound work ethic who brought levity to the job and to life more generally, he never took anyone too seriously, especially himself. He could have easily thrived as chief. It was Bardo whom, perhaps ironically, represented a token hire—a gesture to the affluent community that drug use and broken windows would not sully Hynek's quality of life.

She retrained her thoughts on Scott. *Is he deranged? Pure fantasy?* He was a serious man, someone entrusted with lives. Trained to have sound judgment and a steady hand. *Do I indulge this bizarre song and dance, or start pressing him?* She resolved to let Scott move at his own pace and for the story to run its course, however fantastical. Although a homicide, the investigation did not demand urgency, at least not yet. Best to let Scott dig his own grave, with the more admissions, the better. Justin was recording every word with an old iPhone 8 they used for taking statements.

Hence, Scott went on. As he spoke, his demeanor and expression did not change—stoic acceptance—but his blinking quickened. Indicia of agitation, Bardo thought.

"So we're watching this thing for, I don't know, three minutes. Then suddenly, *boom!*" Scott clapped powerfully. Justin had been slouched over but his head jerked up.

"It shoots up and away through the clouds at forty-five degrees. We're talking so fast it looked blurry. And the thing is," he swallowed, "there's this *hole* in the cloud cover. The God damn thing shot a circular hole right in the cloud cover." His index finger traced a circle in the air. "You could see the sun through the hole. On this totally grey day, a single beam of light shooting down to the runway like a searchlight from heaven.

"We're all standing there, and no one's said a damn word. Phones ringing and chirping, the mechanics' radios going berserk. But we were in this *daze*. Or at least I was. A fog. And I felt so, what's the word?" He closed his eyes. "I guess, small. I felt really small."

"And then?" Bardo asked.

"Well, that's not everything about Ryan Field. This is even stranger. When I was staring at this thing, I heard a voice.

You're going to think I'm really crazy now: it was my grandmother. Her name was Inanna. Grandma Ina. She's been dead since I was thirteen, so you do the math. I hadn't heard her voice in *decades*. I didn't even realize I remembered it.

"I was looking at this thing in the sky spinning like a top, and my grandma spoke to me, clear as Christ on the cross. She said, 'All I want to believe is that you are better. You are my emissary.' And then there was this noise like a dial tone. A soft, pulsing dial tone.

"After the thing was gone, we were all standing there. A couple of the stewardesses were crying. And then we staggered away like zombies; no one said a peep. And I was so tired, *so* tired. I've never run a marathon, but I have to think that's how I'd feel afterward.

"I was supposed to fly two hours later, but I couldn't do it. Had to check back into the airport hotel, and then I slept for sixteen hours. And when I woke up, I had this terrible sun burn." He pointed to his face. "I wasn't visibly burned; I wasn't red or anything. But my skin felt tender.

"I went back to the terminal and asked around about what happened—to see if there'd been any word from the FAA or the Air Force. NASA. The CIA, the UN. Hell, I don't know. I figure the President had been briefed. But nothing. No one knew anything about it. Not a peep on the internet. And I'm kind of doubting my sanity a little."

Bardo considered this account: couple of dozen folks should be able to back it up—refute it, more likely. But his body language bespoke candor. *Nothing obviously deceptive.* Bardo felt a chill on her arms. Goosebumps.

The question remained, of course: what's the nexus to the dead man? And Scott's supposed amnesia?

"Scott," Bardo said, "move us forward in time now, please." She sounded patient yet stern, like a grade-school teacher.

Scott cleared his throat and then groaned, clutching his jaw.

"You pulled a real number on me, Shelly. I need a doctor for my face."

"We had one check you out a few hours ago. You'll live for now. Aspirin?"

Scott shook his head and massaged his gullet.

"Move forward in time. Yes, I can do that." Scott had been sitting on the corner of the cot, arms resting on his thighs. He tried to stand up, but the handcuff snapped him back down. He looked at Bardo. "Is this really necessary?"

Bardo shot Justin an acquiescent look, who passed a key to Scott through the bars. Scott unlocked the handcuffs, handed the key back, stood up, and stretched his arms. He approached the bars and, gripping them at shoulder level, pushed into the ground with his ankles. He looked down as he pushed, his curly hair pressed in between the steel slats.

Justin and Bardo exchanged glances, and two of the Hamfield officers shot one another looks as well. Their expressions all conveyed the same sentiment: what could possibly come next?

$$\triangle \ \triangle \ \triangle$$

Scott cracked his knuckles and then resumed pinching his temple.

"Well, let's see: that was, uh, about two weeks ago." He sat back down on the cot. "I'd need a calendar to be positive about the dates. Anyhow, when I got back to Washington, I was still tired. I don't know what that, uh, that *thing* did to me." He issued a joyless, flaccid chuckle. "I had to take myself off the flight rotation. 'Unfit due to physical incapacity.'" Scott mimed quotation marks. "Probably three days after I got back here, these new, uh," he sighed, "new *events*, I guess you'd call them, started."

"What kind?" Justin squinted at Scott.

"For one, my appliances began doing things." Scott scratched his head. "Wait, no, first, let me say, I had terrible insomnia. I was up, initially, like forty-eight hours straight. Then I kind of drank myself into a coma."

"What's your poison?" Josh interposed.

"Bourbon. Evan Williams." Josh nodded approvingly.

"I crashed in a stupor for a few hours, just from the liquor. Then I went another couple of days without sleep. At that point, I went to a walk-in clinic and got sleeping meds."

Bardo asked, "What day was that?"

"I don't know."

"Which clinic?"

"The one in Hamfield. 'GoHealth' or something like that."

"Which doctor?"

"Some Indian guy. Last name was Embarr-, Umbarrasado. Indian name, I don't know. Hard to pronounce. I could find out. So could you."

"And the medicine?" Bardo continued to probe.

Scott shook his head. "Didn't work."

"No, what's it called?"

"Ambien. Or generic Ambien, I think."

"Thanks Scott, please continue." She noticed Scott's nostrils: the edges and creases connecting his nose to the upper lip. The skin appeared slightly raw and crusty.

"So, anyway, I was awake a lot."

"What'd you do to pass the time?" Justin asked.

"Read. *The Brothers Karamazov*. The whole thing. The book's in tatters. Watched Fox News, the internet, you know. Spoke to my ex and kids."

Bardo took a sip of coffee. "You tell them about Ryan Field?" He nodded.

"What's your ex's name," Justin asked.

"Miranda. She kept my surname. Better than Slutsky."

Bardo knew of Miranda. "Amicable divorce," Scott had insisted to her. She'd heard different elsewhere: that Miranda was sleeping with an old flame (a used car salesman, straight out of *True Lies*). That she wore the pants and was emotionally abusive. That Scott was no shrinking violet, but that she was the alpha. A dominant, not infrequently cruel, partner—which, perhaps, Scott liked. That he discovered her infidelity and would have worked through it, but that she ended the marriage. Bardo knew all this. And now, by all appearances, Scott had killed a man and undergone a full psychotic break . . . not necessarily in that order. Good thing the Maccabee kids were grown, she thought, as this would be a tough pill to swallow.

"So you told Miranda about what happened on the tarmac?" Bardo asked.

"Yes."

"What'd she say?"

"Supportive. Didn't think I was crazy. Her grandfather went through something similar when she was a girl. He was scouting oil sites near Mt. Rainier—"

Justin interjected, "Let's continue forward in time, Scott. We need the time continuum to move forward here," he drew a horizontal line in the air, "not backward."

"Well, like I said, things began happening in my house. I've read this kind of stuff described as 'high strangeness.' These were definitely strange things. Above and beyond seeing a damn UFO."

The words induced unease among the group. Scott finally voicing something that, until then, had been the elephant in the room. Bardo, however, was unfazed. Under her emerging theory of the case, Scott had undergone a mental break precipitated by the trauma of his divorce. His tale was nonsense. But they'd do well to keep milking statements that, if necessary, they could contradict with evidence from their own investigation. The State's Attorney in Baltimore had a saying: "It's the statements, stupid." Get suspects to talk and they'll tie their own noose.

"The appliances came first. Turning on suddenly. I'd be in the living room, walk to the kitchen, and come back. And the TV was suddenly on. It had just been off. *I* didn't turn it on. I live alone." He blinked a few times in thought. "And I got calls."

"To what: cellphone, landline?" Justin asked. "You still have a landline?"

"Landline. I'd pick up and there was this kind of, I don't know how to describe him, but, I suppose, a kind of a pulse. Metallic pulse, if that makes sense."

"Him?" Justin squinted as he spoke, tapping his foot nervously. *Justin's wearing his best poker face. But this is spooking him.*

"Yeah, *him*. It was like a man's voice through the metallic sounds." He paused, grinned, and said, "You know what it was like? That Frampton song where he talks with his guitar. You know the one?"

Josh and Bardo both blurted out: "*Do You Feel Like We Do.*" Bardo added "jinx" and winked at Josh, who shook his head.

"Who was he?" Justin demanded.

"I don't know."

"What'd he say?"

Scott swallowed and massaged his temple. He stared at the officers' shoes and then looked up and blinked once. Twice. Thrice.

"Numbers, at first. Just numbers. Some kind of pattern."

"How many numbers in the pattern?"

"Sixteen, I think it was. I counted at one point. A couple of calls like that. I'd try to speak, but he just repeated numbers."

She examined Scott. *Another claim that's easy enough to check. Phone calls to a landline with approximate dates. Easy peasey, one, two, three—*

"Fourth or fifth call, it was, when he started actually saying stuff, other than just numbers." He looked down again. "Said his name was 'Astrar' and that he was from somewhere far away."

Bardo shot Justin a glance. Justin shot Bardo a glance. Josh shot Bardo a glance. One of the other Hamfield cops shot Josh a glance. Lots of silent glance-shots.

"He said I was," Scott paused, "chosen. Chosen to see what I saw. That the earth is going through profound changes, and that I got selected. That I would help 'stoke the rebirth.'"

Josh rolled his eyes.

Bardo had heard enough. She decided to test Scott's self-awareness.

"Scott, we're not pulling any punches. Before we go on, I want to lay something on you. What do you think the chances are that some of this stuff, maybe even much of it, didn't objectively happen? That it happened in your head? You said it yourself: you're not sleeping, you're drinking, you're taking Ambien. Could you have, you know, *imagined* some of this? I mean, you're a reasonable guy, we both know that." Scott nodded. "You're a pilot, for Christ's sake. People trust your judgment. Lives depend on it. And to us, well, skip, this doesn't sound so reasonable. You appreciate that, right?"

By now, Scott's slow nod had transitioned to a steady shake. He spoke just above a whisper. "I don't think so, Shelly."

He believes it.

A phone on a nearby desk began to vibrate, shaking the metal surface and causing the desk's innards to rattle. *Buzz.* Stop. *Buzz.* Stop. A few seconds passed. Bardo eventually snapped, "Someone gonna get that?" Josh walked over to the desk, disengaged the ring, pocketed the device, and sat back down. Bardo retrained her attention on Scott.

"Fair enough, scoop. Go on. What's next?" She smiled. "I'm almost afraid to ask."

Maccabee smirked. "Where was I? The night he identified himself as Astrar. I slept like a baby that night. First time in a long time."

Justin put one finger in the air. "Wait, let me just clarify something. Did you talk to Astrar, or did he talk and you listened? Or both?"

"Mostly he talked. I did ask him why he chose me."

"And?"

"He said it's because I'll need to escape to the sky. I figured he meant because I'm a pilot."

"Makes perfect sense," Josh sniped.

Justin pressed him. "Escape from *what*?"

Scott's lips twisted into a crooked grin, even as he winced from the pain in his jaw. By now, he was back on the edge of the cot, elbows on his knees and a palm cupping his chin. Bushy reddish hair poked out from the lining of his neck and arm sleeves. Bardo considered whether she'd ever noticed just how truly hairy Scott was. She visualized him as a teenager undergoing puberty, sprouting hair from every square inch of his body. Hair consuming him while Scott wondered, with trepidation, whether it would ever stop, or whether he'd metamorphosize into a giant hairball, a human tumbleweed. A mutant.

Scott ignored Justin's question. "The next night. That's when it all happened."

△ △ △

"I was in a deep sleep," Scott said, "and it was the dead of night. Something coaxed me out of it.

"I opened my eyes to a bluish light. It was coming through the blinds. So I looked out the window into the woods beyond my yard and there was this, this shimmering blue ball. I guess you'd call it an orb. Alternating between dark blue and indigo, flickering like a lantern. It looked like it was on the ground maybe a hundred feet into the brush."

"How was the orb dressed?" Josh snickered. Bardo shot him a look usually reserved for her daughter. "My bad, sorry," Josh said, "just trying to lighten the mood a little."

Bardo asked, "Did you go outside, Scott?" She glanced at a clock on the wall: almost 9:00 a.m. He'd been speaking for an hour.

Scott nodded. "I don't know if I even walked. It was more like I floated through the wall into the yard."

"To be clear, you went downstairs, opened the door, and walked outside. Or you floated through the wall? Let's not mince words at this point."

"I'm pretty sure I floated." He furrowed his brow. "Yes, for the record: I floated through the wall." Bardo blinked a few times as she studied Scott's face. Josh shook his head and started to laugh, but, when Bardo turned toward him, went silent.

"Go on," she said.

"Well, from my window it looked like a shiny orb. A tiny blue sun. It was beautiful, actually. But the closer I got, I'm realizing—it's not an orb. It's a rectangle. It's a *door*. With a knob and everything." He shook his head and registered an anemic chuckle. "Have to laugh to keep from crying, know what I mean? Anyway, the blue was from a halo or corona around the edges of the door. The door was floating a couple of feet off the ground."

Bardo blinked. "And what'd you do?"

"What do you think I did, Shelly? I went inside."

△ △ △

Bardo, Justin, and Josh stood in the break room and sipped coffee. One of the Hamfield men had brought Scott an egg sandwich and orange juice, which he was consuming feverishly. After Scott described having "ventured upon a star gate," as Josh put it, Bardo had paused the interrogation. Scott was visibly famished—his hands were beginning to tremble—and the trio wanted to trade observations. Each viewed Scott's account through a different lens.

"The man is lying through his teeth," Josh said. "You see that smirk, Justin, when you asked him about what he was 'escaping' from? He's toying with us."

Bardo shook her head. "I know Scott. He's a serious man. This is a pilot we're talking about, for God's sa—"

Josh drowned out Bardo, "I don't put much credence in that. He can fly a plane—so what? Remember that story a few years ago about the copilot who locked the pilot out of the cockpit? Steered a plane into a mountain to commit suicide. What was his excuse?" Bardo opened her mouth to respond, but Josh spoke again. "And why's he calling you 'Shelly,' Bardo? You got a history with him or something?"

Didn't think this would come up so quickly. Bardo knew she'd be frozen out of the case once she divulged her past with Scott. *I'm not ready for that. Not yet.* She raised the cup to her mouth, muttered that she knew him from Shaker's, and took a long gulp, polishing off the rest of the coffee. "You're misunderstanding me, Josh," she continued, "Scott's probably certifiable; I'm not disputing that. Having a pilot's license doesn't, I don't know, uh," she strained for a word, "inoculate him against being an evil bastard. But you think he's *knowingly* and *deliberately* lying to us? I don't think so. He's telling us what he believes is the truth."

"That creepy grin was a dead giveaway about what's going on in this guy's head," Josh responded. "I've seen that look from my worst collars. Remember the punk who shot up that pharmacy and claimed it was bath salts?" Bardo and Justin nodded. "That was my arrest. He gave us this song and dance about gumdrop houses and talking beagles. Turned out his ex worked at the pharmacy. He'd been texting and phoning her, obsessively. Maccabee's doing the same kind of thing."

"It's all premature anyway," Bardo replied, "considering that we haven't even ID'd the John Doe. So who knows. I can say that, pilot or no pilot, he's an even-keeled guy. And he's *simple*. He's not—"

"And then there's door number three, folks," Justin finally chimed in.

Bardo squinted in thought. "And that is?"

"The big blue door in the woods. Don't you want to know what's inside? Do either of you have even the slightest idea what he might say?"

They shook their heads. Justin was manipulating the cross at the end of his gold necklace, which he normally kept tucked under his shirt. He raised his eyebrows in a look of cavalier suggestion. "There's also the chance, I'm just putting it out there, that he's telling the truth. Not what he *thinks* is the truth. The truth."

"Hah!" Josh blurted out. "You're dicking around, right?"

"Which part of it?" Bardo asked, kneading her temple. The dog mutilations had dulled her skepticism to these kinds of things. Back in Baltimore she would have laughed Justin out of the room. But in trying to wrap her head around the dog killings, she'd read up on three decades of livestock mutilations in the Midwest. Claims of unmarked black helicopters. Of aircraft using light beams to float steers into collapsible trap doors. People insisted they saw this stuff. Even some credible ones. Was it possible that Scott was speaking objective truth? *Not impossible.*

"Which part?" Justin parroted. "Hell, all of it. First and foremost, I'd like to know what's behind the blue door. But the thing in Louisiana, the calls. We can check this stuff out. We *have to* check it out."

Bardo nodded. "Easy enough. The Baton Rouge thing. His work records, flight schedule. His wife and kids, landline, cell-site—the usual. We'll need a few warrants."

Josh grinned incredulously and shook his head. "Oh Lordy," he mumbled. "Jesus and baby Jesus. Let's get on with the show."

$$\triangle \ \triangle \ \triangle$$

Justin tapped "record" on the crusty old iPhone. "We're go, Chief."

The group had reformed: Scott Maccabee perched on the corner of the cot and the five seated officers forming a loose semi-circle outside the bars, with Bardo in the middle. She looked at Scott and asked whether he was ready.

"Yup," he muttered.

"We're dying with anticipation," Josh said. "Where'd the door take you? Let me guess: the Pleiades? Andromeda?"

Scott massaged his jaw. "You know son," he squinted to read Josh's name off his uniform, "Officer Urban. What are you, late twenties? For your edification, I was flying support in Sadr City when you were in Pampers. So some semblance of respect is in—"

"Like the respect you paid that man in your living room? You're on the wrong side of the bars to be—"

"Stop. *Now*." Bardo stamped her foot and glowered at Josh. "This ends now or you get out. You're about *this* much more mature than my teenage daughter." She pinched her thumb and index finger an inch apart. Josh looked at his feet.

Bardo turned back to Scott. "Go ahead, champ." Josh rolled his eyes.

Several seconds passed. Then he spoke.

"The bottom of the door was, maybe, two feet off the ground."

"Just floating there?" Justin asked.

He nodded. "So I turned the knob and it opened. Just blackness inside. Like a door into outer space. I peered around the frame and it's the forest. Inside led somewhere else. Like a tunnel or gate."

"You might even call it a *star*-gate," Josh piped in.

Bardo didn't even turn her head. "Get out."

Like a soldier at attention, Justin launched to his feet. Justin was a large man—a solid six feet, two-hundred pounds—with his bulletproof vest adding girth. Josh, in contrast, offered little in the way of physicality, notwithstanding some colorful tattoos peppering his forearms. With dirty blond hair pulled back in a man-bun, a chiseled face, and a pointed nose, Josh had good looks, but he was neither tall nor particularly muscular. If anything, his hairstyle and inked forearms bespoke a certain chic sensibility. Justin was like another species of man. Club-wielding Neanderthal to Josh's *Homo habilis*.

With as much baritone as he could muster, Justin directed the officer to "wait outside."

Josh pursed his lips in a wry smile.

"Bardo," Josh said as he stood up, "or should I say 'Shelly'? This is a great story, but it was already done back in the nineties." Josh collected a half-filled water bottle and walked toward the reinforced door separating the bullpen from the vestibule. He shot daggers at Scott along the way. "Kurt Russell was the Air Force colonel, James Spader was the scientist." As the door inched closed, Josh's voice trailed off. "Text me when you guys actually start to question him." The glass front door slammed shut, followed by the slower moving reinforced door.

Still standing, Justin stared at Bardo. He seemed perplexed.

"Does he mean the *Sex, Lies, and Videotape* James Spader?" Justin asked.

Bardo chortled and shook her head. "Oh, Justin. Honestly, I'm surprised you saw that one."

"Vintage Soderbergh," one of the other cops volunteered. Scott appeared confounded by the whole exchange.

Bardo addressed Scott.

"I'm going to say it yet again, but please go on. No more interruptions."

"Where was I?" Scott asked. "Oh, yeah. The blue door."

Justin clapped eagerly, "Where to next?"

As if delivering a ghost story around a campfire, Scott surveyed the faces of his remaining audience. "This is where it really gets weird."

$$\triangle \; \triangle \; \triangle$$

He peered around one edge of the frame. The door itself— consisting of a fiberglass-like material, its surface sleek and slightly rounded—was swung fully open. The front of the door, positioned almost parallel to the frame, cast a powerful blue corona several hundred feet into the woods. Insects were omnipresent in the band of blue light. They filled the air and clasped every tree limb, piece of shrubbery, and exposed rock.

Scott Maccabee could somehow see . . . more. His vision was heightened, as if he could perceive all life in the forest no matter how miniscule. He wondered how his brain could process so many stimuli at once. The shimmering scales on the back of a dragonfly. The thorax of a grasshopper, shuddering rhythmically. The individual hairs on the leg of a spider. Everything sharper and clearer, amplified somehow. It made the woods resemble the landscape of an alien planet, a second earth. *Was it just the blue light? Some optical effect?* He noticed, too, that his other senses were dulled. Where was the dank, rich smell of Doursham on a humid June night? He smelled nothing. And the familiar tactile sensations of the forest—the scraping of branches and leaves, the tingling of the ubiquitous mosquitos— felt there yet numbed and distant, as if he had a second skin.

Only one thing was for sure: Scott was not afraid. He felt something intrinsic signaling that he was meant to be there. It was the door, *the gate*, pulling him in. But he also knew it was not the gate itself. No, it was someone or something inside. Beckoning him. Every instinct told him so.

He continued admiring the visage, the infinite swarm of motion illuminated by, and bathed in, that comforting blue glow, like the reassuring beam of a light house to a vessel at sea. He saw six, no seven, pairs of flickering yellow eyes perched at the intersection of several thick tree boughs. They stared cautiously into the light and primitively assessed the situation. A family of raccoons.

Scott looked back into the doorway. Darkness. Black space. It had coaxed him from a deep sleep and lured him here—the culmination of this high strangeness since Ryan Field.

He reached inside. His arm vanished up to his elbow, although he could still feel a weight tugging softly on it. Nothing overpowering. As if his veins bore tiny traces of liquid magnet with a steel plate just below the door. When he stepped through, he was heading down. *Time to move forward.* The thought rattled around his head—forward and backward, up and down, in and out. Time. *Time.*

He lifted one sandaled foot over the lower edge of the frame and felt the magnet-like force on his thigh. With one arm and one leg in the void, Scott froze. He was Krishna in a dancing pose. Suddenly, the force, whatever it was, sent an orgasmic ripple outward from his core.

He grunted contentedly and allowed his body to fall, flipping forward into the darkness. He dropped into the void.

The ecstasy engulfed his senses. Strobing, concentric pulses that shot outward to his toes, fingers, and scalp—unfurling pleasure waves.

Time seemed to have passed, although he couldn't discern how long. Time continued to pass. The euphoria began to wane and, with it, lucidity returned.

He heard nothing. He felt cold against the exposed parts of his body; heels, calves, elbows, forearms, the crown of his head. The force from the void—the magnet or whatever it was—pinned him down against something. It must have been metal. And it was increasingly cold, outweighing the physical euphoria. His eyelids rolled open. He saw nothing but a blurred double-vision awash in deep greys.

Scott concentrated on uncrossing his eyes and putting images in their proper place. He was on his back against a gunmetal grey table, not unlike something in a veterinary examining room. The force pressed his torso and the side of his face to the metal surface. He tried to lift his head and separate his thinning crown from the table, but couldn't overcome the force. Just beyond his strength. He was staring at a nondescript grey wall. Some kind of gentle glow from his unseen left illuminated both the wall and, to a lesser extent, the brushed metal table beneath Scott's shoulder. No other source of light.

He strained to rotate his neck counterclockwise. It was challenging but possible. Over the course of a minute, expending all the power in his neck, he managed to incrementally swivel his head to the left, which brought the other half of the room into his field of vision.

And when he did, the sight brought Scott Maccabee to tears.

△ △ △

The left side of the room consisted of an expansive viewing window that spanned almost the full length and width of the wall, roughly fifteen feet by fifteen feet. Outside the window, at a distance Scott could not begin to estimate, was a blue and white marble with an occasional jagged patch of green and tan, set against a uniform black canvas.

He was looking at earth.

Miraculous, miracle, God—the only words Scott's mind could summon. He began to visualize lifelike images. First, of Miranda, and his children, Michael and Lindsey. Then of his mother in the Memory Wing of the Crane Retirement Home, vacantly staring out a window while chomping on gum like a horse. Of Miranda greeting him on the Vandenberg tarmac after his first and only tour overseas. To his surprise, images of more minor figures surfaced as well, as if his brain was casually flipping through a handful of Polaroids. Christos Eros, his training partner in the 144th Fighter Wing. One of his professors at UC Santa Cruz. His father's brother, Uncle Frank the alcoholic, like the title of some tangential figure in a royal family. Frank had broken his neck cliff diving in Big Sur when Scott was a boy. His first grade teacher, Mrs. Amberfield. *That old goat.*

Scott struggled to get to the window: he strained against the force that still pinned him down, even attempting to use his thoughts to overcome it—mind over matter. To get a closer, unrestrained look at the splendor of his planet. *My planet.* He considered the words. That marble was everyone, every last person in his life and member of his ancestry. Generations had gone from dust to fertilized eggs to endlessly complex sentient beings. And only to wither and perish. To return to the soil, reintegrated with, and recycled by, other forms of life. Each at its own stage of its own unique journey. But everything, ultimately, a cosmic dust. Life, growth, death, absorption, and renewal. And there it was: all those cycles, that ebb and flow, in one flawless marble. Small enough to put in his pocket, a sight he never thought he'd see in his wildest dreams. Scott moaned plaintively as tears streamed down his cheeks, tracing the curvature of his lip.

A whooshing sound—something sliding open and then quickly closing, like a hydraulic door—jolted Scott to his senses. Five gentle but deliberate steps grew louder. Scott reflexively tried to wipe the tears and snot from his face, but his arm met the resistance of the force. His shoulder merely jerked up and down. Trembling under the weight of what, to Scott, was a moment of existential clarity, he asked meekly, "Who's there?"

Suddenly, everything went white.

Someone had dropped a white towel over Scott's head. He repeated himself, but now as a directive.

"Tell me who's there." Silence. "I'm Scott McConnell Maccabee. I'm a pilot from Washington in the United States of America. I'm from, uh," he paused, "that planet out there. Which I think you know." Silence. "Explain why I'm here. *How* I'm here." Silence. "Talk. Now!" Scott's voice cracked as the gravity of the situation dawned on him. This person could be anything. No person at all, perhaps. And he was powerless. The sense of calm and direction to which he'd first awoken in his bedroom (hours ago? days? weeks?), and the euphoric trance he'd felt only moments earlier, were subsumed by mounting panic. His chest tightened.

"Who are you?" His tone desperate. The continued silence killing him.

Then a voice.

"Sir, I know who you are. Sir."

It was a young man. Speaking English with an American accent. High pitched and betraying insecurity, even anxiety.

"Sah sah, sah, sir," he stuttered, "you're in orbit."

Scott inhaled and spoke assertively. "Tell me your name, young man."

"Sir. Evan Benjamin, sir sir sir sir." The repetition sounded less like a stutter and more like a broken record. A malfunctioning piece of technology. "Evan Benjamin Eldridge. Sir. Su-, su-, sir."

"Relax Evan." Scott spoke as if addressing a child. "Just relax, young man."

"Sir."

"Evan, how did I get here?"

"Well, the, sir . . . the blue door."

"How does the blue door work? Wait, no, tell me something first." He had too many questions and needed to prioritize. "Evan, where are you from?"

"From the America, sir."

"*The* America?" Silence. Scott listened to his own breaths. Nothing from Evan—not a breath.

"Pull this towel off my head so we can see one another."

"Sir, su-su sir, that wouldn't be a, eh, good idea, sir."

"And why not?"

"My C.O., suh, suh, sir sir sir."

Scott *knew* it. This was a military operation of some stripe, however bizarre.

"*Who's* your commanding officer? Son, which branch? USAF? Navy?"

Scott heard the hydraulic sound. A door opening and closing. Footsteps approached.

"Are you awake, Mr. Maccabee?" A different and much older voice, with a Midwestern accent. Far more confident. The inflection bore the crisp precision of a high-ranking military officer.

Evan's C.O.

More footsteps and the hydraulic sound again.

Evan leaving.

"I am awake, yes. You in charge?"

"I am indeed, Mr. Maccabee."

"I was Air Reserves. I flew in Iraq. Iraqi Freedom."

"We know."

A bitter realization hit Scott: he was the subject of some kind of experiment. That fellow officers were treating him like a subhuman, putting a towel over his head as if he was little more than a lab rat. His anger was gathering.

"What in the name of *Christ* am I doing here, then!" Scott bellowed, his breathing increasingly labored. Silence. "*Answer me! I fought for this God forsaken coun*—"

"Operation Yahweh."

Scott paused.

"Operation *what?*"

"Yah-weh." The man enunciated each syllable. "It is a Hebrew word that means God. Which is beside the point."

"How does the blue door work? Was that you guys in Baton Rouge? Are we in that, that *disc*, whatever it was? Are you Air Force?"

"Mr. Maccabee, Yahweh is our attempt to test-drive a new technology, if you will. But not the kind of technology of which you are thinking right now." A few seconds passed in silence. "Are you familiar with temporal-oriented remote viewing?"

"Huh?" Scott grunted.

"It is a form of clairvoyance. Time-directed extrasensory perception, if you will. We believe that most, if not all, human beings possess the skill in some latent form."

"Tell me what this is—"

"Mr. Maccabee," he interrupted, "are you familiar with Osmond Romanek?"

"What? What the hell are you—"

"Are you, sir?"

Scott shot back, "*No!* I don't know who that is or what any of this is about. Listen, are you Air Force? What's your name and rank?"

"Is not what I am saying more interesting than who I am?"

"I want to call my wife."

"You do not have a wife, Mr. Maccabee."

"Fuck you. Ex-wife. I want to call my kids. Take this towel off my head and let me stand up. *Now!*"

"I cannot allow that to happen."

"Who are you!" he shrieked.

"I am Evan Benjamin Eldridge."

Scott quieted. *Is my mind playing tricks on me?*

"No you're not. That's, uh, that's that kid. That stuttering kid."

"There is no 'kid' here. Just us. We are alo—"

The voice halted mid-sentence. The words transmogrified into a guttural sound like a cat retching, regurgitating a hairball. But this was much deeper and fuller throated—a tiger, not a housecat. It was also rhythmic. Two fast, one slow. Two fast, one slow. This continued for a minute before abruptly ceasing. The voice then resumed and completed the sentence without skipping a beat: "—ne in the observation room."

What in God's name. Scott swallowed. His mouth was like cotton.

"Why won't you let me . . . see you?" He was almost whispering now. Silence. "Please, just answer me." The retching recommenced. But it was closer this time: just above the towel.

Scott then felt a wet spongy mass against his ankle; it was the size of a dry-board eraser. His muscles spasmed wildly, yet the force suppressed any movement beyond a dampened shudder. He began to scream as hysteria overcame him.

"*What is that*, get it off, please, please, please please *please*, *take it off*, please help me, *please!*" He couldn't discern whether the object was attached to something—an appendage connected to something larger—that was probing and testing Scott's body, or whether it was the entire creature; some kind of slug or eel. Whatever it was, it had suctioned itself to his ankle and its body was undulating with a heartbeat-like rhythm. *Buhbuh, buh. Buhbuh, buh.*

The voice spoke; it was closer this time. Under the towel somehow. Inside his head.

"You are in severe discomfort, Mr. Maccabee. Would you like to return home?"

"Please, yes, *please!*"

"Alright. You have three options: three doors from which to choose. Please close your eyes."

The creature was progressing, slowly but surely, up his leg. It was just past his calf.

Scott closed his eyes, body trembling and on the cusp of shock. The measured voice continued.

"Do you see the three doors, Mr. Maccabee?"

"What doors! I don't see anything but bla—"

Three blue doors materialized in his mind's eye. Each resembled the blue door in the woods.

Scott spoke feverishly, "Yes yes, I see them. I do see doors, they're blue. I'm *imagining* them, they're not real, but yes! This God damn towel is on my head!"

"Good, Mr. Maccabee. The doors do exist. Now please select which to enter."

"Why are you doing this? I served my cou—"

The voice, now nested in his brain, cut short Scott's pleas. He could not expel the voice. His thoughts were not his own.

"Choose a door. Your time has almost lapsed. No second chances."

The surface of each door bore carved hieroglyphs painted crudely in red, yellow, and blue. All three were images of naked men's bodies with animal heads. To the left, the head of a large stork-like bird. To the right, the head of a reptile with a forked tongue spouting from a slit of a mouth. And in the center, unmistakable: a wolf bearing its fangs. As he examined each image, the creature continued up his leg. It had reached his inner thigh, just below his groin. What felt like pincers, a miniature trident or the teeth of a lobster fork, entered the slit of his boxers. It gently probed his scrotum, which had shriveled to smaller than a gumball. At the same time, another appendage—this one cylindrical, firm, and muscular, like a snake—entered his shirt near his naval and inched its way along his ribcage.

Scott's body would have shaken and rocked violently, but the force constricted him and absorbed his energy like a car's suspension. The sensation of the pincer, and the thought of it tearing into his scrotum, now escalated his panic to outright shock. Meanwhile, the snakelike appendage continued its journey up his chest, taking a few moments to probe one of his armpits. Something on its tip was sticky and moist, secreting a paste with the texture of Elmer's glue.

Something changed.

Scott's mind suddenly slowed down. He cast off the paralyzing, frantic terror as if shedding an exoskeleton. He could think again. Some kind of calming force was facilitating his decision-making.

Must choose a door. But which?

The pincer widened and, still gently, adjusted its grip on his scrotum. Tiny hairs at the base of the pincer brushed against the inside of his thigh. Meanwhile, the creature's spongy underside tightened its suction on Scott's leg.

The bird. I choose the left door.

"Interesting. Good for you." The voice was patronizing; like a waiter to a child placing his own order.

"Please, then, enter the left door, Mr. Maccabee. You will want to move promptly." The pincers now fully enveloped his testicles and began to squeeze.

He approached the door on the left and extended his hand toward a brass doorknob of the same shape and tarnish as the one that led into his childhood bedroom. The pincers tightened and pierced the skin, sending a shock through Scott's body. The image of his arm and hand jerkily recoiled from the doorknob. He reached out for it again, but the door began receding to his left. Something was dragging him away. He concentrated furiously, but it was unavailing. That something, whatever it was, pulled him to the middle door. The wolf.

It doesn't matter at this point, Scott thought.

The middle door was already open, revealing a familiar black void. When he placed his arm into the darkness, he felt the suction lifting him upward. And then a powerful pleasure wave hit. A repetitive orgasm pulsing outward from his groin, the sensation was even stronger than in the forest and nearly smothered his ability to execute the mind-movement.

Using the final shred of control over his avatar, Scott willed the muscles in his haunches and propelled himself forward through the door. The suction lifted him up and away.

And   then   everything   went   black.

CHAPTER 9. TUESDAY, JUNE 29, 2021.

A nd then what?"

It was Bardo asking. Scott's account was like a Stephen King novella—*The Observation Room*, its name would have been.

Justin wore an intense expression, less fascination than dread.

Scott aped the question.

"And then what?" He ran a hand through his thinning curls. "And then . . . I woke up in this fucking cell."

No one spoke. They continued looking at Scott and examining every little crease in his face. Every bit of skin. And those eyes that, to Bardo, were so different now than in Scott's kitchen. Hazel now. Blue then.

"That's FUBAR," one of the Hamfield officers eventually muttered. His tone was not one of disbelief.

Feeling a faint tingling, Bardo looked at her hands. They were trembling.

And then she felt a sudden, profound jolt. And her body began to rock.

The earth is moving.

Bardo locked eyes with her deputy. One of the Hamfield men shrieked, "Holy shit, is this happening?" He and the other officer stood up and grabbed each other's arms for balance. The room swayed and underwent a relentless, pounding rattle. Small items on the desktops took stutter steps before crashing to the floor. A snow globe in Bardo's office, a Christmas gift from Sasha, shattered. Staplers, tape dispensers, coffee mugs, pencil cups, all hit the ground. As if navigating a fun house, the Hamfield officers wobbled in half-steps toward the reinforced door.

Justin grabbed Bardo's arm.

"Chief, we gotta move. *Now!*"

Scott had retreated to the farthest corner of the cell with his back against a concrete wall. He caught Bardo's eye for a split second as the rocking continued. Slabs of dry wall began raining from the ceiling and crashing to the floor, spitting up plumes of white dust and debris. Bardo shouted to Justin over the crescendo of toppling office equipment.

"We have to get Scott! Keys in my office!"

A tearing bass—the earth shifting and turning—suddenly drowned out all else. The copy machine tipped over and rocked violently. It didn't make a sound amidst the tumult.

Trying to use her momentum to fling herself across the room in one fell swoop, Bardo bolted toward the office. Almost instantly, she reeled violently to the right. Propelled by an especially jarring shake, she glided across two adjacent desktops into the wall. She crumpled to the floor like a crash test dummy, her head cracking the drywall.

Stars twinkled for Bardo. She lay face down and limp on the trampoline of a laminate floor. Yet, moments later, she found herself slumped over Justin's shoulder as he fought their way to the vestibule.

Bardo lifted her head just as the roof above Scott collapsed.

△ △ △

"Hey El, did you get any Honeycrisps? Or do we just have those old Fujis?"

TJ Freeman crouched his oversized frame in front of the fruit drawer of an ultra-modern silver refrigerator. A touchscreen panel on the inside of the fridge marked the time: 9:00 a.m. "Not seeing any Honeycrisps, El." His voice trailed off.

Elise was barely audible from a few rooms away.

"Just Fuji babe, sorry. I'll get them next time."

He browsed among the dozen or so apples, poking and checking for bruises. He picked up the choicest specimen, unpeeled the "Fuji" sticker, and walked to the blue porcelain sink. Three conjoined sinks, to be exact, each separated by a small ridged divider. He placed the apple under the left faucet and waited for the motion sensor to trigger the water. A few seconds passed. Nothing. TJ shook his head and tried the center sink. It flowed instantly.

Channeled through a glass skylight spanning almost the entire ceiling, sunshine lit the Freeman's kitchen and painted it a rich gold. A branch from an enormous oak peeked across one corner of the skylight. The house was perched a few hundred yards south of the lake on top of a small hill, eight miles east of Hynek Proper and six miles east of the Field Club. They had built the house not long after getting married—which was itself not long after they met. TJ had been at the tail end of a brilliant NBA career. By then, a veteran journeyman whom the Golden State Warriors had signed to a one-year contract, bolstering the team's bench for an anticipated playoff run. Elise was "of counsel" at a prestigious west coast law firm. Her title meant less than partner, more than associate, as she'd explained to TJ when they first met at a tech magnate's party in Palo Alto. "Not quite ready for primetime," she had said. Within one year, she'd resigned from the firm and was carrying their first child. They married two months later.

Timothy John retired not long after. He and Elise built the four-thousand-square-foot house on ten acres of lake-facing property. This was where they had raised their two children—the most famous of a handful of celebrity families in Hynek. Since the kids left home, TJ's life had become ritualistic: eighteen holes at the Field Club on Tuesday, Friday, and Sunday; dinner at San Telmo's on Saturday, an Italian restaurant on Post Road; one-hour workouts each morning, alternating between cardio and weights; occasional antiquing trips to search for maritime artefacts.

He had an affinity for old sea vessels and collected helms, anchors, onboard guns, signage—really any maritime relic that could fit in his front door. His dearest item was a piece of weathered hickory that had once been nailed to the bathroom door of a merchant marine ship in the late eighteenth century. Crudely carved on the wood was a woefully misspelled message from captain to crew: "For drainin ya pikel ONLEE [Read: ONLY]. Pinch ya lofe off starborde. -Capt Lancaster."

In 1763, after docking in the Mexican city of Tampico to onboard a cargo of honey, Captain Atherwild B. Lancaster contracted a gastrointestinal virus. He literally shat his brains out—the story being that, with every bout of diarrhea, the old captain became more and more delirious. By Lancaster's lights, he was in psychic communication with an albino pilot whale named Sammy that was accompanying the ship on its journey to Nova Scotia. One crewmember thought he actually saw Sammy, but it turned out to be the rotted carcass of a massive sea turtle. The Captain ultimately succumbed to the virus (as did four crewmen), and the survivors tossed their bodies off the starboard into the North Atlantic. TJ loved the sign so much that he would have proudly hung it in their living room. Instead, the piece of hickory and its bizarre provenance were relegated to one of the several dozen drawers in TJ's walk-in closet. "You can buy it, baby, but I never want to see it again." That was Elise's admonition several minutes before TJ paid $1,000 for what was, in his eyes, a priceless and richly ironic piece of history.

Elise entered the kitchen carrying a framed canvas and a beverage tray with two cups of Starbucks. Dressed in a picnic-table checkered blouse and grey Lululemon leotards, she had "held up," as TJ's golfing buddies put it. Elise's bluish eyes offered a striking juxtaposition with her mocha skin, and the delicate bone structure in her face had an almost elfish quality. That beautiful face, however, was marred by several small blackened marks on her temple and cheeks. The fading byproducts of Botox injections. Elise placed the frame on the counter and handed a latte to her husband.

"Thanks El. Whatcha got there?"

"Just picked up the portrait of Rosie. Still playing around with where to hang it." The canvas showed a youthful black Labrador Retriever on an exquisitely manicured green lawn, with the Freeman's house in the distance. TJ held up the portrait at arm's length and shook his head. Elise hugged him and, standing on her toes, gently kissed his neck.

"It's ok, babe, I know," she whispered.

He used his thumb and index finger to rub the corners of his eyes. "It's just a dog, it's ridiculous. She was such a good girl, though."

"Babe, I know. I loved her too." Elise ran a hand across his shaved scalp.

"I like Michelle," TJ said, "but I still think she doesn't have the time or resources to *really* investigate. I want Popper followed. If he did this to Rosie, I'm sure it wasn't the first or last."

"You're still thinking about a private investigator?"

He nodded. "The league always had a bunch of retired NYPD detectives on retainer. If they thought one of the players was being harassed or blackmailed, stuff like that—first line of defense before going to the cops. You know what those younger guys are like, the clubs, drinking. Walking shit-storm magnets."

"I'm not opposed; but would we tell Michelle?"

"I don't see why. A couple of men for a week or two, maybe a grand a day. Drop in the bucket."

"If we do this, babe, it's to make sure this doesn't happen again to anyone else."

"Exactly," TJ replied with a nod.

She sat down at an oval table beyond a marble-topped island with induction-stovetop tiles. Removing a phone from her pocket and tapping the surface twice, a paper-thin LCD display on the far wall switched on. An androgynous CNN anchor's voice picked up mid-sentence.

"—tain Banes's last communication, according to Houston flight staff. Now that's quite different than what we've been told in the past. Evidently, the ship had some kind of, um, alternative channel for private communications. 'P Com B,' we're told it was called. This is something, you know, you would have expected, although we'd not gotten confirmation that this was actually the case. Until now.

"The public communications went through a radio frequency that NASA streamed to Facebook. But, apparently, the crew had access to this encrypted channel through a separate, I guess you'd say, apparatus of some kind built into the lining of their suits. And the audio of Peter Banes's final transmission, which wa—"

She tapped her phone and the station changed to a cooking show: a chef in a white apron hacking into a cut of raw beef while staring straight ahead into the camera and laughing. His apron speckled with red, which grew with each exaggerated hack.

"—oulder is one of the choicest cuts, known as the 'petite tender.' Down in Buenos Aires, where I really cut my teeth on steaks, no pun intended, they call it '*la paleta*,' just a fine"—*hack hack hack blood blood blood*—"tender, soft cut, a bit less expensive than a mig—" Elise said "mute" and the audio silenced.

"El, turn CNN back!"

"Babe, I've had enough Valor. Your son is obsessed too. He's been texting me nonstop. I bet there's gonna be some mundane explanation despite all these insane theories."

TJ tilted his head. "Why don't the kids ever text *me*?"

"You know why. It takes you forever to respond. And you ask too many questions. You're a texting 'black hole,' as Timmy put it. You want some advice? Actually carry your phone. And don't always end your texts with a question mark. It's annoying."

"Well, I'm not carrying my phone more often."

"Try the patch."

TJ shook his head. "If I don't want to carry a phone around, I'm *definitely* not wearing that thing on my skin. It's not about the size. That's not the sticking point, you know that."

"We live in a different age, babe. It left you behind some time ago. You're such an old fart now," she said with a wink. The chef continued silently hacking and laughing.

"I shared one clamshell Obama Phone with Elton and Chris. Now people are mainlining phones. Ever thought you'd see the day?"

"Gwen Gurfein has the patch. Loves it."

"That's not my point."

"I know. Just saying babe."

TJ tried to sip the latte, but realized his hand was trembling. Foam doused his chin.

Propelled by a force not his own, TJ flew backward into the fridge like a ragdoll. He called out for Elise, who was bear-hugging the kitchen table. Everything shook. Wine glasses, cereal bowls, unmoored appliances: all smashed to the floor in a cacophony of destruction. Elise pressed the side of her head against the table and craned her neck toward the fridge to see her husband, who had fallen forward into the stovetop island. He looked up and met her eyes.

"Basement!" he screamed over the creaking of the house's foundation and shattering of kitchen items. And the sound of splintering wood.

"TJ, I ca—" The kitchen table upended and flung Elise against a chinaware bureau, which collapsed onto her. As if by detonation, the skylight then exploded into glass shards that rained down on the overturned bureau. TJ had wrapped his arms around the stovetop island and was using his wingspan to grip the lips on each side. Spurred to action by a grinding noise just behind him, he pushed off the floor onto the island and rolled across. He had just cleared the corner when the fridge toppled over and shattered against the marble overlay, the six-hundred-pound machine narrowly missing his legs. Another jolt sent TJ into the air and back-first onto the tile floor, the impact knocking the breath out of him.

A bellowing groan preceded a thunderous snapping that lasted several seconds. The Freeman's oak—that is to say, the giant beast of a tree next to which the Freemans had deigned to build their home—was splitting.

And part of the tree was heading directly for their kitchen.

△ △ △

A pack of six-year-olds—a baker's dozen—piled into the Aquarium House. It was dark except for the faint glow from the black lights on the far sides of each tank. Whenever the door opened, a narrow flash of piercing sunlight, like a lightning bolt, flickered into the room. Al was in his usual position: holding tools for Bernie who, in turn, was reaching into the starfish tank and poking one of the creatures. When the occasional bolt of sunlight struck the tank, Bernie shook his head.

"I keep asking the Board for the money to erect a vestibule. We need a damn buffer for the sun. Been asking for three years now."

He manipulated one of the starfish's appendages between his thumb and index finger, checking for the telltale rippling of flesh that signaled life. "Not healthy for these critters to get hit with light. Especially Otto."

"Especially what?" Al asked. The kids were a loud, messy commotion in a room that, only seconds earlier, had been empty except for the two men. Lots of excited pointing, exclaiming, and faces pressed against glass.

Bernie raised his voice. "I said, 'Especially *Otto*.' This must be the daytrip from Camp Tuckashoa. Very fun."

"Otto, yeah sure," Al yelled.

"Everything alright, Kemosabe? You seem a little off."

Bernie was right; he did feel off. *Dom? The Valor? No, it was Mom. Something still felt different.*

"A lot on my mind, I guess."

"Thinking about your folks? You were talking about some heavy stuff when the bear ate my leg."

Al chuckled, although even the memory of that conversation now seemed hazy to him. *What is happening to my mind?* He looked at Bernie and blinked. "That thing with Rocky; was it the scariest thing that ever happened to you?"

Bernie shook his head. "No, pal. Wish it was."

Al remembered Bernie's prosthetic leg and apologized.

"No need to say you're sorry, my man. Kind of ironic: if I *hadn't* lived through worse, then that episode with Rocky probably *would* have been the worst. It's a paradox. At least I think that's the right word."

Al pondered the idea. "So it's not the worst thing that happened to you only because the worst thing that happened to you changed you physically such that," Al considered his phrasing, "what could have been the worst thing to happen to you was not?"

"What you said, Kemosabe."

"But the real question, Bernie, is whether that starfish is dead. You've been stroking it for a while."

Bernie mumbled a rote, "That's what she said." He shook his head. "You make a good point. You're not even supposed to touch these guys, I should know better. I think this fella punched his last ticket, as they say." He extracted his forearm from the tank as Al handed him a towel. "The *real* question is what you think your dad did or did not do."

Al instinctively touched his ear. *Pearl's still missing.*

"Bernie, did you find a pearl by Rocky's enclosure? Or did anyone find a loose pearl, as far as you know?"

Bernie shook his head. "Hand me Otto's clam meat, please."

Al reached into the toolbox, removed a can of chopped clams, broke the seal on the lid, and pushed the can into Bernie's chest.

"Easy there, pal. Something got you angry?"

Angry about what happened back home. But why *exactly? It was Dad, what he did. No, what he was* going *to do. Did he do it?*

"Alyosha, you there?" Al snapped out of the morass of questions and half-formed answers. He was still holding the can against Bernie's chest. Children scampered around them as if they were fire hydrants on a street corner.

"You've been lost in deep thought or something. I thought you were gonna have a seizure."

"I hadn't thought about what happened at home, like *really* thought about it, since the last time we spoke. It's just that—"

He squeezed Al's shoulder. "Listen, man, I'm sorry to remind you of it; you don't have to say anything else. I'm here for you pal, as long as you know that. We're all haunted. It's the human condition. No explanation needed."

"Bernie, it's not that . . . it's just that . . ."

"Compadre, stop right there. Let it be. Whisper words of wisdom, but let it be."

"Can if I step out for a second, Bernie?"

When Bernie nodded and turned his attention to the toolbox, Al charted his way to the door through a flock of kids, emerging in blinding sunlight and shielding his eyes. As he trotted to Rocky's enclosure, he began to panic: he couldn't remember what happened to his parents. He remembered the emotions, including the raw, unmitigated hatred. The overwhelming urge for vengeance. But the events precipitating those emotions: nothing but a fog. *Am I losing my mind? Is this dementia?* He worked backward. *I came to Hynek. I dropped out of university. Uncle Dmitri moved to Germany. The investigation. The detectives questioned me. Mom di—. Mom left. No, that wasn't it. Dad left?*

What were they investigating? Dad, right? Me? His thoughts became entangled and led nowhere.

He had reached the enclosure. Al circled the perimeter until he found the patch of bushes into which he and Bernie had fallen, which was bent inward in a delta shape like a dented car hood. He got to his knees and used his hands to sweep the grass beyond the initial railing. Nothing. Next, he hopped over the rail and crouched, groping at the dirt beneath the bushes. Still no. He crawled under the bushes and emerged on the other side just before the ledge on which Bernie had balanced when the quake struck. He peered down into the moat that opened onto the cage: *Pringles can. Dried leaves. Tangled mass of string. Rotting piece of fish. Ugh. Selfie stick. How'd that get there?* He crouched back down and reversed course.

An elderly man was a few feet away holding onto the safety railing for balance. A thick book was tucked into the crook of one arm: *The Singularity Is Near.*

"Young man," he admonished Al, "that does not seem like an intelligent thing to do. You lose something?"

The man had a long face with avian features: a curving, beaklike nose and small beady eyes, like gunpowder pellets, that rested in deeply receded sockets. The skin on his forehead, unlike that on his wrinkled face, was taut, as if staples were buried somewhere beneath the thin white hair on his scalp. He wore black slacks and a black button-up shirt. Al noticed his Roman collar.

"Hi there, Father. I work here actually." Al pointed to the laminated nametag above his heart. "I did lose something. A pearl. A single pearl."

"Let me guess: your sweetheart's?"

He shook his head. "No sir, my mother's. And it has a lot of sentimental value."

"How'd you lose her, son?"

The old priest looked Al in the eyes and waited for an answer. After a few seconds, Al finally said, "I don't know anymore."

"Grief's a mysterious beast," the priest replied. "I understand."

"No, I don't think you do."

"Of course I do." He squinted at Al's nametag. "'Alyosha Dragunov.' Hmmm. I hear your accent. Subtle, but it's there. Indulge me this: is your family from the Caucasus? Tbilisi, maybe?"

"No sir. Close. Kiev."

"Ah, Kiev! Beautiful city. Beautiful country, really. Ravaged, but magnificent." He flashed a smile of yellow teeth. "The people are kind. Inferior peasant blood, but a fierce spirit nonetheless. That's what my father always said."

Al was taken aback. He said nothing.

"Vitaly Petrov, pleasure to meet you. I go by 'Father,' but you already seem to know that." He hobbled over to Al, guiding himself along the rail. He shook Al's hand and flashed another mustard smile. "My parents hailed from Voronezh. 'Alyosha.' Hmm. A good Roman Catholic, I presume?"

"Jewish."

The old man recoiled. "Do excuse me, Alyosha. I have nothing against the Jews. But these days, Kiev is not exactly, well . . ."

"That's why I'm here, not there. Father, I do need to get back to work."

"Tell me something first, Mr. Alyosha Dragunov," he said, enunciating each syllable with staccato precision. "You *do* know your namesake? You must."

Al knitted his brow; a few seconds passed. "Are you talking about—"

Father Petrov's jaw dropped.

He shouted over Al, "Look at that! My *God*, that can't be right!"

Fifty feet from Rocky's enclosure, dozens of creatures scampered past in unison. It was a bizarre migration of rodents, from field mice and chipmunks to squirrels and rats. An animal phalanx shaped like the tip of a spear. Zoo visitors stood on each side and pointed in amazement.

"They're moving in formation!" Father Petrov gasped. "And in the air, look!" He pointed above at an assembly of birds of all kinds—sparrows, crows, gulls, starlings, ibises, hawks—flying in a massive V-formation, like a football field-sized airship. "This is a bad!" the priest cried out. He grabbed Al's arm and uttered a few sentences in another language. Al could make out "receding ocean" and "shelter."

Then the earth shook.

And Father Petrov crumpled to the ground like a house of cards.

$$\triangle \ \triangle \ \triangle$$

The earth pounded with abandon. It was like nothing Al had ever felt before.

As he hugged the dirt, Al thought to himself: if the earlier quake was a three, this was a twelve. Father Petrov whimpered "help me Lord" a few feet away. Another twenty feet past the priest, each shake sent a skunk bursting several feet into the air like a popcorn kernel on a stovetop, chattering and spraying indiscriminately. After a forty-five-second eternity, the shaking lulled. The throbbing bass in Al's eardrums ceased. The priest sobbed. Car alarms blared and children screamed.

Al stood up and sprinted to the Aquarium House. The glass door had not only shattered but separated from its hinges and was flat on the cement walkway. He stopped just short of the doorway.

"Bernie, you in there?" No answer. He entered with tentative steps, glass shards crunching under his soles. Sparks flickered on a far wall. Sunlight streamed into the room in a tight beam, illuminating an empty metal stand that had, until a few minutes ago, held a two-hundred-gallon rectangular tank with a miniature basking shark.

Bernie was off to the side of a nearby tank. He was squatting and facing away from the door with a full plumber's ass. Al noticed at least two other stands that also held shattered tanks.

"Come on, Bernie," he said urgently, "we need to get out of here."

Al looked over Bernie's shoulders and saw that he was juggling one of the small brown sharks, struggling to get a handle. Each time he seemed to have a grip the shark squirmed free and flopped onto the floor.

"Damn it! Help me out bud, won't ya?"

Al scanned the surrounding floor and realized it was littered with writhing, gasping fish.

"Bernie, there are too many. You won't get them all."

"Some is better than none."

Al tugged on his shoulder. "It's not safe in here. There could be another quake any second." He spoke quickly.

Bernie looked up and said sternly, "Alyosha, either help me or get out." Just as he spoke, Bernie gained control of the shark by clutching its whiskered face in both hands and pressing its torso into the fold of his armpit, like a running back with a football. "Bingo! Now let's find this fella a lit—"

And the earth moved again. It was as if gravity had been switched on and off; both men shot into the air and then down to the floor. Al went careening to his left into a wall. Bernie toppled backward, smacked the crown of his head against the floor, and crushed a starfish.

The pounding bass resumed as the planet's innards, its tectonic plates, shifted position. A chain of side-by-side tanks began to rock. Al crawled toward Bernie and squeezed the zookeeper's hand to get his attention. The two men locked eyes, with Bernie then following Al's gesture toward the tanks rocking in unison. The tanks were moments away from tipping over and clipping the lower half of each man. Bernie nodded and they began wriggling backward, crablike, toward the door, tracing the beam of sunlight as their lodestar. The tanks then fell, crashing and shattering on the ground without sound or vibration, the churning bass drowning everything out. A cavalcade of small fish and crustaceans, coupled with broken glass, rode a wave toward the exit and collided with the men.

The foundation of the building began to shift: with each spastic shake, it slid a few inches. Noticing that the doorway and frame were growing increasingly misaligned—causing the exit to the windowless Aquarium House to shrink—Al flipped onto his knees, tugged on Bernie's shirt, and pointed emphatically to the sunlight. Like manic babies, the men crawled on their knees for the doorway. A driving shake sent them tumbling out of the vanishing band of sunlight, but they righted themselves and, a few seconds later, scrambled through the doorway onto the cement walkway. They emerged under a cloudless blue sky.

And that's when the earthquake got really bad.

△ △ △

Al and Bernie spent the next three minutes underneath a pair of heavy wooden benches a dozen feet from the Aquarium House's entrance, the quake rattling the men against the undercarriage of each bench.

Al did what was logical: pushed his hands upward against the wooden paneling of the seat so that his back was pressed firmly against the dirt, stabilizing his body. He shot an occasional glance at Bernie, who, inexplicably, had wrapped his arms around his own shoulders as if he was making out with himself. With every jolt, Bernie's head smacked against the wooden frame. A wound had opened on Bernie's temple and blood streamed down the bridge of his nose. Al would have yelled at him to ask what the hell he was doing, but it would have been like shouting at a passing train.

As the world shook, Al witnessed some notable happenings:

- A terrified zebra ran past with its equilibrium in shambles. The quivering animal sought refuge under the shingles on the far side of the Aquarium House, tucking its front legs under its torso like a nesting hen.
- The Aquarium House collapsed on the zebra.

- A translucent, hair-like substance floated to the ground as if it was raining cellophane noodles. Al squinted into the cloudless blue sky but couldn't discern from where this mysterious substance was originating. Upon hitting the ground, the noodles almost instantaneously took on the consistency of sea foam and then evaporated.
- Three children that had been in the Aquarium House were now a few hundred feet away near Penguin Pond. They were crouched and holding hands, faces smeared with tears and snot. Each mouthed one word—"mommy"—over and over.

As abruptly as the chaos began, it ended. The bass generated by the shifting plates disappeared, replaced by blaring car alarms and shrieking children. Al stood up and took a few cautious steps as he braced for more shaking. He froze for a minute with his hands open in front of him. Nothing.

He reached under the other bench and helped Bernie to his feet. His boss' face and shaggy beard were smeared red, and his arms remained wrapped around his own shoulders.

"Bernie?"

A dumb smirk crept across the corners of Bernie's mouth. He unfurled his arms to reveal a mess of glistening flesh and slimy tentacles.

Al looked bewildered. "Is that Otto?"

Bernie nodded and smiled triumphantly.

"Couldn't leave my main mollusk behind. We have to get him to fresh water."

Al examined the messy bounty of octopus.

"Bernie, I'm pretty sure he's dead. Look at his eye," Al said as he pointed, "it might as well have a big 'X' across it."

Bernie's smile vanished. "No, that can't be. I felt him during the quake, he was . . ." He peeled some suckers off his forearm, which popped like plastic suction cups and left behind bright red hickeys. Otto's tentacles drooped lifelessly. Bernie frowned and shook his head. "Well that's just splendid. Shit."

Al, meanwhile, had turned around and surveyed the zoo. Every structure in sight had collapsed. It was in ruins.

"It's like a bad dream," Al said.

Bernie placed Otto's carcass on the bench and looked around as well. What had been frustration turned to profound sadness. The event's magnitude dawned on him.

"God damn," Bernie muttered as tears welled up in his eyes. He wiped the back of his hand across his eyes, painting his eyebrows with bluish ink and pinkish jelly. He stunk of ammonia.

Al tugged at Bernie's wrist. "We need to help people. Those kids."

"Quiet Al. Listen."

A distant voice cried out.

"Someone help me! Please! I don't want to die!"

They ran toward the wails.

There, by Rocky's cage, lay Father Petrov.

A tree had been unearthed from its roots and crashed into the steel bars. It had ripped the cement foundation from the ground and caused a twenty-foot patch of bars to collapse outward. The flattened metal now formed a readymade bridge out of Rocky's enclosure.

A bough had split from the trunk and landed squarely on top of the old priest. It was like a massive dough roller on Father Petrov's mid-section pinning him to the dirt. The priest heard them approach.

"Help me, *please*, help me! I, I think I'm in shock. It crushed my legs." His eyes were puffy and wet. "*Do* something! Pull this tree off me!"

Bernie looked at the bridge and then back at Vitaly Petrov. He whispered urgently, "Father, keep your voice down."

Al and Bernie examined the bough and exchanged an incredulous glance. It was far too heavy. There was simply no way.

And the bridge. The bridge was death, Al thought. *We have to get out of here.* Al peered under the bough: blood was pooling near the priest's crotch. Al shot his boss another look.

"Kiev boy, look at me. What do you see down there? What was that look? Tell me *now!*"

Bernie squeezed the priest's shoulder. "Father, relax, we're going to get you help. Just stay calm and keep as quiet as you can." He reached into his pocket and rooted around. Several crumpled wet bills spilled onto the ground. Next came a waterlogged pack of cigarettes: "Happy Days Organic Smokes." After a few more seconds, he retrieved a small phone and began tapping and swiping at the screen. "It's dead. Al, yours work?"

Al held out his arm and swiped at his wrist. He looked at Bernie. "No signal."

"You've *got* to do something, please," the priest begged.

"Al, let's move the branch. Let's . . . try."

The two men positioned their bodies just below the bough and crouched like sprinters preparing to race.

"You ready Al?"

"Yes sir."

The priest hollered: "*Do it! Do—*"

And then the growl drowned out everything.

The three men froze. The priest's already ashen face lost its last bit of hue. The look in his eyes morphed from one of panic to horrified realization.

Rocky ascended the bridge of bars. The bars that, for years, had locked him inside but now were his path to freedom. He ambled nonchalantly as if taking a daily constitutional. With his full body coming into view, the bear was not much smaller than a Volkswagen Bug. An awesome, terrifying creation.

Bernie remained absolutely still. Al, in the meantime, inched backward with both hands outstretched in front of him as if to say, "No problem here."

Father Petrov stammered, "Protect me! Don't leave me. Please! *Please!*" When Rocky's shadow swallowed him, the priest went silent even as his lips continued moving. As if he was trying to wish away this nightmare come to life. Tears streamed down his cheeks. As Rocky drew still closer, wearing what Al could have sworn was a content smirk, Father Petrov's eyes widened. His eyes spoke volumes. Yes, this is happening, they seemed to say. Yes, I am about to feel tremendous pain and then undergo death. Yes, the world will go on without me. Yes, I am about to become a memory. Yes, this is irreversible.

The bear stepped onto the bough that held down the priest, who expelled a sharp groan from the tremendous weight. Rocky knelt above the priest's head and, with his snout only a few inches away from the priest's face, sniffed four times. Al was frozen in horrified anticipation. Bernie bore an exaggeratedly droopy frown, with laser-like focus on whatever was about to transpire.

What came next none of the three expected.

A giant floppy tongue unfurled from Rocky's mouth. The bear began to bathe the priest's nose and lips in saliva, its breath like rotten chicken.

Father Petrov opened his eyes. They betrayed a glint of hope that this could turn out okay after all. He even registered a nervous giggle.

And then Rocky bit off his face.

The first thing that Rocky swallowed was the outermost layer of Vitaly Petrov. With a single tearing motion, the bear ripped off his skin, nose, and one eyeball. The priest's brain, his grey matter, was left exposed and partially severed. His lips, teeth, and mouth were gone. The tongue flapped around in an open gullet, as if the man's head was little more than a cross-section to illustrate the human anatomy.

By the time Al and Bernie sprinted past the rubble of the Aquarium House, the priest's upper half consisted of nothing more than some splintered ribs.

△ △ △

Aiden hugged the crumbling wall of dirt. He was on a narrow platform of soil a dozen feet beneath the fairway. And it was collapsing.

After the shaking commenced, he'd taken a cue from the raccoons and run south toward the forest. As he lurched and sporadically tumbled along the golf course, a vein deep within the ground had ruptured and collapsed two hundred feet into a thrashing underwater river. The newly formed canyon walls were thirty feet across and dropped precipitously into churning brown water that flowed south, away from the lake. When the second quake stopped, Aiden, in awe of the earth's transmogrification, doubled back to the edge and peered over, even instinctively reaching for his phone to record video. Two seconds later, the loose soil under his feet had crumbled into the abyss and taken Aiden with it. Now, all that stood between him and a nightmarish descent into the underwater river was a craggy, vanishing ledge.

Terrified that any movement would cause the ledge to drop away completely, his face and chest were flush against the wall. He jammed his fingers into the wet soil searching for a grip, but only pulled out clumps of worm-packed dirt. The sound of the whitewater ricocheted off the walls of the newly formed canyon. This wasn't supposed to happen this way, Aiden thought. He was too smart, too special, too rich.

"*Help!* Anyone, *please!*" He craned his neck to the left and saw the ledge disappearing. It would be a matter of seconds. "*Mommy!*"

He clawed at the wall. The edge was three feet away. Two. One.

Aiden jumped upward with outstretched arms. The act of pushing off with his haunches triggered the soil under his feet to drop away. He tore at the wall.

And, as if from God, down came a hand.

That hand was connected to a rippling Popeye of an arm that grabbed Aiden's forearm near the crease in his elbow. A second hand followed and grasped his wrist. The navy blue bill of a hat came into sight. Then a New York Yankees emblem.

It was Dom.

Dom grunted and yelled, "Come *on*, now," as he tapped into the reserves of strength in his biceps, triceps, deltoids, shoulders, and upper back. "There we go! *Fuck* yeah, come on now!" With a final huff, he pulled Aiden past the edge and onto the grass. Both men lay prone and panted furiously.

After several seconds, Dom stood up, helped Aiden to his feet, and shepherded him fifty feet south, where they again collapsed and resumed gasping. On their backs and staring into the blue sky, sun beating down, the men's furious breathing subsided over the next two minutes. A few translucent noodles floated gently toward earth and landed in the grass, undergoing what seemed like immediate petrification and evaporation.

Dried snot coated Aiden's upper lip; his eyes were red. Dom stood up, reached for Aiden's hand, and pulled him up effortlessly. Aiden stood in Dom's shadow and looked at his wide, homely face. He then stepped forward and wrapped his arms around Dom's jukebox of a frame, pressing his face into Dom's chest.

"I thought I was going to die. I owe you my life." He was sobbing and squeezing Dom.

"You're welcome, bro." The gears slowly turned in Dom's head.

Aiden stepped back. "What's your name?"

"Dom."

"I'm Aiden Campbell."

"You almost bit the bullet, huh. Glad I could help. Are you a guest at the Field Club?"

He nodded and asked, "Do you work here?"

"Well, I *did*. Landscaping." He frowned and shook his head. "Something tells me I'll be looking for a new job."

"What are you talking about? You deserve a God damn medal for this."

"Look around, bro. Look at what the quake did to the course. The whole club is probably totaled. I didn't think there were quakes in Washington."

"Where are you from, Dom?"

"New York. Ever hear of Yonkers?"

Aiden nodded. "Sure, I'm from Manhattan. Born and raised on East 84th."

The gears in Dom's head clicked into place.

"I came out for a job. My dad, he's, um, sick. Been sick for a while." He thought back to those old commercials he used to see on Channel 9. "Mesothelioma, from working in the Brooklyn Shipyard." He grinned on the inside—impressed by his own ingenuity. "I send money back home for his medical bills, you know. And now I'm screwed because of this quake. My dad's screwed, you know?"

Aiden put an arm around Dom's shoulder. "Easy there, big guy. Listen to me, Dom, I have money. And I owe you my life. But I need to find my wife first." He patted Dom's back. "We're staying in Bungalow 7. Find me when this settles down."

He hugged Dom again and, this time, Dom hugged back. Aiden felt like a child in Dom's embrace. Dom held on for a full minute.

By the forty-fifth second, Aiden began to feel uneasy.

△ △ △

TJ and Elise were alive.

The entire oak didn't fall on their house—just the top half. Having been buried alive under a bureau inured to Elise's benefit: she escaped harm except for some scratches and bruises to her forearms. TJ had landed on the floor between the stovetop island and the wall, the latter partially caving in and, similar to Elise, yielding refuge from the falling debris. First from the raining shards of skylight glass, then from the tree.

When the shaking ended, each held their breath, terrified of calling out and receiving no answer. They waited several minutes, praying and taking strange comfort in just a few more moments of uncertainty. TJ was the first to speak.

"El?"

He heard his wife exhale and then burst into sobs.

"TJ, I'm here! Oh, *thank God*! Baby, you okay? You hurt?"

"I'm okay. Beneath lots of stuff, but not really hurt. Can you get out?"

Within a few minutes, they had emerged from the ruins of their kitchen and embraced, their bodies pulsing with an electricity not felt for two decades.

△ △ △

Elise had her face glued to her phone as she circled the property and searched for a signal. TJ, in the meantime, stood with his back to the lake and assessed the damage to their home. The kitchen was demolished. Fortunately, he thought, they had a second kitchen in the basement. So not too much of an inconvenience to wall off the main kitchen while they renovated. He pondered how far the quake could have reached. He thought about his kids in Seattle and, for the third time, asked God for them to be alive and well.

Yet his focus suddenly shifted to a distant sound that echoed across the lake: air horns. At this distance, they were like the party-favor toots, albeit in a frenzied staccato. Almost like Morse code. When TJ turned toward the lake, goose bumps spread across his body. His jaw dropped.

A churning, coursing whirlpool occupied nearly the full width of the visible lake, its diameter thousands of feet. The vortex spun clockwise and descended into a black hole at its eye. It resembled the gateway to some horrible netherworld. Sailboats and speedboats, like toy ships, coasted at different points of the vortex and orbited the eye. The tooting continued in panicked succession.

One of the boats, a fishing skiff with a small tan deck, neared the eddy's center and spun rapidly on its axis, completing progressively smaller circles around the hole. Two flares shot into the sky from the skiff, followed by a third, and then a fourth. Communicating back, the nearest boat shot off two of its own flares and tooted four times. As if chewing food, the vortex flipped the skiff onto its portside. TJ could just make out two sticklike figures, man and child, shaken from the vessel into the water before disappearing in the abyss, down the hellish drain.

After one more short lap around the eye, the capsized boat followed its passengers and dropped precipitously out of sight.

TJ crouched down and rested his hands on his knees. The hairs on his neck stood at full attention. Memories of the Twin Towers surfaced in his mind's eye. Helpless people facing certain death. He cried as three more flares rocketed into the air and petered out. TJ counted the boats. Six. No, seven. The whirlpool had pulled three swimmers into the widest edge of its orbit—an event horizon beyond which, barring divine intervention, they would never return.

When he squinted closely at other rings in the vortex, he could see additional swimmers, like figurines, bobbing as they gained speed in their swirling descent. He saw, as well, at least five unmanned jet skis, and six, no eight, massive pink sturgeon at the surface. The fish were far larger than the humans, albeit just as helpless.

Elise approached with her eyes still trained on her phone.

"Babe, no signal anywhere. I'm freaking out!" She had yet to see this horrific vista, a macabre triptych plastered across Lake Hynek like Hieronymus Bosch's imagination come to life. "Babe, did you hear—"

"Look up," TJ said.

She did.

"Oh my God. *Oh!*" Elise fell to her knees, tears streaming down her face. She moaned plaintively. "It's the, the end, TJ . . . end of the . . ." Her words disintegrated into weeping, which soon became whimpers. "We . . . have . . . to help. Somehow."

TJ ran his hand through her hair. "It'll be okay, my love."

CHAPTER 10.
THURSDAY, JULY 1,
2021.

The quake that hit Hynek was the beginning of the end. Or vice-versa.

The epicenter lined the Oregon coast, triggering the collapse of an underwater shelf hundreds of miles long in the Pacific. Land abutting the ocean within just under one mile—and everything on top—entered the water. This was true for the entire coastline of Oregon and large coastal swaths of southern Washington and northern California. For communities farther away, the shaking pulverized homes, buildings, roads, infrastructure. Round 1 of the devastation.

Round 2 assumed the form of a tsunami: trillions of gallons of displaced salt water. Because the fault line was so close to shore, the wave was instantaneous—or at least it felt that way to those who survived the quake. Waves during Japan's historic

2011 tsunami reached almost one-hundred-thirty feet. Those here eclipsed two-hundred. They lashed into the coast for nearly three miles, sweeping away civilization to saltwater graves.

That day, at the same time, earthquakes of comparable magnitude, and unleashing comparable destruction, struck the Gulf Coast, São Paulo, Chengdu, and Cyprus. Human science never could explain these events. They were somehow related, of course—or so everyone insisted, pointing to common sense. Others said it was mere chance or synchronicity. Wait long enough, some physicists urged, and disorder would become order. That is to say, entropy would reverse itself: toothpaste back in the tube, genie back in the bottle. The bell un-rung. All matter in the universe, some asserted, would contract and condense back into a mote of mind-bendingly astronomical density. Time, too, would eventually go the other way. Odds are it would happen. If you had infinity to wait, they were perfect odds.

And so the occurrence of five simultaneous earthquakes on one lonely planet was, in the grand scheme of things, hardly shocking.

△ △ △

Twenty-four hours after the quakes, Michelle Bardo held a town meeting in the playground outside of Hynek Elementary. The brick walls of the school's auditorium, historically used for community meetings, had toppled inward and covered the last two rows of seats, destabilizing the roof. Town members communicated news of the meeting by word of mouth, with both cellular and internet service not yet back online. Landlines still worked, as did forms of radio communication. Those prescient enough to have kept walkie-talkies patted themselves on the back.

After the quakes, the President issued a solemn radio address. He spoke of the mass death; the expansive damage to the Northwest and Southeast, and, more broadly, to the civilized world; the disruption to modern forms of communication, with the prospect of sustained disruption to the networks and supply chains that provide power and food; the sheer inexplicability of concurrent earthquakes in so many places. He talked of bravery as well. How so many Americans, in the face of unprecedented destruction, directed heroism not only at loved ones, but at strangers. Heroism sometimes successful, but too often not. He praised the courage of the first responders. Of the military and National Guard who were fighting to save lives and restore order.

The first comment at Bardo's meeting was somewhat less profound.

"CVS is closed. How do we get our toiletries—you know, enemas and so on and so forth?"

The prune of a woman who uttered these words was not a day less than ninety-five, her face and arms speckled with chocolatey liver spots. She wore a billowy muumuu emblazoned with a pattern of tiny planet earths, sloppily drawn and colored. A design fit for a child's sleeping bag.

Bardo, who stood in the sandbox at the front of the playground surrounded by dozens of worried citizens, blinked twice. Sasha was a few steps behind her mother, hands pressed against her mouth in an unsuccessful attempt to suppress laughter.

Bardo craned her head and whispered, "*Don't* embarrass me, Sash." She turned back to the crowd. "Mrs. Drutherpickel, I understand your concern. But I need to address some other matters before I take questions, before this becomes a dialogue. So let's table that for now."

"I'm not just speaking for myself, for Pete's sake," the old woman responded, "we need our toiletries. You know, enemas and such." Sasha doubled over, face buried in her knuckles.

"Mrs. Drutherpickel, please sit down. Justin, yes, help her onto that swing over there and hold it still for her," she pointed at an empty swing, "that one, thanks." Bardo redirected her attention to the crowd. "I want to thank so many of you for showing up. Now, needless to say, it's been a long twenty-four hours. Who heard the President's address?" The crowd registered a smattering of nodding heads.

"I'll just begin by saying, well, things could have been worse in Hynek." The statement triggered incredulous murmuring. "Now, that's not to say we haven't lost a lot," she rubbed her hands together nervously, "but the things I'm hearing about the coast. We don't know the real extent of the damage inland, but the things I'm hearing, and I'm sure many of you are hearing . . ." Several people began to cry. "That's not to say we didn't lose anyone. To the extent you all haven't heard, our mayor, Nick Condon, passed away yesterday, which is why I'm speaking and not him. They think it was probably a heart attack brought on by the quake. My condolences to his family. And we've got quite a few more missing, it pains me to say. And, hell, I know some of you lost your homes. But thank God it wasn't worse." Someone muttered church and state. "And thank Allah," Bardo continued, "and Yahweh, Jobu, all that." She exhaled and looked at her hands.

She was about to resume when an angelic voice distracted her. It was a little girl in the front of the crowd singing in French:

> *Entendez-vous dans la plaine*
> *Ce bruit venant jusqu' à nous?*
> *On dirait un bruit de chaîne*
> *Se traînant sur les cailloux.*

The girl was six years old with blonde curls and a peaches-and-cream complexion, serenading a tattered, stuffed bunny. She went on:

> *C'est le grand Lustukru qui passe,*
> *Qui repasse et s'en ira*
> *Emportant dans sa besace*
> *Tous les petits gâs*
> *Qui ne dorment pas.*

Bardo fought to regain concentration. She looked at the girl's mother and said politely, "Would you, please?" The mother nodded and gestured for the girl to be silent with a finger across her mouth. The child nodded obediently and simulated zipping up her lips. Bardo turned her attention back to the crowd.

"I think by later today we'll have a better idea of the true damage closer to the fault."

"Can we talk about the lake already?" It was a middle-aged man leaning against a seesaw in front of the sandbox. Bruce Mercer, owner of the Field Club.

Ingo's father, Moses Lee, piped up from the back of the group

"People died, Bruce. Our livelihoods are all suffering. Show some respect."

"People died in the damn lake," Bruce retorted, twisting his head to look for Moses. He turned back to Bardo. "And I'm not talking about my club. I'm talking about what's happening to the water and whether we're safe. One of my fairways looks like the Colorado River. How do we know if the ground is stable, Michelle?"

An attractive woman in the middle of the crowd announced, "We saw people die on the water!" It was Elise Freeman. Her words trailed off into sobs.

TJ wrapped an arm around Elise and said, "There were people and boats getting sucked into the whirlpool." Several more townspeople began moaning.

Bardo nodded slowly and took a deep breath. "Okay, folks. The lake. This is like something out of *The Twilight Zone*. So, apparently," she started to read from a piece of paper in her hand, "the quake ruptured the lakebed floor, which leads down to what, according to the Army Corps of Engineers, is a 'confined aquifer.' They told me that the aquifer abuts some kind of underground cavern. The lake water is emptying into the aquifer, and then the cavern. This is what's causing the whirlpool. They estimated that, based on the rough diameter of the whirlpool and the size of Lake Hynek, it'll be fully drained in a matter of hours."

A male voice from the middle of the crowd blurted out, "I still don't get it. Where's the water going?"

Bruce spoke again.   "Some's going to that cavern, like Michelle just said. Some's running south, perpendicular to the lake. Like I mentioned, I practically have a river crossing one of my fairways."

"Yes, the lion's share is, I guess, going into that cavern," Bardo said, "but how far down, who knows. The Army said this is not unheard of—at least, you know, geologically speaking." She tittered joylessly. "This is obviously going to change what kind of town we are. But that's a topic for another day." She scanned the faces in the crowd. "I will say this: stay *out* of the lakebed. We've got neither the resources nor expertise to be rescuing folks who go gallivanting down there. Please do us all a favor: just don't do it. No one go searching for Josie. And with that, I'll move onto the food issue." She grit her teeth. "As most of you have seen, Safeway is closed.   That's at my direction." A discontented murmur rippled through the group. "I did it for a good reason. Fuel and food deliveries are going to be disrupted. They *are* disrupted." The murmur assumed a more worried tone. "We've got to make ends meet for, maybe, a couple of weeks."   The murmuring sharpened into anxious chatter. Bardo opened her hands in front of her. "Look, I'm not just doing this willy-nilly. I'm following the *FEMA Handbook*, which contemplates this type of situation."   The townspeople continued   mumbling   with   displeasure,   Hurricane   Katrina uttered a few times.

Budd Hopkins, with a red bandana wrapped around his forehead, stood on an elevated wooden platform at the top of a neon yellow tube-slide. He looked like a pirate in a crow's nest.

"Hey Chief," he interjected, "can I broach something on this topic real quick?" Bardo nodded. "Let me start by saying that all of us have cars. Generally one or two. Many have compacts, some have small SUVs and whatnot. Me personally, I've got an Escape Hybrid." He clapped his hands together. "So, anywho, I do realize this town has people with, what you might call, higher means."

"Where's this going?" Bardo asked.

"I'm getting there. As I was saying, we got folks with money. So whereas I have my little hybrid, others have a few cars. I get that. I do. Now when you talk about disruptions, Chief, you'd think the reasonable thing to do, the *responsible* thing, is for these folks with lots of means, who have lots of cars, to show a little restraint. Some judgment. Right?

"With that in mind, I'm cleaning up my shop late last night. It was, I don't know, 2:30 in the morning. And here comes this parade of gas-guzzlers: a Range Rover; another Range Rover; one of those fancy Mercedes G65s, which is another giant SUV for those who don't know; a Suburban; a Porsche; and, finally, a Harley, the Cadillac of choppers."

Leaning against his blue Infiniti behind the playground, Dom's ears perked up at the description of this luxury fleet.

Budd went on, "So I'm thinking to myself, 'Who is filling up their Porsche in the middle of the night? Who's filling up their God damn *Harley*? And I hate to put people on the spot, but I do think it's warranted here. I'll direct everyone's attention to Mr. and Mrs. Timothy John Freeman."

Elise stared sheepishly at her feet as she and TJ became the target of a sea of disapproving eyes. TJ could barely contain his fury as he shot daggers at Budd on his wooden perch.

"My point is that the Freemans, and those like them, should save a little for the proletariat. We can't all be so good at bouncing a ball."

"Not cool, Budd," TJ barked, "not cool at all. You could have done this a lot differently."

By now, the crowd was chattering in condemnation.

"Can we sustain another round of fill-ups from the Freemans? I don't know," Budd said. "What are we going to do about *that*, Chief Bardo?"

Bardo frowned at Budd. "I think we should all use our judgment in these matters," she said. "And I happen to agree with TJ: there were better ways to do this."

"I'm sorry, but sometimes you got to single out folks. I mean, how long is this 'disruption' gonna last? Mother Nature dropped an atom bomb. For those who don't have a mansion on Cedar Drive, this could get very hairy, very fast."

Dom blinked in thought.

TJ shouted, "You shut the fuck up right now, you hear me? You say one more thing about us and I'm coming up there!"

"What, I can't speak?" Budd shot back. "Just because I'm not rich, I have no rights? Chief, you hear him threaten me?"

The crowd was buzzing. Someone near the front said smugly, "I drive a Tesla." Elise buried her face in her hands.

A cloud cover passed that, until then, had been shading the playground. It was as if they were emerging from an eclipse, the summer sun now beating down on the group. Those not wearing sunglasses, including Bardo, shielded their eyes. As she began to speak, Bardo rummaged in her pocket for her aviators.

"Enough Budd, you've said your piece, you—"

TJ spoke over her, his cadence rapid and agitated.

"Now that we're all here like one big happy family and doing some shaming, I see we have a dog killer in our midst. Yeah, *you*, you sick prick."

TJ, who towered above those around him, pointed past Budd to a gazebo on stilts. Standing in the center was Popper, dressed in a stained *Black Dog* tank top and his perennial khaki shorts. With a Chaplin-esque expression of exaggerated surprise, Popper's eyebrows shot up as he pointed to himself with both thumbs. *What, me?!*

"You killed my dog you son of a bitch!"

He charged at Popper. The crowd instantly parted in his path. Bardo hopped out of the sandbox and ran to intersect him. But Justin was already there, standing in front of the gazebo in a defensive posture.

Justin held out his hands. "Calm down brother, chill."

"Don't 'brother' me! If you guys did your fucking job, he'd be in jail. He would—"

"TJ, stop, *now!*" It was Elise. Her shriek rang out across the playground like a gunshot, halting TJ in his tracks. As Justin escorted TJ back to Elise, she addressed the crowd.

"It was bad judgment on our part, we're really sorry. We, just . . . we weren't thinking." She scanned everyone's faces. "We're sorry."

"Apology accepted," Budd replied. "Hopefully your husband feels the same. Now that he's done deflecting." He grunted self-righteously.

By now, Bardo had returned to the sandbox.

"Okay, well that was cathartic," she said, eliciting a few awkward chuckles. "Now, about the Safeway. Everyone knows Justin Treanor, of course." Bardo nodded to her deputy, who was whispering something to TJ. "He'll be overseeing the opening in two hours. We're going to allow twenty customers into the store at a time for twenty minutes each. Let's see how that plays out."

A voice emerged from the back of the crowd. It was the lawyer, Jay Taylor.

"Just out of curiosity, Chief Bardo, on what authority have you ordered the supermarkets closed?"

"The Governor declared a state of emergency. With the mayor gone, I'm exercising his power to suspend cer—" She ceased mid-sentence and considered her words. "Well, suspend certain rights. I shouldn't be afraid to say that aloud." There was renewed grumbling from the townspeople. Someone uttered taxation without representation.

"Now, if everything wasn't swell enough," she continued, "the Fire Marshal and National Weather Service are reporting wildfires in Oregon that are moving north. As of an hour ago, about a hundred miles south of Hynek." Some groaned while others nervously chattered. "Please listen to AM 660, which is where we'll be broadcasting news and emergency management info out of the City Center building. And, for the time being, we're stationing the Police Department there as well."

"What happened to the police station?" someone asked.

"Good question. That brings me to my next topic." She took a deep breath and exhaled. "Yesterday morning, before the quake, we arrested Scott Maccabee for murder. Suspicion of murder, I should say." Several people gasped and then the crowd went silent. "Some of you know Scott, I'm sure. He's a pilot. I was responding to a radio run—a 911 call—and discovered Scott in his home with a deceased male." She cleared her throat.

Budd asked, "Who'd he polish off?"

"That, we don't know yet. We had a forensics team coming from Olympia when the quake hit. But they went back."

"Did Scott identify the guy?" Jay asked.

Bardo glanced at Justin, who tilted his head equivocally.

"Scott," she responded, "well, he was, uh, incoherent. He had a concussion, which we think played a role." She coughed uncomfortably. "Anyway, my point is that we had Scott in the stationhouse cell. The quake caused the structure to cave in right over him. We thought he might have died. But he didn't. He escaped."

The crowd buzzed with worried questions: "So he's loose?" "A fugitive's loose?" "Does he have a gun?" "How'd he kill the guy?" "Where could he be?" "What about the children?"

Bardo pushed down with her hands, gesturing for quiet. "We don't understand why Scott did what he did, or who the victim is. But rest assured, we do *not* have reason to believe that Scott's some kind of serial killer. We're not dealing with Jason Voorhees. There are certain, eh, indications pointing to a definite motive." A boldfaced lie, Bardo thought. "With all that said, you should, of course, assume he's dangerous. If you see him, don't approach him. Act cool, stay away, and notify us immediately."

"Is there a bounty?"

Bardo squinted to see who asked the question. It was a musclebound man in a flat-rimmed Yankees hat leaning against an old blue Infinity. Dom.

"Sir, if you mean *reward* for information leading to his arrest, the answer is 'no.' Although you'd be doing your civic duty and I'm sure everyone here would be grateful."

A skinny white arm went up near the back of the crowd.

"Yes, you," Bardo said, "the one raising your hand so politely. What say you?"

"Hello," the voice projected nervously, "I'm Alyosha Dragunov. I need to make an announcement about the Hamfield Zoo. I'm speaking on behalf of Zookeeper Bernard Higgins."

"Go ahead, sport."

"I was at the zoo yesterday with Mr. Higgins during the quake."

"And?" someone blurted out.

"Animals got loose."

A matronly woman next to Al asked, "Nothing too dangerous, I hope?"

Al shook his head. "A polar bear."

The crowd registered a collective gasp. After three seconds of silence, the same woman blurted out, "Christ on a stick." A few people sniggered nervously.

"Thank you for that information, Aly-ya. Al-yo—"

"You can call me 'Al,' Chief Bardo."

"That's easier, thanks Al. Any other escaped wildlife?"

"Not that I know of, ma'am. I haven't spoken to Mr. Higgins since yesterday. He was assessing the situation when I left."

"Okay, thank you again. Al's comments bring me to another topic: concealed carry. We're suspending the ban. *I'm* suspending it. I see a compelling interest in Hynek's law-abiding citizens carrying their properly concealed firearms." An approving murmur swept through the crowd. "Folks, just please don't make me regret this decision." She readjusted her belt and flexed her pelvis, loosening a wedgie, and then wiped a bead of sweat from her brow. The sun had nearly reached its apex.

"Seeing that we're starting to sweat, I'm going to adjourn until Saturday, same time, same place. Let me just say: we'll get through this, folks. When I graduated from the academy, my old boss told me something that's really kind of prophetic considering what happened yesterday. He told me that, when despair hardens into pain, and the journey through the long da—"

A voice drowned her out.

"This better be about our toiletries—enemas and such!"

△ △ △

As the meeting drew to a close, the last few hundred-thousand gallons of water spirited down the giant hole that would eventually become known as "Alpha Drain." It resembled an enormous sink hole with the square footage of twenty football fields. The lakebed around Alpha Drain, which had contained three-hundred cubic miles of water, now lay exposed to the sunlight. It was part of earth's troposphere once more after submerged for ages.

The lakebed varied in depth, with no shortage of peaks and troughs, some quite steep. In the eastern half, a few dozen small islands, some populated with cabins, had peppered Lake Hynek, formed from underwater hills that crested and plateaued just above the water's surface. Those islands now resembled mushrooms tops: craggy slopes that sprouted into flattened earth with grass, sunflowers, and shaggy sourwood trees. The contrast between the lakebed's maroon sediment and the verdant island tops was unnatural, evoking an isolated patch of jungle surrounded by snow on all sides. Most of the lakebed was a deep red, with the lingering wetness giving the sediment a bloody, almost cartoonish, appearance. Some said the color called to mind images that the Mars Rover had transmitted to earth, along with those of the Rover's younger sibling, the Trailblazer.

Numerous troughs littering the basin floor had retained lake water; without direct paths to Alpha Drain, they became moderately sized ponds and creeks. The sun-kissed ground closer to the bottom of the lakebed was a malleable sludge—a composite of wet sediment, shells, mashed sturgeon eggs, and fish bones. After a few hours under the sun, the sludge's bloody hue had lightened slightly in tone, approaching a color nearer that of a boiled red potato. It also stiffened as it baked in the summer heat.

Once drained, crabs were by far the most ubiquitous of the creatures now in plain sight. Most were palm-sized and an exotic cerulean blue; they scurried in and out of the craggy surfaces that made up the newly emerged hills. Others were far larger and with surprisingly rotund shells, like oversized Honeycrisp apples, and spiderlike legs. Many of Hynek's famed pink sturgeon got snagged in parts of the rocky terrain, leaving them sprawled awkwardly in hilly nooks. They choked and coughed, sometimes over the course of many hours—giant, wondrous, suffocating fish. Those sturgeons were a sight. Over seven feet and with rose-colored backs that bore swirling symmetrical white dots, neck to tail. Quarter-sized eyes that were milky white (no pupils, as if their eyes were mucous sacs through which you'd expect tadpoles to poke holes and shimmy out). They had thick whiskers, like uncooked bucatini, which gave them a shaggy, almost comical appearance—a touch of disco, even. Lake trout, far smaller and, by contrast, plebeian in appearance, also found themselves stranded. Unlike the sturgeons, the trout generally ran out of air in less than an hour after the quake. They strained for breath while jerking their bodies with animatronic movements, struggling to flop into one of the leftover pools. Only a small handful succeeded.

These fish and crustaceans attracted birds of all stripes from near and far, as if news of vulnerable prey had spread through chirp-of-mouth for hundreds of miles. Or, perhaps, it was the advancing wildfire that spurred those birds north, trying to escape from their own unique form of airborne asphyxiation. Either way, the number of birds grew. They flew clockwise patterns above the lakebed like Corsairs over the Pacific Theatre. Some of those birds were common to Washington: condor; osprey; golden eagle; red-shouldered hawk; northern harrier; the list goes on. One bird, however, was far larger and more peculiar.

With the wingspan of a large car, its wings were featherless on top—not unlike a bat with sinewy, tar-colored skin. Underneath, those wings had bushy orange hair. Not feathers, but rather coarse fur with the texture of a doormat. Its torso and neck resembled those of a crane, only far larger. All told, its body was several times bigger than a large Thanksgiving turkey. The creature's saurian face was its most alien feature. Each side of its head was a two-foot-long obtuse triangle, with its mouth containing three successive rows of tiny teeth that resembled miniature spearheads. Its eyes, nestled just above the mouth, were separated by a sharp ridge jutting out of its temple like a fleshy mohawk. The ridge ran along the skull and ended in blunt appendages akin to a buck's shaved antlers. And the beast's eyes were truly something else. Two inches across and spade-shaped, each eyeball bulged outward in a highly unnatural fashion. They were a waxy yellow color with a honeycomb pattern.

The tribe that once lived along the northern shore of Lake Hynek considered this animal a god.

Upon pointing the creature out to a son or daughter, a Tuckashoa parent would say, "Behold, my love. The Thunderbird."

CHAPTER 11.
THURSDAY, JULY 1,
2021.

Al walked from the playground to his motorcycle and picked up his helmet from the tattered leather seat. Bernie had instructed him to spread the message about Rocky and otherwise not return for a while. He'd lamented that, while it was probably the last thing Al wanted to hear, he should look for another job once the dust settled—that the zoo would be hobbling to rebuild for the foreseeable future. Moreover, that Al shouldn't let his "demons" get the best of him. And, of course, that he'd do well to keep his eyes peeled for Rocky.

His job with the Field Club met a similar fate. A few hours before the town meeting, Bruce Mercer had gathered the operational staff, from landscapers and painters to janitors and busboys. He expressed hope that their loved ones were safe, thanked them for their hard work, and said that, unless already notified to the contrary, they were no longer employees of the Field Club. The golf course was a tort waiting to happen, the restaurant had sustained extensive structural damage, and he did not envision fully restoring the facilities (assuming he chose to do so) for at least two years. Considering that the lake would soon be gone, he doubted that restoration would make commercial sense.

Al's scatterbrained thoughts jumped from one foggy item to the next. *My demons? What did Bernie mean?* His mother's pearl. The priest. *That misanthropic coward. But no one deserved that.* The priest's tongue, skin shorn off like plastic wrapping from a toy. Nose gone, eye sockets empty. His tongue, though, had escaped the first bite intact. *It was flapping around. He was silently screaming.* The tongue in that pulpy red cavity. Something happened in those moments before the quake. When the priest had insulted the Ukraine, Al had wished for something bad to befall the man. Or maybe not wished, but at least a vision had flashed through his mind's eye. A bloody face. Raw flesh. *It was that tongue: I saw that flapping tongue. But how could I have known?*

A hand gently squeezed his shoulder. Al flinched like a cat.

It was Lilly in a straw hat that shaded her face. Aiden, in a tight polo shirt, stood behind her and peered at Al. The look on his face suggested validated disapproval. "I told you so," it seemed to say.

"Hi Alyosha!" Lilly chirped. Her bubbly demeanor stood in sharp relief to the zombie-like townspeople who, in a somber procession, were exiting the meeting.

Al shot a glance at Aiden and answered cautiously. "Hi, Lilly. Hope you're okay. You seem . . . okay."

She lowered her voice. "Terrible, truly, the whole thing." Pointing to Aiden, she said, "Alyosha, please meet my husband, Aiden." Al waved meekly. Aiden stepped forward and shook his hand.

"Nice to meet you, Alyosha." Aiden paused. "Listen, brother, I'm sorry for what happened at the restaurant a few days ago when you spilled food on me. Very rude on my part."

Al shook his head. "It's just Al. And nothing to apologize about, I was the one at fault. Anyway, so much has happened since then. Feels like a different age, really." Aiden nodded and stepped backward.

Lilly spoke. "Alyosha, I want to—"

He cut her off. "Like I told Aiden, just 'Al.' Only my mom calls . . ." He trailed off awkwardly. *Called. Calls. Called.*

"Sorry Al. Listen, I want—no, *we* want your help." She cupped her hands like she was saying a prayer. "We're going into the lakebed. Will you come? We'll pay you."

He jerked his head back in surprise.

"Why do you want to go in there?"

"Remember at the bar, Al, I mentioned having done something stupid? Well, we—" She stopped and corrected herself. "*I* dropped something in the lake when we were in a rowboat. A ring."

"What kind of ring?"

She hesitated. "An heirloom. Doesn't matter what kind."

"Worth a lot?"

"Yes. A lot of sentimental value too. We hired divers to help us find it. That was before the quake. We haven't been able to get in contact with them. And, I mean, there's nothing to dive in anymore. So there's that."

He stared silently at Lilly, and then at her husband, and then at her again. He eventually said, "Why me?"

"Because Aiden's too scared for us to go alone," she answered with a fleeting chuckle.

Aiden stepped forward. "For the record, I am not." Just as quickly, he receded into the background.

"Because Aiden's cautious," she clarified.

"I still don't understand," Al interposed, "why *me*? Do I look like I can protect you?"

"Do you have a gun?" she asked.

"No."

"A knife?"

"Well, I mean, I could *get* a knife, yes."

"And you're from the Ukraine?"

He nodded.

"And that's a dangerous place, right?"

"It is these days. A few years ago it—"

"Have you ever fought?"

"Like a fistfight? In Kiev, maybe once or twice." Al thought for a second and then tittered. "Come to think of it I almost had to hit someone with a crowbar right before the quake because he was . . ."

"Great, then you're *perfect*!" She drowned him out. "Aiden wants to ask some big Italian guy who helped him during the quake. But I much rather have you." She winked. "We'd want you to carry some supplies and watch our backs. Be an extra set of eyes. We're leaving before dawn tomorrow; it should only take a few hours."

Al blinked a few times and tried to muster a smile while he weighed the risks. His mind's eye shot back to Bernie's severed prosthetic.

"I'm sorry, Lilly, but no. You heard what the police chief said; it's not safe."

"Five thousand. Risk-reward."

His eyes widened. "Rupees?" Lilly giggled while Al took a deep breath and exhaled slowly. *How can I turn this down?*

"I, I still do—"

"Seventy-five hundred," she interrupted.

"What the hell?" Aiden protested.

"Oh, shut up Aiden, we've got it," she said dismissively. "How about now?"

Al couldn't turn this down. But he could get more. Enough to put him over the edge so that he could finally track down his father.

"Make it ten thousand, Lilly. If you've got it, like you say. I just lost both my jobs."

"Give an inch," Aiden scoffed.

Lilly turned and examined her husband's face. His head tipped forward in acquiescence. Then he stepped forward. "We'll pay you when we get back to our bungalow tomorrow. Now let's hammer out a plan."

△ △ △

Bardo sat at a Plexiglas desk on the second floor of the City Center building. The building itself was intact, although papers, office supplies, and furniture were strewn everywhere. She riffled through some cabinets and found a hard copy of the most recent *Tuckashoa County White Pages*. She knew that Scott Maccabee had two children, including a daughter, Lindsey. She also knew that Lindsey had married the heir to a famous tool manufacturer. But Bardo couldn't recall the name of the brand. It was on the tip of her tongue.

She stood up and scanned the room. Off in a corner was an electrician—an elderly Asian man with a tool belt drooping from his hips. He was unscrewing a breaker box.

"Excuse me sir," she called out, "what kind of tools do you use?"

"What's that, ma'am?"

"What brand tools do you use?"

"Personally, I like Armstrong. Made in the USA. That's what I've got at home."

"Is that what you've got there in your belt?"

"No ma'am. I use town tools when I'm here, and they buy some second-rate stuff. Portuguese brand that's made in China or Malaysia or something."

"What's it called?"

He unsheathed a wrench from his belt and flipped over the handle, lowering his glasses to examine it. "Duarte."

Bingo.

"Thank you, sir. That's exactly what I needed to know." The janitor nodded and turned back to his work.

Bardo opened the white book to "D" and searched for Duarte. *Do-, Do-, Dr-, Dr-, Dr-. Lots of those. There we go, Du-. Duane. No. There, Duart. Duarte, Pedro and Lindsey.* She picked up a cordless phone from its cradle and dialed the number. One ring, two, three, four, five, six, seven. She hung up. *Shit.* Bardo flexed her jaw and looked toward an arched window. The sun, spilling diagonally across the room in a narrow beam, illuminated a patch of tired grey carpet before tapering off as it climbed a nearby wall. A self-contained universe of dust mites floated aimlessly in the light band.

Someone had carved something on the wall at the tip of the light, captured within the last few inches of the illumination. The very end of this light wave's journey across the solar system, Bardo thought. She squinted.

"Carlos M. wuz here," it read.

"Hah!" Bardo hollered. "What are the chances?" She'd known a Carlos M. a long time ago in Baltimore. An undercover cop: Carlos Medina. *He killed a man over some stupid shit. It changed my life.*

Her mind skipped to Sasha. *My little Mayan princess.*

Her first act after the quake had not been an official one: she'd sped to the high school and searched empty rooms until she found the summer school classroom, which was filled with twenty of the town's juvenile misfits. In the field just outside the windows, a trio of once towering trees had toppled and narrowly missed eradicating the classroom. All but one of the desks rested on their sides, and a large monitor, which had hung in the back of the room, lay shattered on the floor like a broken mirror. Teachers and administrators comforted several of the students; most were crying and trembling.

Not Sasha. She stood alone by a window with arms folded across her chest, examining the destruction in the field. When she heard Principal Ken Lee greet Bardo at the door, she swiveled her head and caught her mother's eye. Sasha smirked and raised her eyebrows as if to say, "Look at these chumps."

Bardo ran to her daughter, squeezed Sasha with all her might, and silently shed tears into her silky black hair. Sasha offered a reluctant, tepid embrace. After thirty seconds, she pushed Bardo away and asked to go home. *My little sociopath.*

But then came the ride home. To Bardo's shock, someone different emerged from the husk that was her daughter.

As soon as they'd shut the car doors, Sasha's breathing began to stutter as if she was hyperventilating. Confused, Bardo had asked, "Sash, what's up with your breathing?" When she twisted her head to inspect her daughter's face, she saw tears streaming down her cheeks. "Goblin, you okay?"

And with those words, the wall came down: the perpetually irritated expression that she presented to the world—her steadfastly defiant posture and body language—crumbled and vanished. In their stead emerged an unsure, fragile, and terrified little girl. The girl Bardo hadn't encountered since Baltimore and that she'd come to believe her daughter had shed like a second skin, gone and relegated to fond memories.

Sasha wept into her mother's shoulder for the next thirty minutes. She described her fear during the quake, including how she was convinced that two of the trees would surely flatten the classroom. But how, when she tried to flee, her muscles didn't work. It was an unfolding nightmare over which she was powerless, and she had just wanted Bardo there. She'd wanted her mom.

And then she spoke about the suffocating anxiety with which she woke up every morning. Panic about what others thought of her: a trashy, adopted newcomer to the school, someone who came from a blue collar family. Whose mom was just a cop, not a millionaire hedge fund manager or software designer. And the shame she felt because, at the same time, she felt that she and her mom were, in fact, stronger and better. That they were real, whereas others were playing roles of the perfect son, the perfect daughter, the perfect family.

Bardo listened and cried, cried and listened. In a state of exquisite relief.

She reached for the cordless phone to call Sasha. Before she could touch it, the phone rang.

Bardo pressed "POWER" and answered, "Hello?"

A woman with a warble-like voice spoke guardedly.

"Uh, hi. Did you just call me?"

"Are you Lindsey Duarte?"

"Yes. Who are you?"

"Mrs. Duarte, great, thank you for calling back. I'm Michelle Bardo, Hynek Chief of Police."

The woman's composure shattered. "Oh God, it's Dad, isn't it? He's dead, right? I knew it, oh my God!"

Bardo shouted over her, "No, no, Mrs. Duarte, you don't understand. I know your dad and he's not dead. Please, just relax."

"What?"

"In fact, him being alive is throwing us for a loop. Let me explain, and I'll be blunt, which comes easy to me. Before the quake, we arrested your dad."

"What?"

"I was responding to 911 call. I found Scott, your dad, dragging a dead guy through his living room."

"*What?*"

"I know. Listen, we had him in a cell at the station when the quake hit. It destroyed the building. When we went to search for him, he wasn't there. He got out. He's *alive*, dear." She waited for the woman to absorb the news. "You still there?"

"Yes."

"Okay. So, at the moment anyway, he's a fugitive. I take it you haven't heard from him. Where are you located?"

"A bit east of Seattle. I've been calling his place nonstop. I have two terrified children otherwise we'd have driven to his house. *Who* was he dragging?"

"Dear, listen, we don't yet know the decedent's identity. Middle-aged Caucasian with a really hairy mole on his face. Ring a bell?"

"No. What did my dad say happened?"

Bardo considered her words. "Peculiar stuff. Paranormal stuff."

"Oh God, Dad," she whimpered, starting to cry again. "He had some kind of meltdown after one of his flights. He was really cryptic with us about it. You know he lost his job, right? That he was drinking?"

Justin approached holding up a walkie-talkie. He pointed toward it and mouthed some words. Bardo whispered "not now" and shooed him away.

"Listen, Lindsey, all that is beside the point right now. Do you know where he could be?"

"Where Dad could be? Honestly, between flights, I think he used to just sit in his house and read, watch shows. He went on a few dates a couple of months back. I don't know if that turned into anything. Melissa Welling is her name."

Bardo nodded. "I've heard of her."

"I found Melissa's number and tried calling her after the quake, to see if he was with her. No answer at the number in the phone book."

She thanked Lindsey and urged her not to worry, that there must be some kind of rational explanation for the "decedent" in her father's home, as she put it. That her father was alive and that, hopefully, they'd clear everything up soon. She hung up and looked at Justin, who was leaning against a file cabinet.

"Melissa Welling," she merely said.

"The waitress?"

Bardo nodded. "Maccabee's fling, evidently."

"Worth a shot," he muttered. "Me and Cutty went to Zamora before dawn." He was referring to another Hynek officer, Nick Cuttino. "Real Navy SEAL-type stuff: creeping around and then busting in with guns in the air. No sign Scott's been there."

"Why were you pointing to your radio?"

He unclipped the walkie-talkie from his belt and turned up the volume. The grainy sound of a National Weather Service broadcaster, succinct and staccato, became audible.

". . . spreading north. Now vegetation fire, eclipsing one-hundred-thousand acres. Mandatory evacuations for homes in the communities of Duneville, Kepler's Park, and Weston Range. Aerial resources increased to sixteen helicopters and five air tankers. Water and retardant. Northern cordon points in Kepler's Park are Halfmoon Pond Drive and Brower Place; California Road and Barfield Cove; Abilene Crescent and Mile Square Road. More than fifty structures in the burn zone. Burn zone expanded to include Bixby (ten miles), Garrapatos (twenty miles), and Hynek (thirty miles) . . ." He muted it.

They stared into one another's eyes.

"This is gonna get bad, huh Justin?"

He frowned and nodded. "I got Sarah packing. You'd best do the same with Sasha. And the town."

Bardo put her thumbs into her belt loops and exhaled.

"First things first. Melissa Welling."

△ △ △

A man spoke.

"And the Book tells of this, of cataclysm and Armageddon. The fact that man, these terribly fallible creatures that we are, would—by our own hand—invite this. Our greed, avarice. Our lust for *things*. For objects and status. Things to take and to pet and to kiss and to display. To call our own. To wear on our bodies. Raw, foul braggadocio. And now the tinkering with our genes, tainting God's hand with this, this, *scientific* grotesqueness, unnaturalness."

A woman interposed, "Amen to that."

He continued, his tone louder and angrier.

"We foresaw this day. When He would *smite* us in great numbers, even those young and sick and, you would think, the most innocent. He would make an example of us. That not one of us—no matter how young, no matter how sick—is ever truly innocent.

"It was our common ancestor, after all, who ate that fruit and forsook His simple rules. Who followed that *snake*. It was they who plunged us into this chaos, this, this . . . repellant *perversion*. Want and lust, and its champion, science, stitching our rectums and then filling our plate. Feeding us more and more. That wickedness cast out of His kingdom."

"Hallelujah."

"Fortunately, those who've listened to 990 KMT, who've been listening all along, you've prepared for this day. You've purchased your 'Faith Taste Survival Barrels.' High-quality, nutritious canned meals, guaranteed to last for fifte—"

Dom turned the dial.

"—ady for the worst, certainly. It's spreading because of the drought and, frankly, the depleted resources. *Tremendous* resources being deployed closer to the coast. It could not have come at a worse time. The inland towns and cities are not—"

He clicked "FM."

> *—chine will, will not communicate*
> *These thoughts and the strain I am under*
> *Be a world child, form a circle*
> *Before we all go under*
> *And fade—*

Dom mashed his palm into the "OFF" knob. He shifted into second as he slowed to cross a speed bump. The cold sore had healed and crusted over; it had taken everything in his willpower not to pick it. He could exercise self-control when necessary. In fact, the way Dom looked at it, his entire life these days was one giant exercise of self-control. No more taking what he wanted.

When he was on the inside it'd been different. *Dog eat dog.* The guards were the gods, of course. But big, strong men were the demigods. And Dom, lucky for him, was a big, strong man. He reflected on one of his finer moments: the whiffle-ball game. Not long after Dom began his term, some loudmouth spic talked shit to him.

"Look at that Shrek-ass looking nigga throw the ball! Yo, that nigga can't throw! Puta faggot ass nigga." Trying to make a name for himself. *Thought he was safe because he was with his two spic friends.* As if *that* would scare a demigod. Later in the game, when that spic hit a ball to deep left and rounded first, Dom delivered a running clothesline that knocked him out instantly. He crashed backward without bracing himself; the hollow pop of a skull hitting concrete at full force rang out across the rec yard. Dom got on top, flipped him around, and, with one hand on each side of his jaw, pressed down until he split the mandible—*crack*—causing the guy's mouth to part like a snake swallowing a watermelon. He took a spare whiffle ball out of his pocket and, in one deft motion, jammed it down his throat. By the time someone fielded the hit, Dom was already back at first base.

As it turned out, he'd fractured the guy's skull, causing his brain to bruise and swell. He died a couple of days later. No one ratted on Dom, though. And no video of the attack.

That was the first of four during his stint. He got away with them all. The spic was because of an insult. The three others, in contrast, arose not from retribution. No, the others each had something Dom wanted. The first two had objects: one, an heirloom wristwatch; another, a Rubik's cube. The third had something more intimate—and he died rather than relinquish it. So it goes, Dom thought. I take what I want. I'm a demigod. Puta Faggot Ass Nigga Demigod takes what he wants.

He turned onto Cedar Drive. Using the nails of his thumb and middle finger, he dug under the scab on his lip and peeled it off. Rolling the dead skin between his fingers, Dom savored the crusty tactile sensation. *The little things in life.* He continued parallel to the lake's southern shore and, after five minutes, stopped at the base of a long driveway that led up to stately white mansion. *It could be no other. NBA royalty lives here.* Perched in the center of a carefully manicured lawn not much thicker than a putting green, the sweeping vista of what was once Lake Hynek framed the background of the house. The fallen bough of a giant oak protruded from the roof. He smiled and looked for somewhere to leave his car.

For a demigod, this was the start of something good. He could just tell.

△ △ △

Elise Freeman read a few more words of *The Dancing Wu Li Masters*. She held the book several inches from her face, her neck and head propped against a scrunched pillow at the end of the couch.

However, if the principle of local causes fails and, hence, the world is not the way it appears to be, then what is the true nature of our world?

There are several mutually exclusive possibilities. The first possibility, which we have just discussed, is that, appearances to the contrary, there really may be no such thing as "separate parts" in our world (in the dialect of physics, "locality fails"). In that case, the idea that events are autonomous happenings is an illusion. This would be the case for any "separate parts" that have interacted with each other at any time in the past. When "separate parts" interact with each other, they (their wave functions) become correlated (through the exchange of conventional signals) (forces). Unless this correlation is disrupted by external forces, the wave functions representing these "separate parts" remain correlated forever. For such correlated "separate parts," what an experimenter does in this area has an intrinsic effect upon the results of an experiment in a distant, space-like separated area. This possibility entails a faster-than-light communication of a type different than conventional physics can explain.

In this picture, what happens here is intimately and immediately connected to—

The charming attraction of sleep beckoned her. She placed the splayed book on her breasts and then reached into the lining of her yoga pants. She retrieved a yellow tube of lip balm and, with one hand, removed the cap, twisted the tube, applied the balm, replaced the cap, and re-pocketed the tube. She could do this in the middle of a gunfight. Muscle memory.

Her eye caught the LCD embedded in the wall of her large pink yoga studio. Still just static.

A pleasant drowsiness continued expanding and overwhelming her senses. She let go.

Elise found herself in a recurring dream—one she'd had since her teenage years. Her dreams were long the subject of some controversy in her family. Elise's mother, who had visited a psychic biweekly until her death, always insisted that her daughter was prescient ("clairvoyant," she'd said). These dreams, her mother claimed, foretold major events in Elise's life. That is, if Elise could only learn how to interpret them. She encouraged her daughter to visit a particular psychic in Seattle "of sterling reputation." Elise always refused, dismissing the entire premise as hogwash. But, deep down, she enjoyed the idea of being special—of possessing an extraordinary faculty that made her different. Unique.

In this particular dream, she was always ascending in a hot air balloon. As it rose, she grew increasingly anxious and then began to panic, scared that it would not stop rising and, physics notwithstanding, breach the edge of the atmosphere. It was not the prospect of some kind of horrible suffocation in the vacuum of space that alarmed her. No, instead, it was the thought of losing gravity. Of floating out of her wicker-basket cocoon, untethered and exposed.

Sometimes she was alone in the balloon, but often not. When she was younger, her father was an occasional fellow traveler. Later in life, it was TJ or one of the kids in the balloon. It had once been a dictatorial partner at her old law firm. Another time: Popper.

In this iteration, her co-passenger was an inanimate object: a small cardboard box. She felt a gust of wind as the basket accelerated upward, which triggered an unpleasant sinking feeling in her gut; it was the ascent countering the effect of gravity. The sky darkened as the balloon neared the limit of the atmosphere. Panic would have normally set in by now, but this mysterious box had captured her attention. She knelt and examined it. *What could possibly be inside?* She shimmied the box; its contents, what seemed like one solid object, slid from side to side. Next came a gentle purr, as if Elise had jumpstarted a toy motorboat. She slowly opened the flaps and peered inside.

It was a kitten. An orange tabby no bigger than a fist, staring up expectantly from its haunches. She picked it up and swaddled the animal, peering into one of its eyes. Peering back was a shimmering gold iris and slender black diamond of a pupil. It had a pink eraser nose and absurdly long whiskers that drooped to the bottom of the box. Its head was surprisingly big for such a tiny body.

The purring grew louder. She cupped its chin in her hand and stroked its neck, feeling a powerful muscle contract and expand as it purred. It then opened its mouth and delivered a bellowing roar. She felt hot breath against her face; spittle made its way into her mouth.

She dropped the animal and scrambled backward until they were catty-corner in the basket. After licking the back of its paw and fastidiously grooming its ear, the kitten looked up at Elise, opened its mouth like a tiny bird, and roared again. It then began stumbling toward her, its Lilliputian paws slipping on the curved bamboo. She retreated to a four-foot-wide elevated platform with cup-holder indentations that encircled the perimeter of the basket, just beyond the arched lip that functioned as a handrail. On her hands and knees, Elise stole a glance over the edge. She was *not* nearing space, as it turned out. She was instead floating five-hundred feet over the lakebed. Directly on top of Alpha Drain—the great black void.

When she looked back, the kitten was on the ledge with her. Only a few inches away. Holding onto a taut nylon rope that connected the basket to the balloon above, Elise stood up. She tried to step around the animal, but her legs felt heavy, frozen. And now the kitten began to grow. Each time she blinked, it was larger and more developed—more muscular. First like an adult housecat, then a lynx or bobcat, then a mountain lion, then a panther, then a lion, then a tiger. It didn't even make sense that it could fit in the basket, much less on the small ledge. She blinked once more.

She was no longer in the basket—instead she was falling into Alpha Drain. A strange calm overtook Elise as gravity sucked her into the black hole.

She opened her eyes, stared at the pink ceiling, and blinked rapidly to moisten her contact lenses. She lay still and reflected on the dream. *The balloon again. And what was it this time? A kitten. What would Mom have said about this one?*

And then she heard the roar.

$$\triangle \ \triangle \ \triangle$$

Elise opened her eyes wide; the sound was *not* in her head. It was muffled and coming from outside the second floor window, somewhere on the vast brick patio below. She remained still. She did not want to confront what might be down there. Hoping that, if she simply didn't react—if she hid her face in her hands—the problem would go away. An adult could handle it. But then she thought of TJ. *He could be in danger.*

She compelled herself to sit up, placed her feet gently on the carpet, and tiptoed to the bay window, which was covered by an oversized blackout curtain. She drew a sliver of fabric and peered through the glass. Straight ahead was their sweeping lawn; it was on the crest of a hill that sloped down through a patch of forest to what was once Lake Hynek, but now a craggy, descending maroon landscape. The darkness of Alpha Drain—a well-defined circle of black set against a sea of red—lurked in the distance. For someone floating above and looking down, Alpha Drain was the pupil of an ungodly eye. She tried to swallow, but her mouth was chalky. She took a deep breath and traced her eyes to the patio below.

And there it was.

Resting on the Freeman's chaise lounge sofa: an adult Bengal tiger. Like a mutant housecat, it lay on its side with one of its grapefruit-sized paws hooked toward its mouth. The animal alternately licked and gnawed on one of its claws, biting and twisting its head to splinter and then sever the keratin. Elise watched like a mannequin, transfixed. *Never in my wildest dreams.*

A sickening thought jolted her back to reality: TJ possibly stepping through the sliding glass door onto the patio. She tiptoed out of the studio and down a long wooden hallway to a banister overlooking the grand foyer below. Elise issued a single controlled yelp—terrified that, even from here, the animal would hear. "*Timothy!*"

Several seconds passed in silence.

"*Timothy John!*"

Still nothing.

With the footwork of a ballerina, she pranced down the curved staircase to the entrance hall. Once off the creaky steps and onto solid marble, she ran frenziedly to TJ's office and tried to open the door, but it was locked. She exhaled in relief. She rapped once and whispered urgently for her husband to open the door. She heard movement and rustling, a radio clicking on, and then the stoic tone of a broadcaster discussing the wildfire.

"I'm coming, relax," a muffled voice said with annoyance.

He opened the door several seconds later. A vintage boom box, Radio Raheem-style, was on an antique mahogany desk, which was littered with papers and pens. An NBA Finals MVP trophy nearby served as a paperweight for some yellowed newspapers. A glistening bottle of Lubriderm, which seemed conspicuously out of place, sat next to the boom box.

"What is it, El?" he asked. TJ was in an old game jersey, checkered pajama pants, and Nike sandals.

She surveyed the desk. "What are you doing in here, and why do you have the door locked?"

"I was just listening to—"

Elise shook her head and cut him off: "Doesn't matter. Listen to me: there's a *tiger* on our patio!"

"What?"

"There is a gigantic wild cat on our chaise lounge! I swear to God this is happening, TJ!"

"Holy shit!"

"I *know*!"

"You didn't leave any doors or windows open, did you?"

"No."

"I got to see this," he said. "Hold on." He galloped to the other side of the office and, from a display on the wall, retrieved a rusted sugar-cane machete—an antebellum antique.

"Babe, what are you doing?"

"What do you think? Protection."

Thirty seconds later they were perched by the curtains in the yoga studio. Elise said "get ready" as she slowly withdrew the curtains and watched his reaction. TJ's jaw fell and eyes widened. For five minutes they stared silently at the giant cat. He eventually tapped on the window, eliciting a thunderous roar.

Elise grabbed his hand and whispered, "What are you doing!" He didn't respond. And they simply watched.

Finally, TJ said, "You saw that it deflated my basketball, right. It's chewing it like a toy." He turned to Elise for the first time in a long time. "Could that *thing* down there have gotten Rosie?"

"This is from the zoo, babe. Remember what Michelle said at the meeting? Must be."

TJ rested his chin on his knuckles and continued watching.

Suddenly, someone rang the Freeman's bell.

△ △ △

TJ sprinted through the hallway, dropping the machete on a ceramic side table by the banister as he bounded down the stairs to the front door. He unhinged the heavy lock, swung open the door, and, without a word, grabbed the man outside by the shoulders and yanked him into the house. It was Dom.

"Whoa, Mr. Freeman, sir!"

His back against the closed door, TJ caught his breath while examining Dom.

"I, pulled, you, in, because . . . not safe. Outside. Why, am I, so, out, of shape?" He panted for several more seconds.

"Mr. Freeman, I'm—"

"Don't I know you?"

"The golf course, sir. A few days ago." His voice tapered off as he tried to gauge whether he'd refreshed TJ's memory. TJ squinted and scratched behind his ear. "With the—"

"Dog?" Dom cut in. "You said 'us big guys need to look out for one another.' Remember?"

"Ah yes! The landscaper, of course. Please son, remind me of your name."

"Dominick DeRuglia, sir."

"Yup, yup, Dominick." He grabbed Dom by his colossal shoulders. "Listen to me: there's a *tiger* in our backyard!"

Dom laughed. "That some kind of code?"

"No code, no euphemism. An actual tiger. It's on our patio. My wife thinks it must have escaped from the Hamfield Zoo."

"That's, like, amazing sir."

He patted Dom on the back. "Good thing you showed up exactly when you did. You could have had a close encounter with the damn thing! Anyway, that's what's happening around this neck of the woods."

"So crazy. Really."

He nodded. "So how can I help you, Dominick?"

Dom had spent an hour mapping out how this visit might unfold, toying with what felt like the endless permutations of his first move. How his initial action would spill into the next, and then the next, and the next. That first domino to set everything in motion. Nonetheless, he couldn't answer TJ's simple question. He fumbled for words.

"Well, I just, uh. It's that. You see, I, well, I just wanted to, um, to . . ."

As he tried to articulate a coherent sentence, Dom glanced around him. The vestibule spilled into a checkered black and white marble floor surrounding a winding wooden staircase. Canvassed paintings of wildlife adorned the walls, with a maze of hallways leading away from the foyer to other wings of the house. Off to the right Dom noticed a framed Golden State Warriors jersey on a wall. Straight ahead, through another door, a majestic dining room table dressed in gold tablecloth and covered with fine china—articles that wouldn't have looked out of place in a Victorian palace.

TJ began to grow impatient and, after several more seconds, said, "Why don't you think about it and, in the meantime, we go check out the tiger? That must be throwing you for a loop."

"Exactly, sir. That'd be excellent, I'd like that."

TJ gestured for Dom to follow him. The men quickly went upstairs and along the corridor to the yoga studio. Holding a cordless phone, Elise eyed Dom—nearly as tall as her husband and far more muscular—with an unsettled look.

"TJ, who is this?"

He wrapped one arm around his wife's shoulders and led her toward Dom.

"El, this is Dominick. He works at the Field Club; we met the other day. Remember the dog Jay and I saw on the golf course? *This* was the young man who helped him out."

"Oh, wow," she said, her posture loosening and expression lighting up. "You're the one that helped out that pup?" She shook Dom's hand. "It's a pleasure, Dominick. You must be a real animal lover, like us. Well, you picked the right day! Take a look at our *other* unexpected guest." She walked over to the window and drew the curtain. The tiger was still on the chaise lounge, although it had changed position: the right side of its face and body were pressed against the cushion. Its left eye, which pointed up, was shut. Every few seconds the eye opened momentarily and peeked at the bay window. Dom laughed.

Elise whispered, "He's been looking up here ever since TJ tapped on the window. Scoping us out."

TJ and Elise stepped even closer to the window. Yet Dom took two steps back. A massive LCD set into the wall, suede sofa, wood-paneled floor with a full-length mirror covering the far wall. He surveyed it all. How the rich lived. How a demigod should live.

Elise noticed that Dom was not watching the tiger. She gently tapped TJ's shoulder and motioned in Dom's direction with her chin.

"So, Dominick," she said without turning, "where'd you bring that dog?"

He didn't answer for a few seconds. "Uh, you know. The pound."

"The *pound*?" she almost squealed.

"Yeah. The pound."

She looked at Dom. "I hope you mean the no-kill shelter."

"Sure."

She considered her next question. "The one in Hamfield?"

"Exactly, ma'am."

"There is no shelter in Hamfield, much less a no-kill one. What are you talking about?"

Dom doubled down even as he became increasingly inarticulate, grasping for words.

"Maybe I got the no-man-clay-chair"—he fought through the pronunciation—"wrong or something, ma'am. But there's this, like, um, you know, this place with animals in Hamfield. Like dogs and cats. And parakeets."

"The pet shop in Hamfield—is *that* what you're talking about?" With her hands on her hips, Elise squinted at Dom.

He knew he was digging himself a deeper hole. Fuck it, he thought. *Won't matter anyway.*

"Yeah, the pet shop."

"So, to be clear," Elise snapped like a prosecutor, "you brought a starving dog you found on the golf course to a pet shop? Number one, that doesn't make sense. Number two, I'm friendly with Janet Marsh who owns Hamfield Pets. She didn't say anything to me about this. And she *would* have."

TJ stepped back from the window and took his wife's hand.

"El, sweet love, ease up. You're cross-examining our guest." He put his arm around Elise's shoulders and looked at Dom. "This is what happens when you marry a lawyer, Dominick. Why don't you just tell us what brought you here today."

He had an answer this time.

"Well, sir, you mentioned on the golf course that, you know, you may have some work for me. And I just lost my job. The Field Club's shutting down. I was following up, like you told me to do." He paused for a moment. "Sir."

Elise asked accusingly, "How'd you know where we lived?"

"On the golf course, your husband mentioned the street. And the guy at the playground said your street, too," referring to Budd Hopkins. She winced at his mention of the playground.

He continued, "This was the, you know, like the nicest house on the street, probably the whole town. I took an educated guess."

TJ nodded with ostensible satisfaction.

"A man's got to work, right El? Come to think of it we could use some manpower to clean out the kitchen, right?" He looked at his wife for approval. "You must have seen the tree, Dominick. We're going to tear down the room and rebuild, but it's still got everything in it. Fridge, furniture, stove, so on and so forth. We need to move everything into one of the garages. We could throw you a few bucks to handle that. What do you think, El?"

Elise grinned superficially at Dom.

"Maybe. My husband and I would need to discuss it and speak to our contractor. So we couldn't give you an answer right away. TJ will get in touch with you. After this craziness subsides." She gestured toward the window.

Dom clasped his hands together and bowed.

"Mrs. Freeman, thank you sincerely just for considering it. I know this is a strange time for everyone. And, you know, I didn't mean to, like, intrude or be so direct." He spoke more confidently, evincing an almost magnanimous charm. "I'm just, you know, trying to earn an honest living." A sprinkle of sentimental flourish.

TJ seemed impressed. He looked at Elise with eyebrows raised, telegraphing his assessment that this "Dominick" was indeed a decent, hardworking young man. She looked back with sterile eyes and a hollow smile.

"We understand," she said, "hopefully we can help. TJ will walk you out now."

"El, what about the tiger?"

"It's fine," Dom responded, "I'll run to my car. It's on the other side of the house. As long as someone keeps an eye on the tiger when I go. Mr. and Mrs. Freeman, can I please use the bathroom first?"

Elise nodded. "Down the hall, third door on the right."

He bowed deferentially and disappeared into the hallway.

△ △ △

Once the sound of Dom's footsteps receded, TJ whispered, "Doesn't seem like a bad dude, right?"

Elise eyed the door and then glared at her husband. "Are you kidding? He was lying to my face about what he did with that dog. Didn't you hear that?"

"Yeah, I heard it," he offered sheepishly, "I guess that's a bad sign, huh?"

"A 'bad sign'? It says at least two things. One, he's dishonest—right at the outset. You want him in our house? Two: what did he *actually* do with that dog? After what happened to Rosie—"

"That was Popper."

"*Was* it? We don't know beyond a reasonable doubt. This guy could be some sicko. No no no. Tell him now or later, I don't care. And either way, get him *out* of our house. In fact, you should be keeping an eye on him right now."

TJ shook his head. "Christ, El, relax. He's just a big dumb jock, like me. He's not Lucifer."

"I don't know *what* he is. Out. Our kitchen looks like a bomb went off, we've got a tiger in our yard, and now this creep."

"We should call the kids," he said, "they're going to freak when they hear about the tiger."

Elise nodded as she turned back to the window.

"Our friend looks like he's asleep. For real, this time." She looked back at TJ. "I called 911. Got a damn answering machine. Go figure. I left a message."

He approached the window and wrapped an arm around Elise.

"Kind of magical, though," he offered, "our very own patio tiger. Sounds like a band Junior would like."

Elise pushed back against the windowpane and nestled in his chest. They sat on the sofa, exhaled collectively, and waited.

Two minutes passed. Three. Four. Five. Six. Ten.

Elise flashed worried eyes. "We should check on your guest."

"Relax, babe. I'm sure he's just dropping the kids off at the pool."

She recoiled and slapped his arm. "Ugh, gross! He better not be. Big guy like him. Okay, let's give him a couple more minutes."

Five more minutes went by.

Elise looked wide-eyed at TJ. "Let's go," she said.

She tiptoed behind TJ as he crept along the hallway runner toward the bathroom.

Light peaked out from under the bathroom door. They heard the muffled sound of the bathroom fan. And a weak, echoing cough. Every four seconds, a throat clearing. And then more gentle coughs.

"Uh, hello in there," TJ projected his voice as he knocked, "you coming out?" No answer. "Dominick, you okay?" Just coughs. Throat clearing then coughs. "Hello?" After knocking again, TJ glanced at Elise. Her eyes bespoke mounting panic.

"I told you," she whispered frantically.

He swallowed and slowly turned the doorknob, the cylinder inside the lock clicking into place. He pushed and the door creaked open.

△ △ △

Bardo and her deputy entered the lobby of the three-story apartment building across from Nardo's Pizza. She scanned the names on the mailboxes. *2B, Welling.* Melissa was a longtime waitress at Tuckashoa Bistro on Post Road. She was also a casual acquaintance of Bardo.

They went up the stairs and Justin knocked on Apartment 2B. Silence. He knocked again. This time, he identified himself.

"Police, ma'am."

Still no answer. Time for Plan B, Bardo thought.

She hustled down the stairs, went outside, and trotted to the back of the building. A thin metal ladder from the fire escape stopped in the air eight feet above the ground.

Bardo sized up the distance, retreated several feet to get a running start, and then sprinted toward the ladder. She leapt into the air and grasped the bottom rung with both hands, swinging back and forth like a chimp. Once stabilized, she put her light weightlifting to use. Although she could do only three pullups, she needed just one. She hoisted herself up, grabbed the next rung, and lifted her knee onto the first bar. She exhaled and set to climbing.

Upon reaching the second floor, Bardo put her back against the wall just outside two conjoined rectangular windows; one was enclosed with only a mesh screen. She craned her neck around and peered inside.

Under Plan B, Justin would continue knocking every twenty seconds, affording Bardo an opportunity to see what exactly was happening on the other side of Melissa Welling's front door.

And it was just as she'd hoped.

Scott Maccabee stood frozen a few feet from the door. He was listening to the intervals of knocking, at attention like a cat on a hot tin roof. She could make out his thinning crown and chia-like hair sprouting from the collar of his shirt. She spent two seconds considering her options. Then she acted.

"Scott, we have you surrounded! Hands in the air, *now*!"

Scott's shoulders sank. His head went down while his arms went up.

"I'm unarmed, Shelly," he shouted.

She ordered Scott to open the front door and he complied. Justin charged inside with gun drawn, threw Scott to the floor, and handcuffed him. Bardo, meanwhile, lifted up the mesh screen and slipped through the opening. She stood over Scott whose arms were pinned behind his back and broad shoulder blades pinched together.

"We thought you died at first," she said.

Scott muttered, "Probably would have been better off."

"Keep your chin up, Scott," Bardo said as she put her hands under his face. When Scott didn't move, she clarified, "No, literally, keep your chin up." She helped elevate his head while Justin wrapped his arms around Scott's waist and lifted.

As they got him to his feet, Bardo asked, "Where's Melissa?"

"Spokane. I knew she wouldn't be here."

They led him downstairs to the Camaro, which was parked in front of Nardo's.

"This is going to be a squeeze," Bardo warned.

Scott looked incredulously at the car.

"Seriously? Shouldn't you be driving something more, you know, official? Like something with four doors?"

She tapped Scott on the shoulder and pointed toward Nardo's.

"Want a slice before we go?"

Before Scott could answer, Justin had one foot in the restaurant door.

△ △ △

The prisoner and his captors sat at a round table enjoying plain slices and Diet Coke. Every thirty seconds, Bardo raised a slice to Scott's mouth.

"To be honest, Scott," she said, "we don't really have anywhere to take you. You saw the stationhouse."

Scott chewed and swallowed. Then he dipped his head to the straw and slurped twice in rapid succession.

"How bad was the quake?" he asked. "You guys took my phone. And nothing was working at Melissa's."

Bardo and Justin exchanged amused looks.

"He doesn't know, Chief," Justin said.

"Well, Justin, you do the honors."

Justin described the concurrent earthquakes. The draining of Lake Hynek. The encroaching wildfire. Noticing Scott's increasingly panicked look and taut posture, Bardo reassured him that she'd spoken to his daughter. When he learned that his family was alive and well, Scott slouched back in his chair and belched.

"When you gave your statement," Bardo said, "you mentioned a name. One of the men in the, eh, craft, said a name. 'Ozzy' something or other. Do you know who that is?"

"Osmond Romanek," Scott clarified. "I don't have the slightest. Bite please." She fed him a piece of crust and Justin used a napkin to dab tomato sauce from Scott's chin.

Justin looked Scott in the eyes and said, "Let's say it all happened just like you said, that we take everything at face value. Baton Rouge, the phone calls, the blue door, the room— wherever that was. 'Project Yahweh.' All that." He narrowed his eyes. "Why you? Why'd they choose *you*?"

"I've thought about that," Scott responded, "and the closest I could come to rationalizing what happened is to think about it this way: a mouse in a maze. Does a mouse ask why it's in the maze? The scientist looking down from above—well, *he* understands. He's got a hypothesis of some sort, and he's using the maze to test that hypothesis. Try to explain that to the mouse."

Their police radios chirped. It was Winnie. Something about a message on their 911 line.

Scott wrinkled his nose in surprise. "Did she just say *tiger*?"

$$\triangle \ \triangle \ \triangle$$

The Freemans didn't know what they expected "Dominick" to be doing in the bathroom when they opened the door. But they didn't expect what they found.

An empty room.

An old iPhone X with a screen like a spider web rested on top of the closed toilet seat. It was producing the looped sound of coughing and throat clearing.

TJ let out a deep breath and gave his wife a puzzled look.

If he had known that, in this particular reality, it would be the last time he would glimpse Elise, he would have told her how much he loved her.

TJ suddenly yelped and twitched.

It began on his back: immediate, without warning, and jarring, almost like several simultaneous bee stings. It then continued with unrelenting intensity.

It was Dom. Antique machete in hand, hacking. Like a butcher at a giant slab of beef. *Hack. Hack. Hack.* The blade tore through TJ's basketball jersey.

After the initial blow TJ swiveled. He saw his assailant mid-motion, raising the giant knife. Preparing to swing again and wearing a workmanlike expression on his face.

Elise shrieked. She retreated frantically from the blade, tripping and falling backward into the bathtub. She pled through choking gasps for him to stop. Clawing at the porcelain as if she could get even farther away. But there was nowhere else to go.

The next swing yielded a six-inch gash along TJ's abs. The jersey soaked up some of the blood, the rest streaming onto his mesh shorts before dripping to the tile floor. He shouted "no," raised both arms in a defensive posture, and stepped back toward the sink. This blow struck the side of his left forearm below the elbow. It hit bone. After a few milliseconds, the skin parted like a blossoming flower and overflowed with red. TJ looked at the wound in disbelief. He kept repeating "no."

But, like a machine, Dom continued. Controlled yet devastatingly powerful swings. The third, fourth, and fifth lopped off four fingers on one hand, his thumb and index finger on the other. Blood spattered in all directions. Elise screamed hysterically for Dom to "please just stop." But it continued, unabated. TJ kept offering up his arms to defend his face and body, and Dom kept chipping away at flesh. Within seconds, TJ slipped on the blood and struck his head on the sink as he fell. No working hands to brace his fall.

From the floor, TJ starting kicking like a furious stallion at Dom's shins. Dom took two large steps back and then began swinging at the flailing legs, earning direct blows. TJ recoiled and tried curling into a ball under the sink, tucking his knees in front of his stomach. And Dom continued hacking. Hack the shin. Hack the calves. Hack the naked feet.

Three hacks later, one foot was severed and dangling, connected by a ropey string of flesh. Pressed against the wall under the sink, there was no escape route. He tried desperately kicking with his remaining foot, and Dom swung at it three times. Slice to bone. Splitting, parting skin. Blood. TJ shouted "no" like a mantra.

He had no more functioning limbs with which to protect himself. Dom crouched, tilted sideways, and swung the machete like a bat. Four times in rapid succession—aiming for areas of exposed skin on the upper thighs and chest. All four landed squarely. The flesh split, the wounds peeled open, and blood gushed.   Adrenaline sustained TJ's continual, fruitless thrashing, struggling to protect what was left of his shell of a body.

Dom had been swinging for ninety seconds. He stopped, panted heavily, and wiped the sweat from his forehead.

Elise was no longer crying. Placid from the shock, she simply repeated "why" over and over.

"I'll tell you real soon," Dom muttered under his breath.

He backed away from the sink and beheld his prey. TJ's head had escaped unscathed and his back bore only one long gash inflicted at the onset of the attack. Most of the cuts were to his limbs and extremities. He was awake but losing substantial blood. Elise was asleep; her mind had shut down.

"No," TJ repeated mindlessly. His speech was slowing. He seemed unable to comprehend the damage done. He tried to move, pawing at the wet floor with his stumps. Dom dropped the machete and put his hands around his own waist. He examined the pulpy mess. His creation.

"You were *such* a good defender, Mr. Freeman. Those long arms and legs. I remember when you defended LeBron in the Conference Finals. You were the only one who could stop him. Look at you now."

"No." TJ's lucidity was gone. He was on his side, like one of the giant sturgeon gasping for breath. "No."

"Before you go, where do you keep the keys to your Range Rover? I always wanted to drive one. I guess I should ask *which* Range Rover! Mr. Freeman? Sir?"

"El, El."

"I'm talking to you, *bro*. Well, guess I'll have to wake up Mrs. Freeman."

He stepped toward the bathtub.

$$\triangle \; \triangle \; \triangle$$

They had their guns drawn.

Bardo led Justin as they walked briskly to the Freeman's front door with a handcuffed Scott Maccabee in tow. All three scanned the lawn intently.

"Keep your heads on a swivel, boys," she advised.

"Couldn't you just leave me in the car?" Scott grumbled.

As Justin rang the bell, Bardo looked back at Scott. "This is so much more fun. You get to meet a sports legend. And maybe a six-hundred-pound cat."

Justin rang again and then knocked. They waited for a minute without speaking, the midday silence broken by the call of a mourning dove. After another few seconds he looked at Bardo, shook his head, and gestured to the side of the house. She nodded.

"Let's do it," she said. "Scott, I probably don't need to tell you, but stay close."

They walked along the western perimeter of the sprawling property. It took them on a gravel driveway that culminated in a barn-like yellow garage with six retractable doors. One door was open and revealed an empty parking space; a large black SUV and silver Porsche visible on each side of the empty space. The trio passed the wreckage of the kitchen as they crossed the fastidiously maintained backyard, perched atop a large hill that led down to what was once Lake Hynek, but was now a maroon wasteland. Birds of prey in the hundreds, if not thousands, circled above the gaping black hole several miles away.

As they rounded the corner of a rectangular sunroom that spilled into the lawn from the main structure of the house, Bardo gestured with the barrel of her gun at a brick patio coming into view. She breathed quickly, heart racing. Justin was pointing his own gun from one direction to the next in swift movements, sweat streaming down his temple and along his nose. Scott was simply hustling to keep up.

Nearing an arrangement of oversized furniture on the patio, Bardo was the first to see it.

"Justin, look," Bardo said softly, pointing to the ground next to a chaise lounge. The brick patio was awash in haphazard red streaks. Tiptoeing closer, Justin gestured toward a fist-sized pulpy mass and a torn piece of orange fabric. She noticed a tangle of wet brown hairs on one end of the mass. A trail of red led toward the grass and away from the house.

Justin manipulated the handle on a sliding glass door. "Locked, Chief."

Scott whispered, "Deputy Treanor, look up."

A bay window on the second floor was ajar; red curtains rippled gently in the wind. Bardo was looking as well. She considered their options.

Bardo approached a small window near the sliding door and, holding her gun by the barrel like a club, smacked the window once, then twice. The glass shattered on the third try. She reached through the broken window and jiggled the lock on the sliding door. After a few seconds, she'd disengaged the lock, opened it, and stepped inside.

"Everybody in."

△ △ △

Bardo, Justin, and Scott formed a semicircle around the open bathroom door. They didn't say a word.

Still handcuffed, Scott took a step back and dropped to his knees. He began vomiting mozzarella braids.

Justin patted him on the back. "Easy there, Mr. Maccabee." He removed a handkerchief from his pocket and dabbed at the remnants on Scott's chin.

"I've never seen so much blood," Bardo eventually said stoically. "From this angle, looks like the wounds are mostly on the hands and feet." She crouched and tilted her head. "Oh, Lord. His feet are, well, pretty much gone. Fingers too. TJ, you poor bastard." She looked at her deputy. "Who could have done this?"

"Tiger . . . in the house?" he offered.

She shook her head. "Those are defensive wounds. Some*one* did this to him. With a knife."

"Elise," Justin uttered.

Bardo nodded. "The mess outside. It's Elise. Part of her. Let's find that window."

With Scott still on his knees, Bardo and Justin followed a trail of bloody shoeprints—large Nikes—along the hallway runner. They entered the yoga studio. The prints continued to an open bay window that looked down onto the bloody patio. From this vantage point it was easy to see that the red trail led to the northern edge of the backyard. It was no longer visible once it passed the crest of the hill that descended into the lakebed.

Bardo sniffed twice as she contemplated the scene.

"Justin, stop me if you think I'm crazy. They let in the perp. Probably has something to do with the tiger. They saw the perp outside, maybe working, and then pulled him in. For his own safety. Little did they know. Perp attacks TJ in the baño. Perp throws Elise out the window. And, I'm loathe to say it: tiger drags Elise out there." She pointed toward Alpha Drain.

"It fits, Chief." Justin scoffed under his breath. "What the hell is happening to us?"

"You know, even before the quake, Budd gave me his weird theory. In so many words, he said Satan's flexing his muscles. Which is why things keep getting crazier." She gazed at the

otherworldly landscape—the giant black pit like the eye of
Sauron.   "I dismissed it as a joke.   But maybe he knew
something I didn't."

She scrunched up her face in thought, before her eyes
suddenly lit up.

"TJ and Elise: they put hidden closed circuit cameras all over
the house. After what happened to their dog."

Justin looked at her with a pained expression. "So we'll have
a snuff video, I suppose."

It didn't take long to find the control panel and monitors for
the CCTV, which the Freemans had hidden in a mahogany
wardrobe in TJ's office. In horrible astonishment, they replayed
the motion sensor-activated footage:

- A large white man ("John Doe") accompanying TJ to the
  yoga studio, where Elise was standing with a cordless
  phone. (Bardo: *That's the guy from the meeting, Justin.
  The big guy who asked about the 'bounty.' Right?*")
- John Doe leaving the studio and walking down the
  hallway to the bathroom, entering the bathroom briefly
  and turning on the light, exiting, and closing the door
  from the outside.
- John Doe walking to the stairs and picking up a large
  knife from a table.
- John Doe entering a nearby room on the second floor.
- TJ and Elise opening the bathroom door.
- John Doe approaching the Freemans from behind, using
  the knife to slash TJ and knocking them into the
  bathroom.
- John Doe emerging from the bathroom with Elise over
  his shoulder, carrying her to the yoga studio.
- Elise waking up.
- Elise mouthing words to John Doe, who looked at the
  camera.   The man mouthing words back angrily.
  (Justin: *She must have warned him about the cameras.*")
- Elise mouthing several more words to John Doe.

- John Doe pushing Elise onto her back and then stomping on one of her kneecaps, inverting the bone. (Justin: "*Dear God.*")
- John Doe opening the bay window, picking up Elise by her hair and the seat of her pants, and heaving her through it.
- Elise landing face-first on her chest on the patio below. The impact causing her to momentarily lose consciousness. (Bardo: "*She's still alive!*")
- A tiger stepping off the chaise lounge, straddling Elise, and biting her neck. (Justin: "*I can see the blood. Christ almighty.*")
- The tiger tearing, licking, and chewing on Elise's neck. One arm free of its paws and flailing frantically.
- Elise going still.
- The tiger picking up Elise's body by the neck, carrying her to the northernmost edge of the Freeman's yard, and disappearing from sight.
- John Doe entering the master bedroom, opening the top shelf of a dresser, and removing two items—a pistol and a smaller nondescript object—which he placed in his pocket.
- John Doe leaving the house, crossing the driveway, and entering the garage.
- A garage door retracting.
- A heavily tinted Range Rover driving away.

CHAPTER 12. FRIDAY, JULY 2, 2021.

Al, Lilly, and Aiden walked south along the splintered wooden planks of the boardwalk that lined the lakebed's southwestern edge. All three carried powerful Maglites, although switched off because the moon was nearly full and illuminated the boardwalk. Al wore a backpack filled with water bottles and dried snacks. He and Aiden each had sheathed Bowie knives tucked into their waistbands. To their right: dense overgrowth and chirping crickets. To their left: the massive, descending pit. The stars were bright.

The boardwalk eventually ended with a set of rickety steps that led down to a narrow pebble beach. They had said about three words since their 4:30 a.m. rendezvous in front of Budd's. Once on the beach, Aiden took the lead and walked twenty feet ahead. Lilly clicked on her flashlight and shined the beam at Al's sneakers.

"Nervous?" she asked in a giddy voice.

Al nodded as he swept the lush forest with his eyes, trying to pinpoint the source of a gentle ruffling in the distance. "You, on the other hand, seem to be enjoying this."

"You know what?" she chirped, "I am. I've been on a thousand of these golf trips. And I hate golf. *Detest* it." She shot an indignant glance ahead. "I sit in hotel rooms. You know what I did during our 'golfing pilgrimage' to Scotland last fall? Read *Crime and Punishment.* In five days. It's a long book. Good, but long. Yet this is . . . different. Exciting. Am I nuts?" She spoke quickly.

Al continued surveying the bush. "I always wanted to go to space; I thought it was my destiny. Which is kind of what we're about to do—except going down, not up."

Lilly didn't answer. After a few more minutes, she whistled for Aiden to stop. "Where should we enter?"

The trio trained their flashlights on the lakebed. The pebbles continued for a dozen feet at a thirty-degree downward slope, resembling the transition between the shallow and deep ends of a manmade swimming pool. The ground then abruptly disappeared, which marked the point at which a far sharper descent commenced.

The lakebed produced a foul, suffocating odor: mildew and decomposing flesh. Aiden registered a muffled gag and then hacked a wad of phlegm onto the pebbly ground.

"Smells like that dead rat in the crawlspace, remember?" Aiden asked Lilly, who sniffed the air, grimaced, and nodded.

Al pointed his light in all directions, anxiously checking for anyone or anything. Opposite the lakebed, his beam lit up a reflective object tucked in the distant overgrowth. It was a chrome-plated headlight reflector on a luxury SUV. Strange place to park, Al thought.

Al continued surveying the landscape and then declared, "Here's as good as any."

Lilly made the sign of the cross.

△ △ △

Appearances notwithstanding, the descent was not challenging. Although steep at points, the lakebed floor alternated between craggy hard sediment and rock (with no shortage of places to step securely), and a muddy crimson sludge that squished under their shoes, supporting their weight. Aiden compared it to stepping on Playdough.

They passed two giant sturgeons. One was lodged in a crevice between two boulders; it was little more than a handful of picked over bones swarming with flies. The other was in a leftover pool the size of a Jacuzzi—alive, although just barely. Part of the fish's body, its spiky pink spine and rear fin, were above water. So were its eyes: milky, alien-looking pupils. It had nowhere to go and breathed with labored gasps.

Lilly crouched next to the pool and touched the skin between the creature's eyes. She looked despondently at her husband.

"It's beautiful, in a way. I wish we could help it somehow."

"It's a fucking fish," he sniped. "The smell is getting worse."

Al stood a few feet away, shining his light in every direction like a methodical sentry. One hand clutching the leather handle of his knife.

After a few minutes of steep descent the terrain levelled off. It was uniform rock with indentations that formed small streams, each only a foot wide and deep, which ran downward along the gentle slope. Sensing his wife's frigid body language, Aiden commented on how the streams ran parallel, sometimes only an inch away, yet never seemed to cross. Two paths—side by side.

"Isn't that strange?" he asked and took her hand, but she recoiled. Aiden issued a frustrated scoff and walked far ahead.

Lilly looked at Al. "He sucks," she said.

Al smirked. "Has he always?"

"No," she answered hesitantly, "well, maybe." She kicked a loose rock. "I knew he treated others a certain way. But he treated me differently. Not anymore." She exhaled slowly. "I'm sorry I said anything. Tell me about *you*, Al."

"What about?"

"You came from somewhere so different. How'd you end up here?"

Al smirked. At eighteen, he explained, he'd matriculated at KTI. "It was kind of like Ukraine's MIT," he put it. His goals, at least back then, were crystal clear: study mathematics. Then graduate school for astrodynamics. Next, apply to every publicly and privately funded space program. Train and go to space. Simple as that. "I sometimes feel as if, in some other dimension, a carbon copy of me lived that life. This other version of me out there, the one I always envisioned." In *this* life, however, Russia's annexation of Crimea had spawned a virulent anti-Semitism, and a fascist political party soon rose to power in Ukraine. It enacted laws stripping Jews of their rights: to hold public office; to practice certain professions; to possess "disproportionate" wealth. There was an exodus to the U.S. and Israel. His family stayed. "My dad is Vladimir Nettishovo Dragunov—'Nettie'—which doesn't mean anything here. But back home he was a really well-known politician. A lot of people thought he was going to be president one day. Then it all changed."

"Do you think he would have been a good president?"

Al didn't answer. He thought of how, when things got bad, his father had shed his veneer of compassion that, until then, he'd always presented not only to the public, but also to his own family. Beneath was something raw and ugly. *Undischarged, disrupted ambition.* It was a scary thing. A bitter man filled with painful, rotting apathy that he turned outward to those around him. And, by then, it was just the four of them. Gone was the fawning public who stopped him in the street for a selfie and an autograph.

Those last few months were bad: they spent twenty-three hours a day holed up in their townhouse, trying to wait it out as if the ideology was a virus that would run its course. But the yellow paint on their front door; the roving, deputized mobs of fifteen-years-olds—those didn't change. *Just give it some time and it would all go back to normal, Mom insisted.* And it was his mother who'd taken the brunt of Nettie during those months.

Anna with her fine blonde hair, slender frame, and probing blue eyes, Al's spitting image.

Then *it* happened. But what *it* was, Al didn't know anymore.

They walked silently for another minute with Aiden still far ahead, his light scanning the Martian terrain and acting as their lodestar. Aiden suddenly stopped and trained the beam on the ground directly at his feet.

Lilly eventually asked, "What happened to your family? Are they here?"

"Want to hear something weird?" Al tittered uncomfortably.

"Okay."

"I don't remember anymore. It's just this wooly canvas in my mind. There's something on the canvas, but it's hazy and out of reach. Does that make sense?"

"That's what trauma does."

Al sighed. "You don't understand. I *did* remember. And then a few days ago, it just," Al snapped his fingers, "disappeared. This is my *life*, Lilly." He thought for a moment. "You know how the glass on a shower door can be frosted? Not opaque because you can still see a rough outline of a body on the other side. But you just see an indistinct body. It could be anyone. Your best friend or the Queen of England."

By now, Aiden had crouched down and illuminated a patch of blood red sediment in front of him. He stood up, turned around, and shined the beam into their faces.

"Quit it," Lilly snapped as she shielded her face. "Did you find the ring?"

Aiden shook his head. "No. But you're gonna want to see this."

△ △ △

Aiden traced the light over a landscape littered with bones— a graveyard of four-legged animals. Some skeletons intact and resting on the lakebed floor, mostly white and ostensibly not too old. Others consisting of a few handfuls of yellowed, lichen-covered nuggets lodged in hardened sediment like dinosaur fossils.

Lilly examined a skull. "Long face," she said pointing, "that's a snout, right? And fangs, canines." She crouched and tapped lightly on the top of the skull. "Wolves?"

Al scrutinized an older specimen. In a depression on the skull, he noticed a rusted circular object that resembled a silver dollar. He picked it up, used his thumb and index finger to scrape off the crust from both sides, and shined the light on it. It took a second, but when he realized what he was holding, Al chortled.

"Nope, not wolves," he said, "take a look." He handed the object to Aiden.

Aiden read aloud: "'Hello, I'm Kareem Abdul Ja-Bark. (509) 635-2210.'" He turned it around. "'If you can read this, I will lick you.' This was someone's *dog*?" He handed the tag back to Al.

Lilly surveyed the skeletons and uttered, "Ugh, sick."

Al flashed his light across the lakebed and mouthed some words to himself. "I'm counting fourteen."

"Someone obviously dumped 'em," Aiden said.

"Not at once," Al noted, "different states of decomposition and oxidation. Some have been here a lot longer." Aiden watched Lilly's face as Al spoke. She was nodding. And biting her lip. "Whoever it was, they must have taken a boat out here," he said.

Lilly reached for Al's hand to take the dog tag. As he opened his fist and dropped it into her hand, she slid her fingers along the creases of his palm. Aiden watched. He smirked and, almost imperceptibly, shook his head.

"Water," Aiden barked abruptly.

Al took off his backpack, removed two bottles, and handed one to Aiden. He tried to give the other to Lilly, but she waved it away.

"You have some first, Al," she said.

Al shook his head and placed the bottle firmly in her hands, while Aiden, who had taken a quick slug from his own, twisted the cap back onto it.

With Lilly mid-gulp, Aiden flung the bottle at Al's head. Despite the darkness, Al swiped at the air in front of him and caught it only a few inches from his face.

Al said nothing.

A shot across the bow.

△ △ △

Dom sat underneath the shelter of a small ledge with his back against a concave rock. He'd walked for an hour, using the flashlight on his phone to guide his path. Stench notwithstanding, the lakebed had offered some small pleasures. For one thing, an opportunity to use his machete to spear fish. Some were already dead, although some were alive in small puddles. A big one, with peculiar, milky eyes, was just barely breathing. He'd inserted his blade deep into one of those eyes, piercing its brain. The fish had kind of farted in response. It made Dom laugh.

After growing bored of walking, he'd sat down and began sifting through the loose sand and soil between his legs, uncovering mollusk shells and crab remnants. He'd examined the sleek black SIG handgun recovered from TJ's dresser, counting the number of shells in the clip. He'd eventually remembered the other booty from the dresser, rooting around in his pocket for it. He'd shined the light on it while slowly rotating it with blood-stained digits. Admiring every diamond, every bit of gold wording. "NBA Champion." So cool, he'd thought. *My ring now.* It was sad TJ was gone . . . or at least *how* he went. He shook his head.

Pathetic way for such a great one to go, huh Dad? Dom remembered the last thing TJ had said after just about every pint of blood in his body was pooled on the floor like a tiny red lake:

"Let's just talk." *About what? About the fact that you've got no hands and feet?*

He meditated on how everything had unfolded. It'd not been according to plan. He hadn't expected to be brought into the house willingly, which had thrown him off his game. *Dad would still be proud, though. Man, Mr. Freeman was such a great defender. A fucking legend. And now he's gone. He was an honorary demigod. Actual demigods come first, though.*

And that cunt's face. Like I'm not good enough. Like I'm some kind of brainless idiot. They always think they're smarter than me. But a demigod isn't stupid. If her man was a real *demigod, he would have known. He would have dodged that first swing. And then we would have had to fight. To wrestle.*

Dom put the ring onto his wedding finger, pocketed the phone, and started to unzip his fly.

Yet he stopped. Hearing echoes carrying voices through the lakebed, Dom twisted onto his knees and peered above the lip of the small ledge.

Fifty feet away were three people scanning the lakebed with powerful flashlights. Squinting, Dom could make out the figures of two men and a woman. One of the men was tall and gaunt, almost like a grasshopper. He heard the tall one say, "Look at the different states of decomposition and oxidation. Some have been here a lot longer."

I know that voice: Drago! He could barely contain his excitement. *The life of a fucking demigod!*

He watched in fascination for another few minutes as they drank from water bottles and then continued to walk, heading down a steepening decline.

Suddenly, the ground trembled and Dom heard the sound of moving earth. *A landslide!* The group's lights blinked out followed by panicked, fading shrieks.

Dom zipped up his fly.

CHAPTER 13. FRIDAY, JULY 2, 2021.

A   l was locked in a closet and banging on the door to get
     out.
         Where am I? How did I get here?

He struggled to remember something, anything. But he
could summon only one memory: a dinner years earlier with
Mom, Kaz, and Uncle Dmitri. They had just been in the audience
of the *Verkhovna Rada*, the Ukrainian Parliament, where his
father had delivered a speech about infrastructure. It had
seemed rousing to the adults in the chamber, yet the words and
ideas had confused young Alyosha. *Where was Dad? Ah, yes, he
was going to meet us at the restaurant.* Mom and Kaz were
laughing about something. *What was it?* A mime. Walking by
the restaurant window, Kaz was chirping with delight as the
mime feigned bewilderment, finding himself trapped in an
invisible box. Mom, for her part, was in a state of contentment

as she watched Kaz, occasionally guffawing at her daughter's reactions. It was such a simple pleasure.

And then a waiter pushed a food cart to the table, which carried a large white plate covered with an inverted metal saucer. *I don't remember this.* The waiter grasped the handle of the saucer, bowed, and then ceremoniously withdrew it.

Underneath: a dog's skull. Words scribbled across the forehead in black magic marker: "If you can read this, I will lick you." Kaz shrieked.

And Al awoke in darkness. He was on his back in a slimy puddle of water and algae. He sat up and instantly felt severely hung over. A grinding pain radiating from his forehead.

The moist, packed sediment under their feet had given way to a landslide of mud, sand, and small rocks. He was at the foot of a newly formed slope that stretched upward one-hundred-feet at an intimidating, seventy-degree angle. Al touched the throbbing area above his eyebrow and traced a large bump with his fingers. He remembered only the first one or two seconds of their tumble downward as they rode the crest of the landslide. He must have hit his head along the way. He looked up the hill again and noticed a maroon sliver through the lakebed's newly formed opening. It was the morning sky. Birds were already circling—tiny black silhouettes framed against a bloody canvas.

Realizing that the flashlight he'd been holding was gone, Al undid his soaking wet backpack and found the spare. He used the light to explore his new surroundings: a dark, cavernous chamber shaped like a cauldron. Tracing the curves of the nearest wall until it connected to the ceiling, Al estimated it was hundreds of feet from the ground. And directing the beam diagonally across the chamber was not unlike pointing a flashlight into the night sky; the light seemed to go on forever. Al thought of the Polyphemus, the cyclops. *This could have been his dwelling.*

Al began combing his surroundings for Lilly and Aiden. The landslide had formed a small ridge of mud and sand off to his left, which he stepped over as he scanned the craterous floor with his light. About twenty feet away, Aiden was lying awkwardly on his side with his back to Al, stuck in heavy sludge. The sludge had swallowed one of his legs and, as he flailed, his other leg and waist were increasingly submerging as well.

Lilly was in even worse shape. She was a few feet beyond her husband with her face lodged in the sludge, nothing visible but her mess of curls (dirt-infused and now far more auburn than strawberry). Her feet, too, were trapped in the quicksand-like sludge, but her legs, midsection, chest, and arms were free. She had managed to press both hands against a large flat rock near her head and was furiously pushing against the rock as she fought to dislodge her face. She would suffocate without help.

Aiden grasped for his wife's body, desperately seeking his own solid object from which to gather leverage. He grabbed the side of Lilly's neck with his right hand and pulled himself toward her. He then placed his left palm onto her dirty curls and pushed down on the back of her skull, straining intensely and gradually freeing his leg. His leg-extraction was inversely proportional to Lilly's face-submersion.

With his leg clear, Aiden flipped stomach-first onto Lilly's midsection and butt, where he stayed perched for a moment like a shipwrecked sailor clinging to a piece of driftwood. He then stepped on her butt—one foot in a shoe, the other just a sock— and propelled himself to a nearby rock. There, he collapsed on his back and panted, trying to catch his breath.

Al hurried past Aiden and got onto his knees at the end of the rock. He took Lilly's hand by the wrist and started pulling, yet couldn't overcome the suction. She was no longer flailing but only flopping limply.

"Aiden, help me *now!*" Al screamed.

Aiden sprung to his feet, crouched next to Al, and grabbed his wife's other hand. Aiden said, "On three. One, two, three, *pull!*"

Both men howled like baboons. Lilly's neck and collar were freed, then her face, and finally her feet; her gasping echoed throughout the chamber. They dragged her onto the rock and laid her down. With her entire head dark brown, Lilly was like some kind of bipedal swamp monster for which cryptozoologists had long searched. Small breaks in the mud sustained her open eyes and mouth. She sucked in air desperately.

For the next five minutes, they sat without speaking and listened to their breaths. Lilly removed a soaked towel from Al's backpack and tried in vain to clean off her face.

She eventually stood up over Aiden and stared down at him. She spoke quietly.

"You pushed me down."

Aiden scoffed, "I rescued you! I couldn't have done that if I didn't get to this rock first."

She whispered a melancholy "okay," took a deep breath, and exhaled. "Okay," she repeated, "I see. I see what this is." She looked directly at Al through her brown mask even as she addressed her husband in a lifeless, robotic voice. "What matters, Aiden, is that we're all safe now. You're safe."

Lilly's eyes rolled up as if she was lost in thought. After a few seconds, her focus seemed to snap back into place; she peered up toward the brightening sliver of sky, and then into the utter blackness of the cavern.

"We literally stumbled into this place," she said. "Think about how far we are beneath the lakebed. And look," she pointed toward the neon violet pocket of dawn past the crest of the landslide, "it shouldn't be too hard to hike out. Once we've looked around."

"No fucking way," Aiden declared. "You almost died. And that's not why we're here, Lilly. We haven't found what we're looking for."

"I agree with your husband," Al said as he sniffed the air. "And the smell. It's worse down here than up there. It's like pure rot."

She looked at Al. "Grow a pair," she said playfully.

"Excuse me?"

"You heard me. Don't they have testicles in the Ukraine?" She grinned through her mask of mud.

Al grinned back. "Sure we do. We call them *yaytsya*." He massaged the lump on his temple.

Lilly got on her knees within inches of Al and examined his forehead in the half-light. "What'd you hit?"

Al shook his head. "Knocked me out whatever it was. The last thing I remembered was the ground giving out. And then waking up in a puddle."

"Here, let me feel." Al knew she was playing with fire, but before he could push her away, Lilly had placed her lips on his forehead. Even though she was smearing wet earth all over his head, the touch of her lips sent pulses throughout his body. "More lost memories, huh?" She took his hands. "Thank you. For being a man."

Veins rippled across Aiden's forehead and neck.

Al said, "Lilly, we have to—"

It happened in the blink of an eye.

Aiden wrapped both hands around Lilly's neck, whipped her backward like a rag doll, and flung her at the ground with what appeared to be every last ounce of strength in his upper body. When her back hit rock, Al heard the whoosh of the wind being knocked out of her. She gasped for air and caught her breath. After a few seconds she began to weep quietly. All the while, Aiden stood over her, straddling Lilly with one foot on each side of her chest and staring down at her crumpled body.

Instinctively, Al had stepped forward and lifted an arm, but then stopped himself. What he'd just witnessed was clearly not the first time Aiden had done this and would not be the last. And he thought of Aiden turning on him like a rabid dog. Next, his mind defaulted to excuses and rationalizations. *Is this even my fight? She baits him. I can't fix this broken, toxic thing they have. It's not my place.* He shrunk backward. Aiden continued towering over Lilly as she whimpered softly.

"Just leave her alone, Aiden, please," Al finally said.

Aiden's back was to Al. "Stay out of this. It doesn't concern you." The whimpering had tapered off to an occasional sniffle.

"It's okay, Al," Lilly called out.

Aiden stepped forward, turned on the lone remaining flashlight, and walked farther into the cavern. Al scurried to

Lilly and crouched next to her; she stared vacantly at the sliver of brightening sky.

"You okay?"

She whispered, "I had it coming, I did."

"No one deserves that."

"I can hear you both," Aiden said from ten feet away. "Now shut up and look." He was directing the beam at a low angle deep into the void. "There's something out there."

△ △ △

It was three-hundred feet into the cavern, large and inanimate—some kind of structure or vessel. Too far away for them to discern exactly what. They all squinted at the prick of light from Aiden's flashlight.

"Whatever it is, it's big," he said. "I see bars. Like a handrail or something. And I think I see lettering."

Lilly looked up at Al. "Still want to leave?" Al flashed a grin and shook his head.

He helped Lilly to her feet and they stepped from the base of the landslide onto the chamber floor where Aiden was standing. All three walked cautiously toward the object. Aiden continued to trace its contours with the light.

Lilly stopped and laughed. "How on God's green earth did a *boat* get down here?"

"That's no boat," Al countered, "that's a *ship*."

He was right. It was a mid-twentieth century tanker, four-hundred feet long and standing perfectly upright. The rusted and scarred hull, littered with hundreds of bowling ball-sized holes like construction paper cutouts, was nestled in a supporting layer of hardened sediment that resembled a frozen sea of mud. A crisscrossing maze of rotted wooden beams, which looked like toothpicks from far away, had toppled over and covered much of the deck. A true ghost ship.

Lilly and Al stood fifty feet back as Aiden began to circle the ship.

"Must be a chimney or some kind of smoke stack over there," Aiden said as he illuminated a water tower-like cylinder jutting up from the deck near the stern. He disappeared behind the ship's far side and then emerged by the bow after two minutes. Shining the light on the ship's lettering, he slowly read aloud. "SS, Ma-. M, A, looks like three letters covered up with rust, and then an N and an E."

Al said, "SS Marine something, most likely."

Aiden continued, "SS Marine, and then S, U, something, something, H, U, R. What could that be? Suh, suh-. Uh. Wait! Sulphur, right? Does that make sense? SS Marine Sulphur Q. And then looks like a U, something, something, and then an N. And that seems to be the end of it. SS Marine Sulphur. Queen? *SS Marine Sulphur Queen*? Could that be the name of this thing? Does that mean anything to you two?"

"Alas, my sweet internet," Lilly lamented sarcastically.

Al noted that it looked like an oil tanker. Same long body and wide rounded deck at the front. Aiden grunted in agreement.

"Aiden, shine the light over there," Lilly called out, "behind the railing." He pointed the light beam on Lilly and then followed the direction of her finger to an area near the middle of the ship. "Are those statues?" she asked, "some kind of, like, statue garden or something? Does that make sense?"

Six human-shaped figures were huddled near a bench ten feet inside the ship's outer railing. A seventh was next to a ladder several feet away from the rest. Al struggled to process what he was seeing. They had dark brown patches like pieces of burnt toast, but a texture that was almost waxy. As if human-shaped figurines had been dipped in a vat of liquid chocolate. Al scratched his head. Even more perplexing, he thought, was the relationship between the figures and parts of the vessel. The one near the ladder, for instance, was almost *inside* the ladder: multiple rungs passed directly through the figure's midsection and chest. Similarly, two were seated on the metal bench, but the backrest ran directly through their arms and chests.

Another figure consisted of only a neck and head emerging from the deck, like a plant that had just barely breached the soil.

"This is like Pompeii," Lilly whispered in a distressed tone. "But stranger. If those are real," she gulped uncomfortably, "then they're *fused* to the ship."

Aiden, who had rejoined them, wrapped an arm around his wife. "You happy *now*?"

She shed his arm and walked away. Suddenly, Lilly shrieked. Her voice echoed resoundingly.

"Light, light, light! I stepped on something!"

Aiden swiveled the Maglite toward Lilly's feet and illuminated a cat-sized blue spider crab frantically shuffling away. Lilly sighed in relief. Al, conversely, lit up like a Christmas tree.

"When you yelled did you see what just happened?"

Lilly and Aiden each shook their head.

Al directed Aiden to turn off the light. The cavern went black except for the tiny yellow strip at the foot of the landslide that, from this distance, was like a discarded glow stick.

"Look at me," Al said. He lifted up his chin and shouted "echo."

A fist-sized, salmon pink orb—faint and nearly translucent—materialized from Al's mouth. Like a pinball flicked at half-strength, it glided straight up through the air until it struck a stalactite and exploded into a concentric field of blood red dots. The dots sprayed outward, some ricocheting off one another and others becoming trapped in the ceiling's upside-down garden of solidified mineral deposits. As if Al's lungs had birthed and then expelled a peony fireworks shell.

Lilly's one word captured their collective astonishment: "How."

"It's like some kind of visible sonar," Al whispered.

"I bet it has something to do with the air down here," Aiden said. "You feel it? It's charged or something. The dry parts of my body feel staticky."

"The hairs on my arm are standing on end," Lilly responded, "I don't know if that's the energy down here or whatever."

Aiden looked up and screamed, "Hello!" A pink orb shot up from his mouth like a projectile before colliding with the ceiling and dispersing into a field of maroon particles.

"Hamburger!" Lilly yelled while looking forward. She spit out an orb that zipped across the cavern horizontally. They eagerly watched and waited for the orb to hit a wall and burst into a concentric field of dots—the payoff. Instead, after shrinking to the size of a marble as it gained distance, the orb suddenly vanished.

"Must be some kind of crease in the wall," Al said. "Should we check it out?"

Aiden clicked on his flashlight. "What the hell. Let's roll."

$$\triangle \; \triangle \; \triangle$$

Aiden led them a few hundred feet past the vessel in the direction of Lilly's "hamburger orb," as Al called it. There was indeed a gap in the far wall. The rock on each side of the opening curved smoothly outward like the arc of a giant bow, massive columns that could have adorned the entrance to a Nabatene crypt two millennia earlier. The opening led into a claustrophobic corridor.

Lilly peered at the columns.

"We may just find the Holy Grail," she whispered.

Aiden flicked off the flashlight, looked up, and shouted "hotdog." An orb shot upward and traveled vertically for several seconds before it crashed into the ceiling and burst into a ring of unfurling particles. He turned the light back on and stepped forward into the ravine.

Inside, only twenty feet separated the walls, which grew progressively narrower as they continued slowly advancing. After a minute of walking, Aiden reached to his sides and touched each wall with his fingertips. The passage then quickly shrunk until it was just barely wider than his shoulders. It ended in a ladder pressed against a flat rock wall glittering with mica flakes. The ladder ascended thirty feet; it led to an arched and neatly carved door-like opening in the rock, resembling the entrance to a barn loft.

By now, they were in a single-file line: Aiden, Al, and Lilly.

"Does it feel sturdy?" Lilly asked.

Aiden squeezed one of the side rails. He then rapped his knuckle on a few of the rungs.

"It's not steel or anything. It's lighter. Like aluminum. Seems to be in okay shape. Can't say how long it's been here." He stepped on the bottom rung and pushed down. "Feels strong."

"Something's not right about this," Al said, "the whole thing."

"Too late," Lilly parried before ordering her husband to get moving already.

Aiden secured the Maglite in his front pocket so that it was shining directly up the ladder and then began to climb. Three minutes later he reached the top and vanished from sight.

Al and Lilly waited anxiously in the darkness. Al felt her breath on his neck. Short and excited.

Then they heard him.

"There's some, uh, interesting stuff up here. Come up."

Lilly called out, "We need light, Aiden."

He peered over the edge. "I'm dropping it, get ready."

Aiden dangled the lit flashlight in the air and then released it. Al caught it and, like a relay baton, handed it off to Lilly. He told her to train the beam on the ladder as he went up and then to follow him. He ascended and disappeared.

△ △ △

Al emerged in a gently lit tunnel with an arched ceiling that was only a hair's length taller than his head. It stretched straight ahead for two dozen feet before curving sharply right.

Five square picture frames, evenly spaced from one another, adorned the left wall. Under each frame an apple-sized vessel, semi-translucent, protruded from the wall. They were the shape of lion's paw shells and their innards flickered like candles, emitting a soft blue glow that was the lone source of light. Aiden was nowhere to be seen.

Hunching forward, Al approached the first frame. He discovered that the candle was no candle at all—in fact, it was not a light source with which Al was familiar. Inside the soap dish-like vessel was an acorn-sized indigo pearl. It randomly pulsated and flashed. He couldn't discern any obvious power source.

The picture frame above the pearl was just that: an austere wooden frame with a glass cover. It bore a photograph: a glossy, high-resolution aerial photograph of what, to Al, looked like an unremarkable patch of water, perhaps the ocean from an airplane. A two-inch plaque at the bottom bore a laser-engraved number: 353,219. He considered the image and number. They meant nothing to him.

He stepped forward and examined the next frame. Another aerial photograph, but this one depicting a sheet of ice. The plaque carried a different engraved number, 4,542,843,451, followed by "ou" and "-87,252."

The third frame was yet another aerial photograph, although Al immediately recognized the image. It was Lake Hynek . . . with water. The photo must have been taken some time ago, Al thought, as there were no homes, no Field Club, no golf course. Just water and dense forest with the distinctive ridge running parallel to the northern shore. "4,542,919,551 ou -11,152."

The fourth frame: a reddish crater surrounded by forest and a small handful of houses. Hynek post-quake. "4,542,932,769 ou +2066."

The fifth and final frame: a patch of unremarkable water once again. "4,542,934,269 ou +3566."

Al called out for Aiden. No response. He squatted so that he could stretch his neck. The tunnel clearly was not built for someone his size.

He rounded the bend.

△ △ △

A few feet past the curve, embedded in the right side of the rocky wall, Al encountered a simple brown door with a brass knob. Just barely visible from the blue light of the pearls, baroque white script emblazoned the door's surface: *salle d'observation*. He looked at the door on his right, then down the tunnel that tapered off into absolute darkness. He looked back at the door and took a deep breath. He turned the knob and pushed.

The door opened into an antechamber not much larger than a telephone booth, containing a brushed metal wall with a small black box. Al lifted up a hinged cover on the box: it revealed a backlit panel with three colored, illuminated buttons that formed a triangle. The top button was green, the two others red and black. Something was feeding power to the lightly glowing panel. He tapped the green button.

The brushed metal wall, which was actually a door, made a whoosh sound as it retracted and disappeared into a narrow crease. Beyond was a considerably larger room, grey and dimly lit from above by a concealed light source.

On the far side of the room, his back to Al, Aiden was running his fingers along the seamless white wall. At the sound of the door, he spun around excitedly. The two men traded mystified glances.

In the center of the room was a rectangular examining table—gun metal grey. The wall on the left side of the room was flat and glasslike, not unlike a large window. Or display monitor.

Al spoke first.

"What *is* this place?"

Aiden shook his head. "The door says 'observation room.' In French."

"To observe what? Who could have built this?"

Al walked to the table and placed an index finger on the surface: cool to the touch. He circled the table and then crouched down, tracing his finger along a cylindrical bar fused to the floor that held the structure in place. His digit encountered indentations on the otherwise smooth surface of the bar. He squatted and looked underneath the table, examining the bar. He counted six tally marks. *Someone counting days.*

Running his hand along the table's undercarriage, he felt a compact piece of paper wedged into a curled lip; it was like a miniature paper football. He pried it out. Al's hand held a yellowed, anhydrous piece of paper that had been folded over numerous times. As he opened it up, the page split in half.

The door whooshed open. Startled, Al looked up and saw Aiden going back into the antechamber and beginning to examine the control panel. The door whooshed closed behind him.

Al held the two halves of paper together. It contained a handwritten note in minute block print:

March 12, 1973

My name is Dr. Osmond Oleksander Romanek. I live in Hynek in Washington. Shendo Estates. My wife is Theresa Romanek. I have one daughter, Rose.

I am a doctor of science—a plasma physicist. I am Chief Engineer at Vision Labs. I research and experiment in the areas of electrostatic motion, dynamic counterbary, and barycentric control.

My research has brought me terrible harassment. Men called my home and threatened me. They threatened my wife and daughter. Black sedans followed us. These men approached me in restaurants, the supermarket, the drugstore. They told me to stop what I was doing or that I would "pay." That my family would "pay." That if I didn't leave "it" be, I would turn up "in the ground." I have no doubt that these are agents of the United States government who view my research, if fully realized and disclosed to the public, as too significant a risk to the world order.

I was abducted four days ago, March 8th. At the time, I was returning by car from Olympia. It was the early morning when some kind of aircraft shined a spotlight into my car and blinded me. My engine died and I lost consciousness.

I woke up where I have left this note, assuming it is one day read, somehow. It is, remarkably, a space vessel of some sort, in orbit. I have a view of the earth—I never thought I would see such a thing in my life. As I write these words, I look down on what I believe to be the Cape of Good Hope.

This craft must be part of the black budget. A man has spoken to me over an intercom. He has asked me questions about my research. He does not respond to my pleas to go home, or for food or water. He repeats a number. I don't know what the number means. I don't know what any of this means.

I do not think I am going home. I have already seen too much, know too much, although I know nothing. I am scared and weak. If this note someday reaches earth, please convey to my wife and daughter that I loved them. I loved them so dearly. I wish I could have seen them one last time. Rose, good luck in life and in all your endeavors, my sweet baby.

Let God have mercy on my soul.

Scrawled under the text were numbers: 2325193362897114.

△ △ △

Al delicately folded the note in thirds and placed it in his pocket. He stared straight ahead and wrestled with the implications. The tanker, the orbs, the photographs. And now this room, and the note. *It makes no sense.*

And then it happened: the wall in front of him lit up with a surreal image.

Earth from space. Al shrieked.

The doorway whooshed open.

"Did that do any—" Aiden halted midsentence when he saw the image. "Holy shit! I was playing around with the control panel!" He stepped into the room and placed both palms against the giant monitor. "The black button creates a fancy holographic list of words. One of them is 'ORBIT.'" He laughed in delight. "Looks just like the real thing, right? What the hell went *on* down here?"

Al approached the screen. It was as if he was looking down on Brazil—cotton ball clouds obscuring sweeping portions of the rich green interior. The Amazon River snaking its way west, the countless channels appearing like hair-thin striations from so high up, the blood vessels of a continental retina. The resolution was flawless: indistinguishable from the real thing. *Pure beauty.*

Just then, it hit Al like a truck.

"Lilly," he uttered.

Aiden's eyes widened. "Shit."

$$\triangle \, \triangle \, \triangle$$

Dom had waited until Al reached the top of the ladder. As Lilly had tucked the Maglite into the waistband of her mud-caked jeans, Dom bum-rushed her from the shadows, wrapped his arms around her shoulders, and slammed her head into the canyon wall. She didn't even have time to shout for help.

He was covered in TJ Freeman's dried blood, and his wide nose was a hive of blackheads. With two more fever blisters— raw, bubbling skin sprouting from his lips—Dom was Grendel personified.

He took the flashlight from her waist, hoisted her petite body over his shoulder like a sack of grain, and headed toward the ghost ship.

Dom had seen Aiden Campbell—the same man whose life he had saved—ascend the ladder first. Then Drago. *My little bitch.*

He wanted to have a talk with Drago, but he'd been the second to go up the ladder. Leaving that filthy woman, instead, ripe for the picking. *Take what I can get.*

He hauled Lilly to a bed-sized rocky surface near the ship and slowly laid her down, cupping the back of her head. He turned off her flashlight and placed it on the ground along with his gun and knife, and then lightly smacked her cheek with an open hand. Nothing. Next, he delivered a swift jab to her solar plexus. Although her eyes remained closed, she let out a guttural belch and spit up watery liquid onto her chin. She turned over, threw up for several seconds, and then gasped for air.

Dom flipped her back around effortlessly.

"Hello, anyone in there? Anyone home?" He rapped on her forehead with his knuckles, his fist half the size of her head.

Lilly opened her eyes to darkness; they were bloodshot and wet with tears. She wiped vomit from her mouth and gagged again. Reaching into the air, she touched Dom's face. Her fingers traced the flattened nose, sweaty bald scalp, and thick neck.

"Who are you?" Her voice trembled. Chewed up carrots and snot slid down her cheek.

Dom wrapped one hand around Lilly's neck and started to squeeze. He ordered Lilly to "just fucking obey" or else he would "end her." Then he slowly loosened his grip. As he did, she hollered like a cornered wolf.

"*GET OFF ME!*"

As if breathing fire, her mouth birthed a grapefruit-sized neon pink orb.

Dom recoiled in shock. He tried to stand, but his foot slipped on the rock and he fell backward. He landed on his tailbone, smacking the back of his head on the ground. He watched the orb shoot straight up like a fireball, strike the cavern ceiling, and burst into a mesmerizing wave of expanding dots.

And in the pink afterglow, he saw something. It glided past.

It was snakelike with an undulating torso, scales, and bulbous head. The head was more round than oval. Whatever it was, it traversed the air like an eel through water.

"Witch," Dom whispered in terror.

He groped frantically at the ground until he found his gun. Then he sprinted into darkness.

△ △ △

Seconds after Al thought of Lilly, they heard her shriek. The men scrambled along the bluely lit tunnel, down the ladder, and through the darkness, using the ravine wall to guide themselves.

As they neared the ship Aiden instructed Lilly to keep yelling so that they could track her. She screamed "here," then added some "Marcos" and "Polos," and finally a few "hotdogs" and "hamburgers" for good measure. The orbs led them directly to her.

Lilly was oddly calm as she recounted her abduction at the hands of a hulking, faceless captor—a dastardly pirate of some kind.

"I could use a couple aspirins," she noted.

They began their hike out of the cauldron, soon emerging at the top of the landslide in a world of blinding sunshine. An odd menagerie of circling birds watched from above, occasionally descending to feast on rotten fish.

The craggy surface soon led to the pebbly beach and then the boardwalk toward Post Road. By noon, they were regrouping in the Campbell's bungalow.

CHAPTER 14. FRIDAY, JULY 2, 2021.

Aiden had taped the fragile note back together. Lilly turned it around and read it for a fourth time.

"Could he still be alive?"

Al nodded. "Let's say he was thirty-five in 1973. In that case, he'd be eighty-three today."

Aiden, for his part, was more concerned with whom to call.

"The police? The media? The FBI?"

Lilly wondered aloud whether the FBI really had an X-Files unit.

"I'm not being facetious," she added.

Al smiled. "I have a friend who might know about Osmond Romanek and Shendo Estates; his family's been in Hynek for generations. And he may have some theories about what we saw in the lakebed. He's kind of like a younger version of Agent Mulder. If Mulder didn't have a job. And had never worked for the FBI. And was a lot lazier."

Lilly looked at him. "Well, get him over here."

Al paused. "Let me just warn you: he's a bit, uh, different. Marches to the beat of his own drum."

She picked up the cordless phone from its cradle and handed it to Al.

Twenty minutes later, Ingo Lee was on the plush armchair opposite the bungalow's king-size bed. Lilly was on the corner of the bed with an oversized towel draped over her breasts, which covered her body to just above her knees.

She had called 911 to report her brief abduction and spoken with an operator who sounded utterly overworked and overwhelmed. When she'd explained where the incident had transpired—"a cave beneath the lakebed next to the shipwreck of a giant ghost tanker"—the operator had been either unimpressed or not processing the information. ("Okay, señora, let me just get that down on paper. You said 'shipwreck of a giant ghost tanker,' right?") All the Hynek police units were busy with other emergencies; she asked for Lilly's patience.

Lilly then showered and was dressing a small wound on her temple. Aiden, meanwhile, was in the bathroom with the door shut and humming Paul Simon's *Graceland*. Still in his filthy lakebed garb, with the grime darkening his chalkish skin, Al stared at the ceiling from a beach towel laid across the carpet floor. And Ingo held Osmond Romanek's note in front of his face—albeit peering at Lilly's legs through the scotch tape that held together the tattered paper.

As she applied Neosporin to her head, Lilly admonished Ingo jokingly.

"Got a little Peeping Tom here, huh? Little Peeper McGee? You better cut that out before my husband sees."

His eyes instantly shifted to the words in the note.

"Ingo, you dirt bag," Al said, "quit it."

"I, I, I. . ."

"Yes?" Lilly asked pleasantly.

Ingo couldn't string together any words. He slunk back into the chair, cheeks beet red.

Al lifted up his head and looked at Ingo. "Any hypothesis?"

He put down the note.

"Well, for one thing, I know Sh- Sh- Sh. Sh-endo Estates."

Lilly spun toward him. "Where is it?"

"A few miles east of my house along the s-s-s-shore. It's just one big house. It has this giant sp- sp- spire and a gold roost-, roost-, va-, va-. Ugh." He exhaled slowly. "Roo-ster. Weather-vane."

"And everything else?"

"The ship," Ingo said with a smile, "now *that's* interesting. You ever hear of the Philadelphia Experiment?" He sounded giddy.

Lilly shook her head.

"It was this naval experiment in the forties. The navy used a ma- massive amount of electric power from generators to excite coils wra-, wra-, wrapped around a ship's hull. The idea was to set up a pulsating mag-, magnetic field. Turn the sh- sh- ship into a giant electromagnet. The field would, in theory, make the ship invisible to radar." His cadence quickened. "Here's the rub: it did way more than expected."

He stood up and paced by the window, hands gesticulating excitedly.

"When they did this to a sh- ship in the Philadelphia harbor, it *disappeared*."

"Where'd it go?" Al asked.

"The sh- ship teleported hundreds of miles to North Carolina. Then back to Philadelphia. And it went *back in time*, too."

"This sounds insane," Lilly interjected, "but go on."

"The tanker you saw comes to mind because the Philadelphia Experiment crew got si-, si-, sick after they sh- sh- shut off the field. Some went missing. Others insane. But *some* were, like, fuh- fuh- few- fused to parts of the ship. They'd, like, merged with the bulkheads and bunkbeds. Railings stuck through their bodies and stuff."

"Sounds familiar," Al murmured.

Lilly met Ingo's eyes. "Like when the transporter malfunctions in *Star Trek*, essentially," she said.

Ingo nodded. "Not an inapt comparison."

By now, Aiden was by the open bathroom door in checkered boxers, his physique statuesque.

Lilly looked at him and exhaled. She began speaking in a measured, sterile tone.

"Honey, Ingo knows where to find Shendo Estates—it's just one house. He's going to take us there so we can ask about the note."

Ingo blinked in surprise.

"I don't recall agreeing to any su-, such thing. But I'll interpret your st-, st- statement as a polite request. And my answer is yes, I'll bring you."

Aiden covered one nostril and snorted forcefully into a hand towel with the other, sounding like an agitated bull.

"Not happening," he said nonchalantly, "this little game is over. I'm paying Al and we're getting out of here. I don't care about the ring at this point. We'll take a hit when we file the claim with Lloyd's, but so be it. We need to be home."

"All flights are gr- gr- gr- grounded."

Aiden looked at Ingo. "Who is this ugly motherfucker and why is here?"

"Aiden!" Lilly sprung to her feet, causing her towel to unravel and drop to her stomach. She quickly lifted up the towel.

Ingo, who had been muttering something about a "perfect score," went quiet. His eyes widened like an owl. Aiden stepped in front of Lilly as she refashioned the towel. He then marched to the open closet, tapped a code into the wall safe, and removed a wad of cash. He huffed as he counted out hundred-dollar bills.

"This isn't the fucking *Hardy Boys*. We start driving east. We'll return the rental car in Manhattan and pay the fees."

Lilly mouthed a silent apology to Ingo as Al stood up and leaned against the bungalow door. She gave Al an "I'll handle this" glance. She bit her lip, her expression uneasy yet increasingly resolute.

Aiden walked past her and handed Al a girthy stack of bills.

"You let someone nearly rape my wife; but here you go, as promised. Good luck with everything." He grimaced at Ingo. "*You*, freak. You get out too."

"That wasn't Al's fault and you know that," Lilly said. "And I'm going with them. I'll call you once we've checked it out. It won't take long."

"No you're not."

"Or what Aiden?"

"I'm your husband."

"Or what?"

"Don't do this now. Not in front of . . . them."

She scoffed. "You stepped on my head."

"I pulled you out!"

"You stepped on my head to save *yourself*. I would have died if Al wasn't there. I would have died because of you." Her voice quickened.

"Do you hear yourself? I just paid Alyosha—handsomely— for being there! That was *my* idea to bring someone else along."

Lilly slowed her cadence, her tone calmer yet still assertive.

"You wait here, I won't be long. Stay inside, answer the phone, and I'll check in soon. Then we'll go. I agree: we need to go home. But this comes first."

Aiden's jaw bulged as he clenched his fists. He issued three piggish snorts and looked down. He was near the bathroom door, ten feet from his wife.

Then he charged.

Not this time.

Al sprung forward and cut off his path. Without flinching, Aiden lowered his shoulder like a running back to drive into Al's chest. But before he could execute, Al dove at Aiden's feet. He wrapped both hands around Aiden's left calf and yanked, sending Aiden toppling face down. He landed on Al's back, whose body crumpled under the weight.

"You little fuck," Aiden growled.

He clasped Al around the waist, planted his feet on the floor, and then shimmied so that he was above the back of Al's head. Then he grabbed Al's neck and held him in place while using his other hand to deliver a series of rapid hooks to the side of Al's head, just above his ear. Lilly and Ingo each yelped for Aiden to stop—neither moved. Al's skull sounded like a coconut as it absorbed each hit. After eight blows, he released Al's neck, who collapsed face-down onto the carpet, clutching his head. Aiden stood up, took two steps back, and delivered a corner kick to Al's ribs.

Lilly was crying, face nuzzled in her palms.

"I'm so sorry," she croaked.

Aiden stepped over Al and walked toward her.

Aiden began to speak. "Lilly, get in the—"

"Don't touch her." It was Al.

He was on his knees with both hands clutching the bowie knife like a candle.

"So help me God, Aiden, if you touch her again, I'll cut you down."

Aiden scoffed until he turned and saw the knife.

"I've seen him get cr-, crazy," Ingo added from his frozen stance by the window. "Eastern European nihilism-type stuff."

Aiden faced his wife again and issued a hollow chuckle.

"Just fucking go," he uttered. "Go with these freaks." He looked at Al and then back at his wife. "You should have married a busboy. I'm sure he would have given you everything you wanted." He glanced at Ingo's malformed chin and shook his head. Then he walked back into the bathroom and slammed the door.

CHAPTER 15. FRIDAY, JULY 2, 2021.

W hat happens if this place, like, totally burns down. Do we go back to Cecil?" Sasha stared at her mom from her perch on the bed.

Bardo picked through a large cardboard box, removed two vinyl photo albums, and placed them on the bed. She looked up at Sasha as she pondered the question.

"Well, let's see. I guess if seventy percent or more of the houses burn down and people move somewhere else. Then probably yes."

"So we're talking about a seventy-percent destruction threshold?"

"'Threshold,' huh? Good vocab, Sash."

"What about if *just* the school burns down?"

"Then you, my little lady, are getting a job. Or I should say, my little Starbucks barista."

"Ugh, as if."

Sasha studied her mother's profile as Bardo stretched to root around in the bottom of a dresser drawer. With the skin on her face and neck pulled back, the scar behind Bardo's ear came into view. It began on her scalp and ended half an inch past her hairline.

"Mom."

"Uh-huh?"

"How'd you get that scar again?"

"Got hit by a car crossing the street in Cherry Hill. On duty. I was running an undercover operation."

"Did it hurt?"

She turned to her daughter. "I told you about this, Sash. I don't remember. I got a bad concussion and the doctors had to induce a coma for a day. I was crossing the street and the next thing I remember: boom, I'm waking up in a hospital bed."

"Yeah, I do remember that." Sasha nodded. "Didn't you say that that was when you decided to adopt me?"

"It was," she replied with a grin. "Never thought I wanted a little goon like you. But after the accident—it was right after I woke up, in fact—something changed. It's weird how life works, huh? And then, not even a year later, you were in my life. Worst decision I ever made." She winked. "It is something to think about. If that car didn't hit me, you probably wouldn't be here. And I doubt I'd be in Hynek. Our trajectories would have been totally different. A different decision, a different life."

"I'd probably be carrying a spear. And collecting shrunken heads."

Bardo was rifling through a desk drawer.

"I don't think that's the way it works in Ecuador. You might have been a farmer. I could just see you holding a potato up." She imitated a squeaky girlish voice, "'Is my potato done growing yet?'" They laughed.

"Sash, for real, you're absolutely, positively, one-hundred-percent sure you packed everything you want?"

"Yep."

"You took Winky?" She was referring to Sasha's tattered one-eyed teddy bear.

"Mom, give me a break, I'm fifteen." She paused. "But yes, of course I got him." She flashed a crooked smile.

"And your pot: got that too?"

"Is that a trick question?"

"What do you think, Sash?"

"Maybe I should ask *you*, Mom. Evan's little brother, Noah, said he saw you eating donuts at Budd's. And that you looked, like, totally baked. Finely toasted."

Bardo grinned. "What, a pig can't pig out sometimes? Isn't Evan the one with two moms?"

"Yeah. So?"

"So nothing. Just asking."

Sasha was silent for a few seconds. "That could be me one day," Sasha eventually said, almost mumbling and sounding hesitant. She was making herself do this. Saying something she didn't want to say—something she'd rather ignore. Putting herself on the line for her mother.

Bardo's head jerked back from the drawer. She looked at her daughter.

"Do you feel that way?" She'd never confided in Bardo like this before.

"I've been, like, confused, Mom." She exhaled self-consciously. "I've felt different things, but there's this girl I really like. And I think it's . . . real. I don't think I've ever felt this about a guy."

The walkie-talkie on the desk chirped.

"Chief, Justin here. Over."

Bardo looked at the walkie-talkie. *Bad timing.*

He repeated the transmission. It sounded urgent.

Bardo picked up the handset and stared at the buttons. "Click to Talk" or "Off."

She looked back at her daughter, who was still visibly uneasy about the discussion she'd started. Or tried to start. *Shit.* Bardo exhaled in frustration.

Time to make a choice.

"You know what Sash: hold that thought just for a second." She picked up the radio and, sustaining eye contact with her daughter, pressed "Click to Talk."

"It's Bardo, talk to me."

"We got news on the John Doe. Over."

"And?"

"And it's . . . odd. Kind of a long story. Come to City Center ASAP, we'll show you. Over."

Bardo sighed and glanced at Sasha, who was fidgeting with her cuticles.

"Okay, on my way." She put down the walkie-talkie.

"Sasha, I don't want to shortchange this discussion, wherever it's going. Hold tight and I'll be back in a jiff."

Sasha laughed even as her eyes betrayed disappointment.

"Back in a jiff, Mom? That's the gayest thing I ever heard."

$$\triangle \ \triangle \ \triangle$$

Bardo drove east among middle-class houses not unlike her own. She passed at least six homes with family members busy loading SUVs and minivans with suitcases and stuffed black garbage bags. *This is really happening. It's like a bad dream.*

"Chevy, turn on AM 770," she said to the car's infotainment system. The radio clicked on.

"—control so little of it. He was really disheartened. The wind and the dryness, together, are pushing it consistently north. And if this was any other time—historically, I mean—there'd be more resources, as he made clear. But everything is just in, I mean, disarray really. The diminished manpower, the rescue equipment and trucks all in use. National Guard still working to pull out trapped folks. So it's just a matter of priorities. Property and homes from which able-bodied citizens can evacuate safely—in the end, well, it's just property, not life.

"At any rate, assuming no further acceleration, we're looking at forty-eight hours for Ogdenville, Ferndale, and Walla Walla. Maybe another twelve to fifteen for Hynek and Hamfield.

But, to be clear, this could change, as the Governor underscored. The wind picks up and these estimates could be halved, easily."

Bardo grimaced. "Chevy off."

$$\triangle \ \triangle \ \triangle$$

The makeshift police station on the first floor was bustling. Busy answering calls, Winnie looked like she'd gone days without sleep. Her voice was hoarse and eyes bore deep black bags. As Bardo approached, she heard Winnie finishing a conversation, her English occasionally devolving into Spanglish:

". . . uh huh. Si. I mean, yes. Claro. Well, that's why you need to keep listening to the radio. We're in contact with county and state authorities, pero no estamos controlándolo al nivel local. Not at the local level, no." She paused and listened, looking up at Bardo and choking out a tortured, exasperated smile. "Ma'am, we need to free up this line for emergencies. Okay, yes, good luck to you as well. Bye bye." She hung up the phone.

"Let me guess," Bardo said, "el fuego?"

"Jefecita, it's like non-stop."

"Sounds like you're saying the right thing. I know you're tired, but keep it in English."

Winnie nodded and looked at her notepad.

"Since I saw you last, jefecita, four calls about exotic animals. Nick Arnold saw either a small hyena or a jackal. Janet Su said, wait, let me find the quote. Aqui es: 'There's some kind of primate in the rocking chair on my porch. It has a bright red ass.' We were all thinking baboon, right? I wish we could just Google it. Paul Steinman, the trainer, said he had an impala in his yard. He walked right up to it and pet it."

"So a tame impala?" Bardo found herself giggling as Winnie recited the laundry list of escaped animals.

"This one's not so funny, jefecita. Alastair Cavallo saw some kind of giant yellow snake."

"How about an engorged tiger? Or polar bear?"

Winnie shook her head and said, "We've got a four-hour wait for our boys. There's too many calls. Some are muy seriosas. A woman got assaulted in the lakebed. Almost raped."

"Almost?"

"The guy ran away."

"Ugh. I told them *not* to go down there. Winnie, take one of the boys off looking for the Freeman's Range Rover. Add him to the radio runs."

Winnie nodded and picked up a walkie-talkie as Bardo walked away.

Bardo continued past a small waiting area filled with civilians, including Cliff Bentwater. His eyes were closed and hands were clasped over his paunch. He looked peaceful—albeit mildly absurd in checkered corduroy overalls and an Elmer Fuddish hunting hat.

Seeing Cliff reminded Bardo of something. She approached him.

"Cliff, hey there. You with us?" She snapped her fingers a few inches from his face. He opened his eyes in tiny increments as if emerging from a deep slumber.

"Oh, hi there Chief Bardo," he whispered.

"Don't leave without talking to me."

Cliff nodded and, just as gradually as he'd cracked his eyelids, closed them.

Bardo walked through a backroom in use as a makeshift holding area for Scott Maccabee, who was handcuffed to a heavy metal desk. When Scott saw her, he tried to stand up but got jerked back like a leashed dog.

"Shelly, how long you gonna hold me like this? What's happening? I want a lawyer."

Without stopping Bardo noted to Scott that she was on her way at that very moment to find out something about his situation. "Hold tight scoop," she added.

"How about a drink? I could kill for a Maker's."

"Be a little more judicious with your words," Bardo uttered as she entered an adjacent conference room and shut the door behind her.

By a window overlooking the street, Justin was conversing with Josh Urban. The two men looked up excitedly.

"Boy do we have something interesting for you," Justin said with a smile.

$$\triangle \ \triangle \ \triangle$$

"Let's have it." Bardo was on a stool near the conference room window, gently tickling her own arm. "What's the deal?"

Justin looked at Josh and said, "All you."

Josh clapped his hands together. "So," he began, "after you inauspiciously dismissed me from the interrogation, and after the whole fucking world shook, I went to the Medical Examiner to check out our John Doe. And I'm feeling the fabric on the guy's pants. They're clearly nice pants to begin with, but the fabric—it's like insanely fine quality. Hand-stitched. So I find the label and it's this word in an alphabet I don't recognize. Not a Romance language. I'm thinking, Turkish? Russian? Something Slavic.

"We've got this old Russkie detective over in Hamfield, Boris Petrov. His brother's even a Roman Orthodox priest. So I show him a photo of the label. No dice. Can't read it. Says it's Slavic, though."

Bardo shot Josh an impatient look.

"Boris suggests I call the Russian consulate in Seattle. Good idea, I think. Well, I call them, spend about an hour figuring out how to work a fax machine, and send them a photo of the label. And they say the same thing: not Russian and they don't recognize the brand."

"Josh," Bardo interjected, "this town is *literally* about to burn down. Get to the point."

"Easy there, Chief. The Russian consulate guy says, not our patria. *But*, he tells me, *but*, it possibly looks Ukrainian. Try their consulate. So," he clapped again, "I fax the Ukrainian consulate the photo. I get some woman there on the horn. She says, yes, that's Ukrainian.   The word is "ha-lad-key," or something like that."

"Which means what."

"Smooth.   It's the name of an über expensive boutique in Kiev. Only the rich and powerful go there. Pants from Smooth are like $1,500. And I ask her: is there any reason you know why some gentleman wearing a pair of Smooths would turn up dead in southeast Washington? And I describe our John Doe. The hairy mole on his face—which may as well be a tattoo of a giant dick. And the woman kind of does a verbal double-take when I mention the mole.   She goes, 'There was this Ukrainian politician with something like that.' She remembers growing up and seeing political cartoons lampooning him. The hairy mole was always like, you know, the most memorable thing in the world. Real Rapunzel-like in the cartoons. So I fax a picture of John Doe's face over there."   He paused several seconds for effect.

"And?"

"And . . . *boom*!   It's him!   Problem is: no one at the consulate remembers the guy's name. So what does a shrewd investigator with no internet do, you ask?   Well, off to the Hamfield Public Library.

"Next thing you know I'm scouring microfiche.   To be honest, before then, I didn't even know what the hell microfiche was. But now I'm poring through Herald Tribunes from the past couple of years. And, eventually: *boom* again! Take a look."

He handed a piece of paper to Bardo.

"That's him, alright," she murmured as she scanned the photo. "Went missing, huh? 'Vladimir Nettishovo Dragunov.' Dragunov. *Dragunov*. Why does that sound so familiar, Justin?"

"Does it?"

"Does to me," she said, "anyway, let's see. 'Influential lawmaker.' 'Removed from office.' 'Statute 331A.' 'Jewish.' 'Proto Progressives.' 'Opposition voice.' 'Reported *missing*.' 'Suspected abduction.' 'Politically motivated.' What's the date on this? December 23, 2020. Huh."   Bardo paused, attempting to synthesize the new information with what she already knew.

"Explain to me how he ends up dead here, with fresh wounds, two days ago?"

Josh and Justin shook their heads.

"Wait, wait, wait," she suddenly said, "*now* I remember. Dragunov: that polite kid from the meeting! The one who told us about the escaped animals, right? What was his first name?" She thought aloud. "He gave some complicated name and then he was like, 'People call me blah.' What was it? I remembered thinking something at the time. Something about a song. People call me something. That music video: the one with Chevy Chase."

"*You Can Call Me Al*?" Justin proffered.

"Yes! *Al* Dragunov. We need to find him. Justin, go to the Hamfield Zoo."

"Roger that, Chief."

Bardo addressed Josh as she stood up and headed briskly for the door.

"Officer Urban, sir, you've done some sound investigative work. I owe you."

"Just doing my job."

Bardo stopped at the door and smiled. "Very magnanimous. You've got skill. You're a shit interrogator, though. But this makes up for it." She winked. "Almost."

$$\triangle \ \triangle \ \triangle$$

Bardo bounded out of the conference room and, ignoring the pleading Scott ("lawyer Shelly, lawyer"), reentered the waiting room. She quickly doubled back to Scott.

"What does the name 'Vladimir Dragunov' mean to you, Scott?"

He squinted in confusion. "What are you talking about? I've never heard that name in my life."

"What about the Ukraine?"

"What about it?" he spit back.

"When's the last time you were there?"

"Are you kidding me, Shelly? What in God's name are you talking about? I've never set foot there. I don't even know if I've ever met a Ukrainian person."

"You're telling me you've never met a Ukrainian person in your life?"

"I mean, I fly planes Shelly. Um." He paused in thought. "Last year, in Istanbul, I held a plane at the gate for some passengers who'd arrived late on a flight from Kiev. They were connecting to New York. I was standing by the cockpit and shook a few hands when they came sprinting onto the plane. Some fat guy and his son and daughter, I think. Were they Ukrainian? I don't know. So, technically, have I met a Ukrainian person? Possibly, I suppose."

Bardo said nothing. She turned back around and headed out the door into the waiting room.

As she went, Scott began to shout, "Are you kidding, Shelly? You're going to ask me that stuff and then just wa—"

She slammed the door behind her, scanned the waiting room, and spotted Cliff, who was snoring gently with both chins resting on his chest, fat bottom lip hanging open. She tapped his shoulder.

"Oh, hello there, Bardo. This feels like *déjà vu* all over again, as Yogi Be—"

"Cliff," she interrupted, "you've spent your whole life in Hynek, right? Answer me this: you ever heard of an 'Osmond Romanek?'"

Cliff furrowed his brow in thought. "An Osmond? No."

"Crap."

"I've heard of a Romanek, though. Just not Osmond."

Bardo's eyes lit up. "Where?"

"When my daughter was seven or eight, or around that age, she was friendly with an Ashley Clarke, if I'm remembering that right. Now, let's see." He looked up in thought. "Ashley's mother was Rose. Rose Clarke. Rose and Dan. They had money. Now let me think—and mind'ya, Bardo, this is decades ago— Rose's maiden name was Romanek, I believe. Rose Romanek. I heard someone mention her name a couple years back. That she got cancer."

"Anything else you remember? Where she lived, perhaps?"

"Well, where she lived a long time ago. They invited Barbara and me there for a dinner party. Us and some of the other parents, you know. Real fancy-type house out there southwest of Shendo Ridge. Big gold rooster weathervane. You know the one? It's kind of hidden on the lake's north shore."

She patted his shoulder enthusiastically.

"This is so helpful, Cliff, you don't even understand. You ever find . . . what was her name? Lady?"

He shook his head and looked down at his hands.

"Why you here?" Bardo asked.

"Reporting a sighting."

"Land or sky?"

Cliff looked confused. "Land. Some kind of giant lizard."

"Godzilla?"

Cliff chuckled. "Not Godzilla, no. I'm thinking Komodo dragon. Fascinating, really."

"You have a gun Cliff?"

"Rifle."

"Looks like we'll be evacuating pretty soon. But, in the meantime, my advice is to stay home, keep your doors locked, and keep that rifle close. Things are getting hairy."

Cliff laughed and snorted.

"*Getting* hairy? Bardo, we left hairy behind some time ago."

"Funny thing is, Cliff, you don't know the half of it."

△ △ △

The flying humanoid had sent Dom running like a bat out of hell.

For a good minute he'd sprinted through absolute darkness, which had felt like running in place. That was before the inevitable: he tripped on a spider crab, fell face-first into the rocky ground, and knocked himself out cold. He'd woken with a swollen eye socket and bloody cheeks. His head pounding, Dom lay on his back and breathed through his mouth to avoid the rank smell—mildew with a cutting, ammonia-like finish. He stared at nothing until nothing became a kaleidoscopic array of crisscrossing colors and oscillating strings, the byproducts of floaters and flashes in his eyes.

No flashlight, no machete.

But he had the gun. He used his thumb to manipulate the safety and exhaled in relief.

The bubblegum orbs, which he'd seen Drago and the two others spitting out like fireballs, were strange, for sure. But it was that flying beast—like a snake or an eel, something horrible—that had spooked him to the core.

My eyes must have been playing tricks on me. He stroked the SIG.

Time passed. Hours. His head hurt and body felt limp, weathered. He danced in and out of consciousness.

And his thoughts wandered.

Dom wanted to use the gun on something or someone. He'd killed with a gun only once before. The second or two after he fired the shots—it was the best part. The guy was still moving and screaming and living as if nothing happened. Like Wile E. Coyote running off the cliff and pedaling his feet in the air. Meanwhile, the bullet perforated an organ and blood was already sloshing through the hole, escaping. Three seconds at most, he thought. Headless chicken. Then the guy slowed down. And he got this *look.* This horrible epiphany. Probably wasn't even pain. Just an understanding that he was seconds away. That nothing could turn back time.

Colors swirled and danced in Dom's vision, pulsing glow sticks weaving trails and patterns so real he could almost touch them.

His head still throbbing, Dom tried to sit up. Instant vertigo. He rested his head back into a patch of sludge, which yielded comfortably under the weight of his skull.

He suddenly felt like someone else was with him in the cavern. Someone familiar. Then came the voice.

"Dommy Boy! *My* Dommy Boy!"

Dom turned his head to the left.

It was only five feet away: a luminescent apparition of a broad-shouldered man with a beaming smile. He had paper thin grey hair parted neatly down the center, a large wide nose, and an unnaturally black goatee. Craggy cheeks with strong, deep lines enclosing the smile.

Dad?

"Ah, my big boy, you look great! The same handsome devil!"

Are you really here? How'd you get out of prison?

"What, I can't be in two places at once?" He winked. "I heard you were down here. I wanted to say hello to my big boy."

I just saw TJ Freeman, Dad! The TJ Freeman.

"I know. I saw what you did. I saw it all, Dom."

Are you proud?

He didn't answer.

"What's next for you, Dommy Boy?   That's the *real* question."

What do you mean?

"That young man who was just down here. 'Drago,' you call him."

What about him?

"He has something you don't."

I could crush him, Dad. I'm so much stronger. I'm a demi—

"Dom, listen to me. That young man: he's been where I am right now."

Mr. DeRuglia's speech pattern began to change. What had been a blue-collar New York accent grew softer, and then more feminine. At the same time, the cadence assumed a rigid, almost robotic quality.

I don't understand. Where are you?

"A jumping off point, Dominick. To different paths. Kind of like a crossroads. And that young man, Drago, has created something new."

I don't get it.

"Let me put it this way: you are a wanted man, Dominick. The authorities will find and kill you. It is just a matter of time. What if you could forge a new and different life . . . would you like that?"

Yes.

"You could give yourself anything."

Money?

"You can have that. Endless money. Power. Sex. Pleasure. Be a good boy, Dominick, and take it. Find that young man. And take it."

Okay, I will.

"Do you promise?"

Dom spoke aloud.

"Yes, I promise. Daddy, I love you. Do you hear me? I said I *love* you Daddy."

Dom still saw his father. But any other observer would have seen something different.

A fleshy stack of coiled brown scales supporting a symmetrically round head—like a perfect marble. The face of a horribly mutated woman: beady black eyes spaced too far apart and situated *beneath*, rather than above, a pair of dime-sized, nostril-like cavities. A mouth without lips. Wet brown gums devoid of teeth. Something rhythmically contracting and then expanding inside that mouth. Something alive in there. Medusa come to life.

And a big, bloody, brute of a man—gun in hand—calling it "Daddy."

CHAPTER 16. FRIDAY, JULY 2, 2021.

Ingo stepped back and admired the spire shooting up from the slate roof of Lake Hynek's majestic white colonial resting on the precipice of the northern shore. Only a few days earlier it had overlooked shimmering turquoise water. Now it faced a craggy maroon landscape that descended into a preternatural black hole.

He squinted toward the southern sky beyond the lakebed. Many miles in the distance, cloudless blue abruptly changed to charcoal grey. Smoke from the encroaching fire.

"Ingo, get up here," Al yelled, "we're ringing the bell."

Ingo hustled past a massive cast iron rooster lodged in the grass—a patch of missing slate tiles on the roof marked the point of impact from the weathervane's journey down to the lawn—and up a steep wooden stairway leading to a wraparound porch. Al stood patiently at the door while Lilly peeked through a security window that spilled into a large vestibule. From within the house the sound of muffled footsteps grew louder.

"Someone's coming," Lilly whispered.

After a few locks clanged and unhinged, the giant oak door swung inward. A plain looking man in his late twenties eyed them suspiciously. His focus lingered on the Band-Aid across Lilly's forehead and the considerable bump above Al's eye.

"What do you want?"

Al began to speak, "Hi, we're fr—"

"Do you know Osmond Romanek?" Ingo blurted out.

"Excuse me?" The man's expression was not one of confusion—he seemed to know exactly who they were talking about.

Al shot Ingo a frustrated glance.

"I'm sorry about my friend, he's a bit abrupt. I'm Al Dragunov. That's Ingo Lee. And this is Lilly Campbell."

Lilly fluttered her eyelashes and waved sheepishly.

"We're, uh, how best to explain it. Let's see. Well, number one, we're good people."

"Okay."

"Number two—and this will sound a little crazy—but we found an old letter written by Osmond Romanek. In the letter, he said he lived in Shendo Estates. Which is this house, right?"

The man nodded.

"We're trying to find out if Osmond Romanek actually lives here, or did live here. And who he is. Or was."

"Where'd you find the letter?"

"In the lakebed," Lilly answered. "*Under* the lakebed, actually."

The man's eyes softened as he considered her answer for a few seconds.

"I'm Gavin Clarke. I live here with my mom, Rose. And yes, I certainly know Osmond Romanek."

△ △ △

Gavin invited them into the house and led them to a large living room with a lofty vaulted ceiling of painted white wood. The floor was strewn with the remnants of shattered ceramic bowls and vases, as well as a baroque, wax-encrusted candelabra so large it looked like a lawn ornament. In one corner, a ten-foot-tall freestanding bookcase had crashed onto its side and scattered dusty hardcopies the full width of the room. As Al entered, he noticed a few of the names: Dostoyevsky, Kean, Pirsig, Greene. Gavin rushed to remove a plastic sheet covering an upholstered white sofa. He had them sit down.

His mother, Gavin explained, was born Rose Romanek. Rose's father—his maternal grandfather—was Osmond. Rose and Gavin's own father had divorced almost a decade earlier, at which point Rose moved back into this house, which was her childhood home. The home of Dr. Osmond Romanek.

Lilly asked if Dr. Romanek was still alive.

"In all honesty, we don't know." Gavin asked eagerly, "Can I see the letter?"

Ingo stood up.

"Can we sp-, sp-, sp-. Can we speak to your mom?"

Gavin was momentarily surprised by Ingo's stutter. Then he said, "Wait here." He ran into the vestibule and up a curved staircase.

Lilly looked at Al and Ingo. "This is his grandfather's house, but he doesn't know whether he's alive . . . how does *that* work?" They each shrugged.

Gavin trotted back down the stairs and into the living room.

"My mom said she'll speak to you. You have to come upstairs, though. She's sick."

Ingo's head perked up. "I don't want to get sick."

Gavin shook his head. "It's not like that. Melanoma. It's advanced."

"That's terrible," Lilly whispered.

Gavin led them up the staircase and then along a winding hallway with a high oak ceiling, the walls adorned with black and white photographs of big game hunters posing with their spoils. One looked just like Teddy Roosevelt next to a lioness carcass.

A long yellow carpet covered the floor. It bore a repeating pattern: a copper colored sun with a fatherly face perched over a medieval town. Colorful circles, cylinders, and crosses peppered the sky. Below, on a hillside, two plumes of smoke rose into the air.

Ingo paused and examined the design. His eyes lit up.

"Gavin, is this su-, su-, supposed to depict the 'Battle Over Nuremberg'?" By then, Gavin was ascending a second staircase and didn't answer, with Al and Lilly on Gavin's heels; Ingo scrambled to catch up.

When they reached the next floor, they passed a door that led into a large parlor with a pool table. The parlor fed into yet another diverging hallway in the labyrinth-like house.

Just past the entrance to the parlor, they stopped at an open doorway to an airy bedroom with a large bed in the farthest corner. Oversized casement windows surrounded the bed on two sides—windows that, only days earlier, would have offered a breathtaking view of Lake Hynek.

Instead, the vista was unearthly and jarring. Maroon sediment that descended until reaching the freakish monstrosity of Alpha Drain, at which point the Martian-like landscape dropped precipitously into blackness. It was enormous: a perfectly circular empty socket spanning nearly the full width of the lakebed. Flocks of large birds—like flies against the backdrop of the massive pit—tirelessly circled above.

And, in the bed overlooking Alpha Drain, was Rose.

△ △ △

She looked like an old sad doll in the giant bed.

Rose Clarke had clearly been an attractive woman at one point in her life. But she was obviously very sick. Her face was emaciated: cheeks concave and the outline of her skull pushing up against the skin on her forehead. Gaunt arms and feet, like matchsticks, poking out of green silk pajamas. She was propped upright with pillows behind her back and a thick wool blanket covering much of her lower half. Around her bony neck, a delicate silver chain with a black cross. The nightstand was littered with orange prescription bottles and loose tissues, props of the infirm and dying.

Lilly and Ingo remained several few feet away as Al approached the bed and extended a hand.

"Thank you for seeing us, Ms. Clarke. I'm Alyosha Dragunov. I just go by Al." He paused and waited, but the woman said nothing. Her eyes narrowed. "I live in Hynek. I used to work at the Field Club and the Hamfield Zoo. Until the quake." He pointed to Lilly and Ingo, identifying them by name.

Rose finally reached out and shook Al's hand with her wispy, cold fingers.

"A pleasure, Al. And nice to meet you two, as well." From her throat, she cleared what sounded like a stream of loose phlegm. "You can call me Rose. Formerly Rose *Romanek*, which my son tells me is why you're here. You say you found something my father wrote . . . in the lakebed?"

"Under," Lilly interjected.

"Uh huh. And what were you doing down there?"

"Exploring," Al said.

Rose chuckled. "Good answer. You know, if I wasn't like *this*," she gestured to herself, "I probably would've done the same. Lord knows what's hidden down there."

"It was west of here," Al explained, "closer to the boardwalk."

"And you believe my father wrote this letter?"

Al nodded.

"His name is on it, I suppose?"

He nodded again.

"Ms. Clarke, is he alive?"

"Just Rose, dear." She sighed. "Wouldn't I love to know. Dad's a man of mystery."

"What happened?"

"He's a physicist, Al. Brilliant man. Worked for an engineering company headquartered closer to Seattle. He spent his career trying to develop a new form of propulsion. Have you heard of gravitics? I'm sure none of you has."

All three shook their heads.

"Well, neither has anyone else. Real 'hush-hush'-type stuff, as Dad used to say. The bane of our existence. They targeted him because of his research."

"What do you mean?" Al asked.

"When I was girl, they took him. And brainwashed him. That's what Mom always said."

She suddenly broke into a spastic coughing fit. Despite the earlier phlegmy sound, these coughs were now dry and unproductive, almost like strained honks. She reached for a handful of tissues, placed them up to her mouth, and muffled the sound. After a minute, she resumed speaking.

"I was eight. Dad was supposed to be driving back from a work trip. He never showed up. Gone. A week later, Mom answered the bell. Lo and behold, it was him on the porch, standing there in filthy clothes, dehydrated." She shook her head. "It was his work. His *experiments*. He was too close. They wanted to send a message."

All three guests echoed one another: "They?"

"The government. Military."

Ingo grinned smugly.

"Why do you think he was brainwashed?" Lilly asked.

"Well," Rose exhaled and cleared her throat, "he had some crazy ideas about the abduction. About *where* they brought him. He said they took him to a spaceship. That he woke up in orbit above earth. This was 1973, mind you."

"Hah!" Lilly cackled.

Rose glared at her with puzzled eyes.

Al spoke up. "Rose, about the note: we found it in some kind of observation room under the lakebed."

"What do you mean by 'observation room'?"

"It was sparse. Just a metal table and a big display monitor that looks like a window. There's a control panel outside the room; you can turn on an image of earth from space. It's just as if you're looking out the window of a spaceship in orbit—it was impossible to tell the difference when we saw it this morning. You can imagine how it would have looked to someone locked in that room in 1973."

A beaming smile lit up Rose's face. For a moment she looked young again as she first giggled, then laughed, then guffawed. Yet she soon choked on her own breath and devolved into a violent coughing fit. Even as she fought to catch her breath, Rose's smile never vanished.

"Oh Dad, you old bastard—not so crazy after all!" She thought for a few seconds. "So it was a trick; a *simulation*? Why would they do that? Wait: can I see the note?"

Al handed the yellowed paper to Rose, who put on thick glasses and began to read. Tears welled up in her eyes and streamed down her cheeks.

"Dad, Dad." She breathed deeply. "They locked him down there. What are these numbers?"

"Can I see that, please?" It was Gavin, who had been standing outside the bedroom door. He walked over to the bed, took the letter from his mother, and examined it by the window overlooking Alpha Drain. Then he handed it back to Al. Gavin wore an unaffected, sterile expression.

"My grandfather's been gone for a few months. He had a small lab in a cabin on one of the Bantam Islands. It's called Trigger Island; it's not even half the size of a football field. The cabin's got a generator and some of his equipment."

"Where's Trigger Island in relation to here?" Lilly asked.

Ingo spoke for the first time. "A few miles e-, e-, ea-. Fuck me in the—"

"Excuse me, young man," Rose admonished him, "we don't talk like that in this house."

"Sah sah sorry. The Bantams are a few miles ea-, east."

"My grandfather bought the island years ago. It's got a small dock. He used to take a motorboat out there."

Rose pointed at the note in Al's hand. "The letter mentions Dad's job at Vision Labs. He had a trust, so he didn't need the money.

"And he was never the same after the abduction. He withdrew. Continued his research, but alone at his lab on the island. And he became very, very secretive." She met Al's eyes. "He was a damaged man. We call it PTSD these days. Of course, there was no such thing back then."

"So anyway," Gavin piped in, "my mom moved back here a few years ago. And after she got sick I moved in too. My grandfather was in his early nineties, but still spry. He used to take his little boat to the lab three, four days a week. When I started living here, I'd give him a ride in the morning and then pick him up in the afternoon.

"A few months back, I brought him to the island one morning. Nothing seemed out of the ordinary. But when I returned to pick him up he wasn't on the dock. I remember thinking immediately: this is bad. He must have had a stroke or something. I checked the lab and . . . *nothing*. Not there. No sign of a break-in or anything missing. Just a note." He looked at his mother. "What exactly did it say, Mom?" Gavin didn't wait for an answer. "Something like, 'Dear Rose and Gavin, I'm taking a trip somewhere far away. But I'll always be very close to you. I don't know if I'll return. I love you both dearly, I'm so proud of you. Please don't have anyone look for me.'"

"What'd the police say," Lilly asked.

Rose shook her head. "We never reported him gone. His last sentence was a request and we honored it. Frankly, I thought he might show up again. Like when I was a girl."

"Where do you think he went?"

"I can't even begin to fathom, Al," Rose answered with a chuckle. "Maybe he shrunk himself to the size of an ant and is busy exploring the lab floor. Maybe he teleported to the moon. Or maybe he drowned himself and just didn't want to admit it." She examined Al's face with a furrowed brow. "Where you are from? What's that subtle accent I hear?"

"I moved here from the Ukraine."

Rose and her son exchanged astonished glances, and then Rose shook her head incredulously.

"My father came here with his family in the forties. They were living on the Channel Islands at the time, in Guernsey. But that's not where my family's actually from. They came from *Kiev*. Dad was born and raised there."

Al shook his head, smiling.

"I feel like fate brought you here. Or perhaps it was Dad. You see, all his research—his notebooks, his machines, his thoughts and ideas—it's all in that cabin. And everything's written in a Cyrillic alphabet that's indecipherable to Gavin and me. I have to ask: do you read Ukrainian?"

Al nodded.

Rose, in turn, hooted in delight. "Amazing. Truly." She lifted an index finger in front of her mouth, turned her head, and cleared her throat into a wad of tissues. She then continued, "Go out there, Al. Look through his materials. See if you can salvage something, anything." She pointed to the window. "Looks like the fire's really coming. And if it can cross the lakebed, his work—it'll all be gone."

She looked back at her son. "The boat's obviously no good now. But Gavin can show you on a map where to find Trigger Island. Go out there."

Al looked at Lilly and Ingo, who were each nodding subtly. He looked back at Rose.

"We'll do it."

△ △ △

With only a towel wrapped around his midsection Aiden slouched into the oversized club chair, sipping from a rocks glass. A half empty bottle of Booker's rested on the table next to him. He was on his third drink.

Drinking alone always left him pondering his lives— personal and professional. He began by considering what kind of new business the firm could expect from the quakes. Tremendous insurance litigation, of course. Some of their clients, major life insurers, could very well be bankrupted given the scale. Massive liability, as well. Never ending plaintiffs' work. And someone had to defend those suits. Those were his thoughts during drink number one.

As he imbibed drink number two, he reflected on the lakebed, the ghost ship, the observation room. It felt like some Sierra computer game his older brother played when they were growing up. Or a cockamamie J.J. Abrams screenplay.

Numero three.

His thoughts turned to Lilly. *That bitch. I saved her. How could she not see that?* Sure, he had to step on her head, but that was the only way to save himself, and then to save her. It was like on an airplane: if the oxygen masks drop, place the mask on yourself first, and only then place the mask on your child. Common sense.

The phone rang. He picked it up.

"Hello?"

"It's me." Lilly's voice was crackling with excitement.

"When're ya' coming back?"

Lilly broke the news: she had one final task to complete with Al and Ingo. At that point, she'd return to the Field Club and they'd commence their long drive east. She recounted what they'd learned: Osmond Romanek had indeed lived in the house on the lake; he'd vanished from his lab on a nearby island; and the dying wish of his daughter was that they visit the lab. She detailed how, at that moment, Al and Ingo were at a kitchen table with Dr. Romanek's grandson and a huge crinkled map of Lake Hynek unfurled in front of them. It was the kind of adventure she'd always imagined.

Aiden listened silently. After Lilly finished talking, she waited several seconds for a response. Nothing.

He eventually spoke. He was seething.

"What chou did ta me infrondof those *faggots*," he belted out.

"How much did you drink?"

Aiden had knocked down the bourbons in rapid succession and it was catching up to him—in spades.

"I'm your husband! Thiz isn't a movie. It's *real. Live.*"

"I know, Aiden. This is my life as well."

"Com'back *now*."

"I will, soon. Get some sleep in the meantime."

"I lu'rve you," he mumbled.

Lilly paused. "I'll see you soon." She hung up.

△ △ △

The world spun like a top. Aiden sprawled himself across the bed, taking deep breaths to ward off the encroaching nausea. After twenty minutes of huffing and puffing, his mental and physical constitution settled back into loose normalcy—still very drunk but with a slightly diminishing effect. No longer at risk of losing all control. He didn't enjoy that messy, undisciplined feeling.

He eventually turned on the radio and started nursing a large bottle of water. The broadcaster was engaged in a freeform mix of reporting and opinion:

"—north, or west. As you can expect, I-683 is very crowded, but moving. We have reports of a car that hit the divide just east of the Smithtown exit. This was at least thirty minutes ago and apparently no emergency units are out there. Cars are just driving around the wreckage, driving on the shoulder. Not much order out there.

"And it's understandable: as we've seen in so many other instances, folks, there are just not enough emergency responders to handle everything all at once. The diversion of resources to address the catastrophe on the coast—it's left us inland communities exposed. No question about that.

"And the general feeling of *lawlessness*. And the fire. And, of course, our inability to communicate, to use the modern forms of communication we've taken for granted for so long. Don't you feel naked and exposed? Scary times.

"I've been speaking to you about those horrible people—the worst of humanity—taking advantage of the chaos. And we've heard those insane, just *insane*, reports of cannibalism up in

Eureka and just north of the border in Roosville. Those are unconfirmed, folks. But *cannibalism*. People using spike strips to stop cars going north. Ambushing vehicles.

"Did you ever, *ever* think you'd be hearing that? In North America? Wild stuff. As far as we know, food scarcity is *not* an issue, at least not yet. So that begs the question: *why*?

"Now, again, the cannibalism—that's not official, those reports. We have credible accounts, but the authorities have not confirmed it. When you hear cannibalism, you start thinking of Seventh-day Adventist. Daniel and Revelation. That's where my mind heads, at least. I don't know about you.

"Is that what we're witnessing? The system collapsing and people, well, reverting to some kind of baser instinct buried in our DNA? What law and order has kept at bay for so long. And now we're seeing mankind with the shackles off. *Cannibalism.* For God's sake, the earthquakes were a couple days ago! We've been without the internet for a couple days. And that's what some of us have become? Grilling man-meat?

"And now we've got another report; this is just in. Oh, boy. NBA fans—and fans of humanity and civilization, for that matter—this is tragic. Just *tragic*. A home invasion in Hynek and, from unconfirmed reports—again, nothing official yet—TJ Freeman and his wife were killed. Looks like an armed burglary, according to what we're hearing. If this is true, my condolences.

"You know, in some perverse way, this kind of horrible story makes sense. What I mean is that if you're a rich celebrity, you've got a target on your back. If law and order is breaking down, then people like TJ—who I always heard was just a really, really good guy—they're going to be targets.

"They tried to take our guns for how many years, people? Every mass shooting, every lone wolf attack, every teenager gunned down in Chicago or Detroit. The left's solution was always the same: take our guns. Subvert the Constitution. And look where we find ourselves, right? Cannibalism and home invasions. You crash your car: no police, no ambulance. Others just drive around you.

"Is that the new normal? I sure hope not. But we're getting a taste of it and, at the very least, I hope some of this gives us a renewed appreciation for the wisdom, the *sagacity*, of our Founding Fathers. Of those—"

Someone knocked on the bungalow door. Aiden stayed still with his eyes closed. He believed, initially, that he'd merely imagined the knock.

Another knock, but harder.

He stood up and fought off the dizziness. He silenced the radio and walked to the door in his towel.

"Who's there?"

"Mr. Campbell, hello. It's Dominick DeRuglia."

"Who?"

"After the quake, don't you remember? I pulled you out of the ground. You told me to come by."

Aiden unlocked and opened the door. Outside stood a mess of a man: a swollen black eye; a red cornea from broken blood vessels; blood smeared across his face and neck. Dom's shirt, once crisp and white, was a uniform brown, as were his khaki shorts. His socks were coated with a solidified layer of dirt, shell fragments, and grass.

"Dominick, whoa! What happened?"

"It's a long story, Mr. Campbell. Can you help me—like I helped you?"

"Of course, come in, come in." He ushered Dom into the room. "Hold on a sec, sit on this." He took Al's dirty towel from the floor and placed it on the corner of the bed. "Sit down, big guy."

He looked Dom up and down.

"So what the hell happened?" Aiden was taken aback by the crushed blood vessels in Dom's eye. It gave Dom a demonic air.

"I fell."

"You fell? Where?"

"In the lakebed." He spoke slowly and with a detached timber, as if his mind was floating elsewhere.

Aiden had sat down in the club chair opposite Dom. When he heard Dom mention the lakebed, he lurched forward.

"Really, you were in the lakebed? So was I."

"I know," Dom grunted.

Aiden considered the implications of these words, his mind racing.

Dom, in the meantime, used a dirt-encrusted fingernail to pick at a scab on his lower lip. As he did so, a shimmer of light caught Aiden's eye. An absurdly ostentatious gold ring, speckled with diamonds, on Dom's finger. Aiden squinted at the ring. He could make out three letters spanning the top.

N. B. A.

Ultimately, it took only six seconds for Aiden's mind to process and synthesize his observations and memories. For everything to click.

But it was already too late.

By the seventh second, Dom had removed the SIG from his waistband. He fired one round at Aiden's diaphragm. Squarely between his finely sculpted abs.

After two seconds, a nickel-sized puncture overflowed with blood. It streamed down Aiden's stomach into the white towel.

He didn't react at first. He just stared at Dom. It felt fantastically surreal, like he was watching a movie. This couldn't possibly be happening.

Then he felt the sharp sting. And saw the blood.

"I need to shower," Dom said cavalierly.

Aiden looked up at Dom and then back down at the wound. He pressed both palms onto the leaking hole, trying to stanch the blood flow.

"Where'd Alyosha go, Mr. Campbell?"

Aiden lay back in the chair. He pulled off the bloody towel and pressed it down on the wound. His thighs and penis were painted red.

At the sight of Aiden's genitals, Dom sat forward. An erection pushed awkwardly against his muddy shorts.

"Don't die on me, Mr. Campbell. I need to know about Alyosha. Did he come back here with you?"

"You. Shot. Me. Call 911," Aiden gasped.

Dom laughed and slapped his knees.

"Oh, jeez, Mr. Campbell. Bro, seriously. You think *I'm* gonna call 911? *Me*, the demigod?"

"Please." Aiden was wheezing.

Dom stood up and walked over to the chair. He pressed his crotch on the armrest only a few inches from Aiden's elbow.

"Listen bro, how about we make a deal? A little *quid bro quo?*" He chuckled. "You tell me where Alyosha went, and I call 911 and leave you here. I can't guarantee you'll make it until the EMT comes, but you'll have a shot."

Aiden swallowed once, the effort needed to force saliva down his throat approaching herculean.

"Okay," Aiden croaked. "Trigger. Island." His strength diminished with each word.

Dom edged closer, grinding into Aiden's arm.

"Where the fuck is that, brah?"

"A few miles east. The lakebed."

"What's out there?"

"A cabin. It's . . . a . . . lab."

"Like science shit?"

Aiden tipped his head forward.

"Now call . . . help." He coughed, which caused blood to bubble out of his mouth and dribble onto his chin.

Dom shook his head.

"Nah, I don't think I'll be doing that, Mr. Campbell." Aiden's eyes widened. "Do your best to stay awake for this."

Dom lifted up Aiden by the shoulders and threw him face-first onto the bed. The comforter muffled Aiden's guttural moans.

Dom stood behind him and looked down, smiling.

"Just hang in there, bro."

CHAPTER 17. FRIDAY-SATURDAY, JULY 2-3, 2021.

Their trek to the lab was uneventful. Mostly.

Ingo drove them several miles east of Shendo Estates, parallel to the north shore. It was late afternoon, although the sun remained powerful. He parked on the side of the road and they hiked past an abandoned cottage to the lakebed. They walked another mile along the lakebed edge as they searched for a reasonably safe-looking entry point.

As they descended cautiously from the pebbly beach into the craggy red terrain, a cluster of small islands—steep dirt mounds topped with green foliage—were visible in the distance to the south. Even farther south, the blue sky suddenly transformed into an ominous greyish black.

Birds circled overhead, periodically diving, disappearing from view, and then ascending with flesh-filled beaks. The stink of decomposing fish and mildew was worse than ever. Ingo was the first to complain; Al and Lilly ignored him.

Al kept glancing straight up and pondering how they looked from the birds' soaring heights. Perhaps like three ants marching in a line.

At one point, they encountered a deer-sized animal with its head pressed into the crevice between two jagged boulders. It looked up warily and revealed a narrow face with an elongated snout: an anteater. Al chuckled at the sight. This was Baxter, he explained, another zoo escapee. Al had often cleaned his enclosure.

"Baxter, where's Betty?" Al asked in a coddling voice. "Where's your lady friend?" The anteater stared at him with confounded eyes and sniffed the air a few times. Ingo sneezed and the animal scampered off.

They continued for another twenty minutes. Dusk began to encroach, the sky turning a deeper hue of blue.

It was Lilly who eventually spotted a small wooden dock built into the side of a steep hill. It was barely visible up a challenging sixty-degree incline. She gestured to the structure.

"That's it, I think," she said, wiping sweat from her brow, "I haven't seen any other docks."

The men nodded. Ingo grimaced and noted his hope that there was a bathroom in the cabin. That he had to "drop the kids off at the pa- pa- pool." Al rolled his eyes.

Lilly wrinkled her brow. "There's a pool there?"

It took another few minutes to hike up the hill to the dock, which spilled onto a miniature pebble beach encircling the small island. The pebbles gave way to overgrown grass and holly bushes, the latter seeming out of character for the island.

The foliage surrounded a single-story wooden cabin painted dark green. With a black slate roof and heavy brown Spanish shutters concealing the windows, the house blended into its surroundings. In fact, it was nearly camouflaged.

By then, night had just about arrived.

Wielding cheap plastic flashlights courtesy of Gavin Clarke, Al and Lilly used the feeble light beams to explore the cabin's external contours. Al then approached the door and, using a pair of keys attached to a Seahawks keychain, unlocked the door in two places. He pushed it open.

The inside consisted of a single room. An unfinished ceiling was crisscrossed by thick oak beams, with dozens of spider webs bridging the open space between beams and roof. Their flashlights illuminated several metal desks covered with appliances that resembled VCRs. Four rusted file cabinets were tucked in one corner. A Mr. Coffee that had seen better days rested on one of the cabinet tops. A layer of soot covered everything and, with each footstep, their beams captured a fresh burst of unsettled dust.

Gavin had insisted he touched nothing since his grandfather disappeared. It was exactly as Osmond left it.

Several stovetop oven-sized objects draped in opaque white sheets were situated randomly about the room. Ingo lifted up one of the sheets and inspected the object underneath—some kind of peculiar looking metal appliance. Scientific equipment of some kind.

Only one freestanding object was not covered: a rectangular apparatus, metal and black, no larger than a shoebox. It was perched three feet off the ground on two pairs of stilt-like legs. A weathered wooden chair and open toolbox rested next to the apparatus.

Al examined the chair: the seat was littered with crumbs. Popcorn kernels.

Red and white cables joined the apparatus to a car battery on the floor a few feet away.

"Only thing that looks used, really," Lilly whispered as she pointed at the device.

She reached beneath the legs of the chair and removed an antique marble notebook with a pen tucked inside. The pages were thick and waxy.

Lilly opened the notebook and shined the light into it. She turned to Al.

"The writing looks alien to me."

She handed the notebook to Al, who scanned the first page.

"It's Ukrainian alright," he muttered. He rubbed a page between his thumb and middle finger. It was not paper, but rather velum. "The first entry is dated December 7, 1967." He flipped through the pages. "The entries: they're not every day. Sometimes months between them. But they're kind of like," he scanned some sentences, "observations. About life, work. Equations, too."

Four caged-metal construction lamps dangling from the ceiling beams suddenly lit up and showered the lab in an intense halogen glow. Ingo was in the corner of the room wearing a triumphant grin.

"Let there be light!" he declared. "The ge- generator Gavin mentioned."

Al nodded gratefully before returning his attention to the journal. Ingo, meanwhile, sat on a small orange couch near Al and tucked his hands under his thighs. "Let's do some reading, Yoshi."

Lilly sat next to Ingo and looked at Al expectantly.

"Please speak clearly and don't mumble," she said, "you do that sometimes." She removed lip balm from her pocket, applied some to her bottom lip, and puckered up with a popping noise.

Ingo, for his part, had unsheathed a piece of Bazooka Joe. He popped the gum into his mouth and chewed vigorously.

"Ándale," he instructed.

Al wiped some kernels off the wooden chair and sat down with the notebook on his lap. He turned a few pages and cleared his throat.

December 7, 1967

Father always urged me to memorialize it all. I suppose I finally will.

I am seated in a room at Hamfield Memorial. Tess gave birth— our first—a few hours ago. She and the baby, Rose, are sleeping soundly. A glorious day, truly is. I wish Father and Mother could have lived to see it.

I am proud of Tess. The labor was difficult, but she was strong. I expected no less, but it was still wonderful to watch her meet this newest challenge. She will be a fine mother. I hope the same for myself. A worthy father, that is! The boys at the lab will surely have their fun with me when I return. I can just imagine.

It is fascinating to ponder how, when Tess delivers our second child, I will have, in all likelihood, achieved the ends of my research. In a perfect world—in _my_ perfect world—I would be known beyond the narrow circles in which I now work. I would be to gravitics what Tesla was to electromagnetism.

A man can hope! I do feel I'm getting awfully close. If celebrity finds me, it will be strange, indeed. But that is secondary, tertiary even. I want to give Rose and her generation a better world.

Al flipped through several pages:

March 24, 1973

I'm still amazed to be writing again. I've not a modicum of doubt that, even now, I remain the target of continuing and pervasive surveillance. Privacy ever again? They let me live, but could discredit me at their leisure. Paint me as a kook. Perhaps access my mind.

The whole horrible affair has got me thinking. For one, how did they exercise control over my old Buick? That has stirred my thoughts. It suggests a field of some kind. To scramble the radio, the hydraulics. To remotely shut down a combustion engine.

I went back to Vision Labs. It took everything in my power not to tell Frank and Max (they believe I took to a sudden, frightful illness). If only to disclose what the government is up to. The *technology and shenanigans. Decades beyond what they reveal. A century ahead, perhaps?*

I still believe in the future of gravitics. I thought they wanted to crush my work and cow me. But I toy with the idea that, just maybe, their motivation is more opaque. More complicated than I thought at first blush.

Whatever their motivation, I continue to feel peculiar. I was at Stalingrad during the war and yet this feels even more transformative. The oddest symptom are the vivid dreams— they do not fade. They are less like dreams and more like memories of some perverse future. Of Tess dying. Of Rose—a grown woman—sick and dying. Of explosions and earthquakes. Of an all-consuming cosmic jihad. And then of darkness.

Who knows what these dreams portend, if anything. But I cannot escape them. They are always there. They do not dissipate upon waking.

I sleep very little. My appetite is poor. Yet something is pushing me forward, driving me toward an outcome. Good or bad, I do not yet know.

And the numbers! I know the string like a mantra. Forever imprinted on my brain.

August 15, 1973

Friday was my last day at Vision Labs. An amicable parting, you could say. I rarely showed up anymore and communicated very little to the boys. Since the event I have not been particularly tolerant of life's quotidian necessities. And my work is moving in a direction that my colleagues found increasingly uncomfortable. A parting of ways was inexorable.

My "dreams" are amplifying in nuance and intensity. I am convinced, however, that they are not dreams at all. I see ball lightning. Pink orbs.

I'm beginning to think the lake is playing some role in all this. My body, senses, critical faculties all seem excited and heightened when I'm standing close to the water. Almost as if the lake vibrates with a resonance that matches my own.

"Skip forward a bit in time," Lilly urged.

"I can do that." Al flipped through several pages.

October 1, 1974

I've moved the last of my equipment. I'm confident that being surrounded by the water will stoke my ideas and accelerate progress. Hynek is an area of exceptionally high electromagnetic energy, and, if my theories prove correct, also an epicenter for gravitons, those mysterious little buggers. I wonder how an anomaly like Hynek came to be? I do wish I could consult Joey Rhodes, the geologist at WSU. I am sure he would have some insights. But I am going to do this alone.

I am nearing a breakthrough. Although far slower than anticipated, it is close.

October 7, 1979

Five years since my last entry—difficult to believe.

I'm convinced that the water's properties can facilitate travel. She showed me. Josie. Two kinds of movement: lateral and vertical. She moves laterally at will and can straddle several different planes. She called it "shifting." Geospatial or temporal. A vertical shift is different.

As she explained it, a vertical shift is not that far removed from the old Flatland concept. She was "born" one step up, if you can describe her creation as a birth. She said things exist three steps up. In the seventh step. We've had many discussions.

I saw her in the house. At first, she came to me as an apparition: as Mother. But I eventually saw the real her. God knows it frightened me, but I grew used to it. To her.

Tess believed I was sick and she convinced others as much. The fallacy that my mind was "broken." She thinks I've been "treated." Lithium.

I am more lucid than anyone in this Godforsaken place and time. I can test Josie's information—the revelation she bestowed on me.

No more distractions and sideshows. I now have the blueprint. I will devote myself to this unfailingly.

January 1, 1989

On the cusp of a new decade and days away from a prototype. I knew it would be a long journey. Just one man working through the equations and fabricating the equipment.

Rose is a dynamic young woman, but her mother's exit has stunted her in some ways. I will never forgive Tess. To leave herself there for Rose to find . . . it pains me.

I have upped my lithium once more. It has yielded a steady consciousness in which to carry on my work.

Rose said she will follow her beau to Seattle. I've gone to the island for 22 straight days. Just a bit more time.

"I'm going to fast-forward again."

April 17, 1991

The hopper is finally functioning. As expected, it yields some kind of spatial tear directly above its jets. The effect is quite beautiful: a shimmering, almost sparkling, translucent patch of space. Like Lake Hynek's surface suspended in air.

Each shifting phase lasts 5.32 seconds. To date, I have introduced only inanimate objects, live insects, and live birds. To be exact: 10 assorted pebbles; 25 quarters; 25 potted plants (peace lilies); 30 black beetles (American carrier); and 15 parakeets (budgerigars).

I introduced most subjects individually, although paired some of the animals. I used a pole with an attached clamp that has a trigger-release mechanism. When the subject enters the gate, I typically feel a slight attractive tug, whereupon I depress the trigger and release the subject.

Not all subjects reappeared. Seven of 10 pebbles reappeared a few seconds later (always at the foot of the hopper). I cleaned each pebble before introduction; three of seven came back noticeably dirtier. They were covered in a layer of brown grime or soot. The remaining four appeared indistinguishable from before their introduction. Mass did not materially change. All seven registered slightly higher output in Becquerels.

Of 25 quarters, 13 returned. Of the 13, five showed visual changes. Three were dirt-stained. Two were rusted heavily. One of these two appeared extremely oxidized. Based on visual comparisons to known samples of oxidized metal objects, this quarter showed signs of <u>2,000 years</u> of aging. Without proper equipment and qualified assistance (I am no chemist) this is a loose and potentially inaccurate estimate. But intriguing nonetheless.

Not one of the plants or beetles came back alive. Fifteen plants returned; all obviously dead, some covered with a red dust. Mass differences were as expected given the change. Radioactivity: unchanged. Five beetles returned in varying states of decomposition. One retained traces of humidity as if it had expired within the past few days. The remaining four were only dried exoskeletons.

Finally, the parakeets. Of the 15 introduced, seven instantly rematerialized. Two were still alive and, to the naked eye, appeared materially older. Four had expired and were at various stages of decomposition: three with feathers and flesh, one a skeleton only. The seventh was fossilized, remarkably. As I understand it, this would have meant that its expiration occurred <u>at least</u> 10,000 years earlier. But I am neither a chemist nor geologist.

I have been unable to determine an outcome pattern.

June 3, 1991
I increased my lithium once more. Sleep continues to elude me, and I am dreading the next phase: mammals. Dogs first. Such loyal and intelligent creatures. I must work up the nerve. And determine how best to procure them without arousing suspicion. I will need quite a few.

August 20, 1991
Yesterday, on my way to the market, I encountered Bill Dhryme's untended Scottish Terrier roaming his lawn. I thought: now or never. So I did it! I took the damn pooch in my car and spirited him away. Friendly little fellow. I am making preparations. I must do so quickly, lest I lose my will.

August 22, 1991
It was a terrible morning. I introduced the terrier into the hopper. After two minutes (far longer than for any of the smaller subjects), I began thinking that it would not return. Yet, just then, the poor thing rematerialized several feet away.
It was in an atrocious yet incredible state: snout and mouth fused to what appeared to be a steel rod. This fusion of animate and inanimate matter is unlike anything I have ever seen—a first in science? This must have happened at the molecular level. Truthfully, I lack the expertise or equipment even to hazard a guess.
At any rate, and quite astonishingly, the old boy was still alive. Snorting desperately through its lone remaining breathing orifice: half a nostril on its misshapen snout. Its eyes betrayed excruciating pain and fluttering panic. A truly horrible sight. It groaned less like a canine and more like a tortured boy.

But this march must go on!

After several hours of examining the chimera—body slumped over on the lab floor, huffing furiously through that partial nostril—I euthanized it with a pistol shot. I then tied some rocks to the carcass and took it out in the boat.

April 10, 1992,

I introduced another one yesterday; that makes four dogs. Two returned, including the most recent. Re-materialization for this last one was instantaneous and the dog was alive. When I pushed him through the gate it was a young and handsome beagle mix. He returned old and feeble: littered with scars, a mangy scalp, and glassy eyes. I put a bullet in his head and added him to the lakebed graveyard.

I am gathering granular measurements and data with each experiment. After another 10, I will analyze the dataset and consider next steps.

Al leafed through the next several pages.

"This is getting strange," he observed. "Lots of equations in here, not much text. I'm traveling forward in time."

June 24, 1994

These experiments were always heading here. Do I like this? Of course not. But the gate is like a hungry beast: it demands more. Human flesh—

Ingo spoke over Al, "Are you fucking kidding me?"

Al looked up from the journal and nodded incredulously. Lilly, meanwhile, had rested her head on her palm. Her eyes flickered sleepily.

"Go on, Al," she said gently.

—is what it demands. I really am Dr. Frankenstein now. I never wanted this.

But Frankenstein did create life.

I will begin observing homes. Habits, schedules, tendencies.

August 20, 1994

It happened yesterday. I do a disservice by writing so passively. It did not just "happen." I did it. I made it happen.

The "boy" came out alive. For that, I am grateful to God. Nonetheless, I harmed him. A harm both strange and terrible.

It was a stately house on the south shore. A great sweeping lawn with a swing set, treehouse—everything a tyke could want. On Saturdays, he played with his older sister on the lawn. He was maybe two; his sister seven, perhaps. A large maple divides the lawn into halves and, at an angle, obscures any view from the house. From my casing, I suppose you would call it, I knew that the sister sometimes neglected her duties as babysitter: she scurried into the house for a few minutes, or disappeared briefly into the backyard.

A Saturday morning and, as usual, they were frolicking on the lawn. Big sister ran to the front door and looked back at baby brother, who was playing with figures in front of the maple. The perfect angle. I foresaw my opportunity.

As big sister held open the door and glanced at little brother for reassurance, my adrenaline began pumping furiously. This was it.

Once the door closed I dashed onto the lawn, grabbed the chap under one arm, and applied the ether handkerchief. Less than a minute later he was subdued and asleep on the passenger side floor as I sped west. He never even saw my face.

Within half an hour we were headed to the lab; I used a large duffel bag to conceal him during our journey. He woke only once on the open water, beginning to squirm and squeal. After another application of ether, he was quickly asleep again.

Once at the lab, I wasted no time. I did not think, I only acted. I powered up the hopper, primed the discharge cell, and took him out of the bag. I blindfolded him, held him a few feet in front of the shimmer, and waited for him to wake. As soon as I felt his muscles exerting force, I heaved him in.

Still no time to stop and think. Just as quickly as I introduced the subject, he materialized three feet from the hopper.

A boy went in; a man came out.

He was in his early fifties, by my estimate. Thin, short, and homely, with a long and unkempt beard. Black hair that was nappy, almost like dreadlocks. Except bald in the center of his head, like a monk's tonsure.

His beard was littered with debris—some kind of vegetable matter. He was dressed only in a pair of tattered jeans caked in dirt and feces. No shirt, socks, or shoes. Nor underwear, for that matter. Stunningly odiferous. Excrement and body odor.

He said nothing. He merely stared at me with dull eyes. A sweet child moments earlier. Now a mute, feebleminded caveman.

With all that said, he was quite agreeable and docile, smiling blankly like a retard. I am unsure whether his diminished faculties stem from some kind of brain trauma brought about by the travel, or from a malnourished period of development. Could it be some kind of purely psychological condition engendered by the experience?

I gave him water and fed him chocolate, which he devoured eagerly, but just as quickly vomited back up. Too rich for his stomach. Like some pathetic dog, he lapped up his own vomit from the lab floor.

I led him into the boat and we returned to the house. I bathed, shaved, and fed him anew. He soon fell asleep on the floor of the library. I sat and watched my special guest.

When he awoke, I dressed him, drove him 20 miles east, and dropped him off on a backroad in the heart of Doursham. He spoke not one word, nor even attempted to sound out a word or otherwise communicate. He certainly knew some words when I introduced him into the gate. Yet he seemed wholly mute.

Someone will surely find and help him. Even if he is taught to communicate, his account, of course, would appear so outlandish as to be utterly unbelievable.

An overpowering nausea at what I've done is beginning to set in. I am still in a daze of sorts.

I don't have the resolve to do this again. Of that, I am certain.

January 17, 2019

Twenty-six years since my last entry—difficult to fathom.

After that entry, I increased my meds yet again. A few days later, Rose and her husband visited unexpectedly. They found me slumped over my desk. A coma induced by acute lithium toxicity.

When I awoke one week later at Hamfield Memorial, I was a raving lunatic—or so they said. I have no memory of the whole affair. Some kind of psychosis. Perhaps I was spouting my horrible secrets. Doubtful considering I remain a free man. Come to think of it, to the uninitiated or skeptical, my secrets would be little more than the colorful fragments of a mad man's imagination.

Once home, I reflected for a good long time on what I had done. The boy: he haunted my thoughts. The lawn on that Saturday morning kept returning to my mind's eye. Him playing so innocently. When my hands touched the skin of his arm: <u>that</u> marked the point in time when, for me, the act became real, irrevocable. Everything then unfolded so quickly like toppling dominoes. Within a matter of hours, the boy was a man. That first touch of his arm. It kept replaying in my mind. If I could only relive it and step back. Retreat. The memory—the regret— pulling me down. Like those sinking dogs.

I spent more than a year recovering from that episode, reflecting on the boy, and pondering my research. Too far—that was one conclusion. I had overreached in a horrible fashion, guided by the conviction that my research trumped all.

But wasn't I also a coward? The notion that the gate lusted for human flesh. Even if it did: why not my own? I treated that boy as a tragic sacrifice to the altar of human knowledge. I could never fix that. Wherever and whenever the gate went—that was for me to confront.

And I will confront it. Eventually. When the time is right.

Hence, I suspended my experiments. I have dedicated my time to some kind of modest penitence: working with the poor and disadvantaged. Working with the high school in Bellington to build a more robust science department. Starting an annual science fair for Tuckashoa high schoolers, and awarding the winner a full university scholarship.

I have also kept an eye on the boy—the man—with whose life I meddled. He walks the streets of Hynek, a mute and harmless fool. As I write, I am looking at one of the "missing" signs on my desk that the police posted for him years ago. Such a—

Ingo drowned out Al. "*Popper*? That has to be him."
Al looked up and nodded, wide-eyed.
Lilly was asleep, her face nuzzled in a cushion.
Al resumed:

—bizarre sight. I find him weekly and put $200 in his pocket, his hidden benefactor. I know nothing I can do will ever make him whole or absolve my sins. He wanders the streets contentedly; the townspeople do not mistreat him. I suppose his life could be worse.

And now Rose is sick—just as my memories foretold.

She moved back home. And my dear grandson lives with us now as well. I love them both. It is good to have some company again.

I write because it is time for me to take the next step. My faculties are still sharp, and I am still mobile despite my age. My health is holding. So now is the time.

Time to dust off the hopper for some preliminary tests. I will need new dogs. Perhaps half a dozen. I would go to the shelter one county over, yet Rose knows the administrator. So back to my old ways.

March 2, 2021

Gavin just dropped me off. So intelligent and thoughtful. His mother loves him endlessly, as do I.

I said goodbye to Rose this morning. She is so thin now; you can see the veins in her cheeks and forehead. The treatment has left her perpetually nauseous, but she's fighting. She battles to put a smile on her face and to engage Gavin in discussions of the arts, current events. She is no one's victim. I will always be proud of her.

If Rose or Gavin reads this one day, I love you. I do not know where I am heading. My hope is to learn something about this world in which we lead such fleeting lives, and of which we know so little. My experiences in this diary were <u>real</u>*—not the ramblings of some loon. And they taught me that we can see only a tiny fraction of an exponentially bigger, and richer, existential tapestry. If I can learn something about that tapestry, I will do my best to communicate back those findings. To aid our species.*

Although we may seem separated by endless space and time, I know we are forever bonded and entwined. We are unitary. Which gives me hope that, in point of fact, I am not saying goodbye to my daughter or grandson—or that Tess, for that matter, ever truly left. Our nexus endures. But I suppose we will see what time has in store for me.

CHAPTER 18,
SATURDAY, JULY 3,
2021,

A l closed the journal. Lilly was still asleep. Ingo, conversely, was grinning with an expression of childlike wonder. He stood up and walked over to Al.

"So 'the hopper,' it's got to be this little thing, right?" He picked up the metal box and dangled it in the air from the cable that led to the car battery. "Looks like a gh-, gh-, ghost trap. Definitely homemade." He cradled the box and mashed some of the buttons underneath a small red LCD screen.

"Whoa, easy there," Al said with his hands raised.

"Relax, Yoshi, I haven't pressed the 'POWER' button. Yet."

"We're not doing that."

Ingo looked at him in disbelief.

"You're sa- sa- saying you *don't* want to turn this thing on? Are you . . . insane?"   Ingo laughed, a maniacal expression spreading from his crooked smile to his eyes.

"Am *I* insane? Are *you*?"

"I'm turning it on. Come he- he- he-. Fuck." He slowed his cadence. "Hell. Or. High. Water."

Whatever the "hopper" was—wherever the "gate" led—it had struck a chord deep inside Ingo. A profound validation of his belief system. He clutched the device and took a step back defensively.

Al scoffed and shook his head. Lilly snored.

"It's all you then, Ingo." Al backed away.

Ingo placed the box on the floor and looked up at Al. He raised an index finger above his head, pointed it down, and, with dramatic flair, slowly lowered his digit toward the "POWER" button. He dangled his finger above the button for three seconds.

"Keep your pa- pa- panties on."

And he tapped the button.

They braced for whatever was coming next.

△ △ △

The control panel emitted two small beeps, like weak farts. Then nothing.

On the LCD screen, a single red word appeared in MS-DOS-like font.

"PRIME."

They exhaled and traded glances.

"Shit," Ingo muttered, "it says 'PRIME,' Yoshi. What does that mean? Prime number?"

"Didn't you score perfectly on your college boards? Prime it. You've got to *prime* it. It's what Romanek wrote in the journal."

"How? It's just a keypad." Ingo furrowed his brow. "Al, give me that letter—the one from the observation room."

Al removed the tattered letter from his pocket and handed it over. Ingo scanned the paper and then tapped several numbers into the keypad.

The box registered a loud click—causing both men to flinch—and then hummed softly. Ingo hurriedly placed the device on the chair and stepped away. They watched anxiously.

The box began to vibrate gently, tapping unevenly against the slightly curved surface of the chair. Suddenly, the side facing away from the chair projected a flat sheet of shimmering emerald light; the sheet was slightly narrower than the width of the chair and extended several feet toward the front door. It was like the machine was a dot-matrix printer spitting out a holographic sheet of sparkling green paper. The box continued to tremble and hum.

Two minutes passed while Al and Ingo stared silently at the numinous light. The device eventually issued a crackling burst, jumped a few inches into the air, and rotated counterclockwise. The side projecting the light landed face-down on the seat of the chair. The men pranced backward like frightened deer with their hands in front of them.

Without a sound, the chair blinked out of sight.

The box dropped to the floor, bounced once, and landed on a different side, causing the green light to reappear; it was once again pointing toward the front of the room, although the light was flush against the ground. It twinkled a few inches in the air like a cosmic trapdoor.

Al looked at Ingo in disbelief. A half-throated "dude" was all he could muster.

"Going down, anyone?" Ingo quipped.

And then someone knocked on the cabin door.

△ △ △

It was less a knock, more a pound.

Lilly sat up; the left half of her face had deep indentations from the sofa pillow. After blinking several times, grimacing, and mumbling about dry contact lenses, she noticed the shimmering green rectangle on the floor. She looked dumbfounded.

"What in God's name is *that*?"

Neither Al nor Ingo responded. Both stared at the door to the lab.

THUMP. THUMP. THUMP.

Lilly stood up and stretched her shoulders. She looked at the two men.

"Is someone going to get that?"

She approached the door, tilted her head sideways, and listened.

THUMP.

She offered a tentative, "Hello?"

A piercing sound rang out—a single thunderclap.

"Ouch, *shit*," Lilly yelped, retreating a few steps.

She grasped her left forearm. Her upper body was contracting, tensing up.

"What the . . . I think. Oh dear. I think I've been shot!" Her voice evinced more surprise than pain.

The doorknob jiggled and then turned. The door opened.

And there stood Dom—gun in hand.

△ △ △

For Al, the moments leading up to and after the gunshot were dreamlike, unfolding in slow cinematic frames.

He lurched forward to help Lilly, but Dom swung the muzzle of the SIG directly at him. He ordered Al to freeze (bro).

By then, Lilly was sitting Indian style. Blood had already soaked through her turquoise blouse and stained her white Bermuda shorts. She kept looking from her arm to Dom, Dom to her arm. But not at his face. Rather, his chest. She was struggling to process what she was seeing.

Stepping through the doorway, Dom glanced at Ingo—a frozen spectator—and then scanned the back of the cabin. His line of sight intersected with the shimmering green gate; his eyes widened. A satisfied grin spread across his cracked lips.

"Drago, you bowl-chested freak. Is that a . . ." His voice trailed off. "Just like Dad said."

"Dom, we need to get her help," Al whisper-shouted.

"No one's getting help," Dom said cavalierly. "You know what I've been through, Drago? I'm here for a reason. For *that*," he pointed to the green projection, "wherever *that* goes. Dad said that you," he directed the barrel of the gun toward Al, "had already been down there. And now it's my turn, bro."

"I don't know what you're talk—"

"Where did you get that *shirt*?" Lilly yelped as she pointed at Dom's chest. Her breaths were breaking down into labored pants.

Dom looked at his own chest. It was a plain grey shirt emblazoned with two words in elegant Garamond font: "Skadden Arps." When Dom realized why Lilly was pointing at his shirt, his smile turned into a giggle, which dissolved into a heaving guffaw. He even slapped his knee joyfully.

"That's *right*, you're Mrs. Aiden Campbell! Mrs. Campbell, did you know I'm half man, half god?"

"How did you get that shirt?"

"I took it from your husband's bag." He paused. "Of course, to reach that bag, I had to step over his naked body. Your husband had such great lats; really impressive. I should have gotten his routine. Mad respect for the lats."

Lilly stared at him, her pants becoming a stuttering breath. "*What?*"

"His *lats*, I said *lats*. His latissimus dorsi muscle. It's on your back. Your husband had awesome lats."

"Is. He. Okay." The bullet had struck her ulnar artery. She was losing blood quickly.

"If okay means a corpse, then yeah, sure, he's great." He began laughing again. "I'm cracking myself up over here. It's like, 'Who wrote this stuff, bro,' know what I mean?"

Lilly's eyes glazed over as she stared mindlessly past Dom and into the night sky. She slumped onto her back.

Ingo whimpered, "Wh-, wh-, why."

"Who's this stuttering faggot?" Dom pointed the gun at Ingo, who cowered like a beaten dog. "Where the fuck is your chin?"

Have to make a tourniquet, Al thought. She can't lose much more blood.

"Dom, man," Al said with strained composure, "you can't torture a dead woman. You let her keep bleeding and you can't screw her or pull out her fingernails or whatever. You need her *alive*, right?"

Dom grunted in thought.

"You know, Drago, you're no idiot. You always say stuff that kind of, I dunno, gets me thinking. You're sharp, you know?"

Dom surveyed the room again.

"Thing is," he continued, "I don't really care about her. This is all hammies, check this out."

Dom stepped toward Lilly, who was now gazing blankly at the ceiling. He bent his right leg while lifting up his foot—a wood-soled Italian dress shoe.

And then he did the unthinkable. The irreversible.

He rained a single, crushing stamp down on Lilly's face. Her eyes and nose collapsed under the force of his powerful leg. The blow mashed her face straight back into her brain.

Al and Ingo gaped. Lilly was gone.

Dom wiped his bloody shoe on the floor.

"You know why I'm a demigod, Drago?"

Silence.

"Because I can do without feeling. I can take. And kill. No 'wah, wah, wah,' sad trombone. I always knew I wasn't meant for this age, brah. And I was *right*. And *that's* what's down there, *bro*-seph." He paused for a few seconds. "I still want some time with you, Drago. You" —he gestured to Ingo—"I don't need."

Dom pointed the muzzle at Ingo. "See ya, wouldn't want to be ya." He cocked the gun and fingered the trigger.

CHAPTER 19.
SATURDAY, JULY 3,
2021.

Bardo shined her Maglite into the fog. Impenetrable. It was still dark out; when she turned off the flashlight, the world went black. She'd been walking aimlessly for almost an hour, sometimes curving in one or another direction to avoid a craggy precipice or muddy pool. She was beginning to get nervous.

Her visit to Rose had been fruitful. Disparate strands of information were marinating in her brain, congealing.

As insane as it had sounded at the time, Scott had claimed that he was abducted to a spaceship above earth where his captors questioned him about Osmond Romanek. He then magically found himself in his living room dragging the body of Vladimir Nettishovo Dragunov, a once prominent Ukrainian politician who had disappeared from that country seven months earlier.   Vladimir shared a surname with a young Hynek resident, Alyosha, who had appeared at Bardo's meeting after the quake.

Meanwhile, according to Rose *Romanek* Clarke: (1) her father was indeed Dr. Osmond Romanek, a plasma physicist born in the Ukraine (*what is it about this country?*); (2) the ninety-four-year-old scientist disappeared a few months ago from his cabin in the Bantam Islands, but Rose never reported it; and (3) of all people, Alyosha Dragunov and two associates had showed up on Rose's doorstep just hours earlier.   They'd found a note that Rose's father had written in 1973 while held captive in what the scientist was led to believe was a spaceship in orbit above earth—*just like Scott.* Except that Alyosha had found the note in a room *underneath* the lakebed. A room built to appear like the cabin of a spaceship in orbit.

And the topper: Bardo had since talked to Bernard "Bernie" Higgins, Al's boss at the Hamfield Zoo. He'd spoke glowingly of Alyosha—"Kemosabe," as he'd affectionately called him. Had Alyosha ever mentioned a father perhaps, Bardo had asked.

"Well, yes," he'd answered. "As a matter of fact, that one was kind of a doozy."   Kemosabe's father was a famous politician in the Ukraine. And Alyosha had hinted that his father had thrown his mother off the roof of their Kiev townhouse. *Quite the motive for patricide.*

By the time she spoke with Bernie, Justin had already apprised him of his tiger's "misconduct," for lack of a better word.   Bernie, in turn, apologized profusely to Bardo ("You know, for eating that poor woman and all"). Fritz the Tiger was not some monster, he'd pleaded, but just a tiger doing what a tiger does.

"Someone fed her to Fritz," she'd replied. "Sad thing is: you'd think a loose tiger would be our biggest problem, wouldn't you?"

Bernie had registered an exhausted sigh.   "A drop in the bucket these days."

Gavin Clarke had advised Bardo of where to find his grandfather's lab. So she'd driven a few miles east along the northern shore, parked next to the rickety shell of an abandoned water filtration building, and took her first steps into the lakebed. Venturing forth, she'd kept a steady palm on the handle of her holstered Glock. Forever imprinted in her brain: "Fritz" transporting Elise Freeman like a housecat carrying a lifeless sparrow. *If I see Fritz, I'm dropping him like a hot pan. Or a wet bar of soap. Or a squirming groundhog.*

While brainstorming similes to calm her nerves, Bardo had tried to continue in one direction—what should have been south—with the fog steadily building and boxing her in. The smell was beyond anything she'd ever experienced—a Porta Potti brimming with excrement and topped with rotten shellfish. She began redirecting her willpower to concentrate on not breathing through her nose. She soon lost any and all sense of direction.

$$\triangle \ \triangle \ \triangle$$

And so, increasingly swallowed by a supremely stinky fog, Bardo's nerves began to get the best of her. As if on cue, the echoing howls of a coyote pack filled the lakebed. And then a vaguely familiar, albeit far more unsettling noise: a chattering, sinister laugh. Lots of chattering, sinister laughs. Another pack of animals—one hardly indigenous to Washington.

She reached for her radio.

"Justin?"

A couple of seconds passed.

"Yup, Chief. Over."

"What are you doing awake?"

"Sitting next to the kids, watching 'em sleep. We're evacuating when the sun rises. Over."

"Justin, I think I'm lost. I've got about a foot of visibility. You know how Dr. Frankenstein had those beakers filled with white smoke? It's like I'm in a smoky beaker."

"So, basically, a giant bong is what you're saying? Over."

"Yup. Eh, shit." She sighed. "What time you got?"

"4:15, over."

"Almost light. This stuff should burn off with the sun. We got anyone looking for DeRuglia?"

"Three of ours, two Hamfield guys. They've already evacuated their families, so they can keep looking. Over."

"Hey Justin, Sash is home and all packed." She paused for a few seconds. "In case anything happens . . . you know, I don't get back in time or whatever. Go get her. Take her with you guys. And, you know, remind her how much I love her."

"That was my plan already, over."

"But also tell her I'm sorry."

"Sorry for what? Over."

"Sorry I didn't stay and talk. Tell her there was nothing more I wanted. And that I wish I could go back in time to that moment. To do it again."

"I'm writing this down. Will relay the message precisely, boss. Over."

"You're really good, Justin. You know that, right?"

"Thanks Chief. I appreciate that. Right back at you. Over."

"You know: I'm waiting for the day when you miss an 'over.'"

"Not gonna happen." The radio went silent for three seconds. "Ov—"

POP!

Bardo instinctively switched off the radio, turned off her flashlight, and drew her gun.

A gunshot. No question.

She closed her eyes and tried to triangulate from where the sound had come. She headed in that direction at a cautious yet brisk trot.

After two minutes, the flat pit in which she was walking curved up—mildly at first, but, after a dozen feet, at a much sharper angle.

She soon passed the rusted metal legs of a small dock, the poles melded to rocks on the slope. The fog was still omnipresent, but there was a soft yellow illumination just beyond the dock. She'd found Trigger Island.

$$\triangle \ \triangle \ \triangle$$

As Bardo emerged on a pebble beach, the fog ended abruptly as if the edge of the lakebed was the lip of a bubbling cauldron. When the air cleared, a small cabin came into view; the front door was ajar, spilling a band of yellow light onto the beach.

A strapping, muscular man was slightly inside the door. She instantly recognized the build and giant bald head from the Freeman's surveillance video.

She heard him say, "See ya. Wouldn't want to be ya."

"*Dominick DeRuglia, police!* Hands up, *now!*"

Both hands slowly rose. One held a gun.

"Put the gun *down*! Slowly!"

Dom bent over, placed the gun on the floor, and stood back up.

"Now turn around!"

Her eyes pranced to the left and right of him. She made out two more people inside the cabin.

"Who else is in there? Alyosha?"

"Yes!" Al shouted. Ingo identified himself as well.

"DeRuglia, turn around, *slowly*," she barked.

"He just killed Lilly Campbell!" Al yelled. His voice quivered.

Calm and deliberate, Dom turned around and squinted to get a better look at Bardo.

She examined Dom's face: chapped, meaty lips awash in cold sores. Some dried and crusty, others glistening and oozy.

"What have you done, DeRuglia?" she shouted. "What's *wrong* with you?"

Dom smiled. "I'm a demigod. Do you know what that means?"

Bardo took three steps toward the door with the muzzle trained on Dom's chest.

Suddenly, Dom's eyes tracked left for a split second. They lit up with a fascinated twinkle.

Bardo cocked her head as she tried to read Dom's expression.

Two seconds later, she realized what was happening. But time was not on her side.

△ △ △

Bardo spun right. By then, a furry white boulder was barreling at her. It was no more than five feet away.

Rocky's initial hit propelled Bardo eight feet to the side like a cannonball.

She landed on her back and skid across the grass. Her gun flew into the darkness. Before her body had even stopped sliding, the bear had its two front paws pressed down against her chest, tearing through her shirt and into her Kevlar vest.

His jaws snapped twice at her neck but missed each time. Sour breath and hot spittle sprayed everywhere.

On the third snap, Rocky sank two fangs into Bardo's shoulder. The animal began furiously shaking his head, Bardo's torso leaving the ground and swinging like a rag doll.

Rocky's canines had cut through Bardo's flesh, struck shoulder bone, and then slipped, causing his jaws to lose their grip and unlock. The bear continued relentlessly whipping his head and Bardo went flying for a second time. She tumbled head over feet and landed face-down in pebbles. He bounded toward her, reared onto his hind legs, and fell forward.

Bardo groped desperately at her ankle. She then flipped onto her back.

The last thing she saw were teeth.

△ △ △

From Al's vantage point, all he could make out were Bardo's jean-covered legs and sneakers; Dom's body obscured the rest.

A mass of distressingly familiar white fur suddenly came crashing at the police chief like a bolt of lightning. Instantly, Bardo shot out of view. It was as if a giant hook had yanked her off stage-right.

Dom remained facing the door. He was watching the attack unfold. His gun was still on the floor. *This is it.*

Al grabbed a combination wrench from the open toolbox near his feet and charged. Ingo ran forward as well. A pair of raptors going after a *T. rex.*

Dom turned at the last second, saw his attackers, and quickly stepped backward. Al had been aiming the wrench at Dom's head but instead landed a blow against his neck before stumbling past Dom toward the open door.

Dom grunted in pain and, momentarily stunned by the impact, tilted to his left side. He used one hand to clutch his neck and the other to fend off Ingo, who was throwing several awkward punches upward at Dom's chin.

Dom quickly regained his balance. He swung only once at Ingo, fist connecting squarely with eye. Ingo instantly lost consciousness and crumpled like a building in a controlled detonation.

Al had gotten off the floor, cocked the wrench back, and was in mid-swing when Dom swiveled toward him. Dom used an arm to shield his head and blocked the hit.

"Ow, *fuck!*" Dom screamed.

He seized one end of the wrench, yanked it out of Al's hand, and flung it through the door into the night.

Al scrambled backward into the cabin with Dom in pursuit. He misjudged the distance from Dom's long arms, who wrapped his hands around Al's neck. Dom then propelled himself forward onto Al—the men landing like bricks on the linoleum floor.

Maintaining his grip on Al's neck with his left hand, Dom used his right fist to pummel Al's face and forehead. Three successive jabs. He then cocked his arm and drove his knuckles into Al's cheek, splitting the skin.

For Al, it was all in slow motion. Flashing colors danced everywhere—a dizzying kaleidoscope.

The pop of a gunshot suddenly rang out from the beach. Followed by five more quick pops.

Dom paused for a moment and craned his head to look outside, but then returned his focus to Al. He stood up and pressed his bloodstained dress shoe against Al's neck. He looked into Al's dazed eyes.

"I always liked you, bro. But you never really understood me."

He started to push down with his foot. Al gasped. His throat began to collapse under the tremendous force. *This is it.*

Then it happened.

A cantaloupe-sized rock struck the back of Dom's head.

"Get d-d-d-*down*!" Ingo bellowed.

The pressure on Al's neck instantly diminished. Simultaneously, Dom's eyes rolled up into his head, leaving just veiny whites. He took one groggy step forward, tripped on Al's armpit, and collapsed forward—face-first into the shimmering green gate.

It was if he'd plummeted through an open manhole. Dom was gone.

$$\triangle \ \triangle \ \triangle$$

Ingo's right eye was blood red and nearly swollen closed. He looked down at his friend with one eye and smiled weakly.

Al saw stars, confused by what had just happened.

"Dom," Al uttered, "where?"

"The g- g- gate."

Al touched his cheek and examined the blood on his fingers. "How?"

"Rock. In the head."

Al nodded slowly; Ingo helped him to his feet.

Placing an arm around Ingo's shoulder, he whispered, "Thank you."

Ingo embraced him in a tight hug. Yet Al abruptly withdrew in a panic.

"He could come back. Like in the journal."

Al scanned the floor, found Dom's gun, and picked it up. Then he caught a glimpse of Lilly's body and shuddered. Al took a sheet off one of the lab machines and gently covered her; the white fabric absorbed the blood and spread outward.

The two friends walked to a far corner of the room where they stood still and silent. They stared at the shimmering rectangular sliver, waiting expectantly. One minute passed. Then two. Three minutes.

Ten minutes went by. Ingo finally spoke.

"I guess he's not coming ba—"

Something blinked into existence on the other side of the room.

It was cattycorner to Al and Ingo, materializing near the ceiling beams and crashing down onto a piece of covered lab equipment before falling onto the floor. The equipment tipped over as well.

That something was a figure, and it shifted erratically. It was trying to stand.

The friends tiptoed across the room. Al led with both hands squeezing the handle of the SIG.

It was Dom. But it was not Dom.

The top half of its face resembled him: bald head; large brown eyes; Roman nose. That familiar part was much older, though. Wrinkled and with red scaly patches of dry skin. Severe psoriasis or eczema.

The bottom half was . . . very different. Dark brown hair covered the mouth and jaw, which protruded several inches forward—like a dog's muzzle. It had no lips, exposing a handful of blackened, corroded teeth. Most were missing. The tongue was brown and scarred.

It struggled to stand and shifted positions awkwardly. The neck then came into view.

Embedded in the muscles: a rodent's face. It was a rat. Eyes, nose, whiskers, mouth, teeth. A horrible fusion. Dom opened his mouth as if to speak, but nothing came out. The rodent tumor was alive. It squeaked and hissed.

Al gasped. Ingo backpedaled, keeled over, and vomited.

Looking into Dom's eyes, Al did not see a man. He saw a feral animal.

It began to flop around desperately in a continuing struggle to stand. It was much skinnier than the Dom they knew, with rolls of loose skin all over its body. An arm was missing; just a hairy stump that stopped at the elbow. The other arm had a hand, but only two fingers. The rest consisted of reddish globs of tissue—dozens, if not hundreds, of small bubbly pockets proliferating in every direction. His shirt was crusty, torn, and dirt-stained. Nonetheless, Al could make out a few letters: "Skadd." It was once Dom, alright.

After finally grasping the handle of the lab equipment with the crook of its arm, the creature pulled itself to its feet. Its breathing was heavy and primal, like a warthog. Ingo looked up and wiped the dribble from his mouth.

"Shoot him, Yoshi," he implored.

Al shook his head, although he kept the gun trained on it.

"It's not him anymore, Ingo. It can't hurt us. It couldn't even hold a gun if it tried."

"Then put it out of its misery."

Al shouted, "Get out, go!" He gestured with his chin toward the open door. "Go, now! Get out of here!"

The animal grunted, huffed, and scrambled sideways toward the door, its gait like a powerwalking crab.

They followed it out the door and watched the animal shuffle toward the lakebed. It disappeared into the receding fog.

The sky was no longer black, but rather dark purple with specks of crimson. The sun was rising.

△ △ △

Ingo tapped Al on the shoulder and pointed toward a giant, furry white mass on the beach.

The bear was sprawled prone and lifeless like a beached pilot whale. The only sign of Bardo was a single hand—unmoving—sprouting from underneath the belly of the carcass. The fur near Rocky's neck had the consistency of a blood-soaked rag.

"I heard gunshots," Ingo said.

Al nodded.

And then the hand made a fist.

"Ingo, Chief Bardo's alive!"

They crouched next to the dead bear and tried pushing with their shoulders. The body didn't give an inch.

"We need to p- p- pull, not push."

They positioned themselves on the side opposite Bardo's hand, reached across the animal's back, and grabbed handfuls of furry flesh.

Al looked at Ingo. "One, two, *go!*"

They grunted and then howled as they peeled back a flap of torso. Bardo's voice, faint at first, grew louder.

"—ep pulling," she cried out, "I can, almost, free . . ."

She shimmied out from under the bear and moaned in anguish. The men released and stumbled backward as the carcass flopped forward again.

They scrambled over to Bardo. She lay on her back in the pebbles, staring at the stars.

"Are you okay?" Al asked frantically. "How badly are you hurt?"

"Just happy to be here," she said softly. "He took a bite out of my shoulder. And," she exhaled and winced, "cracked, a few, of my, ribs." She probed her ribcage, grimacing. "I'll live. I think."

Ingo surveyed the dead bear and then looked at Bardo. He opened his hands in front of him, mystified. "How?"

"Lost my Glock when he charged me. But I had," she expelled a tortured exhale, "a backup. Leg holster. Rocky, I presume?"

Al nodded. "He had it coming."

Bardo smiled weakly and looked at Al. "I spoke to your boss. Bernie. He told me about the priest. Justice done."

"Can you walk?" Ingo asked.

"Yes. Let's get inside already."

△ △ △

They sat shoulder to shoulder on the sofa nursing their concussions and assorted wounds. Al had wrapped one of the sheets from the lab equipment around the gash on Bardo's shoulder. It was rapidly blood soaked.

As soon as Bardo entered and saw the shimmering emerald light she had demanded an explanation. Ingo tried, in the first instance, to recount what they had learned from Dr. Romanek's journal. After two stutter-aborted sentences, she placed one finger to her mouth and shushed unapologetically.

Al then picked up the account and briefed her on everything. The abduction. The experimentation on the dogs. Popper. Aiden. Lilly. And Dom's fate—the grotesque chimera that had re-materialized near the ceiling.

Bardo stared straight ahead the entire time wearing an unchanging grimace.

When Al finally finished the account, no one said a word for several minutes.

"Well ain't that something," Bardo eventually muttered. She then closed her eyes, grinned, and mumbled to herself, "Fucking Budd." She inhaled and exhaled three rapid times, as if performing a Lamaze exercise. "Oomph. I will definitely need antibiotics. Sooner rather than later."

"Do you have a ra- ra- radio?"

Bardo shook her head.

"Claw went right through it. Probably saved me another a hundred stitches." She twisted her body toward Al. "Listen, I probably should . . ." She coughed, spit bloody phlegm into her hand, and wiped it on her jeans. "I probably should tell you something. About your father."

Al's head jerked up. "What?"

"Your father. He's dead."

Al shook his head incredulously. "What are you talking about?"

"Something tells me you know exactly what I'm talking about," Bardo replied with a gentle chortle. "But listen, skip, if you want to play games, then fine. You've caught me at an odd time." She coughed again; more blood in her palm. "Before the quake. We found him; his body. I know you weren't his biggest fan." She waited for him to reply, but Al merely gazed at the shimmering green gate. "I know what you said he did." Still nothing. "Your mom. What happened on the roof. In Kiev. Like I said, I spoke to your boss, Bernie Higgins."

The hazy outline of a memory began crystalizing in Al's mind. The balcony on the roof of his family's townhouse.

Mom and Dad were up there. Was I up there too?

"He killed her, right?" Bardo blurted out. "Threw her off the roof? And got away with it. But you changed that, huh bub?"

Bardo's words fed the imagery unfolding in his mind's eye.

No. He didn't kill Mom. He tried, though. And I was there. Somehow. I got up there, and I . . . stopped him. I stopped it.

The memories were coalescing like drops of oil touching and bonding.

"Alyosha?" Bardo said.

Al stood up. His eyes traced the floor to the twinkling portal.

"He didn't kill her, Chief Bardo. He *tried* to. But I . . . I stopped him. I think . . . *I killed him.*"

Her eyes widened. "Okay. How?"

"In Kiev." He looked at Bardo. "On the roof. It was . . . December, last year. Before I moved to Washington. I didn't remember . . . until now. Until you said these things."

"Impossible," Bardo replied while shaking her head, "we found him two days ago. Fresh knife wound. And we've got someone in custody: he was dragging your dad's body through his living room. In *Hynek*. I was there." Bardo pointed at her chest. "I saw it. What I want to know is: how do you know Scott Maccabee?"

△ △ △

When Al and Bardo first began speaking, Ingo had crossed the room to a window near the front door. He undid the heavy Spanish blinds and peered outside; the sun was rising and fog had burned away. He opened the cabin door and disappeared outside for a minute. He suddenly ran back inside and shouted frantically over them.

"We have ta- ta- ta- ta- to go, *now!*"

They saw the panic in his eyes.

"Just sah- sah south, the sky! It's black. Like an ec-, ec, eclipse. *The fire. It's here, now!*"

Al scurried out the door and looked left.

It wasn't just smoke. Two-hundred feet away, bursts of orange flames erupted and danced at the edge of the encroaching blackness. The fire had advanced past the lakebed's southern edge.

Al stepped back in shock. "I don't get it—there aren't any trees in the lakebed. How could the fire move so quickly?"

By now, Bardo had staggered to the open door.

"The sediment; it's burning somehow," she offered, "feeding it. We've got to go. *Now.*"

The fire was advancing every few seconds, a malevolent spirit out to get them. A cacodemon.

"We won't make it," Ingo whispered, stunned by the turn of events.

The fire had gotten closer—a hundred feet away. A fireball suddenly shot out of the blackness like cannon fire. A flaming chunk of detritus sailed through the air and collided with the highest branches of a tree beyond the cabin. The leaves burst into flames and started shedding fire on the roof.

The trio watched in stupefied silence.

Al felt the familiar sensation return: watching a movie, rather than living in the here and now. "It's happening so fast," he said quietly.

Bardo was the first to snap back into the present.

"We have to go," she barked, "somewhere. We've got a minute or two." She stared at them.

Al blinked. "The gate. It's all we have."

Ingo's face turned an even paler shade of white, which stood in sharp relief to the violet of his swollen eye socket.

"Dom! You sa- sa- saw what happened!"

"Let's do it," Bardo immediately responded, "we're mutants or we're dead. You can stay here, Ingo. Good luck and God bless, compadre." She limped toward the twinkling green trapdoor. Al and Ingo exchanged horrified glances.

Al sighed. "She's right, Ingo. The doctor: he wrote that some of the animals *didn't* come back, right? They went somewhere else and stayed there. Popper too. He came back okay . . . sort of."

By now the roof was on fire. Chunks of the ceiling began plummeting to the floor. The temperature was mounting quickly.

"Who's first?" Bardo snapped. "Ingo, go now!"

A tear streamed down Ingo's cheek from his one good eye.

"I'll see you guys on the other si- si- side, right?" Ingo was shivering violently. He embraced Al and shook Bardo's hand. Then he approached the edge of the light and cautiously dipped one shoe inside. His foot vanished up to his ankle, causing him to lose his balance and fall forward into the green light. He was gone.

Bardo patted Al on the shoulder.

"Good luck, young man," she said stoically.

"You too," he croaked.

Bardo hobbled to the edge and looked down into the sparkling green tear in space. She exhaled one last time, made the sign of the cross, and allowed herself to tip over like a falling tree. The light swallowed Michelle Bardo. She vanished.

Sunlight was no longer visible; thick smoke enveloped the cabin, rushing in through the open door and around the edges of the windows. The walls swayed and the roof crackled. The entire structure shook. And then the roof gave.

Al had no second to spare—no chance to bid this life farewell. He prayed for mercy and then executed a swan dive into the green gate.

CHAPTER 20. DATE UNKNOWN.

verything went black. His next input was auditory: the sound of hands clapping, and an occasional enthusiastic hoot.

Al lacked any sense of how much time had passed. It could have been lifetimes; it could have been seconds. It felt like both.

His eyes were closed. Darkness. Face pressed against a hard surface. The clapping and hooting continued. A wave of vertigo overcame him. He kept his eyes closed in an effort to outlast the sickening spinning. And still the applause went on.

As the vertigo dissipated, Al cracked open an eye. His cheek flush against a wood-paneled floor illuminated by three overhead spotlights. A brown paper bag on its side, spilling popcorn, a few inches from his face.

Lifting his head, Al saw that he was on a large stage. In an auditorium.

In front of him, the stage ended and dropped to numerous rows of chairs and, above, a balcony with still more chairs. Standing in front of every chair was a man or woman, applauding wildly. A standing ovation. He scanned the crowd and estimated three hundred.

The auditorium, the layout—everything seemed familiar. He'd been here before.

"Help!" It was Ingo's voice off to his side. "Help, please!"

Al looked toward the voice. The first thing he saw was not Ingo—it was Bardo. She was curled in the fetal position. He initially thought she was dead, but then noticed her chest moving slightly.

The white sheet tourniquet was gone, which revealed teeth marks and torn flesh. The wound from Rocky was raw and oozing pinkish syrup. It was an infection unlike anything Al had ever seen. He reached over and shook her.

"Chief Bardo, wake up. Wake up!" No response.

Al pressed his palms against the stage and pushed himself up. The rush of blood to his head forced him to lay back down. Ingo was just past Bardo.

Al concentrated and stood up. He stepped around Bardo to Ingo, whose head, neck, and upper half of his torso were somehow propped upward from under the stage.

"Ingo, I'm here," he said reassuringly as he dropped to his knees.

Then Al grasped what had happened to Ingo. A jarring realization.

The lower half of Ingo's body, from the midsection down, was fused to the stage. It melded with the wood as if the stage had been constructed around his body. He was entombed.

Ingo looked at Al with his one good eye, which was puffy and wet.

"Yoshi, I can't feel anything down there. I don't know wh- wh- where it goes." He was panting. On the cusp of hyperventilating.

What do I do?

"Ingo, my friend, it's okay. We'll figure this out. We'll fix it." Al had blocked out the sound of the applause, but then it struck him that hundreds of people were still staring at them and clapping.

He stood up and shouted at the crowd.

"Help! *Help* us! Stop cheering! My friends—they're hurt! We need help!"

The adoring audience did not react even slightly. They stared ahead, clapping and hooting. Al traced his eyes along the maroon carpeted aisle that ran along the center of the auditorium and split the seating into two sections. The aisle ended at a pair of large side-by-side doors with push bars. A glowing red "EXIT" sign on top of the doors.

I've been here before

Al racked his brain. Washington. University, secondary school—*primary school.* The auditorium!

He looked up at the spotlights, and then at the purple velvet curtains off to the side. He remembered standing in that very spot during choir when he was not even a teenager. *How could this be?*

Al walked slowly to the front of the stage. After three steps, a sensation of rapid swirling again overcame his faculties— another wave of vertigo. He kneeled and closed his eyes. And the people screamed and cheered.

He heard Ingo asking where he'd gone, to please come back.

Al neared the edge of the stage; there was a six-foot drop to the carpeted floor. The spectators' eyes went straight ahead. They appeared to be ignoring him.

"Hello?"

With index finger extended, Al reached forward. His fingertip touched a paper-thin, membrane-like translucent barrier separating the stage from the gallery, setting in motion an expanding concentric ripple like a stone on a pond. The faces and bodies of the audience members undulated with the spreading waves.

Al crossed the stage and descended a narrow staircase to the gallery floor. And past the barrier.

The auditorium was empty. But the sound of the cheering continued.

He walked in front of the stage and examined the membranous sheet separating the auditorium from the stage. He was looking at his own bruised face—a one-way reflection.

The lifelike applause was originating from a fist-sized box above the "EXIT" sign. The same device was shooting colored light at the stage. Some kind of holographic projector working in tandem with the membranous barrier. Smoke and mirrors.

Al walked up the aisle as he fought off the multicolored light stream with his palms. He reached the double-doors, pushed, and entered.

△ △ △

Al emerged in the hallway of his school—just as he remembered it. Lockers lined the opposite wall, interrupted by an occasional classroom door. The hallway stretched to his right all the way to the headmaster's office one-hundred feet away. A glass display case next to the auditorium door, once a repository for sports trophies, was shattered and empty.

Not a soul in sight. To Al, a deeply unsettling emptiness.

"Hello? Anyone here?" He peered down the hallway.

"Young man," said a child's voice from his immediate left.

Al's heart nearly careened out of his chest.

It was a boy. He was no more than seven years old, seated several feet away on the bottom step of a metal staircase.

Al examined the boy and asked, "Are you okay? How did you get here?"

The child stood up, surveyed Al from top to bottom, and said, "I should be asking *you* that."

Neither spoke.

"I'm Al. Did you, uh, come here"—he gestured around them—"with your parents?"

The boy seemed confused and scoffed.

"Parents? Young man, they've been gone for decades. What kind of question is that?"

Al furrowed his brow. "Who are you?"

"My name is Osmond. Osmond Romanek."

"*You*," Al responded as he pointed at the boy, "you couldn't be Osmond Romanek."

"And why not?"

"You're just a . . . kid."

The boy shook his head, confounded.

"What do you mean, 'kid'? I'm a doctor of science. And a nonagenarian. A kid is the *last* thing I am."

Al felt the vertigo returning. He sat on the floor, leaned his back against the wall, and pinched the skin on his temple, massaging his forehead in a circular motion.

"Listen, kid—"

"For Christ's sake man, stop calling me 'kid.' It's bizarre!"

"I met Dr. Romanek's daughter and grandson."

The boy's face lit up.

"You met Rose and Gavin? How? Do they know I'm gone?" Before he could answer, the boy said, "Al, it is? Tell me: what do you *see* when you look at me, Al? What do you *hear* when I talk?" The boy placed his thumb and index finger near his chin and gestured as if stroking an invisible beard.

Al took a deep breath, exhaled, and looked up at the boy.

"I see a child. Maybe seven years old. Short brown hair, no wrinkles. Prepubescent voice. You kind of sound like a girl."

The boy cackled excitedly, put out his arm, and said, "My dear boy, when I look at my hand, I see the wrinkles of a ninety-four-year-old. Every last day of that age. And yet *you* see a child!"

The boy shook Al's hand.

"I was born Osmond Oleksander Romanek. I am the widower of Theresa Romanek; father of Rose Romanek Clarke; grandfather of Gavin Charles Clarke. And I . . . built something. I call it a 'hopper.' It facilitates transdimensional—"

"I read your journal."

The boy went silent, his eyes betraying confusion followed by disbelief.

"Impossible. I've only been gone thirty minutes, at most."

"If you are Dr. Romanek, then you've been gone for months."

The boy took one step back and stared straight ahead, lost in thought.

"Uh huh," he eventually murmured, "I guess I shouldn't be surprised. These temporal disruptions, dilations. I saw it in my experiments." A deep frown formed on his face. "If you read my journal, then you must know about the . . . boy."

Al nodded and met his eyes. The child quickly looked away, ashamed.

"Tell me something, young man, what's your full name?"

"Alyosha Dragunov."

The boy nodded and registered a tepid chuckle.

"Well, that answers my next question. I was about to ask *how* you read my diary. A fellow Ukrainian. What are the odds?"

"Listen to me," Al said, "I came here with two other people. They're hurt. Badly. In the auditorium back there. How do I help them?"

The boy looked at him quizzically.

"Auditorium? Young man, where do you think you are?"

Al felt a burgeoning sense of dread.

"In a school. Or what looks like a school. My primary school in Kiev."

The boy sighed in astonishment.

"Fascinating. You see the inside of a building? Some relic from your childhood? To me: we're on a hillside overlooking Tahoe. Where I used to take my wife on holiday. Unblemished blue sky, bright sunshine. Don't you see the sun?" He looked up and pointed at the hallway ceiling, squinting and shielding his eyes.

"My friends," Al pleaded, "I need to help them." He stood up and turned toward the auditorium doors, but they were gone.

Just exposed red brick. Al sat back down. He felt tremendous pressure on his chest.

The boy put his hand on Al's shoulder.

"Easy there, young man. Your friends: they're surely off on some other plane, some other time and place. Things come and go here. Blink in and out. I've seen others. A prehistoric bird of some kind—scared the dickens out of me. A bald muscle man with a bad case of oral herpes. But you're the only one who's stayed longer than a second or two." He resumed stroking the air beneath his chin. "You and me, and everyone: we're on some kind of arc—trajectory—that's unique for each of us."

Al shook his head. "What does that mean? What *is* this place?"

The boy looked around and then back at Al.

"I don't know how closely you read my journal. The hopper, according to what I was told, would allow a person to 'step' between planes. To move laterally among the dimensions that surround our own. But what is *this* particular place around us that we see so differently? Some kind of waystation, I think." He rubbed his hands together. "Let me put it this way: you know how a carousal has different platforms with horses moving at different speeds? Some faster, others slower. Some dip while others rise. The horses pass one another, aligned momentarily, and then continue on their own plane."

Al nodded.

"I think we're on a carousal, young man. And our horses happen to be in sync. At least for the moment."

"And the vertical step you wrote about?"

The boy smiled. "*That*, young man, is beyond the hopper's power. We can straddle these different places and times situated adjacent to one another, so to speak. But if we could go *up*, to put it simplistically, then we could see everything. How these dimensions touch, how they're entwined. Time, too. From start to end. Here's one way to think about it: imagine a creature that lives in two dimensions: length and height. Like the little Italian plumbers in the videogame my grandson played as a child; you know the one, right?"

"*Super Mario Brothers?*"

"Yes, that's the one. Imagine you're a plumber in the world of the *Super Mario Brothers*," the boy said as he mimed air quotes around the name, "you can move in two ways: left and right, up and down. And then *we* appear—you and I—inhabiting the third spatial dimension. Width, magical width. Those little two-dimensional plumbers can't travel through, much less visualize, width. For them it's an *alien* dimension.

"Think of it: from afar we could watch every little part of those plumbers' existence. Where they came from, where they sleep, where they eat, where they're going, where they'll end up at the climax of their little lives. We could swipe through their world.   Like   magic,   our   hands   would   materialize   and dematerialize in their two-dimensional plane. To them we'd be omnipresent and omniscient. Don't you see?"

Al nodded. He was using his finger to probe the cut on his cheek as he listened; the wound had clotted. He could feel the dried blood and crusty scab.

"Josie: she is to us like we are to those plumbers. She's on a higher plane than we can perceive or understand. She sees us right now, I'm sure. Everything we've done, everything we're doing. Everything we will do. Every path we took or even *may* take. But you know what, young man?"

"What?"

△ △ △

And without answering his own question, the boy was gone. Blinked out of sight.

Al turned to look down the hallway, yet his old school had vanished as well. Everything had changed—transmogrified—into a meadow. He was outside under a baby blue sky.

The meadow was nestled on the side of a mountain, part of a majestic sierra stretching as far as he could see. A sweeping field of chrysanthemums blanketed the ground and ended abruptly at a rocky precipice fifty feet away.

Al felt the sun on his head. It felt good.

He closed his eyes, looked up, and allowed the rays to drench his face. He walked to the edge of the cliff and gazed into the distance.

Dozens of miles away, tucked between two verdant green hills, he could just barely discern a grey path that canvassed the valley floor before disappearing around the base of a distant mountain. Tiny colorful dots sped along the grey path in both directions. Presumably cars, but too far for Al to tell.

When he turned back toward the meadow, something had arrived without making a sound.

A metal craft the size of a large van—seamless and shaped like an egg—rested twenty feet away. Three cylindrical silver legs, pressing down into the sea of mums, supported the object. The sun, which reflected off the metal in every direction, blinded Al. He turned his face and used both hands to block the light.

A man's voice spoke. Plain and monotone. From inside the craft.

"We don't receive visitors often."

"My friends, they're hurt," Al implored, "and I don't know where I am. I don't know what all *this* is." Al's lips weren't moving. He dropped to his knees, exhausted from distress and bewilderment. So many shocks to his system. *I want to go home. I just want to see Mom. I want everything to be simple again.*

"Okay. We see."

Al looked up. The tripod was gone; the egg floated a few feet off the ground. Hovering. And it was glowing—pulsing—a deep magenta, then an electric blue, then a blood red.

Heat. Al's face suddenly felt scorching heat. He buried his face in his hands.

Just take me.

And then the heat dissipated.

He withdrew his hands. And stared in wonder.

CHAPTER 21.
NOVEMBER 15, 2006.

Bardo peered through her windshield with the engine off, watching it unfold across the street. Traffic was building on this crisp October morning. She was in a hooded Starter jacket with the window cracked an inch; condensation kept forming on the glass, making it difficult to see.

She was alone in a tinted-out Dodge Caravan. It had dinky plastic rims that spun counterclockwise when the van moved—and continued spinning for a good minute after it came to a rest. At once transparently cheap and absurdly ostentatious. In other words, it fit in perfectly in this part of Baltimore.

It was supposed to be a straightforward buy and bust. She watched her undercover partner, Carlos Medina, in action. He was a dark-skinned, wide-nosed Dominican in a button-up Bullets jersey, unzipped camouflage jacket, and baggy black denims. Carlos was gesticulating with his hands as he spoke to the target—a slight black man with a bright purple backwards hat and a poor excuse for a goatee. Either a teenager or a small guy with shitty facial hair, Bardo thought. Carried himself with typical street bravado so it was hard to tell. She was unsure why there was so much talking, which seemed unusual. But she'd never been an undercover herself and so couldn't say for sure whether something was wrong. Just a bit unusual.

The ghost officer walked out of a nearby bodega and headed up the sidewalk past Carlos and the target, hands in his pockets and headphones in place. He bopped his head like a metronome to a non-existent beat.

Bardo spoke to the ghost over her walkie-talkie.

"The deal's slower than expected. See if you can hear what they're talking about. Then make a long call at the payphone until you hear from me."

The ghost took his left hand out of his pocket and made a subtle "okay" gesture on the side of his body facing away from the unfolding drug sale. He passed the two men and continued to a phone booth at the end of the block, outside the Black Rose Hair Studio. He picked up the phone, inserted a quarter, and started dialing.

Meanwhile, Carlos and the target continued their back and forth. The target had become animated and was pointing a finger at Carlos's chest.

Shit. Time to bail, Carlos.

Bardo moved her left ear closer to the sliver of open window and concentrated. She made out a few words from the target: " . . . listen, you spic ass nigga . . . "

Don't wig out, Carlos, chill.

A few more seconds passed and the exchange escalated to shouting.

End this.

The two men were now in each other's faces. Bardo grabbed the steering wheel and dug her nails into the pleather. This was not what was supposed to happen.

Then it hit the fan. Carlos briefly looked away from the target and smirked. Suddenly, he bitch-slapped the target with the back of his hand. The black man's eyes lit up and jaw dropped. He took a step back and reached for something in the front pocket of his ripped cargo pants.

We lost control. God damn it, Carlos, I will not forgive you for this.

As Bardo issued an urgent directive to the ghost—"Get him out of there now, target's pulling a weapon"—Carlos curled one arm around his own hip, dug his hand under his jersey into the waist of his jeans, and removed a small revolver. The target, for his part, had already retrieved a folding knife from his pocket. He flicked his wrist, which partially unsheathed the blade. He flicked a second time: the blade opened in full and clicked into place. Bardo knew what was coming next.

POP POP.

Like the ricochet of backfiring mufflers. The ghost, who had been walking briskly, now sprinted toward the gunshots while brandishing his own revolver in the air and screaming "police."

Still facing forward and meeting his assailant's eyes, the target stepped backward. He covered his chest with both hands, wearing a look of confusion and uncertainty. "Is this really happening," his eyes seemed to ask. Adrenaline overpowering the pain. One of the man's legs got caught on a freestanding Siamese water connection; he toppled backward like a mannequin.

Bardo hustled out of the van and charged across the street with her own gun in the air. She kept her eyes on Carlos who, by then, was standing on top of the target, pointing his gun down, and kicking at the man's hand.

A Subaru station wagon, teal and rusted, sped along the far side of the street. Bardo shouted "police" while rooting around in her pocket for her badge. Though anticipating that the car would yield, the Subaru instead accelerated and swerved to the right. She leapt backward behind the yellow traffic lines, slid on loose gravel, and fell sideways into a large pothole. The Subaru, meanwhile, lurched back into the lane and regained control.

As the car sped away, Bardo instinctively looked for its license plate. Liberal bumper stickers littered the back of the car: "Give Peace a Chance," "Save the Bees," "Nader '96."

And, out of the corner of her eye, there it was.

A prominent yellow sticker on the rounded edge of the driver's side bumper. "Watch out for the bears. Bearing Land Bridge National Preserve."

The silhouette of a husky polar bear on its hind legs.

The deluge of images and emotions happened instantly; the dam broke. Years of forgotten memories—things Bardo had never experienced but somehow, inexplicably, knew anyway. Knew intimately. At that moment, the clearest and most prominent: *that fucking sadistic bear.* Her mind traced backward from the attack. *DeRuglia. The fire. Justin. The Freemans. Scott. Hynek.*

Sasha! My baby girl!

She felt a sickening, aching yearning for a phantom daughter. A daughter years from being born. A daughter whom, up until this very second, she'd never even realized she wanted.

Am I a seer? Is that a different life?

A chill crept up her spine. It felt as if the pothole was suddenly filled with ice.

She wrested her focus back to the here and now. Whatever this was—a preternatural epiphany or divine awakening—would have to wait.

This is my operation; I need to make it right.

But the street, her hands, the gun, and the blue sky seemed to be retreating from her vision. Everything was moving backward. As if the Baltimore street was a film projected on a portable screen that was rolling away from her.

Nonetheless, she pushed herself off her butt and onto her knees, and, pressing the barrel of her pistol into the gravel like a tiny cane, hoisted herself to her feet. The world continued to recede as a black tunnel increasingly framed her vision. Everything growing smaller and harder to see, like life through the wrong end of binoculars. She tried to say "help" but didn't hear anything. She couldn't discern whether she was talking or just opening her mouth. She lurched forward past the double yellow lines.

And then came a distant screech.

A red coupe swerved right to avoid hitting her. But not before the driver's side fender clipped Bardo's right leg and propelled her several feet backward. After hitting the ground she spun sideways three times—head smacking the pavement twice—before coming to a rest in another large pothole. Her gun skittered across the pavement and disappeared under a parked truck, while traffic screeched to a halt a few feet from her rumpled body. The driver of the red coupe had stopped and switched on her emergency lights. It was an old woman who appeared to be hyperventilating behind the wheel.

The chill on Bardo's spine became sharper as space-time continued its retreat. Shredded from the road rash, her palms erupted blood. Her jacket and jeans were torn, and she felt the distant sensation of warm liquid running down her face. But no pain.

From across a canyon of black she saw the ghost officer looking down at her and mouthing words. The old woman driver, next to the ghost, also mouthed words and made frantic hand gestures.

"She came out of nowhere," the woman seemed to be saying.

Everything decelerated: their mouths moved at one-third speed. An alien sound emerged: an echoing, rattling Pacman ping.

She continued descending into her mind's eye, the black tunnel unfurling like an accordion as she fell into space. The transmutation of Baltimore—from her everything into a colorful dot a football field length away—nearly complete. All she heard was the ping. All she felt was the cold against her spine.

Yet now she could place the sensation: no, it was not ice. Rather, it was her bare skin pressed against cold metal. And the nauseating smell of putrefaction and mildew. The smell of the lakebed.

△ △ △

A dull grey replaced the black accordion.

Bardo hadn't felt the need to blink for some indescribable length of time. The urge finally arose and so she fluttered her eyelids.

She was in the tattered Kevlar vest punctured by Rocky's enormous canines. The edge of her shoulder, naked and exposed, bore two silver dollar-sized scars. She rubbed the scar tissue, which felt thick and rubbery. Goosebumps rippled across her forearms.

A lot of time has passed.

The thought triggered a pit in her stomach. *Sasha.*

The bottom part of her shoulder rested flush against a cold metal surface. She was on a gunmetal grey examining table in a small, gently lit room. To her left: a massive black screen spanning the entire wall. Some unseen light source near the ceiling generated a muted yellow glow.

Certainly not Baltimore.

It was unclear to Bardo why her mind, almost reflexively, harkened back to that city. To one particular day in her career. When her partner, Charles "Carlos" Medina, shot and killed a felon crack dealer, Malik Beasley, during a botched buy and bust. As she'd testified years ago at two civil trials, her memory ended moments before Carlos fired the fatal shots. She'd woken up in a hospital bed: a car hit her as she was crossing the street, or so she was told. She had suffered a Grade 3 concussion, with doctors inducing a twenty-four coma to minimize any brain swelling.

Her most recent memory, in contrast, was the cabin on Trigger Island. She had found DeRuglia—that sick puppy. Then the bear. Next the fire. And, finally, she had escaped with the boys, Al and Ingo, through some kind of . . . portal.

The boys. They could be here.

"Alyosha? Ingo?" Silence.

Bardo swung her legs over the edge of the table and dropped her feet to the floor.

"Hello?" Still nothing.

An open sliding door led into a payphone-sized room with a sophisticated looking control panel; a holographic word, "ORBIT," hovered above one of the buttons. That room, in turn, connected through another open door to a narrow hallway that led sharply right and left. Bardo hobbled into the hallway, paused, and turned left. She inspected some framed pictures on the wall illuminated by glowing blue pearls in small hanging dishes; an exotic power source, she thought. She glanced at some of the pictures: aerial photos of Lake Hynek, ostensibly, with meaningless numbers typed beneath. Then the tunnel ended abruptly in an opening that spilled into darkness. There was some kind of drop, but she couldn't tell how high. As she approached the opening, the odor of mildew and decomposing flesh grew overpowering. Bardo leaned down, put her hands on her knees, and dry heaved.

She doubled back, picking up one of the pearls to use as a light. The arched ceiling was only three feet above Bardo's head and she wielded the pearl like a torch as she walked, examining the ceiling, wall, and ground. Made of some dark grey rock; nothing remarkable. She passed the antechamber with the control panel and continued down the corridor.

After three minutes the tunnel hooked left at a ninety-degree angle. She slowed down: there was some kind of detritus on the ground several yards ahead. Piles of something old and dusty. She counted: six little heaps, one after another along the floor. Piles of rocks, it seemed. She got nearer.

Not rocks.

She exhaled slowly.

Bones.

Six human skeletons—each with a yellowed patina—lined up symmetrically along one side of the narrow passage. Bardo inspected the first. Three gold teeth in the lower jaw and some kind of synthetic joint near the knee. Inside the rib cage was a black plastic object the size and shape of a wedding ring box, with a metal clip; thin multicolored wires sprouted from it.

Bardo reached into the rib cage and picked up the box. No markings or insignia. Upon prying open the binding on one side, she discovered two miniature computer chips. She used the light from the pearl to study the inside. Minute writing just barely visible to the naked eye.

"Bio Track.™" "NASA."

Bardo furrowed her brow and reexamined the first skeleton.

The Valor had six crew members. But these bones are practically . . . fossilized.

She traced her finger along the dense scar tissue on her shoulder.

Bardo swallowed uncomfortably, her spit like sand from dehydration, and continued along the corridor. Nearing the last skeleton, she noticed a ringed indentation around the circumference of the skull's base. Neat and symmetrical.

Cut with a saw or laser of some sort.

She thought back to her father's father, Grandpa Vincent, a military surgeon. At his office he kept a skeleton that belonged to a homeless man whose body Vincent had autopsied during medical school. The cranial incision on the autopsied skull matched what she now saw.

"Michelle."

Bardo jumped two steps back, her breath lost in surprise.

It was the voice of a man. With a French accent. Thirty feet ahead in the passage, a figure stood in front of a doorway to a bright yellow room; the tunnel led nowhere else. None of this had been there seconds earlier.

All she could make out was the silhouette.

"Come along, dear," he said, "you can dispose of that marble—there's plenty of light where I am."

She looked at her hand: just an empty palm. She looked back up.

Bardo had too many questions.

"Where are we?"

"Michelle, dear, please come along now. I'll explain everything."

"Who are you?"

"An old friend."

The silhouette placed its hands on its hips, telegraphing impatience.

"Don't be scared."

"I came here with two other people. Are they here—are they safe?"

The silhouette nodded. "Alyosha and Ingo. Yes, they're safe dear. Now please don't make me ask again. I've got all the time in the world"—he chuckled softly—"but you don't. So you'll want to come over here and not waste any more."

Bardo edged closer and strained to make out his physical characteristics. He appeared to be in his eighties, maybe older: slightly hunched forward and holding a cane. She put the black box in her pocket and walked cautiously toward the light.

As she neared, her view of the room and its occupant crystalized. He was skinny. A thick white beard hid most of his face. Wearing a navy jumpsuit decorated with official looking patches across the chest and shoulders.

He sat down in a simple wooden chair behind an unadorned but expansive black desk concealing the lower half of his body. The desktop was empty.

The room was circular with a rounded ceiling not unlike the inside of an igloo, albeit consisting of a smooth rock rather than ice. Bardo saw no other entrance or exit. All seamless, bluish rock. A single lightbulb in the middle of the ceiling provided the sole source of light. A string dangled next to the bulb and flapped wildly as if driven by a powerful wind, although there was no other indication of moving air. Bardo stopped just short of the entryway.

"You say you're an old friend. But I don't know you."

Despite the fulsome white curls hiding his lips and mouth, Bardo could perceive a smile from the weathered lines of his upper cheeks.

"I'm an old friend of *all* of you. Watching for a long time now."

Bardo considered his answer.

"What's your name?"

"René."

"René what?"

"Vallee."

"Well, René, what *is* this place?" She raised her hands in the air and gestured all around. "And *where* is this place?"

"I built it, Michelle. I created this whole thing ages ago."

"Why?"

"Experiments."

"What kind of experiments?"

Fifteen seconds passed. René did not answer.

"We're under the lakebed, right?"

René nodded.

"How did I get here?"

"I gave one of you, Osmond, information. So that he could build something. A rudimentary device. So that you could reach me. Rather than me reach you, as has always been."

"Are you talking about the, the," she struggled to find the right words, "the green light?"

He nodded.

"Did you make that pearl disappear just now?"

"That pearl was never there to begin with. I simply allowed the projection to die."

Bardo considered everything leading up to this moment.

"You're not like me, are you?" She spoke softly.

"I think you know the answer to that."

Bardo tittered nervously. She thought back to the skeletons and then tilted her head to inspect a patch in front of René's heart. She could make out "NASA." And underneath: "Banes."

"You took that from one of those astronauts, huh?" She didn't wait for an answer. "René, what year is it?"

"Very far in your future."

"Sasha—"

"She's gone, Michelle. But don't feel bad."

A piercing wave of grief hit Bardo. She hunched forward and put her hands on her knees, breathing faster. Blood rushed to her head. Yet, just as quickly, the emotion vanished. She could feel something outside her suppressing it—pushing back the thoughts and feelings that would have otherwise overwhelmed her will to speak, or even to stand.

"So is her daughter," René continued in an empathic tone. "And her daughter's grandchildren. And their great, great, great grandchildren. So nothing to mourn, dear."

Bardo straightened up and looked at him.

She recoiled.

Behind René, between his chair and the wall, a long, brown, and muscular appendage rose one inch at a time, like a cobra from a charmer's basket. It had moist scales that glistened under the light. When it had almost reached the ceiling, the appendage began to thrash unpredictably. Whatever it was, it seemed to have a mind of its own. But it never touched René. She knew it was coming from him. That it was part of him.

"None of this is what it appears to be," he said placidly. "I'm certainly not."

Bardo took a step back.   Fear should have been overpowering, but instead she felt steadfast calm.

"What are you for real, René?"

"A spirit. Sometimes, at least." He smiled warmly. "So much life always surrounds you, dear. A flurry of life. Things you cannot yet see and measure; but they're there. And you're sick inside because your daughter is gone. To *you*, Michelle, she's gone. To me, she's an immutable flame burning brightly. I see her right now. Every moment of her life, every choice she made or makes—every choice she did *not* make. All at once."

"I don't understand."

A second appendage rose behind René and began slapping chaotically. It then entwined with the first appendage to form an elaborate coil of sliding, pulsating muscle. Naked peristalsis.

He placed both palms on the desk, the back of his hands wrinkled and speckled with liver spots. As he leaned forward, so did the intertwined coils of serpentine flesh.

"This happens to be a locus where many paths intersect. One path you can see: the rock; the tunnel; the observation room; this lightbulb above my head. Many others you can't perceive. In any case, because so many paths intersect here—

have always intersected here—it's easy to bring you and your kind to this place. For the mixing and matching. The changes we make. This has been a hotspot for as long as your kind has existed."

Bardo traced the arc of her memories back to Scott. The craft over Baton Rouge. The blue door.

As if reading her mind, René merely said, "Yes." After a third tail emerged.

"Demons, angels, fairies. Aliens. So on and so forth. You've always known our kind. The answer is yes, dear."

Bardo no longer opened her mouth to speak.

Why?

"Because we can. We give second chances. We facilitate choice. And we watch for our own purposes. Purposes you would never understand. Purposes that, well, would not seem like purposes to you. That don't comply with your 'reason.'"

Of all people, why me?

René issued a hearty laugh. Yet his mouth never moved.

"You're not the only one, dear. We touch so many of you. No one remembers, though. It's funny: we don't switch you off. It's a choice *you* all make. You're still so young—so primitive, malleable." He paused for several seconds. "What was it you told your daughter, Michelle? 'Hold that thought,' wasn't it?"

Bardo nodded. She reflected on those words and their implications. A grin formed at the creases of her lips.

Please, yes. I want to go back to that moment ... more than anything in the world.

A fourth appendage surfaced and slapped spastically at the air. Along with the other three, it was the nightmarish plumage of some horrible bird.

Suddenly, they smacked the wall behind René in unison. Two quick smacks, a pause, then two more quick smacks, and another pause.

"Look up, dear."

Bardo tilted back her neck.

A starry night sky had replaced the bluish rock.   And the force sucked her up.

CHAPTER 22. FRIDAY, DECEMBER 18, 2020.

Al lowered his hands from his face.

The night sky was clear and frigid. He was on a rooftop that spilled onto an oversized deck. With a balcony.

He immediately knew where.

He recognized the sloping tiles, the red door that led to a rickety wooden staircase. Off in the distance elaborate Christmas lights adorned the trees in front of Saint Sophia's Cathedral. The lights were blue and so it had to be the third week of December; Ukrainian custom. His breath was like thick smoke in the crisp winter air.

He heard faint voices.

His parents.

The juxtaposition of their figures was unmistakable: his father's portly body and pumpkin-like head with shaggy black hair, olive complexion, and bushy mustache. The mole on

Nettie's cheek sprouting a single, two-inch-long hair—his calling card.

And Mom. Her slender and stately frame, at least three inches taller than his father. Wispy, platinum blond hair, sharp cheekbones, and vanilla complexion. Wearing her simple black dress—the one she wore on December 18, 2020. The day she died. Almost died.

She was sobbing into her hands. His father was yelling.

Al couldn't make out all the words. He was accusing her of something. He kept pointing at her, jabbing an index finger between her breasts.

Al wanted to call out to them—to Mom—but couldn't speak. He could only croak a few syllables. He heard his father cry out, "Whore!"

And then he seized her by the throat and pushed her toward the railing. She was trying to dig her heels into the cement balcony—futile. He was pushing her to the edge.

This is it. It is now.

Al ran forward awkwardly, his body sore and unforgiving. His father had her hip pressed against the railing, her feet dangling off the ground as her waist tipped onto and over the handrail. Only a few moments more.

Anna saw Al over her husband's shoulders. Her eyes widened with both relief and confusion.

Al wrapped his hands around his father's neck and yanked him backward. The man released Anna, swiveled toward Al, and swatted with both arms. He freed himself and stepped back to examine his assailant's face under the flickering rooftop lamp.

Nettie shouted in his native tongue, "Who the hell are you, old man?"

"It's *me*, you bastard! I won't let you kill her!"

Al's father reached into his vest pocket and removed a folding knife with a leather handle. He unsheathed the four-inch blade.

He yelled "intruder" like a battle cry and lunged at Al.

Al nimbly stepped back and dodged the blade; his father fell onto his knees and dropped the knife at Al's feet. Al retrieved it as his father stood back up and then bull-charged.

Before Al could assume a fighting stance, Nettie drove his head and shoulders into Al's chest and knocked him against a brick chimney chute. He grabbed Al's neck and squeezed tightly.

Al used his left hand in a frantic bid to push his father a few inches away. As colorful dots began clouding his vision, Al stabbed furiously with the blade. Twice in rapid succession.

The second stab punctured his father's chest.

The grip on his neck instantly loosened. After two more seconds, he released Al's neck entirely. Nettie let out a guttural moan; his breath sounded like a deflating tire. He stumbled a few steps to his right and then toppled onto his side.

He lay wheezing. Each breath shortened and softened until there was silence.

His father's eyes never closed; he stared up into the night sky. One unusually large star twinkled colorfully. It blinked out of existence as Nettie expired.

Al stared at his father. Then he looked up at Mom. Her eyes were wide.

"What have you done, old man?" Her voice was serene. A cold winter rain began to fall.

"Mom, it's me! It's Alyosha! Don't you recognize me?"

"No, it's not. It couldn't be."

"He was going to kill you, I swear." Tears streamed down Al's cheeks.

"Maybe," she whispered. She looked down at her husband once more, and then back at the old man in front of her. The old man claiming to be her teenage son. And, finally, she looked straight up into the sky.

In one seamless motion she hoisted herself onto the railing, swung her legs outward, and pushed off, freefalling. The sound of a heavy thud followed.

Al stood still. The cathedral lights in the distance transfixed his eyes. But not his mind.

I couldn't stop it. I never could.

The rain strengthened. Heavy droplets battered his father's unblinking eyes.

So unnatural, he thought.

Al grasped his father from the elbows and dragged him toward the red door. To get him out of the rain.

As he strained and pulled, moving the body only a few inches at a time, Al closed his eyes.

△ △ △

When he opened them, the rain had ceased.

Al was no longer outside; no longer in the cold.

He was still pulling his father. Through a doorway of a narrow hallway. A bloody trail led along a white carpet into another room.

Where am I?

"Scott, do *not* move!" It was a woman's voice.

Al froze, confounded.

"Put him down, put your hands up, and turn around. *Now*!"

Gently lowering his father, he looked up. It was Chief Bardo.

"How is this poss . . . Chief, how are you here! Are you okay? You shoul—"

"Get down on your knees, *now*!"

"What? No, Chief, it's me! What day is it? Tell me *now*!" He walked toward Bardo, but his body was even heavier, stiffer, and more unfamiliar. "Put the gun down, Chief, we need to talk!"

They were in a kitchen. Bardo was backing up toward a screen door.

"Scott, get the *fuck ba*—"

Al's foot slipped and he fell forward. Something hard struck his jaw. The world went white for Al.

And time . . .

△ △ △

. . . heals all wounds, Al's father used to tell their country back home. Al, for his part, begged to differ. But he was still young.

So Al had gone west. And now he rode west.

Hi,

Thanks for reading this admittedly weird attempt at a first novel. I hope you enjoyed it (at least some of it) and that the plot, characters, and themes resonated with you on some level. I've not offered answers to everything—which, hopefully, is not too frustrating—and some strands are open to interpretation. I'd like to revisit the misadventures of Al, Bardo, and Ingo, as well as shed light on the machinations of the observation room's engineer(s).

By way of brief background, I'm a full-time lawyer/consultant in Manhattan. This book began as a daydream in Central Park a few years ago and has been a hobby since then in whatever spare time I've scrounged up. I tend to think there's a world of secrets hiding in plain sight—things we've yet to acknowledge, much less understand. The idea of the unknown thrills and sustains me, which you see reflected in this story.

I'd be really appreciative if you would consider reviewing and/or rating the book on Amazon and/or GoodReads. I'm grateful for any and all feedback, which is extremely valuable for self-published books.

Thanks again for reading.

-Tim Stone